D0201610
©CASE

★ THE FLAMES OF WAR ★

Captain Keenan Carlisle: Survivor of a Japanese submarine attack, Keenan came ashore to begin a fierce and bloody jungle trek toward Burma—driven to kill by what the Japanese had taken away from him . . .

General Preston Belvale: He was there when the Zeros seeded Pearl Harbor with death and destruction. After briefing Roosevelt on the disaster, he traveled with Lieutenant General Dwight Eisenhower and U.S. expeditionary forces against Algeria—and got into action at Oran . . .

General Charles "Crusty" Carlisle: He pretended he was willing to serve out the war stateside on Kill Devil Hill, overseeing the family war effort. But deep down he wanted to be on the front lines, and Preston Belvale knew that well enough to make sure it couldn't happen . . .

Lieutenant Colonel Chad Belvale: Fighting alongside the newly formed Rangers, Chad dodged sniper fire on the beach with the 16th Infantry in French North Africa. Having survived Dunkirk, he took the war back to the Germans—in the brutal campaign across the parched and bloody continent . . .

Sergeant Eddie Donnely: While the fighting raged he was trapped as a motor-pool driver in Honolulu. The hard-drinking, hard-loving young staff sergeant, weaned on his old man's heroic memories, wanted battle in the worst way—and he got it at Guadalcanal with the hastily formed American Division . . .

Penny Colvin-Belvale: While British forces fought bitterly in Singapore, Penny was one of the brave Women Air Corps Support Pilots who volunteered to fly the soldiers out—until she was captured and plunged into a nightmare of brutality and survival . . .

Books by Con Sellers

Brothers in Battle

The MEN AT ARMS series

Book 1: The Gathering Storm
Book 2: The Flames of War

Published by POCKET BOOKS

Book 3: A World Ablaze
Book 4: Allied in Victory

Coming soon from POCKET BOOKS

MEN AT ARMS

BOOK 2

THE FLAMES OF WAR

CON SELLERS

POCKET BOOKS
New York London Toronto Sydney Tokyo Singapore

This book is a work of fiction. Names, characters, places and incidents are either products of the author's imagination or are used fictitiously. Any resemblance to actual events or locales or persons, living or dead, is entirely coincidental.

An *Original* Publication of POCKET BOOKS

POCKET BOOKS, a division of Simon & Schuster Inc.
1230 Avenue of the Americas, New York, NY 10020

ISBN: 0-671-66766-1

First Pocket Books printing December 1991

10 9 8 7 6 5 4 3 2 1

POCKET and colophon are registered trademarks of Simon & Schuster Inc.

Printed in the U.S.A.

To: Sgt. Maj. Leonard P. Frusha, RA6299593,
who had a taste of three wars

THE FLAMES OF WAR

CHAPTER 1

ASSOCIATED PRESS—Honolulu, Hawaii, December 7, 1941: Japanese planes struck again and again at military installations here this morning. Soldiers and sailors fought back gallantly with any weapon at hand. One corporal claimed the kill of a low flying Zero with a single shot from his bolt-action rifle.

Unarmed civilians were not so lucky, and bodies are reported sprawled along the blazing streets of Pearl City. Heavy smoke is rising from the harbor itself, and military patrols have shut off all entry to the bay.

General Preston Belvale jumped when coffee slopped over the brim of his cup, his second of the morning. Another explosion slammed against the cottage. ''Kee-rist! On Sunday morning?''

Leave it to the damned navy to pull a surprise maneuver and wake the entire island of Oahu, he thought. The swabbies would do better dispersing all those fat targets lined up on Battleship Row. But the man in charge there, Rear Admiral Anderson, snickered at the idea of Japs sticking their little slope heads into the lion's den. Chew them up and spit them out, he said. They're about half crazy, but they're not that stupid. A pass at Wake Island or Midway to try to bluff the president into restoring their oil imports; maybe even a feint at Manila, but Pearl Harbor? Never.

During last night's sumptuous dinner party at the officers' club the admiral, commander of Battleship Row, had held forth on Japanese weaknesses, and CINCPAC Admiral Kimmel had his standard two drinks at the Halekulani Hotel, conscious of his responsibilities as Commander in Chief, Pacific. That's what Belvale had been told before he made his early excuses and trundled off to bed in one of the army's VIP guest houses atop the hill.

WHAP-WHAP-WHAP!

A light-caliber machine gun—a 7.7 Kikanju, or more like a pair of them, wing-mounted, the flat echoes of their fire rolling in the sharp backwash of the strafing plane. A ricochet whined off the street outside, quick sparks and chips of concrete. No drill, this, but live Jap ammunition.

"Kee-rist," Belvale said, "I thought they'd hit the Philippines first."

Then he snatched his uniform and yelled for his driver. "Donnely! Where the hell are you?"

Roistering in the fleshpots of the city, he thought; where else? He'd given Eddie Donnely the day off, and by now the sergeant would be sleeping off a night of booze in some woman's bed. He had a deserved name for liquor and ladies. Now here came the bastardly Japs shooting up the place. Donnely would show up in due time. Whatever else he might be, the sergeant was regular army like his father, to the bone.

Jerking on his boots while his ears sorted through layers of noises familiar to soldiers and some that were strange, Belvale heard the start of a war—the scream of airplane engines and racketing machine guns; a *whump!* as a bomb exploded—a siren stupidly wailing an alarm far too late, the popcorn of small-arms fire. And oh, God—a mighty blowup that shook the ground and could only be a great ship tearing its guts out.

They were actually doing it—the strutting little bastards

were actually attacking the United States of America. It looked different on paper. Belvale tore out of the cottage and jumped into the olive-drab staff car waiting in the drive. Where to find the army commander? General Short would be at Schofield Barracks Headquarters, probably—or Fort Shafter, rallying the troops and trying to get a coordinated defense going. It wouldn't be easy; the Hawaiian Command had gotten caught with its grass skirts down.

The fighter planes at Hickam Field and the patrol planes on Ford Island—were any of them chasing the enemy bombers? Belvale doubted it; the Japs were doing a thorough job and would have planned to eliminate any threats to their air strength. The American planes were probably burning by now.

Hurling the '39 Plymouth downhill and skidding it around a corner where he almost clipped an ancient flatbed overloaded with pineapples, Belvale saw a greasy column of smoke inking the sky. The poor kids aboard the sleeping ships in the harbor were catching concentrated hell. Many would fry in burning oil before they were fully awake.

Arm-waving military police got in his way at the gate, and Belvale almost ran them down. This was no time to be checking passes and trip tickets, but peacetime regulations and habits would cling for a while. He found General Short's headquarters, but the general hadn't returned from the golf course yet. Kee-rist—the golf course.

Golf and Wednesday afternoons off, dull routine that could turn deadly with war just over the horizon; the garrison setup here was the main reason that Belvale had come to Hawaii. Now it was too damned late. The Japs were making the changes.

Jittery junior officers hit the polished floor as a plane buzzed the building, its guns hammering. Belvale sat erect in his chair, crossing his booted feet and thumbnailing his mustache. In just the two days he'd been in the islands he had seen enough hidebound, self-contented idiocies to last through the next few wars. Spit and polish, garrison troopers who knew what day of what month they were due to pull officer of the guard; the lulling sameness and security of post life; it all tended to stifle any individual thinking. Go by the book and stay out of trouble. If a thing was done this way a hundred years ago, why try to change it now? Don't call attention to yourself; don't get known as a maverick.

Don't rock the boat, even to keep it from going down.

A phone rang, and when someone answered it, another phone took up the cry. Men dashed in and out of headquarters, some trying to balance the flat tin helmets of the war before. The damned things always hurt when they bounced, Belvale recalled.

"They blew up the *Arizona* and the *Oklahoma!* Oh, the bastards—"

"—caught our planes on the ground—"

"—dying on Ford Island—"

The long briefing room stank of burned oil and a dozen cigarettes going at once; it smelled of fear and frustration. The sharp edge of panic sliced across all action and all emotion. Belvale followed standard operating procedure; he gave his name to the duty clerk and went back outside. Nobody would call on him to do anything. It was also SOP that the high brass would try to hide their screwups from him, FDR's hatchet man. But now there was far too much to hide.

Drawing on his cigar, he watched planes streak across the sky and counted a few puffs of ack-ack. The hell with SOP; this was war, and he meant to get into it with more than a sharp pencil.

A squad of soldiers stood uncertainly just beyond the gate, carrying light packs, slung rifles with fixed bayonets, ammunition belts, and gas masks. Gas masks and bayonets, Kee-rist.

Stopping the car, Belvale called out: "Sergeant!"

"Y-yes sir!" The man was lanky, his Adam's apple bobbing. "Yes sir—General."

"Give me your M-1, please—and a bandolier of ammo."

The sergeant's pale eyes went wide. "I—I don't reckon I can do that, sir. I mean, I ain't sure, you being a general and all—"

"Get your ass in a sling if you lose your weapon? I'll testify that it was shot out of your hands by an attacking plane while you were standing out in the open and firing back."

"Jesus," the man said, "I don't reckon I'd be that stupid—but okay—sir; sure. I'll find me another weapon, if they let me shoot at something. Here you are, General—a full bandolier, too."

Pulling the Garand and ammunition through the window and onto the front seat, Belvale said, "Lieutenant General Belvale, the president's staff. If anybody gives you a bad time."

"The president—holy shit, sir. Hold a mite to the right when you fire."

"Thanks." Belvale gunned the motor and headed for Pearl City. He didn't know what the hell he'd do when he got there, but that made him just like a bunch of other headless chickens, running in circles.

Damn! The family didn't often get caught short like this, or there would be no family of professionals whose duty was to keep the country safe. They'd been at the job before the Crusades, and it must have been easier back then. No, simpler maybe, but never easy.

A Jap plane peeled off and screamed down at the street. Belvale raised his rifle and squeezed off shots.

Eddie Donnely was in jail. He couldn't remember a worse drunk tank. Honolulu's cell was big enough for twenty or so sick and sorry boozers, which wasn't such a good idea if some of them got mean and started a fight. Just in case, Eddie had picked a defensive position against the wall and below a barred window set high in the clay wall. The window would be at street level outside, and the pit cellar was dug deep underground. The walls and packed dirt floor were the problem; they had been pissed on, puked on, and bled on for a hundred years. The odors would never scrub out.

Rubbing gently at his right eyebrow, he looked around to see half a dozen sailors in stained whites. The guys he'd fought? He wouldn't know; swabbies all looked alike to Eddie Donnely in their tight pants and beanie hats. Last night's bunch had been off the battleship *Arizona;* that's all he remembered, and one of them had a mean left hand. The girl—frowning, he wondered what had happened to the cute little *wahine* when the brawl started. Eddie lost too many girls that way.

Somewhere outside in the early morning sun the rumble of plane motors grew louder. As if he could see anything, Eddie stared up at the barred window. The thumping came through the hard clay to his feet—thump-thump; pause—a string of them now, some dim, some heavier. Across the tank the sailors sat up and looked at one another. One had a pack of Raleighs that he passed around. Somebody struck a match.

Ship sirens went off. The plane motors raced, and Eddie was certain he could pick out machine guns of different calibers: the 30s whiplashing; slower 50s; there—a 20mm Oerlikon going *pom-pom-pom!*

He went to the door. "Guard! Guard—damnit! Let us out! This is a goddamn air raid."

The iron view panel slid back. "Bullshit." The MP turned to a hulking shore patrolman. "It's them carrier planes, ain't it, Jimbo?"

"Uh-huh," the SP said. "Carriers been out two days, and them planes are pulling a sneak raid on the fucking army, testing defenses, like."

"Listen, goddamnit! I know machine guns, and those aren't ours. They're Jap!"

"Bullshit," said the MP, and the sirens whined; the rattle of gunfire grew.

Eddie said, "I could sure use a drink of water."

The SP grunted and slapped the palm of his left hand with his thick yellow club. "So could guys in hell. You got about the same chance."

"Five bucks," Eddie said.

"Your money is at the desk," the MP said. "Shook you down myself."

Eddie said, "In my shoe."

"Smartass," the MP grunted, and he pulled back the door bar.

Shoulder down, Eddie hurled his full weight at the door. It crashed open and slammed the MP into a wall. The SP stared until Eddie snatched his club and popped him on the head with it. Backhanding the MP, he left the cell door open and trotted out to the main desk. From the files he grabbed the "Donnely" packet and darted out the front door to lose himself in a gabbling crowd surging this way and that, uncertain and scared.

The MP patrol jeep sat lonely at the curb, so Eddie climbed behind the wheel. Where was he going? If he meant to run, to take cover, there wasn't any. Pushing the front bumper slowly through the crowd, tapping the horn, he glanced up from time to time. Jap planes worked over the island and harbor from different angles, one bunch diving on ships and other flights peeling off to make runs on land targets. Smoke rose from the harbor in giant black ropes and blotted the sky over oil storage and dock areas. The noise hammered and shrieked and blasted, one wild sound ripping over another until they drilled into a man's skull.

Hell must taste like this, he thought—gunpowder and burned rubber; cooked steel and fried human flesh. Eddie picked up speed as he aimed toward Schofield and General Belvale. The gunpowder smell was strongest, and its excitement raced through him like a double shot of *okulihao*, the powerful bootleg juice made from pineapple. The stuff had gotten him locked up in the first place.

War; a fat fucking war come along just in time to make some sense out of boring peacetime duty, the chickenshit of petty tyrants a stripe or two up on a guy. A real by-god *war,* damnit—something of his own to hold up next to his old man's memories. Big Mike Donnely drew all eyes his way when he wore his parade uniform, all the hash marks, medals and the gold vees of combat duty and wound stripes. Now Big Mike was too old to fight, and the torch would pass to Eddie when the old man took his retirement.

But not as the general's driver. Any dummy could handle that job, and Eddie was too expert with mortars and machine guns to soldier anyplace but a line outfit, a heavy weapons company. That's where the medals, rank and glory would be.

Gate guards at Schofield Barracks tried to stop him, but he pointed at the big white "Military Police" stenciled along the hood and made them jump for safety. He'd ditch the jeep behind the VIP cottage and drive the Plymouth sedan wherever the general wanted to go.

Except the car and the general were both gone.

"Oh, shit," Eddie said. He might get away with driving the liberated MP jeep into headquarters, but the clowns he'd popped back at the Honolulu jail and all their friends were probably out looking for him and their vehicle. At least now they knew the air raid was for real. Maybe that would keep them busy for a while, doing whatever the hell it was that MPs did in such circumstances.

For now, since the shooting seemed to have died down, Eddie could make it to the docks and pitch in to help the medics and the firefighters. General Belvale would understand, when Eddie finally caught up with him. And at the first still-functioning motor pool he came across he'd change the jeep's identification. Grinning, he started for the harbor. This was a pretty good way to start a war—jail-break and grand theft auto.

A daredevil Jap punched bullet holes in Eddie's jeep, the Zero howling only a few feet above the smoking dockyard, and out across the roiled bay so low that its landing gear almost clipped the water. You had to give the bastards credit; they went all out.

A sailor fought to drag a heavy hose line closer to a burning hangar, ignoring the strafing planes. Eddie got a shoulder under the line and helped the guy drag until the brass nozzle could spew water over drums of aviation gasoline. That scared hell out of him, but not the other swabbies who came to pitch in. Wet down, they plunged into roaring flames to tip over the drums and roll them off into the sea. The brave damned fools had the job under control, so Eddie climbed over a part of the dock where ruptured boards splintered in a circle like the nest of a huge carrion-eating bird. Beyond it shattered concrete showed another bomb hit. Medics waved him over to take one end of a bloody litter. He stayed with them until his shoulders creaked in agony. There was always another wounded guy to haul to an ambulance.

He quit when he came that close to staggering off the dock and into the bay. The Jap planes were gone by then, and Eddie weaved back to his jeep barely in time to save it. A navy ensign in impossibly clean whites was just sliding under the wheel.

Eddie said, "My jeep. Get the hell out."

The ensign had pimples. "A military police jeep is reported stolen. And watch your mouth, soldier. I am a naval officer."

"I know what you're supposed to be. Climb down from that jeep before I kick your officer ass up between your shoulder blades."

"I—I—" the guy sputtered. "Court martial—brig time for—"

Eddie took two steps forward, and the ensign slid out the other side of the jeep, red in the face and yelling for help, for the shore patrol. People in hell wanted ice water, Eddie remembered.

Hours later, tired to the marrow of his bones and crusted deep with dried blood and sticky black oil, Eddie wasn't sure he would ever smile again. There was nothing a goddamned bit funny or glorious about guys with parts blown away, guys burned so badly they screamed for the release of death, or about men turned so suddenly into sides of raw meat.

Temporarily settling for camouflaging the MP jeep markings with OD paint, Eddie drove back to the VIP quarters on the hill. Inside, the cottage was bare of the general's gear, but he had left a note propped against a bottle of Old Bushmill's atop the little bar. Eddie took a long, strengthening drink of Irish whiskey before reading the note. For long moments he luxuriated in the smoky flavor of peat-bog liquor, the cleansing taste of what might have been sweet numbness at another time and in another place.

The general's handwriting was like the man himself, without frills, bold and solid: "Ordered Washington ASAP. General Carlisle en route here as replacement. You will remain as his driver/aide, using these orders assigning you TDY entitled to draw rations and quarters nearest unit your choice."

TDY—temporary duty—General Belvale had practically given him a furlough until the other big wheel got here, and Eddie was thankful as all hell for it. Every outfit in the islands was already going flat-out crazy, stung into insanity by the bombing. Troops would be heading for the beaches to dig defensive positions. Eddie took another drink of Irish and searched for cigars the general might have overlooked in his hasty packing. Belvale had forgotten nothing. That wasn't his style.

Bringing out a Chesterfield, Eddie settled into an overstuffed chair to light the cigarette and to cradle the bottle of Bushmill's. On the table gleamed the general's welcome-to-Hawaii basket, garnished with passion fruit and the inevitable pineapple. He could hide out here until the brass decided that a Jap landing fleet wasn't hovering just off Diamond Head. He could bluff a motor pool or ordnance outfit into repainting the jeep and cruise anywhere he wanted.

After that bloody mess at the dock, Eddie decided he would just as soon wait for General Carlisle to arrive. He didn't really want to go anywhere. Except Tokyo.

CHAPTER 2

INTERNATIONAL NEWS SERVICE—Fort Devens, Mass., December 14, 1941: The U.S. First Infantry Division has been on full alert since December 7, named the "Day of Infamy" by President Roosevelt. All leaves have been canceled in anticipation of an unannounced move somewhere; officials won't even guess at a destination, at least not for publication.

Called the army's elite unit, the First Division has always trained harder and longer than other divisions. Field maneuvers and physical conditioning have doubled in intensity since the perfidious raid upon Pearl Harbor that flung this country headlong into war. Unofficial sources insist that this proud unit will be the first American outfit to draw enemy blood.

Lieutenant Colonel Chad Belvale said to his son, "That's a damned good idea, Owen. It should get rid of the tension all this training has built up. Bad blood also builds up between men. A company party with all the beer they can drink will cause a small explosion, but it should clear the air. Above all things, this outfit has to go into combat as a well-knit family, each man depending upon the other."

"Thank you, sir," Lieutenant Owen Belvale said.

"How's the new CO doing? Your company will miss

Butch Crawford, and regiment will never send him back; he's too good."

"Captain Deas is feeling his way. He does all right."

"For a reserve officer. Ready-made rank. Where the hell do they all come from?" He knew about Deas: University of Alabama, political connections. On the surface Deas looked okay. But there was something reptilian about him, and Chad meant to keep an eye on the man.

Maybe it was Chad himself, on edge with worry about the upcoming troop movements, about down-and-dirty combat nobody else had ever seen. ROTC brass was not what Chad wanted to lead his platoons, much less entire companies. But the point wasn't turning out enough officers to keep up with the desperate expansion of the army. Good men would die because of inept leadership foul-ups, tough and willing RA men who had to depend upon their commanders to make decisions.

The weight of the family's responsibilities grew crushing in times like this. From old and established bases in Virginia and upper New York state the roots of the Belvales and Carlisles spread far, the tendrils bearing other names. But the mission remained the same, and no matter how the family had pushed against the war-is-only-a-bad-memory cartels, or how many millions in treasure were spent to emplace the right politicians, the nation always backslid into isolation.

Chad brought out a pack of Spuds; the menthol eased his throat after he'd taken over a nervous lieutenant's platoon doing close-order drill. Command voice, he said to himself, and he posed in the middle of the field to march the platoon up, down and around. General Carlisle would call it showing his ass. He offered the pack. "Smoke?"

"No, thanks."

From some remembered hillside the vague scent of apple blossoms drifted. Winter still gripped Massachusetts by the throat, but the bright flavors of last spring held strong memories. A beautiful area, with harder and sharper angles than

Virginia's soft loveliness, but he wouldn't mind living here after the war. Here, or in England? No word on Stephanie for too long, even after he'd written Merriman to please keep track.

He said to his son: "You understand why I didn't give you H Company right off?"

"Of course."

"I'm glad you're there. It still needs a regular army man, an executive officer on the stick, to keep everything on solid ground."

"Yes, sir."

Taking a last hard drag upon his cigarette, Chad field-stripped the butt and fed its shreds to the chill air. Maybe the apple scent was Owen's after-shave. Maybe it was a hallucination brought on by wishful thinking. Springtime was Easter and peace and a renewal of life in new birth. Gray Decembers were for endings cold and hard that not even Christmas could ease. It would be a bitch to die in December . . . *silent night, holy night* . . .

He said, "Damn it. Owen—can't we ever talk?"

"You didn't warn me that Mom was coming. I was Officer of the Day and couldn't be relieved."

"She surprised us both—called me from the guest house—and you did see her."

"Politely, formally—'How are you? That's good, dear. Farley sends his love, and do take good care of yourself at war.' A goddamn duty call, didn't you think?"

A wind picked up behind the recently painted barracks, buildings that had been raw framings thrown together upon an ocean of frozen mud. Soldiers had to finish them, make them somewhat livable through forced amateur carpentry. A dogface soldier could do anything, so long as he believed.

"She came because she's worried, because she loves you."

"And loves you?"

"In her fashion."

Residual love and out of habit? Kirstin seemed happy

enough in her new marriage; she looked good. Little worry lines at the corners of her mouth were only natural for a woman in wartime, a woman who had two sons and an ex-husband in uniform. Army wives could always hear the tolling of the bells.

So could wives who had once been army.

"You are invited to the party, sir." Owen took a step back and saluted. "I'll inform Captain Deas."

Farley wouldn't have acted this way. Farley would show how glad he was that his mother had come to visit. A difference between men made up of the same genes; and their school had nothing to do with it. The northern Carlisles favored West Point over Virginia Military Institute. VMI was a gentleman's school, General Belvale said; Crusty Carlisle said that was a crock of grits and shit, that it didn't matter a fart in a whirlwind about gentlemen, so long as the Point turned out hard-nosed soldiers. The cavalier syndrome went out about the time Grant put boiled rat on the rebel menu at Vicksburg.

Watching his son swing away down the company street where sand and thick squares of sod had been brought in to cover the mud, Chad wondered where the time had gone. So much slid on by while nobody noticed, while kids grew suddenly into strange men and grew away from their family.

Wasted, too, had been the quiet hours in barracks on Wednesday afternoons and the boring classes that weren't real training, the hours piled upon hours of make-work. Although the months spent readying for inspections had some value for esprit, to make that cockiness that walks with soldiers proud of their uniform, they also could have been made more useful.

He walked toward battalion headquarters, returning salutes with absent-minded correctness. He remembered how poor damned recruits got themselves gigged every inspection in ranks, how they practically lived every week-end in the kitchen doing extra kitchen police. To avoid that they had to invest their twenty-one dollars a month in uniforms (less 25¢ for the Old Soldiers Home, 75¢ for laundry, a one-dollar barber ticket to pay for four Friday haircuts; less show tickets good for four movies on the post, and minus books of canteen checks issued twice a month, scrip money spendable in the post exchange and at the crap table).

Whatever was left of a recruit's pay went for a five-dollar campaign hat, a Stetson worn for inspections only; then PX blouse buttons whose gilt had to be burned away with lighter fluid in order to really shine the brass. Cut-down and form-fitting shirts and blouses came later. Some of that time and sweat ought to have gone to making a better soldier, not just a prettier one.

He grinned, the taste of soft and smoky coal touching his lips. Probably the family had bitched about the same things during the Crusades. Why polish the damned armor? A strong arm didn't need a blade sharpened to a fine edge. And like soldiers come and gone long before Kipling, the family troopers were always up for screwing between wars . . . "making mock o' uniforms that guard you while you sleep . . . is cheaper than them uniforms, and they're starvation cheap."

Chad stepped around a patch of dirty snow and smelled soft coal smoke from a barracks furnace. How long before orders came down to saddle up and motor out? Nobody could tell, but there were the rumors: desert training somewhere hot, then hurry over to Africa to give the British a hand there; arctic training in frozen Alaska, then ship out to help the Russians; to the deadly Okefenokee swamp for jungle experience to use against the Japs.

Turning into his headquarters, Chad nodded to the clerks as he passed their desks, then to the adjutant, who rose and followed him into his office. "Colonel—a TWX from Washington. It's on your desk. Sorry, sir."

A teletypewriter exchange message uncoded and in the clear? Something to make Captain Nichols sorry? Frowning, Chad picked up the sheet of paper. Any shipping orders would go directly to the regimental CO—but this was not shipping orders.

Over General Preston Belvale's authorization the TWX read: "Status of Captain Keenan Carlisle (promoted rank of major [Res] WD orders dated 11/4/41) officially changed from Missing In Action, China theater, to Killed in Action. Next of kin notified."

Keenan dead, but they'd thought that before, and it was a damned quick change of status. The army never moved this fast unless it was for a good reason, and that with some real power behind it. Why would the general want Keenan KIA? For Nancy Carlisle's sake? It wouldn't be financial; as Chad had done with his own divorce from Kirstin, Keenan had given his ex-wife whatever she wanted. It had been nothing to speak of with Kirstin, and Nancy wasn't the kind to bleed an ex-husband.

Keenan dead; shit! First cousins, they were about the same age and had been pretty good friends, soldiering together on a couple of posts. No kids for Keenan, and maybe that was better all around. Damn—another empty grave in the family cemetery. General Belvale must have some details on Keenan's death, and if he could be reached by phone, Chad would ask about them, and about Nancy. She was a good woman, and making love that one time with Chad didn't change that. It had been a deep and mutual need, and he would always be glad for what they had shared.

But Nancy wasn't Stephanie Bartlett, either.

At a loss for anything concrete to do, Chad stared out the window, seeing nothing but the little paper tags some pissed-off soldier had failed to scrape off the cheap new panes. The battalion street was still a blur when his desk phone rang.

Chad reached for it. "Yes? Colonel Belvale speaking."

It was the regimental CO. "Belvale—give out as many

furloughs as your battalion strength can stand. It's our last Christmas in Christmas-tree land."

Not asking when and where they would be shipping, Chad just said, "Yes, sir." The First Division was going somewhere, and it sure as hell wasn't back to garrison in New York.

CHAPTER 3

REUTERS NEWS AGENCY—Occupied Bangkok, Siam, January 8, 1942: Imperial Japanese army forces have driven south to overrun all of Burma, Malaya and Sumatra. The South China Sea, Bay of Bengal and Indian Ocean have become private lakes for the Japanese fleet, and the emperor's new dominion stretches from Manchuria south to Java and east to New Guinea. There seems to be no end to Rising Sun victories on land, sea and air.

Keenan Carlisle tried not to live, but exquisite pain forced him to suck in breath. Seawater burned his wounds, and a fierce sun beat upon his naked back. Clawing into gritty sand, he bellied across the beach and collapsed in the shade of jungle brush.

His heart fluttered defiantly and he slipped in and out of being. The real and the unreal cut at him with different agonies, and he could not be sure which gripped him. Yin and yang, and oh God, no matter how hard he tried he could not reach Chang Yen Ling. She had to be out there, so he croaked her name again and again.

He saw their faces, every one—the rare smile of Major Hong, Father Lim's gap-toothed pride, the peasant kids who had lived with many forms of death and had finally found something worth dying for.

For him it had been Chang Yen Ling.

He cried, and the tears burned salt grooves down his cheeks but did not wash his soul.

Dark came shivering upon him and then the sun rose dripping red. Keenan became a scarecrow hunching over every foot of beach for lives that did not exist. He became a carrion bird with only wet scraps of salvage to feed upon. A torn jacket, a half-empty water gourd; and there, gleaming through a foot of water, a long knife. He picked up a sandal with the thong still gripped between pale, shrunken toes. There was no foot, just the toes, and he almost threw up until he saw they couldn't be Yen Ling's.

Some of his open wounds held flakes of steel, and he used the knife point to dig them out. Others were gashes and rips that took the same mud and spiderweb poultices. He thought of Chang Yen Ling's medicine kit, the willow leaves and bark that were the source of aspirin; native cures of herb and dried snake and long, sharp needles for acupuncture.

He thought of Yen Ling, and his eyes filled.

Bit by piece he came to remember sailing in the armed Chinese junks, and the aborted mission in Malaya. He remembered the uneven firefight with the Jap sub, and the final, fiery explosion that opened the gates to his personal hell.

Making sure, denying the ugliness of truth and smeared with soothing mud, Keenan crouched in the jungle's edge and watched the sea that refused to give up another survivor. When twilight came as gray and hollow as his soul he waded into the shallows and killed a little shark trapped in a tide pool. He drank the body cavity fluids and slowly chewed the raw, tough flesh.

He had decided to live, and more—to collect for Chang Yen Ling, if that took the miserable life of every goddamned Jap in the world. With his infantryman's built-in guidance system he figured he was back on the mainland of China, north-northwest of Hainan Island and pretty close to the border of French Indochina. By traveling almost due west and crossing a mountain range or two he would come out near Kunming, the Nationalist headquarters. In a thousand miles or so. If he met communist troops on the way, so much the better. Hell, he had a good knife, a water gourd, extra straw sandals and a bundle of rags that could be used a dozen ways. He was in great shape. He was a self-contained fighting unit, the lowest common denominator, and therefore the base danger—the lone infantryman.

Keenan blessed the experience he had gained by fighting beside the guerrillas. The sweating jungle, a brown, muddy river, the fetid earth itself—they were all his friends and allowed him to become them. He looked once more at the featureless sea that buried his love; then he turned into the black shadows of the jungle. They closed about him as they would any animal, prey or predator.

Without calling forth the danger of a fire he ate everything raw. He got by on small reptiles, large crunchy beetles, grubs, roots and berries; sometimes it was only bark and weeds. Sometimes his diet made him sick, so that he had to sweat it out in deep brush like a hurt animal. Sometimes leeches drained his strength or insect stings poisoned him, and he ate a snake that bit him. He out-toughed them all, sun-blackened and turned hairy. Once he looked down into a pool and flinched from the fierce stranger who peered back.

His ancestors must have spooked the infidels whose lands they had invaded in a search for the Holy Grail and in the name of the pale God. The family, that far-spread, honorable and dedicated family of holy warriors who knew the art of arms even before they clanked off to Tyre. Belvale and Carlisle intermarried and carrying on an intrafamily feud after a thousand years, but putting aside differences to carry the gleaming shield of truth and the spiked mace of duty.

Well, truth and duty had damned little to do with butchery, but Keenan no longer gave a shit. He meant to kill Japs, any way he could.

He scared hell out of two brown natives, a man and a woman so small that he realized he had wandered out of China and was in Indochina. He didn't kill the pair, just took anything useful they had. Long ago he had stopped dividing his world into civilian or soldier; there were only survivors, only the dead, the living, and those about to be made dead.

Keenan was naked but for a twist of rag at his crotch when he smelled the campfire. It wasn't big, but here it didn't have to be. Its smoke was a pungent gray snake climbing the trees and signaling. Inching along, Keenan came on the three Japs. They must be on somebody's shit list, he thought; a probe sent out to find trouble, but not big enough to fight: bait.

They knew it, because they were goofing off. Their rifles were pyramided at stacked arms in the middle of the path, and they had brewed a can of tea. They sat cross-legged in a little clearing, laughing and whispering. Blue cigarette smoke trailed wreaths around their close-together heads. Wreaths were appropriate. Goldbricking and bitching, they could have been any group of soldiers in any army.

Almost.

They were Japs, and he not only had to kill them, he wanted to.

Soundlessly, choking down the threatened thunder of his heart, Keenan rose from tangled brush and from behind drew his knife blade quickly across a Jap's throat. He chopped the second man over the Adam's apple, and before the heavy blood geysered far he hurled himself at the third man.

This one dropped the can of hot tea and rolled across the tiny fire to grab for a rifle. Keenan's weight slammed down upon his back, flattening him. Keenan stabbed him between the shoulders, stabbed him again, and a thin sound escaped the Jap as he struggled. Hooking one hand around the guy's small chin, Keenan pulled the head back and made the jugular slash.

Squatting, his ass just over his heels, he stuck the sharp blade into the earth and worked it back and forth, cleaning it. Getting the blood off his own hide would be something else; he was sticky red to both elbows and across his belly and chest. Before he used thick, watery leaves to scrub himself down he inspected the Jap rifles and chose the best one. He kept it within reach, loaded and locked, while he cleaned up. The main body of Jap troops couldn't be too far off, or at least a combat patrol, and he wanted to be long gone if they came this way.

Flies gathered to feed upon puddles of blood, to buzz a black and crawling carpet over the cut and oozing throats. Scraped down, Keenan collected treasures—the 25-caliber Nambu rifle, and an extra bolt; ammunition and two canteens. He clucked over flat cans of fish and a rolled tube of cooked rice, a handful of black tea. He ripped the back of one guy's billed hat so it would fit and made a cloak of sorts from two shirts; the blood would dry. A single pack held all his new gear.

He finished stripping the bodies and burned the shoes and clothing on the cook fire. Bayonets, extra rifles and gear he took with him into the heart of the jungle, where he paused to hide them in the shell of a fallen tree. Let the fucking Japs wonder what happened and worry about a band of native guerrillas. Refreshed and renewed, he shuffled quickly along a game trace, thinking that he should have taken the heads. That would make the Japs keep looking over their shoulders for head-hunting savages. Maybe next time.

An hour, he guessed, then two; he stopped at the rim of a clear spring to rest and fill his canteens. He had so much equipment that he felt rich. Now was the time and place to prove what the army had always claimed—that a hard-ass dogface was complete in himself, his own scout, connecting file, support unit and getaway man. Listening, he heard only the jungle sounds of birds and insects, a damp stir of wind. If the Japs had found their dead men, he was too far away to hear the fuss.

Banzai, you little sons of bitches.

But if a good-sized body of Imperial troops was working along the Indochina border, there had to be a cause; Nationalist, communist or local bandits making trouble. So the Japanese were alert and on the prowl, making it that much tougher for him to pass through the deep jungle territory and reach the foothills.

Still, he was in no hurry. He would remain in the area and kill Japs so long as they gave him targets. Thinking on lessons learned from Major Hong's guerrillas, he walked until he found a wider trail with a traveled look and set about booby-trapping it. Bamboo made a good Venus fly swat, a square frame with supporting crosspieces. Upon each crosspiece he lashed many short and sharp slivers. The work was then strained back and rigged to a trip vine. It was nasty-looking, and he smiled, picturing the swat lashing across the path and impaling some Jap. Walking point was about to become highly unpopular.

Sweating heavily, he tidied up the area and moved out for another mile or so. When he stopped he ate a can of fish and a bit of the cooked rice; the rich food stuffed him and made him queasy. He napped awhile off the trail before setting his next trap—sharpened stakes with their wide ends buried solidly along both sides of the path and angled just so. Farther along he set another bamboo swat. Its arrow release would startle patrolling Japs and make them dive for cover—onto thin stakes that would pierce their bodies.

Excited now, he worked until nightfall, moving up the trail each time, and each time making something else to spook the Japs, something to kill them.

The next day Keenan created a log deadfall, a pit—and for every trick used he left false ones more easily seen, to at least slow them down, at best to make them jumpy as hell, not knowing which ones were real. Since he was also rich with ammunition he made cunning traps of single bullets to be fired by fire-hardened bamboo pins hooked to hidden trip vines.

And days later, leaning back against a tree to slowly chew the last of his liberated rations, he murmured, "And on the seventh day, he rested. Ah, my dear Yen Ling in your tomb by the sounding sea, I send many of your enemies to escort you in that other land."

Scooping a hole in the damp ground, he buried the can and drew leaves over the raw spot. He went on: ". . . for I was no child and she was no child, in that kingdom by the sea; but we loved with a love . . ."

Then it wasn't cute anymore, and he got up quickly and trotted due west into the rolling hills. After them would rise high mountains and open plains. How far, how long? Five, six hundred miles; months, years—a full time of war that would not end until the blood chit was paid and Keenan said so. Or until Keenan was himself ended.

CHAPTER 4

UNITED PRESS—Honolulu, Hawaii, January 10, 1942: Military censorship has been clamped tightly upon all press releases from this wary and still-on-edge city. This includes battle reports from the Philippine Islands and smaller American outposts in the Pacific. But military morale is sky high, as is civilian attitude. Any damage caused by Japan's sneak attack is being cleaned up, and far from dreading an assault landing by the Japs, men here say they would welcome one.

A carefully worded release from combined army/navy headquarters announced the formation of an investigative board that will determine where the blame, if any, will be placed for the success of the Japanese attack.

General Charles Carlisle not only knew that everyone called him Crusty, he gloried in the label. The stupid, inefficient or simple fuck-ups had more pungent names for him, but he didn't really give a rice-fed rodent's rectum. He would do what needed doing, no matter whose tit got caught in the wringer.

Using a straight razor with a carved ivory handle, Crusty made another pass at his bristled chin. It was the damnedest thing: The older he got, the more different colors sprouted on his chin; not the rest of his face, only his knobby chin. Now, for the first time since the Civil War, the army might return to playing beard games, hiding weak chins and pimples. Beards and long hair had been out since Alexander the Great realized they made great hand grips for enemy swordsmen and breeding nests for lice.

Crusty Carlisle didn't have much choice; it was either be a sad-ass rainbow or keep his face as smooth as the skin on a she-mouse's belly.

Why me, Lord—why me?

I don't know, my son. There's just something about you that pisses me off.

Wiping his face, Crusty grunted at the mirror. "It all works out. I got cut in on the jackpot. It's a blessing, being a rich old bastard; nobody fucks with forty million dollars, certainly not senators. And even those Washington-grown peanuts know that's only my personal end of the loot. If the whole family comes down on some congressional eight-ball, it means he's caught in a shitstorm without an umbrella. They'll buy the earth out from under his feet and make him pay cash for enough ground to be buried in."

"Sir?" The aide assigned him by the Hawaiian Command stood at parade rest, garrison cap in the left hand and properly braced at hip level, polished visor turned out. His tailored tropical worsteds had military creases sharp enough to shave with.

Crusty looked the kid over. They must starch and spit-shine him three times a day, he mused. He walked like his ass was cake and he was afraid to crack the icing. His primary duty, of course, was to keep close tabs on every move that Crusty made, every incautious word spoken, every contact he might reach.

Grinning, Crusty said, "I brought a big briefcase here from Washington, and when I go back I mean to have some high-ranking asses in it. You can pass that along."

Kimmel, damnit; one he ached to bag was Admiral Husband Kimmel. "Husband"—imagine! A hell of a name to hang on a baby—it made a man go through a list of possibilities: like his old man was AWOL that birthday and his old lady had been mightily pissed about it.

Kimmel had been warned by TWX from Washington on November 29 that sabotage or outright attack might be expected from the 158,000 Nisei on the islands. His answer to that had been to have his planes hauled into neat lines—all twenty-nine capable of flying. Easier to guard that way, General Short agreed; he had ordered sixty-two of the new P-40 fighters covered down and dressed right. Easy to protect, out in the open.

And a damned sight easier for a single Jap Zero to strafe the entire line without kicking rudder left or right. The bombing came as an afterthought, and almost all the American planes were chopped up and burned where they sat so well guarded. For a commander to be that fucking stupid he had to work at it.

"Where's my driver—General Belvale's driver?"

Lieutenant Taylor looked as if he was constipated and straining to break the blockage. "Ah—absent without leave, sir; escape from custody, assault upon military police, shore patrol and theft of government property. An added charge will soon be desertion in the face of the enemy, since Sergeant Donnely ran away during the air strike."

"Batshit, junior. He could have stayed safe and warm in the pokey. Why was he locked up in the first place?"

"Ah—assault on naval personnel; drunk and disorderly; also a charge of conduct unbecoming a soldier."

Picking up his briefcase, Crusty said. "You seem singularly well-informed about Sergeant Donnely."

"I try to be helpful, sir."

The brown-nosing little son of a bitch. "I'll just bet you do. Well, let's go see whose ass is the hairiest this morning."

They hadn't sent a car for him, but one of the new jeeps with its top down. No starred flags to flap on its fenders and call forth salutes, showing the old bastard from the States just where he stood in the Hawaiian Command.

The driver was a three-striper in starched suntans, his highball a degree from sharp. The lieutenant climbed in back and gave Crusty the front seat. Better this way, riding a little Austin drafted into the military, but Crusty marked the rest of it down. Lord, do they think they're fucking around with some paper asshole?

Forgive them, my son, for they know not what they do.

Into the warm soft wind Crusty said through his teeth, "Nobody ever called me the forgiving kind. If they think to run a bluff on me, they'd better know I deal from a stacked deck and don't bet anything but blue chips."

"Sir?" said the driver.

And Lieutenant Taylor leaned forward to say, "Sir?"

"Sir, my money-making ass," Crusty said. "Pay attention."

He settled back to enjoy the ride, tasting salt in the air and a reminder of burned ships. The jeep swerved to miss a big chuckhole. No, a shell hole as big as anything in the Argonne Forest. No again; it had been caused by a bomb. The Japs didn't pack midget artillery aboard the midget subs designed to fit only little shits. And who would have figured airplanes flying off carrier ships could do this much damage?

Billy Mitchell had, and he got court-martialed for it. Preston Belvale was right, damnit.

Anything to make a ground-pounder's life miserable.

The jeep bucked over another crater, this one half filled. It was only one of many hurried repairs not yet caught up with, although civilians and servicemen alike worked hard. It was as if all signs of the strike on Oahu were patched and swept and polished, as if the terrible thing, the impossible thing, had never happened.

He saw a fat woman in a red muumuu holding out *leis* for sale. A *lei* was a lay, and he should be so lucky, even with a fat woman in a red nightgown. Those little flowers were called frangipani, and the bright orchids had no smell. Well, he'd been around long enough to separate shit from Shinola, and the command peanuts of Hawaii could throw up pretty smokescreens, but he was well acquainted with the odor of bullshit, no matter how well camouflaged.

A pair of shiny gate guards waved the jeep through, saluting when they caught the gleam of stars up front and bars in the back seat. No check of IDs, so the early panic was over and Schofield Barracks had returned to drowsy complacency.

"Headquarters, sir." Lieutenant Taylor, careful of the crease in his trousers, stood ready to assist a tottery old man from the jeep. Crusty knew the imitation soldier thought this AEF relic was on his way out to pasture, that equally ancient and leftover comradeship had passed on this final job before retirement.

Stomping up the stairs, Crusty turned at the landing and said, "Batshit! And don't give me—*sir?*"

He brushed past more MPs playing statues at the conference room and bulled on inside. No Admiral Kimmel; no General Short. Nobody of general or flag rank, in fact, just a few bird colonels and navy commanders gathered for coffee and sinkers at the far end of the long table. A chubby colonel looked around, saw Crusty and called a weak *"ten-hut!"*

Crusty didn't give them as-you-were; he kept them standing while he stalked step by precise step to their end of the table. He frowned at any man caught holding a coffee cup and frowned at anybody trying to sneak one down. After he grabbed the board president's chair he waited until he placed his sharkskin briefcase on the table, opened it with loud, separate clicks and took out a monogrammed pad and a gold pen.

Only then did he say: "Take your seats."

Two of them scurried, the smart ones. The rest sauntered, and the chubby colonel hesitated long enough to let Crusty know who was supposed to be in that chair.

Aiming his pen point and traversing it along the line of officers to his right, then back up the faces on his left, Crusty fisted the pen like a small war club. "Everybody knows this is not an official investigation. The formal hearing will come later in Washington, and I assure you it will come. This I also promise you: I'm going back with names and numbers, so if anybody here is responsible for the worst fuck-up in military history, I'll have his ass on toast. If you try to cover your absentee boss, I'll have your balls for dessert. Two thousand, four hundred and three dead servicemen and thirty-nine civilians want to know why."

"S-sir?" Chubby raised his hand like a schoolboy. "Colonel Pettis here. Those casualty figures are classified, and—"

"Do I look like some dipshit civilian? I was cleared for Top Secret while you were still shitting yellow."

"Sir, as the duly appointed president of this informal—and I stress informal—hearing, I must protest the general's attitude and language—"

"Noted. Now shut the hell up unless I call on you." Crusty glanced down at his notes, conscious of the gasp that ran around the table. It told him that Colonel Pettis was one of General Short's buddies, a high-ranking dog robber. Good; Short would know to hold his ass with both hands and wish he'd made this meeting himself.

"Eighteen ships sunk or badly damaged," Crusty said, "including two battlewagons. Balance that against Jap navy losses of one submarine and five midget subs. Airplanes—188 destroyed, 15 damaged, to 29 Japs. A lopsided score."

Rapping his pen upon the table, he added, "We know who failed in high command; I want details. I also want the little fish—the officers who ignored radar station calls, the sergeant who wouldn't issue guns and ammo, who ran home and who stayed."

"My God," whispered a commander. "He already knows so much—"

Crusty showed his teeth. "We're just getting started."

CHAPTER 5

REUTERS—Singapore, January 1, 1942: British forces fought bitterly along a ten-mile front across west Singapore Island to destroy a strong Japanese bridgehead. All over the island British positions were assaulted by dive bombers, especially at Tenga Airport, where dependents of military personnel and other civilians were attempting to evacuate. An American C-46 transport plane just landed on the aerodrome was slightly damaged but, according to an RAF spokesman, would be repaired by tomorrow.

The uninjured crew is also American, civilians designated as Women Air Corps Support Pilots, or WASPS. Their duty is to ferry bombers and transports to England and then return in groups for more planes. The pilot, Mrs. Farley Belvale, said that this C-46 delivery had been "sidetracked to Singapore" if needed to fly out the sick and wounded.

Co-pilot Miss Theresa Menasco said only: "Wow, what a welcome!"

Penny Colvin-Belvale patted at her coveralls, but looking good was tough after hitting the dirt. Standing tall and locking her fingers together, she forced her hands to stop shaking. Then she turned to examine the plane; her first official command, and the Japs had shot it full of ugly holes. They hadn't even named her plane yet, and the Japs had tried to kill the poor thing.

"Okay?" Theresa Menasco's teeth chattered. "Are you hurt?"

"No—but it's lucky we were already standing on the ground. Look what they did to our plane. Some of those bullets went right through the cockpit. Are you okay, too?"

"Peed my pants." Penny's co-pilot stared at the sky with big eyes. "Will they come right back? I don't like this place already. Let's go home."

"Soon as we're patched up and loaded we'll get out of here—to England, not home." She watched a British truck marked with a red cross race across the airstrip going beep-beep-beep and flashing a red light.

The fair-skinned driver's tin hat sat on the back of his head, the chin strap hooked under his peeling nose. "Good-oh, ladies. The nippers seemed to have missed. Do hop aboard for Charing Cross Station or our equivalent. Charlie—see to the ladies' kits."

Climbing down, the other medic gathered the Val Pacs and shoulder bags, flung aside when the Japanese machine-gun bullets ripped through the plane's skin and gouged long strips from the blacktop. Charlie was a teenager with cropped brown hair and cheeks that Penny thought would always be rosy, Singapore's heat not counted.

She had never known heat like this, not growing up in Virginia or while undergoing intense checking out on transport planes. She had flown nothing bigger than a Piper Cub and Taylor Crafts, but the air corps was desperate. She never quite got over the North Carolina sun blistering the brown, dusty training field and frying everyone's brains.

But this heat was a wet, furry blanket meant to smother, to drown lungs and force sweat to flow from every pore of her body. If she had any makeup left, it had run down her neck and puddled between her breasts. Given a hand up into the back of the truck, she sat beside Theresa beneath the rolled-up canvas top.

"Bake oven," Theresa gasped, fanning herself with the billed cap that was part of their semi-uniforms. Penny pulled out the front of her coveralls and blew down them. It didn't help.

The driver meshed gears and the truck leapt forward, creating wind that was almost cool. Over his shoulder he called, "One gets used to exotic Singapore. Pity you won't have the time; none of us latecomers will."

Theresa stuck her face into the wind. "What's he mean? I thought this was England's strong point. Is everybody leaving?"

"I don't know. For sure not all aboard a single shot-up plane."

Charlie the rosy kid seemed even younger in the short pants and short sleeves of his faded summer uniform, but it hung loosely upon him. She looked closer as the truck skidded to a stop in a boiling of dust. Did fever put that flush in his cheeks? He was a medic; surely he'd know.

As he crawled off the truck and turned to help them down Charlie wobbled and brushed a hand over his face. "Sorry; just give us a bit. Quinine ran short a fortnight past."

Penny hung her shoulder bag and lifted her Val Pac. Theresa struggled with hers but got it off the tailgate as the boy kept apologizing. The truck dashed around the sandbagged terminal building. Inside, a ceiling fan stirred body-sweat-and-curry-smell air over women and children packed against the walls. Some slept on the dirty tile floor, some hunched upon benches or suitcases. Four women and a boy gathered at a teakettle balanced on stones over a tin of canned heat. Two little girls played with one rag doll. A graying native woman watched over them.

Through the rear door Penny saw a large canvas strung to the building, and beneath it row upon row of wounded men on stretchers, uniformed nurses moving through them. Beyond the field low thunder rumbled, only it wasn't thunder. Men were fighting and dying out there.

Touching Penny's arm, Theresa whispered, "Too many of them. We'll never get the crate off the ground. Where are all the English planes?"

"I'm afraid to ask. Oh, God—I hope they don't want us to choose who gets to go and who has to stay."

"Won't the doctors send the worst cases first? We can come back for the others."

Penny swallowed. "Look around; I don't think we'll be coming back. Singapore is about to fall. All those wounded, the refugees, and that artillery fire sounds too close."

A medical officer wearing glasses with one lens cracked waved a clipboard at her and shouted he'd be with them in half a mo. Penny straddled her Val Pac and spun her Ronson at a Kool; even the menthol tasted warm. She wasn't sorry she'd volunteered for this trip. She just hadn't expected it to be so grim. Atop the roof a siren screamed. A woman said, "Bloody hell," and the two little girls scuttled to their native nanny. One turned back for the rag doll.

Farley ought to be here, Penny thought. Farley Belvale should wait here with his lawful wedded wife and all these frightened people—wait for the Jap planes to come firing machine guns and dropping bombs. Let him discover that all his money couldn't buy him a seat on a plane to safety, or even a vial of quinine pills. Goddamn Farley for confusing her so, for being less a man than the boy who first brought her to his super-military family. Walt Belvale's name was on a stone above an empty grave in the family grove, and double damn Farley for even thinking she would consider dishonoring it.

She was strong, but Farley had pulled at that strength because he had so little of his own. He was a product of Kill Devil Hill and the West Point of the South, so that lack of fiber came as a surprise to Penny. She drew hard upon her cigarette and ran the images of Farley through her mind—handsome in his uniform, an officer and certainly a gentleman, he had courted her in a sweet, old-fashioned way that delighted her mother.

He was at first tentative, apologetic, and felt he was trespassing. I know you were engaged to Walt Belvale, and I respect his memory, he said, but he was killed before we even got into the war, as an observer in Poland. We have to accept his death and go on. And I love you, pretty Penny Colvin. I can't keep hiding that.

Penny hadn't been sure about Farley; she was certain that she belonged at the Hill, that she should have been born into that fabulous family. Maybe that was the wrong reason for marrying Farley Belvale, and a good part of their trouble. The drinking had always been with Farley, but not noticeable as more than what any spirited gentleman of means was entitled to. In public he held it well.

An explosion shook the terminal, and snowflakes of plaster drifted down. A string of bombs landed then—*blam!—blam!—blam! blam! blam!*

"Holy Mother." Theresa Menasco grabbed her arm. "And I asked for this."

Antiaircraft guns around the airfield fired steadily, adding to the din. Penny put her hands over her ears and pulled deep breaths, tasting bitter gunpowder and the brassy tang of fear. The girl with the doll nodded and smiled at her. Penny pulled her hands down, and now the ack-ack guns were louder than the bombs.

In his cups, as the old Virginia saying went, Farley had asked her to fly to Switzerland. Damn going off to be shot, he said; see how many Nigras and New York Jews get killed in this war. We have plenty of money to live high on the hog in Switzerland, forever if we have to.

And she had told him it would have to be forever because the family would never allow them to return.

The siren stopped howling, and the gunfire died away in eerie silence. Now Penny could hear a baby crying. Farley sometimes cried when he was drunk—because he didn't make the first string at VMI, because his mom deserted his father for another man, because Penny didn't think a desk job in Washington was a good idea, either. He turned most maudlin when he accused her of not caring for him the way she had his cousin, accused her of still being in love with Walton, or worshipping the memory of a dead man.

Penny didn't think so. By now she wasn't sure she had ever been in love, except with the patriotic concept of the Belvale-Carlisle family. She had grown up with tales of glory. Her mother was so proud of her own membership in the Daughters of the American Revolution, and the Daughters of the Confederacy. And sickly Daddy Colvin, who never had a martial ancestor, kind of submitted when the talk of genealogy so often got around to wars. Whatever, Penny was glad to wear the Belvale name, however come by.

"You're the Yank pilots?"

Looking up, Penny rose to face a small, straight-backed woman, some kind of officer. Her blue uniform was grimy and her short hair dusty; fatigue lined her face and glazed her blue eyes.

"That's us. Is our plane fixed already?"

"Afraid not; our mechanics are checking the vital parts—between bloody air raids. No cosmetics for the bullet holes, so you must take off as soon as possible."

"When the wounded are loaded?"

The woman put one hand against a pillar to steady herself. Not really beautiful, Penny thought, but so attractive that men must follow in droves.

"Women and children. The soldiers and officials want it this way—rather take their chances with the Jap than gamble their families."

Theresa Menasco crossed her arms over her belly. "Are the Japs that bad?"

"Worse, I'd say. Please come to the billets with me. We're a bit short of things, but a spot of tea and a wash ought to help." Leaning away from the wall, she held out a small, dirty hand. "Leftenant Stephanie Bartlett, acting commander of Singapore's remaining ack-ack units."

CHAPTER 6

The New York Times—New York, February 10, 1942: The former French luxury liner *Normandie* burned at its West 48th Street mooring today. Taken over by the United States after the fall of France and renamed the U.S.S. *Lafayette,* the 84,000-ton ship was being refitted as a troop carrier.

Witnesses said a spark from a workman's oxyacetylene torch started the blaze, which raged from 3:00 A.M. until the ship keeled over this afternoon. One hundred twenty-eight navy, Coast Guard and civilians fought the inferno. One civilian died at Roosevelt Hospital, and the Federal Bureau of Investigation is looking into the possibility of sabotage.

Preston Belvale sat beside Benjamin Alexander in the main briefing room of the War Department. He had picked seats near a ventilator because his cousin had to avoid smoke. Gassed at Soissons, Ben still had trouble with his lungs, and if he wasn't family, he would have been shoved into military obscurity. Belvale admitted the same of himself and his leg wound, his age. Now both of them were needed again, and each had picked up an additional star.

Leaning close, whispering against the shuffling and throat-clearing of high-ranking officers from all services, Belvale said, "Can you believe that it's been a quarter century since we started off to our first war with the AEF? We're such mangy old dogs that we should be quietly dozing in the sun."

"Tried that," Ben answered. "We couldn't stay asleep even before the bombs woke up everybody else."

Belvale sat straight and watched George Marshall cross the stage to the big situation map and loose its opaque covering. Overlay markings signifying enemy positions strung a bloody trail all across the Pacific theater of operations. That was a grandiose title for a faraway area where the U.S. was suffering the worst and possibly the final defeat in its history.

General Marshall touched a long wooden pointer to a scattering of small islands difficult to see from back of the room. His voice matched the man, battered, a bit rough, but knowing the decisive. "The Netherlands Indies—Batavia airfields and city streets strafed, friendly planes destroyed on the ground as usual. Why the *hell* does that continue to happen?

"Borneo—Jap patrols are pushing south toward a port three hundred sea miles from Surabaya. We can write off Borneo and any British left there."

The pointer moved. "Burma—the Japs are still held in check along the Salween River. A report from Chennault claims his volunteer pilots shot down their hundred and first enemy plane."

Marshall coughed, and a Marine colonel in the front row said, "Oh, yeah—Chennault," and light laughter rippled the audience.

"The Philippines," Marshall said, and the room went silent. "MacArthur's lines have been hit by repeated attacks the past few days. The Japs have been stopped each time—so far. Fire from the forts at the entrance to Manila Bay silenced some Japanese batteries."

When Marshall lowered the pointer Belvale stood up, and the chief of staff nodded at him. Belvale said, "Sir—is there any chance of getting reinforcements to MacArthur, supplies and air protection?" He knew the answer but hoped he was wrong.

Shaking his head, Marshall said, "I wish to God there was. We don't have the ready troops, Preston, or even the arms. If we did, there's no way to get them there in time. We're lucky to hang onto our few fighting ships left in the Pacific, much less try to sneak loaded troopships past all those waiting Jap subs and planes.

"Our air support? The carriers need their planes, and beyond those, there aren't any. The planes that weren't turned into junk at Pearl, MacArthur lost on the ground—on the goddamned *ground!*—two days later. He hasn't come up with an excuse for that.

"I remind you gentlemen that whatever is said in this room stays in this room, or the press will also report wholesale courts-martial. I tell you now that the Jewel of the Pacific will be in Jap hands too soon—Manila, Luzon and the Bataan Peninsula. The medieval fortress of Corregidor will withstand siege for a short time, until sickness and starvation kill more defenders than the Japs. After it falls, God only knows what the Japs will do to prisoners."

Three rows up another general rose to his feet and snapped an unrequired salute. Ben Alexander nudged Belvale. "Wouldn't you know it? Tom Skelton is about to stuff his mouth with shoe leather."

Whispering back, Belvale said, "It's big enough for both feet."

Skelton posed at parade rest, shoulders back, hands locked behind his back, military as all hell. "Sir! I cannot understand how red-blooded American troops could retreat before any slant-eyed imitation soldiers that can't even shoot straight. Any American can whip ten Japs and—"

Marshall put both hands on the stick and thrust it out like a bayonet's long stroke. "Tell that to all our dead! If you have nothing else to contribute, sit down."

He rubbed his left hand over his lined face and across

the broken nose. Belvale saw the pointer drop to rest its tip upon the platform floor, Don Quixote's broken lance.

Marshall said, "We have to abandon all those troops who have faith that help is on its way, who believe we won't let them take on the whole Jap army by themselves. It's what MacArthur is telling them, and they believe. Jesus—the poor goddamn Philippine Scouts, the Constabulary. The Japs will butcher them. They might murder our men, too, but death is sure for those gutty little Flips."

Belvale waited a second, then asked, "And MacArthur himself, sir? Does he surrender with the troops?"

Looking back at the map, Marshall said, "I don't know yet."

There was more of the same depressing intelligence. The only bright spot was FDR's alphabetized war board agencies pressuring factory owners into unheard-of production schedules. Marshall thanked the gathering and stepped down.

"Holy shit," Ben Alexander said, "look who's going to close with an invocation! I didn't know he was back in Washington."

Colonel Luther Farrand had developed a peculiar method of humble strutting, a man of God not prideful enough to presage a fall but demonstrating that he was one of the chosen.

"He's wherever the rank shineth. Let us execute a rear march," Belvale said, and he walked through the hallelujah presentation by the family's most visible misfit. Propped at parade rest again, Major General Thomas Skelton frowned at them, and limping on, Belvale gave him back a lifted eyebrow.

Over coffee royale at the hotel bar Belvale rolled a cigar between his palms and sniffed it, then clipped one end and held the cigar in his mouth. He didn't light it. "We told them, Ben. Over and over we beat alarm drums and waved red flags. They didn't hear and would not look. Now the line soldiers pay the blood price, and the sailors go down to the sea in ships—but they don't come back."

Ben sipped bourboned coffee and nodded. "Go ahead and light that damned thing. I'll breathe around the smoke."

"I chew them as often as I smoke them. Will Marshall let you breathe salt air?"

"Not Atlantic or Pacific. He checked with the pill rollers, and they said one hemorrhage will do me in. Hell, they said that twenty-five years ago. Shouldn't bitch, I guess. At least I get a staff job." Ben finished his drink, and the waiter appeared with fresh, steaming cups. "How did the president take your Pearl Harbor report?"

"Sorrow and anger." Belvale ran a thumbnail over his mustache. "He's waiting for the other shoe to drop—Crusty's in-depth testimony to fix definite responsibilities. After that, I suspect a covey of officers will find themselves on retirement."

"Herd is a better word. Coveys of quail fly fast and far—cattle and jackasses stumble along in herds. The whole damned herd ought to be tried, but they won't be."

Belvale drank in silence for a while, rich chicory coffee and ten-year-old bonded whiskey. Both would soon be added to a growing list of wartime shortages. "Move to the Hill, Ben. You'll be close enough to commute, and this city is already overrun."

Raising his cup, Ben said, "Done. That's one good thing about being a widower—no problem with moving. It's about the only good thing. Maybe Minerva will seduce me."

"Kee-rist! That's a disgusting picture. Need help with your gear? I'm getting back to our war room. It's yours to run between official tours."

Benjamin Alexander stood up. "You've swung some kind of deal. You won't be in residence on the Hill."

"Not for long," Belvale admitted. "I have an overseas slot."

* * *

The dawn smell of the ocean was good, and flower scents walked a gentle wind. The woman's perfume was even better because only part of it came from a bottle; the rest was her golden sweat and the special attar of arousal.

Eddie Donnely eased away from the full curves of her body. It was well into daylight, and General Carlisle would be rising to strop his old razor with the fancy handle. The Hawaiian dog robber would already have brought a pot of black coffee, and Eddie had better get back with Crusty's staff car. The hard-nosed old bastard probably had an early meet somewhere, to find one more bit of information that meant one more slice off some brass's ass.

Grinning as he slid into his drawers, Eddie liked that line—brass ass, because that's exactly what lay screwed out on the tangled bedsheets, an exceptional piece of ass that was legally assigned to a field-grade officer.

Vanessa's husband was a full colonel on extended TDY to the big island, a G-3 staff officer suddenly jumped one rank and thrown out of city hall to command troops. Colonel Hammond's paper-shuffling and training-plans experience didn't do him much good out in the boondocks where he headed one of the panic outposts that sprang up after the raid on Pearl. The absence didn't do his wife much good either, but it sure helped pass the time for Eddie.

She sat up, a sleepy woman twenty years older; one hell of a woman.

"Eddie? Oh, dear—must you leave so early?"

"The general needs his car." He stepped into his pants, pulled the belt tight and used his handkerchief to wipe fingerprints off the brass buckle. He winked as her purplish eyes, softer without glasses, lingered on his chest. Then he pulled on the undershirt and reached for his shirt. "You'll come back tonight?"

The bedsheet fell away. She was firm all over, tanned and richly put together. Vanessa had taken good care of herself, but her sensual appeal wasn't the main reason he'd zeroed in on her. She was an officer's wife, the higher ranking the better, and he would have passed up more beautiful, unattached women for her even if she hadn't saved his butt before. The first time he screwed her, out on the dewy golf course, was good but too quick, and she had been just about drunk. From them on it only got better.

"Hup-two, hup-two! Double time, baby." Sitting on the bed, he put his arms around her nude body and caressed her slowly and tenderly. Then he kissed her, sweet and adoring as any schoolboy with a crush on his teacher. But the real learning had been hers, new sensations and experiences that made her bloom like an exotic flower kept too long in the bud. Eddie couldn't understand a husband letting such a passionate woman go to waste, but he had ceased being surprised at male sexual stupidity.

Vanessa torched his mouth with her tongue, forcing him to pull away. "Hey, woman—ease up! You don't want me to desert, do you? General Carlisle—"

"Damn Crusty Carlisle, Jonathan Hammond and the entire United States Army. I want you with me, Eddie."

Touching her cheek, soft as a drifting snowflake, Eddie whispered, "Tonight, darling," and he hurried out the back door before the colonel's houseboy and cook arrived. Post-bombing panic hadn't yet swept away most Nisei workers, although immigrant and native-born Japanese were being investigated as soon as the FBI and military intelligence groups could get around to them.

He backed the GI sedan from the driveway's flowering hedges—great for camouflage—and turned onto Kulilani Drive ahead of civilian traffic that gas rationing had thinned to mostly trucks hauling basic supplies. Blue navy vehicles and OD army trucks and jeeps zipped everywhere, the drivers not leery of civilian police since the islands had gone under martial law.

MP gate guards waved him into the spread of Schofield Barracks, and he drove directly to the VIP quarters. Given a few minutes, he could police himself up the old army way—shit, shave, shower, shampoo, and shoeshine. Eddie was good at doing it all quickly; many a morning he'd made it back to barracks just in time to change into fatigues for reveille.

You'll fuck up good some day, his old man said . . . it's easy to lose stripes, but tough to get them back . . . goddamnit, chasing cunt all your life won't get you anything but trouble.

Parking the car and slipping through the kitchen door, Eddie headed for the servants' quarters. "Sure, Daddy. Of course, First Sergeant Donnely—*you* sure as hell ought to know. You can pretend you don't remember the bitch that broke your balls and my mother's heart. But I do—oh, yeah, father, topkick, husband—I remember every fucking detail about the major's redheaded daughter. Not the same details you'll never forget, of course. I was too young to understand."

The Hawaiian house man came into the kitchen with an empty coffeepot. "Hey, man—general be ready pretty quick. Who you talking to?"

"Nobody you know, Bobby. Stall the general for a few minutes."

Bobby Gee showed perfect teeth in a wind- and sunburned face. "Hey, man, that tough *malihini* going to put plenty big-shot *haole* down the toilet. Them *kahunas* going crazy-*pupule*, them experts that got us bombed. When this new general go by mainland?"

"No *hu-hu*, Bobby—no sweat. You can talk without that beach boy pidgin."

"Yeah, but we mix up you *haoles* this way. Excuse me—you white guys. I like this general too good, man, so if he's cutting out, I quit and get me a uniform, too."

Eddie took a can of Schlitz from the refrigerator and punched two holes with an opener. "Better stock up on these church keys, beach boy. Opening beer with a bayonet gets sloppy. When's the old man going home? Whenever he wants—*makemake*."

"You do pidgin more pretty good yourself."

"Sure"—Eddie sang softly as he ducked into the bathroom—"Princess Pupule has plenty papaya; she likes to give it away . . ."

Eddie didn't feel funny. Even in the afterglow of good loving—and love is what sex always turned into, although it started out as a punishment. He got into a mean mood thinking of his old man and the mother who had stopped smiling when Eddie was just a confused kid.

Under the shower he soaped away the darkness. Toweling, he grinned. Oahu had been a kick after the raid. General Belvale had gone, and General Carlisle hadn't arrived, so Eddie changed the numbers and markings on the jeep he liberated from the downtown MPs and went out to see what he could do.

The Reserve Officers Training Corps kids from school were serious about defending against the Japs expected at any minute. They wore their ROTC half-ass officer uniforms and were armed with some .22 rifles and a shotgun. They needed everything else—rations, shelter halves, and blankets; they needed an imaginative supply sergeant. An early lesson from Big Mike Donnely had been on scrounging, and Eddie scored an A.

He counterfeited orders, bluffed, stole and traded until the fuzzy-faced unit was the best equipped on the island. The mistake he made was celebrating. When he furnished the kids with booze from a bombed-out liquor store they got drunk and fired their weapons.

The MPs had just dragged Eddie out of the stolen jeep and were arguing about who was going to do what to him when Vanessa Hammond drove up, the silver bird gleaming on her post license plate. Officer wives could always pull rank better than their husbands, and Eddie was glad for it. She got him off and away before the MPs knew what hit them. And after that General Carlisle arrived in Honolulu with steam pumping from his ears, so Eddie was only a day late for his protection.

"Sergeant!"

Tucking his tie between the second and third shirt buttons, Eddie said, "Coming, sir!"

Damn, but he enjoyed being near any action that nailed inefficient officers, and he enjoyed the sun, sex and pineapple juice bootleg existence of the islands, but out there beyond the ocean rim a war was being fought. Before he was a lover Eddie Donnely was a soldier, and determined to show Big Mike just how good. He didn't know if he could handle it if something blocked his destiny.

CHAPTER 7

ASSOCIATED PRESS—Manila, the Philippine Islands, February 10, 1942: The United States Army Far East Headquarters [USAFE] announced today that a small Japanese invasion force landed at Legaspi, Southern Luzon. One Japanese plane was shot down by an American fighter over Bancayan in the mountain mining district.

Manila took further precautions to evacuate the old walled city, and Red Cross officials said some 2000 families have been trucked to safety zones.

Hell was born in the jungle that was now Keenan Carlisle's domain. It was hot and stank, and to live there meant suffering little pitchfork cuts and barbed stings. Fire was sporadic, and fungus was a fine substitute for brimstone. And Keenan? He was Lucifer and God and the angel of vengeance. He slithered through Kanai grass as quietly as any reptile, his skin considerably tougher and his poison more deadly because it could be spat up close or at long range.

This stretch of jungle that clung to the foothills was thicker, more lush, and an overhead canopy of leaves shut out the light. Maybe it was always twilight in hell, and not leaping flames. Visibility reached only as far as the scrubby vines ahead, to thorny growth that made small hisses against his tattered clothes. He squatted for a while to peel and eat slim new bamboo shoots. The crunches were too loud in his ears, too loud because this kind of close-packed vegetation absorbed other sound. He was keenly aware of smells, a major survival sense here—rotting plants, animal piss and bird shit, bat droppings and the primeval earth, which exuded the musk of both approaching death and the raw beginning of life.

Keenan's home, yes, but also home for other animals, fauna he had never seen before, and never clearly. They eased through the brush, lean shadows swift and quiet, disturbing because they might be something else.

And the goddamned birds—one that screamed like a crazy woman, another that barked like a dog and a weird little bastard that sounded exactly as if some idiot banged two blocks of wood together. The birds had their uses, though; they ate bugs and were quick to cry warning.

Keenan moved again, low to the damp earth and becoming one with a bush or a tree while he carefully eyed the area all around him, listening and sniffing the air. Even the insects had their warning system: cicada, giant grasshoppers, crickets and click beetles and their neighbors, the tree frogs, all fell silent at the approach of noise not their own.

A puddle of tense silence lasted until the intruder moved on, and then the cacophony lifted behind it—behind the scouting Jap. Even in darkest night a hunter could mark the overlapping pools of silence and know exactly where his prey crept.

But the insects were more dangerous to Keenan than the few Japs he had found and killed. When and where he could he wore an armor of leaves embedded in smeared mud against the malaria-carrying *Anopheles* mosquito, the ticks and flies. The mud coating was always temporary, going dry and flaking away. And he fretted that the face pack might cut off his peripheral vision or make him clumsy at the wrong moment. Keenan knew he already had malaria, but so far he was able to handle the intermittent chills and fever.

Yen Ling, my love—may I chew the leaves of the cinchona tree from your aid kit? They ease the aching bones and cool the scalding sweats. But the greatest blessing would be the touch of your hand upon my cheek. Yen Ling, Yen Ling, my love . . .

Oh, you bastard Japs!

They were bloodsuckers like the jungle ticks. Japs lurked in ambush everywhere—underwater in submarines, dug into spider holes, lashed into treetops, waiting to feast on blood. As the ticks waited on brush for warm animals to pass. Then they dropped and hung on with tiny barbed feet until their flat heads needled under the skin surface and they sucked. Swollen to twenty times their size with blood, they dropped off. He was lucky; the bites seldom infected him, but he couldn't afford the loss of life fluids.

A huge buffalo fly zoomed into his cheek, and Keenan crushed it, but not with a slap loud enough to call attention. He wasn't that far from a Jap bivouac, and the cover of night was coming on. He was like the sand fly, skinny and quick, vicious on the attack. Or the assassin bug; or the nameless little spider never noticed until his bite hurt like hell.

It was always twilight here, so there was no hesitation between day and dark. Night slammed down through the leafy ceiling, and Keenan squatted on his heels, Nambu rifle slung across his back, the hand-slick wooden butt of the long knife in his hand. A Chinese farmer had made that knife, lovingly shaping and sharpening a precious length of steel into a tool. The tool became a weapon when the farmer joined with Major Hong's guerrillas to fight the invaders of his country.

And then the fucking Japs blew him into shark food.

And the peasant's blade became the devil's pitchfork.

Within minutes Keenan smelled smoke. Whenever the Japs thought themselves safely beyond a combat zone they built little fires to cook their rice and to hold back the night, like all men afraid of what they could not see or name.

But Japs weren't men, not even Neanderthal; they were just things that lived under rotten logs in the jungle—like the hairy, poisonous centipedes and deadly scorpions and gray lice; the maggots fat and crawling. They were God's mistakes, and He needed help erasing them.

Woodsmoke thickened the air, and firelight flickered through the vines. Silently Keenan sawed a pathway with his knife; silently he unslung the rifle and bellied forward, pulled along by his elbows.

Tinkle-splash!

The stench of urine, almost close enough to taste.

Rolling his eyes upward, he saw the Jap outlined against light from the cookfire, the Jap straddle-legged to piss.

From the group around the fire somebody shouted, "*Nani o?*" and part of Keenan's mind jerked back to the months spent as an observer with Major Watanabe's Imperial troops in Manchuria. Watanabe had become a semi-friend, a respected soldier. Now Keenan would tear out his goddamned Jap throat.

Nani o—What are you doing, what's happening?

"*Shuben suru, nandesu-ka?*"—Taking a piss, what do you think?

Rifle placed gently upon the earth, knife clutched tightly, edge up, Keenan began to lift himself for the gut stroke. He stopped in time, seeing the clearing as the Jap shook his cock and put it back into his baggy pants, seeing the machine gun set up to cover a crossing of surprisingly wide paths beyond the campsite.

A Chinese supply route for Chiang Kai-shek or Mao Tse-tung, a hidden road where coolies plodded under great loads and shaggy Mongol ponies struggled to pull heavy carts? No travel at night, or these roadblock troops wouldn't expose themselves this way. Keenan considered where the main body would be and decided that outposts like this one were stationed at strategic points along the trails. They would be connected by radio, the command post tucked somewhere behind the line and centrally located. If there was a main body, it was even farther out of reach.

So he allowed the Jap pisser to walk away with his balls. A better kill was possible, maybe even a string of them, if he was patient. And in the jungle, patience was a law of survival. Keenan melted into the fetid earth and did not flinch when the mosquitoes buzzed his face, or when night things slimed and fed upon his skin where the mud did not cover.

The fire burned low, and the Japs mumbled to their blankets by the book, as Keenan remembered—one man taking first watch behind the machine gun, the rest of the squad zigzagged behind him in shallow one-man holes. Six Japs in all; a piece of canvas spread over ammo boxes, water cans and supplies. Keenan waited, and the fire turned to dim coals. One Jap snored, a light, bubbling noise.

Leaving his rifle, Keenan eased from the brush and into the clearing, any tiny sound he might commit masked by the singing of the jungle night. He eeled softly up the line and came to his knees behind the gunner. The domed helmet was canvas-covered, and when Keenan reached up and over to hook his fingers under the front edge the helmet strap bit into the throat and choked off any outcry.

Keenan slashed the jugular, and thick blood hosed out. Letting the body sag, he waited until the spray lessened, then finished cutting off the Jap's head. There was a little trouble sawing through the neck bone.

If this were a GI heavy weapons squad, the next guy would be called the number-two man, bearer of an ammunition box and the water can. Keenan stabbed him through the back of the neck and took his head.

Number three, number four and five all died without a struggle, with no moment to make a prayer to their Shinto gods or apology to their emperor. And if they were to rise in ten days to enter warriors' paradise, they would do so without their heads.

The last man was the snorer, still popping little bubbles. Keenan's lips peeled away from his teeth, and he tasted blood still warm upon his face. Shaking now, he poised the wet blade over the sleeping Jap. Kill the son of a bitch! There are no more around to hear him, he told himself, so take your time and kill him slow, so that he screams like the men the sharks ripped apart in the red waters off Hainan Island.

Not Chang Yen Ling, please, God—not Yen Ling.

Give this little turd his life, a wiser voice counseled Keenan; let him sleep away the night, and when he wakes up he'll see all his dead friends without their heads and know fucking well that he's lucky to be alive. He can spread the horror story, tell about the slavering *yonsei,* the ghost that comes by night and eats the heads of soldiers.

Grunting, the Jap turned in his blanket and almost didn't live to tell his story. Keenan waited a moment longer at the hole, then drifted away and collected the dripping heads to hide them in the brush. Always listening for any move from the Jap, he put food and a water canteen into a pack and found a straw-covered bottle of sake.

Only then did he string lacing through the pins of a few grenades and set an ammo box on a wire hooked to the radio on the canvas cover. Jap grenades had to be knocked against something hard after the pins were pulled, to start the fuse. Whoever lifted the radio would drop the box on grenade one.

Banzai!

With his rifle and enough supplies to last a long time Keenan slipped back into the jungle, still heading west by northwest, and now with a trail to parallel, a Chinese supply trail that the Japanese had marked for machine-gun ambushes.

Keenan meant to find each one.

CHAPTER 8

INTERNATIONAL NEWS SERVICE—Washington, D.C., February 12, 1942: A crisis is impending in the relations between the United States and Vichy France. Increasing activity between the Vichy government and the Axis has led the State Department to review its policy of limited cooperation with the administration of Marshal Philippe Pétain.

Immediate cause of the crisis is a report that Germans were allowed to use French ships to supply Axis forces in Libya. French representatives in Indochina are negotiating with the Japanese to turn over French ships there for action against the Allies in Malaysia.

Chad Belvale was damned tired of sand, fine as dust, hard as glass. Camp Blanding sand. If, in the infinite wisdom of the War Department, Florida was the best locale to train and acclimate troops for desert warfare, the planners could blow it out their collective stacking swivels.

First off, right now it was cold as an old maid's belly button, and the humidity so high that the very air dripped. No matter to the damned sand; wet or dry it whipped along with every breeze, grinding at the pyramidal tents and screwing up weapons. It got into food and grated your teeth, slid into leggings and shoes to make hiking difficult and ground down the men themselves. Maybe the general staff's intent was to turn every dogface soldier as mean as snake shit so they'd be ready to kill the first Nazi, Jap or wop they saw.

They were almost that mean now, and that was a minor problem. A problem because of weekend brawls in Boomtown and Starke, and as far away as Jacksonville. "Damn a soldier who won't fight," as Crusty Carlisle was wont to proclaim, but so many on the sick book and missing duty wasn't funny. A good part of the trouble arrived with the 36th Infantry Division out of Texas, one of many National Guard units newly called to federal duty. Weekend warriors, the regulars called them, and the blue arrowhead, T-for-Texas shoulder patches came back with damn Yankees.

And part of the trouble was a song—a goddamned *song*—"Deep in the Heart of Texas" (clap-clap-clap)!

"Stand up when you hear that song," the Texans said.

"Fuck you," said New York's own.

And the war started with any weapon to hand—chairs, beer bottles, the brass buckles of garrison belts. One memorable battle featured the heavy lids of restaurant ice-cream containers.

Still, the problem was minor, because the division CG's recent order was plain: Keep your hands in your pockets. No more fights or the whole outfit is restricted. Shame on the goofy bastard who got his entire unit shut away from the off-post booze and what women were on the market. His own buddies would stomp a mudhole in his ass and walk it dry.

"You'd think," Chad said to his battalion clerk, "that these bastards would take it easy after breaking their humps all week. Thirty-mile hikes in full field equipment is worth sixty in this damned sand—"

Corporal Guist said, "It just jacks them up, sir. And they figure . . ."

After a long moment Chad said, "Figure what?"

Looking down at his typewriter, Guist said, "Well, sir—

that they might be dead pretty soon. So they'll get drunk and—begging the colonel's pardon—fuck and fight."

"I notice you stay close to home."

"Yes, sir. I intend to make it back. I have a wife."

Chad went to the door flap and looked out. H Company's troops, loaded down with heavy machine guns and 81mm mortars, trudged past battalion headquarters on their way home for the night.

Chad used to have a wife, a good-looking woman still. Only now she was married to somebody else.

Here their older son would soon be along, a lieutenant bringing up the rear of the column, looking after his men, checking on anyone who fell out of the road march. That was the company commander's duty, not a job for the exec or a platoon leader. But Captain Deas found excuses to miss long hikes and rough field exercises.

Deas was another hemorrhoid in the anal canal that led to the battalion executive officer, the master asshole, Major Thornton. He had to get rid of them before the regiment went into combat, and another loser who defiled his position of command. Captain Pettis floated bad checks through the officers mess and picked most of them up next payday. Other poker players said he had the instincts of a thief, but they hadn't caught him cheating—yet.

The rear echelon of H Company plodded by company headquarters and Lieutenant Owen Belvale. Owen glanced up and took his thumbs from the straps of the pack he insisted upon carrying like his men. The boy raised a tired salute as he saw Chad standing in the tent flap, and Chad returned it. The boy was becoming a good soldier, and his brother was en route to Hawaii, where Farley would help make up a new division for the Pacific. Both were proving that VMI was as good a trade school as West Point. In the family tradition, they did their duty.

Combat command was no place for shirkers or hustlers, but the low-budget peacetime army had countenanced both. Chad was happy his kids had done well, for it was past time for not only the regiment but the entire First Infantry Division to shake out the parasites.

As Kirstin had shaken him out? She had been right to divorce him, but it shouldn't have been because she caught him in bed with a whore, or because she thought he had to be drunk to have sex. By now he understood that he had been a leech feeding upon Kirstin and their marriage, ingesting love and contentment only when he wanted it, only between the constant changes of posts he asked for. He needed change and travel because he had nothing to put back into a marriage that had become a convenient duty station.

And when he lucked out, both in his first combat as an observer in Europe and by finding another special lady, Englishwoman Stephanie Bartlett was honorably married. Not empty-bed honorably, but enough so she refused to desert a husband posted to Singapore.

"Time for a couple of coffees?" he said to his clerk. "We already owe the mess sergeant, so one more favor won't put us any deeper."

When Guist went through the flap to cross the company street the dank smell of eastern Florida wafted in—skinny pine trees, wet palmetto and sand. People who didn't live with it said that sand had no odor and no taste. Not so; it was a copycat substance, taking on the stink of everything pissed on it or heeled into it, including frustration.

After months of no word from Leftenant Merriman, the great limey he'd fought beside all through France, a letter came. It told him that his love had been transferred to Singapore. Merriman wasn't sure why. Either she had gone on her own to reach her husband there, or because of conflict with a certain colonel in London. When Stephanie got out of that mess in Singapore he would find out which, and he had warned that officious bastard colonel that the roof would fall in on him.

He picked up the phone and went through division for an outside operator, then called collect to Kill Devil Hill. At least one of the family generals should be home, and for the first time in his career Chad was about to use family connections and wealth to rid his battalion of eight balls, and to get up-to-the-minute news on the one-sided fighting at Singapore. Teletype machines would be clattering in the war room. The Hill's command center was probably as well equipped as the War Department's.

He prayed that Stephanie could get away from the rampaging Japs; stories of their savagery were breaking everywhere the little shits overran defenses in any country. The crown colony was about to fall, and if anybody got out now, it would be a miracle. The British had pulled off one miracle at Dunkirk; could there be another one?

Kirstin Belvale-Shelby brushed at her favorite Morgan stallion, and brushed, and brushed. That seemed all right with Ric Arana, descended from a long line of champions; a performance horse liked to be groomed. His chestnut hide glowed from the polishing and good health, dapples showing even through his winter coat.

"Does it help?" Nancy asked. "If it does, I'll get a brush, too."

Kirstin's fingers tightened upon the leather-back brush until they ached. "I guess not. I sent the stableman home and mucked out stalls myself. I lunged three horses and then cooled them out. Nothing helps, goddamn it. It isn't enough that my ex-husband and both my sons are going off to fight a war—Chad, Owen and Farley—now it's Jim. I sure as hell don't regret that I have but two husbands to give my country. And two sons. So let them hang me for that."

Putting the brush into Ric's show kit, she led the stallion into his box stall and slipped the halter. He nuzzled her arm before she left, and Kirstin took time to caress his muscled neck.

"Jim doesn't *have* to go. For all their brave talk, watch how many U.S. senators apply for commissions—especially in the infantry. What the hell does Jim Shelby know about soldiering? He'll get—he'll get his fool self killed!"

When Nancy touched her hand she hung on, then spun herself into Nancy's arms. She only cried a little, hoping against hope that she didn't have to save up tears to use later.

She lifted her face and stepped back. "We never get it out of our systems, do we? The damned army, the family, the Hill. I put it all behind me, but it follows."

"Because all your men are in uniform," Nancy said, and Kirstin thought her voice was a little strained.

"I'm sorry about Keenan," she said, and she took Nancy's hand to walk her to the house. "Everyone is, and even though he was declared KIA, there's always a chance. Chad was missing in action for a long time, remember?"

"I'm sorry about Keenan, sorry for him and for me. MIA or KIA—there's no difference for us now. I cared—still care—for him. But he was determined to go back to China and try to find some woman there. I think he died trying. He never loved me that way, or he'd have fought everybody on the Hill to keep me there. God! Aren't we something, fretting about men we divorced?"

"Like the Hill, they follow us, too."

On the back porch Kirstin turned and looked out at the stables, at the gently rolling land, the beginnings of the hill country. Then she looked toward the town, the friendly little place she had already grown to love. Boerne, Texas; it was where she hoped to spend the rest of her life with Jim Shelby. It was lovely—many adobe houses, tile roofs and iron railings, appearing old Spanish and dusty cowboy at the same time. It was more beautiful because Jim Shelby lived on this horse ranch just outside of town; more beautiful because they had been married here by a grizzled, close-mouthed justice of the peace. So it took the news a long time to get out, and by then marrying a divorced woman wasn't important to Jim's constituents; the war was on.

"He may not"—her voice shook as she turned back to Nancy, once her cousin by marriage, and another of the Spartan women who had broken with the family—"he may not even be buried in his own land. The Shelbys have their own cemetery, too; not as fancy as the memorial grove at Kill Devil Hill, but just as traditional. And this goddamn war—men dying all over the world, getting blown into little bloody pieces—"

She slammed into the big kitchen that always hinted of chili, and behind her Nancy said, "The books say that most soldiers make it through. General Belvale said so. You have to think positive, Kirstin."

Putting both hands to her head, Kirstin pressed hard, then said, "You're right, of course. You came all the way out here to tell me something, and I unloaded my troubles on you. But I'm really glad you're here, and I'll fix us some coffee. Then you tell me your news. You're not married again?"

"Not that." Nancy smiled. "Maybe not ever again. The burned child and the fire? One bad marriage and one disastrous affair should be enough for any woman."

And one sharp, too short and bittersweet moment of love-making with Chad Belvale, Kirstin's husband. God, how she had needed that hard-driving, deeply moving sex. She had left Keenan and taken up with a man who used her politically and dropped her when the family found out. Chad was the right man at the right time, there to prove that she was still a desirable woman.

There had been nothing tricky, like sex with Marshal Pailey. What was the army saying—screwed, blued and tattooed? Marshal did it all, but as part of a practiced act. Chad was honest and much better—direct and filled with the same hidden, boiling need that her body demanded to release. At odd moments she regretted that there hadn't been more between them, if only more wonderful sex. Then she would remember that Kirstin was her best friend and be happy that Chad had shipped out beyond her immediate reach. She still felt saintly for leaving him immediately after, and the "thanks" lipsticked on the mirror had been a neat touch, light and sophisticated.

She glanced at Kirstin and only felt sneaky, even though Kirstin had discarded Chad. Nancy did have news and gossip but hesitated to tell; it might make Kirstin more alone. She accepted a cup of steaming chicory coffee and sugared it.

Then she plunged ahead. "You're so right about Kill Devil Hill following everybody. Maybe there's some kind of infection there and nobody leaves without catching it. I mean—all that holy warrior stuff, the mission handed down from the early Crusades. I sure got tired of that, but the old general, so sweet and understanding—

"You remember Walt Belvale's fiancée? Well, after he was killed, Penny Colvin joined the family anyhow; she married Farley."

Putting down her cup, Kirstin said, "Farley? Isn't he a little young for her?"

"Maybe a little young for any woman. She probably knows that by now. He went off to Hawaii and I guess the Hill really got to her. She's flying those big airplanes overseas for the army. They're letting civilian women do that. And me—"

"You haven't joined the women's army thing—the WAACS? Not you."

Nancy shook her head. "Something better. After my—after the thing with Marshal Pailey broke up, I went to school. You know I didn't have much education, and that was one excuse for the family to not like me. That and—and because I couldn't have any babies."

She paused to finish her coffee, and for a moment the sugar in the bottom of the cup tasted bitter. "I'm about halfway through nurse training, Kirstin. I think I'll be pretty good at it."

She prayed she would be. This gave her a new direction, a new reason, for her life, and this time she couldn't allow anything to screw it up.

CHAPTER 9

The New York Times—February 18, 1942: Singapore fell today. Sir Winston Churchill's confirmation of the British capitulation came some hours after dispatches from Tokyo and Vichy announced the enemy victory.

Lt. Gen. Arthur E. Percival signed surrender documents before Japanese Lt. Gen. Tomoyuki Yamashita in the Ford Motor plant at the foot of Timah Hill. Tokyo radio said three columns of Imperial troops advanced on the city by land and sea.

No word has been received on the number of Allied casualties, prisoners of war or any who might have escaped to Sumatra. Radio Berlin, quoting the Japanese newspaper *Asahi,* said some of the defending forces and "other hostile elements" were still holding out in the inner city.

Gasping for breath, Penny ran all out to reach Theresa Menasco and their plane. At every desperate step her mind screamed at her: Too late! Too late! And the echoes bounced back: Hide yourself! *Hide!*

The explosions came fast—one ugly red flower after another, the blasts shaking the earth and whipping invisible steel splinters past her head. A jagged hole in the tarmac tripped her, and she fell hard, raking her hands. Another shell blew up in her face and knocked her sideways with great force.

And she went blind.

God! Oh, dear God—she couldn't see!

Agony ballooned her head, pain that was flashing red and screaming. Penny's clawed hands searched for her temples and squeezed them back into place. She tasted blood, but only the blindness mattered.

BLAM!

"Kill me!" she yelled into the blood darkness. "Go ahead, you bastards—kill me! I don't care now—"

BLAM! BLAM!—and then a roaring *whoosh!* that rolled her away in scorching heat.

The plane—oh, dear God!—the plane just blew up with those helpless wounded men on board. And Theresa Menasco blew up with them.

Penny struggled to sit, one hand over her mouth so she could breathe against the heat, the other gently passing over her eyelids. No blood, no wounds, and the red behind her eyes bubbled to a deep pink. Was it only shock? Dear God, would she be able to see again?

"No," she said through her fingers, "no more *dear* God, even to get my eyes back. He let these bastard Japs cremate Theresa and all those poor guys and burn my first plane."

Without warning the red-pink in her head flashed blinding white, and she could see clearly. She almost wished she couldn't, because there was the crisping wreckage of the C-46, what the blast had left of it. The burned gas and oil smell slapped at her with another odor right behind—the terrible stench of sizzled human flesh.

BLAM!

The mortars still hissed down, blowing ragged holes in the runways. Every minute some bigger shells exploded with more fury. Heavy Jap artillery, Stephanie Bartlett said. Penny climbed up and moved on shaking legs back toward the smoking terminal. It had taken hits but was mostly intact.

Stephanie Bartlett—and wasn't this one hell of a place to meet Chad Belvale's mistress?

Hell, she was beginning to understand hell.

She wobbled, and a hot shell fragment shrieked by her cheek. All those women and children inside—some might even be hurt. What would happen to them? The wounded had brought back Japanese atrocity stories, and if they were even half-true—

But surely men in combat tended to exaggerate. Japanese in movies were always polite and bowing, but she couldn't remember seeing one in Virginia. Penny made it to the front doors and staggered past the shards of glass and twisted metal, her knees strangely weak.

"Hold on to me. Are you hit?" Stephanie's arm slid around her, and Penny was grateful for the support. Mistress might not be the right word for this woman. Lover, then. Love had shone in Stephanie's eyes when they spoke of Chad.

"I . . . I don't think so . . . but the shock . . . and oh, Steff—poor Theresa, all those wounded soldiers and my plane blown to bits . . ."

At this moment how could she think of anything sane, like love and family? All around her was madness, but Stephanie was solid to hold.

"I saw it. Bloody hell, they got my last gun and all the lads around it. Here—sit down and drink this. Everyone is half potted, I should think, because it's that much less whiskey the Japs will get."

Scotch tasted like iodine to Penny, but she choked it down and coughed. "The—the children are crying."

"Before this is over, everyone will."

Had Uncle Chad ever cried, for losing Kirstin or young Walt, or because of this married Englishwoman? Maybe it was against regulations for any of the Carlisle-Belvale men. Farley might have cried, if she had allowed it.

Farley, Penny thought; her husband had seemed weak, but he might have been right about war. This wasn't glory, it was hate and hell, it was shameful fear so strong that it numbed mind and body.

As soon as she'd said her name Stephanie sort of staggered and put one hand to her face. Had that only been a few hours ago?

"Belvale . . . your name is Belvale?"

"Why, yes. Do you know someone . . ."

"Leftenant Colonel Belvale?"

"Chad—Uncle Chad."

"Oh, God . . . in this place and at this time . . ."

And they had talked faster and more honestly than they would have any other place and time, Penny thought. She learned of the affair in England and the publicity in London newspapers, the resentment of the British army. And Stephanie said quietly that her husband was here, that she had seen him only twice before the battle started.

The spiteful crack of Japanese small arms fire sounded close, and the deeper banging of a British machine gun took up the challenge.

"Our lads are still resisting," Stephanie said, and she lifted the bottle. "Cheers, you *puir,* magnificent bastards."

She passed the whiskey to Penny. "They were told, damn them—the bloody brass were told repeatedly that all our big guns shouldn't face out to sea. But the ruddy admiralty always knows best, and besides, unseating even a few of those coast artillery pieces from their concrete emplacements was a bit too much trouble. Costly, also, you understand. Any junior officer who complained that Singapore's back was wide open to attack—well, that fool placed his career in jeopardy."

Frowning, Penny thought that Stephanie was running her words together, hurrying to get them said, as if they were turning more bitter in her mouth.

"The senior ones agreed, but they knew better than to

say it aloud. Theirs not to reason why, theirs but to do and—and—oh God!"

The second gulp of Scotch went down smoother. It was losing those AA guns, Penny reasoned, and the soldiers who died at them. She knew that Stephanie had been through month after month of London bombings, so whatever deep emotion racked her wasn't panic. It wasn't the time or place for what-if and why-didn't, either.

Say something, Penny thought, anything. "And the Japs came through that jungle nobody was supposed to penetrate."

A shell exploded too close to the terminal, raking tiles from the roof. Another window blew out, and a woman screamed.

"As if it were the open braes of home," Stephanie said. "Impossible, the generals said. Impassable, the admirals insisted. God—the bloody English!"

"But I thought—oh, you must be Irish or Scotch."

Any kind of talk, any distraction to keep from watching fear whiten the faces of the women bunched against the wall, those women holding their children's faces to their breasts to keep them from seeing the dead soldier in the corner; those women openly sobbing because their men had burned aboard Penny's plane.

Talk on and on, so that no other emotion shuddering within Stephanie Bartlett broke out and left Penny with no one to hold onto.

The British machine gun fired a long string of shots; a machine gun with a lighter, sharper voice answered.

She saw Stephanie try on a smile that slipped off the face too tired and dirty and hurt to be pixie now. "This is Scotch." She took a long drink from the bottle. "Only our bonny whiskey is Scotch. I am a Scot. And there are no Irish, just Scots who have never learned to swim."

Penny tried to laugh, but that didn't work. either. The Japs were closer; firing came from all around the building, and the British gun stopped.

A single tear coursed down Stephanie's cheek, clearing a path through the grime. "It's daft, really. I did nae wish to be right at hand when it happened, but I'm grateful I was this close and that he knew it."

"He? Your—"

"Husband. M-my *ain* husband's company was overrun this morning. A single corporal made it out. He knew aught of the rest and tried to help by serving my last g-gun."

Stephanie sounded more and more Scot.

Taking Stephanie's hand, she said, "Missing in action doesn't mean—"

Not always, but it had meant KIA, death for Walt Belvale; it dug a symbolic grave in the honor grove of Kill Devil Hill.

"They're Japs," Stephanie said. "They are goddamned Jap butchers, and Leftenant Dacey Bartlett is either dead or wishes to be."

CHAPTER 10

(Coded; Kill Devil Hill: SECRET)—Guadalcanal, the Solomon Islands, 7 August 1942: At 0900 hours, the 1st Marine Division and a regiment of the 2nd landed here and at Tulagi. Commanded by Maj. Gen. Alexander Vandegrift, a total of 19,000 men struck hard to capture an almost-completed Japanese airfield at Lunga Point. Initial resistance was spotty, but line officers expect fierce counterattacks.

The airstrip was being prepared so Japanese bombers could hit Allied targets heretofore out of reach. Guadalcanal is dense jungle, 90 miles long and 25 miles wide, and it has a heavy rainfall and unhealthy climate.

As the bells clanged Preston Belvale stepped aside so that Crusty Carlisle could read the teletype. "I'm glad you and Gloria moved down before I left," Preston said. "You'll need help in the war room, and who better than somebody in the family? Gloria's smart and level headed. With most of the women gone, Minerva might even appreciate a hand in running the place."

"Ha! The only hand Minerva needs is one right in the mouth. She won't spook my Gloria, though."

Belvale clipped the end from a cigar. "Those hard-luck Marines will be on short rations and shorter ammo for weeks. The Japs just kicked hell out of Fletcher's task force off Savo Island—jumped five of our heavy cruisers, sank four and battered the other. Fletcher saved the transports and supply ships, but now there's no protection for them. The dispatch is in the files there. Kee-rist—five out of five cruisers."

Crusty grunted. "Fucking navy accidentally won one at Midway, so of course they go right back to sleep. Bet your ass MacArthur didn't appreciate the Guadalcanal invasion. First off, he insisted on heading a gigantic, flashy attack on Buna, using every man jack in the Pacific command, right down to the mess cooks. Second, although he outranks Vandegrift, he isn't bossing the operation. Most likely the priorities are the other way around."

He looked again at the bank of momentarily silent machines and walked over to the big situation map of the Pacific command. Fists on hips, Crusty stared up at it. "You know that his supremeness was highly pissed when Doolittle took his bombers over Tokyo? Although it was only a nuisance raid, a public morale booster or whatever—you have to show me more than some paper houses blown up before I believe the war can be won from the air. I enjoyed it because the Japs shit themselves and old Mac got shoved off the front page for weeks."

Drawing upon the cigar, Belvale said, "Why aren't you herded with those other dinosaurs in the War Department? Air power will win or lose this war, and that's from an old cavalryman who's glad thousands of horses won't be gutted this time.

"And MacArthur—credit him for the Bataan fight and the siege of Corregidor. He did all he could with what little he had. And FDR personally ordered him off the Rock."

Crusty snorted. "Yeah, the battling bastards of Bataan—no mama, no papa, no Uncle Sam, and the fucking Japs chopped off their heads or beat them to death. Because we left them out there bare assed; because we had no goddamn help to send or any way to send it. Mac must have been out of favor with God, senior, or he'd have called down divine thunderbolts instead of scooting off to Australia in that torpedo boat."

Belvale got up and walked to the bar to pour shots of bourbon. Thinking of the Death March reports made him angry and dry-mouthed. The Japanese had a lot to answer for, and the war had barely started. Memories of ancient family history stirred; at Acre victorious Turks gave captured Crusaders over to their dark and deadly women for torture.

The honors of battle were too often sullied by the dishonor of barbarians.

Draining his glass, Crusty said, "Nothing in on Keenan, so we'd better mark him off, damnit. How about a report on that pretty kid who got caught at Singapore?"

"Penny—Farley's wife, Penny. Only tactical word has come out of Britain on the loss of their colony. I hope it's nothing like what the Japs did to the survivors on Bataan. Filipino Scouts sent out reports on torture and outright murder. Bayonets and samurai swords."

"We have to keep track of the Jap commanders responsible," Crusty said. "Hang their scruffy asses after the war. No more of this forgive-and-forget shit. If we'd stretched the Kaiser's neck for starting the last war and strung up a bunch of his generals, the Heinies wouldn't have been so eager to brown-nose Hitler."

Smoothing his mustache, Belvale agreed silently and continued his news. "Chad got his advance battalion of the 16th Infantry safely across. They're at Tidworth Barracks in England. The German subs were too busy along our coast, I guess. Let's hope the rest of the First Division is lucky enough to slip by. It's staging at Indiantown Gap."

"Farley's wife," Crusty said. "I keep thinking about her. That girl acts like she's family blood, a soldier born. Look how she jumped right in to fly one of your goddamned airplanes. But the boy himself—I sweated him out while he was still at VMI. Even before he got married that kid acted more like a civilian than a soldier, but I guess he straightened up. Now his wife is MIA; hell of a note. The casualty list is growing—Walt down in Poland, Keenan somewhere in China and now that gutty girl."

"Farley's on New Caledonia. We're holding up notifying him about Penny, official or otherwise. He can't do anything about it, and there's no such thing as an emergency furlough these days. Where would he go—Sumatra?

"He'll have it bad enough in an outfit being patched together from National Guard units, and scattered ones at that. The regiments are out of Illinois, North Dakota and Massachusetts. That means regional blocks and trouble with hometown discipline. And it's the only outfit in the army without an assigned number. They're calling it the Americal Division."

"Just a nickname? What goddamned peanut thought that up, and what does it mean—Americans on Caledonia? Are they going to homestead the fucking island? Somebody was drunk on fermented coconut juice—that *okulihao* stuff. Bad precedent—next thing they'll pick cute names for draftee outfits: Roosevelt's Rookies, MacArthur's Masturbators or some such. What would the family's rank-happy chaplain think of that pornography? The mealy-mouthed bastard would run praying to every half-assed congressman in Washington."

Belvale stretched his legs and rubbbed the bad one. "*Okulihao* is pineapple juice; it's Hawaiian bootleg and a mean hangover. Nothing to do with coconuts. See if you can ship Colonel Luther Farrand to New Caledonia, or anywhere in MacArthur's command, just so he's too far to get back."

Crusty grinned. "How about transferring him to Tokyo? In the Pacific he'll try to make the native women cover their tits. It's a good thing he never saw that driver you left me in Honolulu. That kid bathes in that pineapple booze and is still ready to kick ass in the morning. There ought to be another bar designed to hang on his shooting medal—Expert Cocksman. He's laying half the women at Schofield and has the other half lined up. Sergeant Donnely—damn! Wouldn't he make some kind of chaplain's assistant? Let's give him to Luther so he'll run that bastard over the hill."

"Donnely is a line soldier, and his old man more so. We're already running out of good line troopers."

"I was kidding. I forgot that you-all plantation masters don't joke much."

Leaning back in his chair, Belvale contemplated the glowing tip of his cigar. Crusty Carlisle acted as if he'd be content to serve out the war here at the Hill, putting together the family's own intelligence reports and having the right people act upon them. But if he could open any kind of slot for overseas assignment, he'd take his almost crippled, arthritic joints right up into the front line. Belvale understood the feeling and had set roadblocks in Crusty's path. He also had Ben Alexander ready as a backup in case Crusty outflanked all obstacles and got what he wanted, combat.

Only two persons might make Crusty think again about going out in fire and glory: his granddaughter Gloria and her baby. Crusty felt he owed her, and he was right; the family's marriage casualty rate was high without anyone being pushed into it, as Crusty had pushed the girl.

Hell on horses and women; just as hard on its young men who might wander beyond the prescribed field of march. Sloan Travis was out of step more than any had been. The boy was closely related to Ben Alexander, but Belvale didn't remember exactly how. Minerva knew all connections to the family down to their cousins, better at genealogy than most Virginia matrons.

Sloan was the family's first known draftee. Every other war had been staffed by family volunteers. And worse to some minds, Sloan was a twenty-year-old bright enough for West Point or VMI who had chosen a mediocre college. He refused a gold bar as a ninety-day wonder from Officers

Training School and was just out of the newly designated "basic training" as a private.

The boy shouldn't be faulted for simply being stubborn. With the right attitude he might soldier as well as the Donnelys, father and son. And it was true that sergeants were not only the backbone of the army, they managed to run most of it. Sloan Travis might have the courage of WASP Penny Colvin-Belvale.

Belvale's fingers tightened upon his cigar, and he said a quick prayer that Penny's love of country hadn't bared her lovely throat to the bloody edge of a samurai sword.

CHAPTER 11

REUTERS—the coast of France, August 18, 1942: Thousands of Canadian troops stormed ashore at Dieppe at dawn today. The attack spread along 11 miles of rugged terrain, and fighting is heavy. The Canadians are supported by a major contingent of British Commandos and some Free French. They were joined by at least 50 U.S. Rangers, the new American counterpart of the Commandos.

Disaster struck at 0300, before the landing itself, when a flotilla of 23 landing craft accidentally crossed paths with a German convoy. Enemy escort ships opened fire, and the light Commando boats were forced to run for it. The element of surprise was lost, and heavy casualties are expected on the beach.

The body of Ranger Lieutenant Edwin Loustalot has already been returned to England, the first American soldier of the war to be killed on European soil. He was 19 years old.

Chad Belvale grabbed Johnny Merriman's arm as the landing boat lurched. "What the hell is that?"

"What the hell is what?"

The boat skewed to starboard, and cold salt spray lashed Chad's face. "Those outlines up ahead—damn it! Ships—four—*five!*"

A star shell flashed blinding white in the dark sky.

"Jerry tubs, not ours. There goes the bloody game. Hold to something, colonel. The skipper's putting about quickly. Don't want your Yank arse in the drink now, do we?"

Helmets clanged and men cursed. Heavy guns opened up from German escort vessels, and ragged flashes of orange fire marked their muzzle blasts. Chad went hard to his knees in the sloshy bottom of the wooden boat.

"Bleeding rotten luck," Johnny Merriman said at his ear. "A few minutes either way and nobody would have been seen. Damn all. Ships that pass in the night, eh?"

Muzzle flashes and gun thunder close by told that the Commando E-boats fought back, but their armament was much lighter. A landing boat exploded to strew fire and body parts over the Channel. Chad knew that men screamed, but he heard them only in brittle pieces of silence between gun blasts. Soldiers weighted with combat loads and field packs struggled not to drown. Men ripped bloody by shell fragments fought to reach another boat, to stay alive. The sounds they made tore at Chad's guts, because no boat could stop to pick them up.

So few of the landing craft were making it; fiery gouts marked aim too damned accurate from the Kraut destroyers, and the gutty little E-boats were no match for them, shattered as they attacked in desperation.

Chad's shoulder slammed the bulkhead as his boat zigzagged, its motor roaring full out.

"He's going in!" Merriman shouted. "No surprise now, and every sodding Jerry on the continent will be waiting, but Major Peter Young is heading for shore. Ours not to reason why, eh? The man's daft."

Orders, Chad thought; trained British style, the Canadians were hell on following orders. But this time, where else could the boat go? Not back to Blighty, and not turned around into that murderous naval fire.

Lifting his head slowly above the rail, he saw the miniature sea fight was ending badly, as important to the dead and drowning as if it were the battle of Jutland. Another time and another war; but always the same kind of dying.

On the right, no other boat left white tracks in the dark water. Theirs had ridden midway in a long column, and now the others were gone, either scattered in hopes of safety or smashed. The gunfire died astern, allowing Chad to pick out the bubbling noises of small boat motors to his left. They weren't alone, but if the troop commander held to his objective, they might as well be. Every boatload in Commando 3 had a specific objective, a definitely assigned strip of sand. This handful of Canadians would assault its share of hotly defended beach alone if need be.

The orders were too detailed, too definite. The entire operation was over-planned and didn't allow for errors, bad timing or luck. But nobody had hauled Chad out here by the nose. He could blame only himself—and recently promoted Captain J.J. Merriman, London Rifles. Together they had fought across France to the evacuation of Dunkirk and become as close as only men who have faced death side by side can.

It had been great to see Merriman again, and in the Boar's Head pub they reminisced about past battles and fallen friends. After a time they spoke of Leftenant Stephanie Bartlett. Chad hadn't been able to locate her, nor had Merriman's earlier bird-dogging. Over a gin and tonic Chad heard again how she had been posted to Singapore, now fallen to the Japs. The information had come late to Merriman, and he had mailed it along with regret.

"That goddamn Colonel Blimp," Chad said, his fingers aching tightly around his glass. "Do me a favor and find where he's stationed. I warned that provost marshal son of a bitch. He probably thought I wouldn't make it back here and that Stephanie meant just a quick lay to me. The bastard will believe me when I run his balls through a meat grinder."

A fistful of water punched Chad's face, and he gasped, tasting salt and the familiar bitterness of fear. Only an idiot was not afraid at a time like this, but a soldier not only held that fear in check, he used it. He made the most of tensed muscles and the rush of adrenaline, of pumped-up strength and super alertness.

Up forward a man puked, and then another.

In that smoky London pub the gin and tonics had marched to the table in platoon strength while the piano player did "The White Cliffs of Dover" and "A Nightingale Sang in Berkeley Square." When they got somewhat drunker soldiers and sailors forgot their differences and gathered around the piano to bellow out "Bless 'em all, bless 'em all—the long and the short and the tall . . ."

It was the first song American soldiers learned over here, and they were apt to sing it in its original form: fuck 'em all. Suddenly the younger doggies were calling themselves GIs. Galvanized iron garbage cans had carried the abbreviation, and the Friday night scrubbing down of barracks were GI parties. Chad supposed it was inevitable that soldiers would apply it to themselves after the draftees came, bringing their own terminology. It was then that Merriman mentioned taking a little sea voyage, but of course an American battalion commander had a high responsibility and a duty to a thousand men in training. If he got caught going off on a raid, the family generals would probably pull on the rope when ETO commanders hung his ass.

But Stephanie was dead or tortured in Shanghai, and Chad needed to rip into somebody. The battalion exec, Major Bill Moore, would cover for him for a few days. It could only be done for damned few days.

Feeling exposed and lonesome, Chad wished there hadn't been so many gin and tonics in London. He gripped his Enfield as the landing craft nosed in below the steep and stony cliffs to the east of Dieppe.

Merriman announced "0445," as if it were important. "We're buggered, and five minutes early."

Out through the landing gate and scrambling over the sides, twenty soldiers splashed down and raced across the rocky beach with Chad and Merriman keeping up. They poured into the black mouth of a deep gully, the only way out. No buried mines exploded, nobody screamed in agony, and Chad hissed out breath that he didn't know he had been holding.

"Bloody barbed wire strung up and down the sides," Merriman said. "Jerry thinks that's enough, does he? Watch those lads climb it like ropes."

Chad caught hold of the cold wire and dug his toes into the earth at each pull. He was careful with his hands, but some barbs stabbed his palms and cut his fingers. As he grunted higher the sky lightened and made him a naked target for any sniper's eye. His skin tightened as he bellied down. The target Germans must be following the sound and fury of the sea fight and not paying attention to their own area.

On top of the cliff Merriman sprawled beside him, blowing through his straggly red mustache. "Bloody hell—should have trained the Gibraltar apes to carry grenades. They could've romped up here and dashed low across that open field."

"Those apes are protected by law," Chad panted. "We aren't."

"Reckon they cost more, too. There's our objective, that coast gun battery."

Breath slowing to almost normal, Chad said, "Looks like a big garrison, too big to hit head-on."

"Two hundred, Intelligence says, which probably means more."

Five yards to Chad's left the CO shouted, "As skirmishers—and fire!"

Merriman muttered thanks to the god of battles that had guided Major Peter Young's wise decision. As the sky cleared the Enfield 303s opened up with sharp cracks, and the troops leapfrogged into the field for dubious cover in scrub brush. Closer in to the emplacement, point men fired short bursts from their M4 Sten guns.

Sprang!

Chad pulled in his head, and Merriman said, "Too close. Be damned to any Jerry with a good eye."

Return fire was quick in coming, and most of the German artillery men stayed tight in cover within their concrete redoubt. The first few who rushed out were cut down. Lining his sights on movement, Chad fired, worked the bolt, and fired again, wishing he'd brought along an M-1 rifle. He wasn't sure he hit anything.

Pop-pop-pop-pop!

Spitting sand, Merriman built a little barricade of rocks around his head, one at a time. "Gewehr 34, their light MG. Bless their square heads, they haven't fired a bleeding mortar, which means they have none."

He squeezed off a shot. "There! Curious bastard, wasn't he? Peeping around like he was in Hyde Park."

From the left front a machine gun with a deeper throat rolled out a longer burst. Chad figured that to be the same-caliber gun, but a heavier, water-cooled Maxim. Bullets whipped close to his head, so he rolled left and came up propped on his elbows to fire back and roll again, this time to the right.

He bumped Merriman's shoulder and lay quiet awhile, watching and listening. When the up-close gunfire slowed Chad could sort out the far rumbling of big guns down the coast. Back on the ship his rank had gotten him a look at the situation map—eight landing points; those on the flanks, including his own, were diversions. The two-pronged main thrust was at the town of Dieppe, and it would be no picnic for the Royal Regiment of Canada.

KA-BOOM!

Chad's ears blanked out for a second, and he felt the ripped-air passing of a freight train balling the jack.

"—the ruddy gun! They've turned a ruddy gun on us—a great fucking six incher at the least!"

KA-BOOM!

This time Chad had his fingers in his ears and mouth

open against the blast. When that big shell hit among them—

But it didn't explode. As Chad gaped, three times more the frustrated German gunners slammed high-explosive shells at Commando 3, only to have them scream out over the French countryside.

Cranking off a rifle round at the gun crew only 150 yards away, Merriman laughed. "Silly bastards can't depress enough to zero in on us."

"Lucky us," Chad said. "How's the ammo holding out?"

"Low, I'd say. Hardly hear the Stens now. Where's the bloody RAF? Pissing off at Soho? One plane could knock out that emplacement."

Chad had wondered at the lack of air support. A practice raid, a dry run to probe the enemy defenses and then pull out. The entire German defenses would stand to on full alert for months afterward. British GHQ would probably learn something in the process. Right now Chad wished he were back in the Boar's Head pub or standing reveille with his battalion.

Christ, Stephanie; our story has been air raids and beach landings and across-the-world separations. What will we be like in peace, like that special, bombless morning in your bonny Scotland? That balmy morning to roll about on my tongue for the pure shouting flavor of the air, while the trembles of the night's loving still walked the spine?

For the love of God, Stephanie Bartlett, for the love of me—don't be dead.

Pop-pop-pop! went the Jerry gun. Chad picked up the muzzle flashes this time and pumped his last rounds at them. The gun fell silent.

A whistle shrilled and shrilled again.

"The major's signal," Merriman said. "Suggest you pull back with the rest, Colonel, sir. I've a few more rounds to make Jerry hop it."

"Come on, you idiot." Chad scuttled back to the lip of

the gulch and cursed the barbed wire that ripped at his uniform as he slid down.

Landing on his feet, he turned and looked up, looked for Johnny Merriman. Something blew on the mesa just beyond sight, a sudden flash of smoke and flame. A grenade? "Johnny! Damn it, Merriman!"

The thing spun down like a floppy bird, and Chad caught it. A severed hand drooled sticky blood—Merriman's ring, Merriman's right hand. Men yelled at him, but Chad went back up the cliff.

CHAPTER 12

UNITED PRESS—Tacoma, Wash. September 14, 1942: Troopships are leaving this port of embarkation as soon as soldiers from nearby Fort Lewis and Fort Ord, California can be loaded. The ships are bound for the Pacific Theater and will be escorted by swift, lean destroyers looking for all the world like deadly gray sharks.

Some of the ships are brand new, the marks of the shipyard still clinging to them. Some are old merchantmen sprouting recently added gun tubs. All will hurry their precious cargo of replacements across the sea to jungle islands where other GIs and Marines are holding the line against suicidal Japanese troops.

Army spokesmen said that these replacements are being drawn not only from training camps, but also from regular army units and individual duty assignments across the country.

Farley Belvale treated himself to another long pull at the bottle. The champagne at the reception had been plentiful, but weak. Straight bourbon suited him better and eased the little knot of worry long growing in his stomach.

They were at one of the family's houses in Carolina, in the resort town of Myrtle Beach, and so far the action was true to movies about newlyweds. Penny was in the latrine, readying herself for her wedding night. It was different for her; this was her second wedding night. That caused him a stab of guilt for marrying his cousin's widow. She would come back into the room wearing something slinky, a sexy nightgown that would enhance her natural beauty. Could he handle that?

He was scared. At this moment he wished that he was experienced. Suppose he goofed it up? He knew about it technically and, in a fashion, was proud that he had saved himself for her, for pretty Penny alone. Put that way it sounded old-fashioned and stupid. He should have been more like Owen, taking casual sex where he found it and moving on without complications. Sex didn't seem that important to Owen; he didn't dodge it, but he didn't make a big deal out of chasing women. Maybe that's why women chased him. His brother wouldn't worry about being a failure tonight. Farley took another drink from the bottle. Owen always did things differently, but that didn't make them right.

He wouldn't tell Penny that he was a virgin. She'd think he had hoped for Walt's death and had planned a sneaky campaign to win over the widow, and that he had been too sure of himself. In reality, he still couldn't believe his amazing luck. Penny had been an untouchable dream, a fantasy somehow turned real, turned warm and willing.

"Farley?"

He flinched. She was so lovely that his eyes hurt, and in that black lace nightie she glowed, sleek and leggy. Her beauty struck him hard and low in the groin. He wanted her: oh, Jesus, how he wanted her.

"The bathroom is all yours," she said. "This is something you'll have to get used to—waiting on a woman while she pretties herself."

"You—you don't need prettying."

" 'Why, thank you, sir,' she said, and she made a curtsy. Except I don't know how to do a curtsy."

She was making it easier on him, making things lighter. If he didn't already love her to his limit, he would love her more for it. She had hung his pajamas and robe in the bathroom, and he was surprised to find he had brought the bottle of bourbon in with him. Resolutely he put it aside on the sink and climbed into the shower. The tub and curtain were still steamy from Penny's bath, and he thought he could smell her perfume lingering. He imagined her all slippery with soap bubbles and with hot water caressing that perfect, pearly skin.

Aroused, he didn't dare scrub long at his crotch but soaped thoroughly and stood a long time to rinse. She was waiting; pretty Penny waited for him to make love to her. Farley toweled dry and drank a silent toast to his wife. Lord, Lord—his wife. He went out to her.

There was wonder in the silken feel of her flesh, a wild flavoring in her mouth and on her erectile nipples. Her fingernails raked gently as his hands explored her warm and hidden places. There was a miracle to her lifting for his entry—

As she had arched her naked body for her first choice, Walt Belvale?

Goddamn! Desperately he pushed at her and at the image of her and Walt making love. Biting his lip, he tried to erase the picture of them moving together, but Walt pivoted that skull face to him, and the grimace melted as the moldering bone emerged.

Oh, Christ.

Penny held him close and whispered. "It's all right, honey. It happens. Just take your time. Hold me tight."

Walt took a long damned time to fade away, to return to his grave. The son of a bitch had had his turn with Penny. Why couldn't he stay dead and let her be, leave Farley alone? It wasn't as if Farley was stealing her or raping her. She had come to him of her free will, and he had held her inviolate until after they were married.

Goddamn you, Walt Belvale. Stay overseas as the dead hero.

She was smooth beneath his fingers, and her kisses were gentle at first, comforting upon his skin, then growing stronger and ever more fierce at his mouth, lashing him with flicks of her tongue.

And this time he succeeded. Even if it was too quick, for the moment he rid himself of the disapproving shade of Walt Belvale.

In days to come he walked the beach with her, reveling in her catlike grace, in her obvious enjoyment of sun in her hair and sea wind kissing her lips. Men stared at her as they passed, and women frowned. Farley held back the urge to strut, to show off his pride of possession.

For she was not possessed; she was her own woman, and no man could own Penny. He felt that more as the nights passed, sometimes wonderful and sometimes not so good. She was patient with him, kind to him, and although he could sense her concern, she said nothing when, late at night, he went into the latrine for a drink to steady him.

He didn't tell her that Walt kept getting in the way, that her first husband insisted upon being the only husband. Farley could have ignored an outsider, but not one of the family. When they went back to the Hill the trouble got worse. It was as if Walt waited in their bedroom, even though it wasn't the same one Penny had shared with him. It was the same dining room under the same ancient banners of conquest and honor. It was the same front porch, tall-pillared and shaded by wisteria vines. When he was home on furlough Walt used to sit there with his feet propped up on the railing and tell stories about garrison life. Farley and Owen had listened respectfully, since they were only cadets and he was an army officer on duty.

Aunt Minerva acted as if Penny had committed an unpardonable sin, although General Belvale accepted the situation, and visiting General Carlisle seemed to pay no attention.

Within days Farley knew that they had to move out and be on their own. Penny agreed, and he had the money to set them up in a town apartment, still a bit too close to the Hill. When invitations came, they couldn't refuse to attend, and Farley thought that Penny brightened each time they drove to Kill Devil Hill. She should have been born to the family, and he should be the outsider, he thought. He wondered if he would have become one of the holy warriors if he had been given a choice.

When his orders came he celebrated. Report to Fort Lewis, Washington; no additional delay en route authorized. Like most of the other family women, Penny didn't make a scene about him heading for a combat zone. Family women expected that.

She might not have been so goddamn cheerful about it.

CHAPTER 13

INTERNATIONAL NEWS SERVICE—Hollywood, Cal., September 20, 1942: Mr. Lowell Mellet, the president's motion picture coordinator, said today that Hollywood's direction is now more than "Will this picture help win the war?"

More than 300 actors and actresses joined in a "Stars over America" war bond blitz. Dorothy Lamour was credited with selling $350 million in bonds, and Hedy Lamarr sold kisses to those who bought $25,000 bonds. Producer-director Cecil B. De Mille donated for auction the much-publicized rubber squid used in *Reap the Wild Wind.*

Several of the stars spoke of major motion pictures in production which will pay homage to the brave Marines now fighting so valiantly on Guadalcanal.

Garrison duty in wartime was chickenshit. Eddie Donnely felt he was swimming against a tidal wave of chickenshit and losing. Sure, his bunk was in a City Hall Company barracks where no outside powers screwed around. No bed check there, especially since he was marked Temporary Duty, anywhere and anytime TDY. Which meant he slept out and rarely had to make up his bunk and was almost untouchable.

Most soldiers would give their left nuts to have his

assigned duty—driving a staff car used mainly to pick up VIPs at Honolulu Airport. He would check out the Plymouth at the motor pool, wash and shine it, then report to the HQ dispatcher. After a glance at the Honolulu Star Bulletin, he found magazines to read, because the war news made him feel guilty. The gyrenes were fighting like hell on some jungle island nobody had ever heard of, and the U.S. Army was bound to send troops to help. Latrine rumor had it that a new infantry outfit was building up on another Pacific island and would jump off soon. Eddie wanted in.

He was a heavy weapons section leader, not a goddamn taxi driver. He said as much on his application for transfer. It must be lost in Personnel, he concluded; he hadn't heard anything. Twice, by phone, he had tried to reach the generals, Belvale and Carlisle, for help, but the switchboards on and off post wouldn't put him through to the mainland unless he could prove an emergency.

His old man was already in England with the 16th Infantry Regiment, and it figured that the 1st Infantry, sharpest division in the army, wouldn't sit there long. No other unit was capable of making the "second front" invasion the Russians were yelling for. Damn! Old and beat-up, his father would go into combat first. After World War I and France that would be twice around for him, nothing at all for Eddie the feather merchant.

What made it worse was that they both drew overseas pay; Big Mike earned his, if only for ducking Kraut bombs in England; Eddie's twenty-percent pay boost was a joke, because Hawaii was only a territory, not a state. The extra pay was ration money for *okulihao*.

He didn't even need that. He had the run of Major Hammond's liquor closet, and Captain Doetz's, too. Besides, Hani Lapili's brother made good pineapple bootleg, and Hani told Big Huhu that there was true *aloha nui loa* between Eddie and her. A good thing, because the Big Huhu was really big—like a brick wall, like a hospital.

That "much love" was true enough, he thought, maybe

more than with the officers' wives. Hani was an accident; she didn't belong to brass, and he hadn't gone after her. It just happened, and he was glad. Hani was the islands, warm and flowery, softly giving without demanding.

It was the damnedest thing; as many women as Eddie had known, as many tricks as he had experienced, Hani hit him with something different. While they were making love, while he was deep within her body, Hani danced, danced as she lay upon her back, rolling her hips and pelvis in one of her sexier hulas. At her sides her palms copied the drumbeats of a luau, and she hummed the music, increasing the rhythm as needed. It was weird, and it was exciting.

"Trip for you, hotshot." Sergeant Raineri had one stripe, forty pounds and six years service on Eddie. He also had a dirty grin. "Sign out for Major Hammond's quarters; seems his car ain't running. Happens a lot lately."

Eddie put down the copy of *Look* and stood up. "Busy guy."

"But kind of blind, ain't he?"

Slouching over to the desk, Eddie set his feet apart and leaned over Raineri. "You must think a medical will get you more than straight retirement. But then, you might be so fucked up that you can't even go fishing."

Raineri blinked and pushed back his swivel chair with a squeak, but only to make some distance, not to stand up. Eddie stared down at him for a long moment before leaving the office.

Damn it, Vanessa Hammond knew that gossip flashed like heat lightning on any military post, so she should be more careful and less eager. Her husband was bound to hear, and if friends put off telling him because his wife was bedding a lowly EM, Captain Karl Doetz's buddies might not be so thoughtful. Hani Lapili knew she had the inside track and wouldn't be overly jealous.

Tooling the staff car along tree-sentineled streets whose warm air was heavy with the perfume of exotic flowers and just a touch of the sea, Eddie wondered if he had stepped in it this time. Vanessa, damn it! The network of officer wives generated real power; a word could climb from major's wife to colonel's wife to Mrs. General.

His transfer was blocked because Vanessa Hammond wanted him to stay here with her. Maybe Marilyn Doetz was in on the plot, although he found it hard to believe that any two women were content to share one man. Marilyn might be crazier because she had never had an orgasm before Eddie's oral sex. Then when she asked it of her husband, the stupid bastard slapped her.

He pulled the jeep all the way into the empty garage and swung the door down. Easing through the back door, he thought of the soldiers past who had done time in Leavenworth or Castle Williams because some officer's lady cried rape when she was caught in the act. At the court-martial an enlisted man's word wasn't worth a fart in a whirlwind against the lady's tears.

Not Vanessa and not Marilyn; as always, it got deeper than sex for them as well. That wasn't the way it was meant to go, not for them, not for him. In the beginning he always meant to hurt, to get revenge for what that brass's bitch had done to his family. But he always cared, and caring was love, and that was a hell of a note.

"Darling," she said, flowing up from the couch in swirling layers of transparent pink silks.

Eddie walked past her to the bar for a double shot of Canadian Club. Then he turned and looked at her, a beautiful woman eager to be loved. He said, "Baby, you fouled up my transfer. That isn't right."

Her eyes widened. "I thought you loved me. Why would you want to abandon me, to leave Hawaii for those filthy jungles? Haven't you seen the Marines coming into Tripler General from Guadalcanal? The poor boys—crippled and dying, racked with malaria." Hands pressed to her face, she said it again: "I th-thought you *loved* me—you said you did."

Going to her, he put his arms around her, smelling a musky fragrance, and beneath that the honest woman scent of Vanessa Hammond. "I do love you, baby. But I've been playing around with—"

"That bitch Marilyn Goetz. I know. That's all right, darling—just so long as I'm the one you really care for." Raising her tearstained face, she whispered, "I can't let you go, Eddie. I just won't!"

He stroked her spine and hips as her body pressed against him. "Honey, I'm a soldier—not just a uniform, but a soldier. And you know we're heading for big trouble. You know about Marilyn, and she knows about you. The dispatch sergeant is suspicious of all these staff car calls. How long before your husband knows and is forced to do something? Please let my transfer go through."

"B-but you can be maimed or—or—killed. I'll never see you again. Oh, my God—"

"Love works both ways, baby. If you love me, let me do my job. I'll come back to you one day."

Softly she whispered, "Eddie," and he knew she'd go along. Sinking to the bed with her, he made tender and lingering love to the lady.

It wasn't raw and frantic, like the first sex he saw. He couldn't help seeing it, because they had him boxed in, and it would have been worse to come busting out in the middle of it. Besides, he was curious, even if it made him feel funny because his father was doing it.

She was young, with red hair blazing over her bare white shoulders, and Eddie had never seen a woman naked all over. She was beautiful, and she did things with his father that Eddie hadn't even heard about in school. He was shaking all over and about to cry, although he didn't know why, when they finished and got dressed to leave the garage.

Two days later he found out that she was a major's daughter, that tough officer who ran his father's battalion. It was weeks before his mother found out and began fighting with Big Mike about what he was doing with Frieda Thornton.

"Let it be, woman," his father said. "You aren't jealous. You act like you're suffering the tortures of hell when I top you in bed, and—"

"I do suffer, I do! That vile act should be for procreation only, and you know it. Fornicating and adultery with that shameless bitch—your soul will burn in hell, Michael Donnely, burn in eternal hellfire!"

Eddie hid his head beneath the covers when his father broke something.

"Woman, you're so damned priest-ridden—"

"And I'm telling the good Father on Sunday, and when I go to confession—"

There came a long silence, and Eddie peeped from beneath his pillow. He could only see their shadows on the wall.

"I intend to marry Frieda," his father said.

"Divorce is a sin! I'll never consent."

"It can be done without you."

"Sinner—the holy church will throw you out!"

Eddie knew why he cried then. He didn't want Frieda Thornton for a mother or his father to go away. Neither disaster happened, because when Big Mike asked Frieda to marry him she laughed in his face. There in the garage where they met when Sharon Rose Donnely went to afternoon services or confession. She was always going to confession. And Eddie always hid in the garage, just in case.

"Marry you—an enlisted man? When I'm ready I'll marry a West Pointer, one of my own kind. An enlisted man—just because I had a little fun with you? You expect me to live in Soapsuds Row? Be grateful for screwing above your caste, Sergeant. The colonel's lady and Judy O'Grady are hardly sisters under the skin, despite the poet.

"There's a certain animal attraction about you, but remember that some women find it thrilling to do it with a big dog. I haven't yet, but who knows? Good-bye, Sergeant Donnely—it has been fun, of a coarse sort."

"Bitch," Mike said, "you fucking bitch!"

"Of course," Frieda laughed.

It damned near killed Eddie's father. It made many years of his life miserable because Sharon Rose Donnely never allowed him to forget his transgression, and certainly she never intended to forgive him, or to allow Christ to do so. Eddie's mother went to her grave blaming the cancer that killed her on the evil that Mike Donnely had done. The sins of the husband, she screamed, the sins shall be visited upon the innocent wife.

Now this other officer's wife lay snug within Eddie's arms, and he could not hurt her, for she was not Frieda Thornton. None of them were, although he kept looking. Drawing gently away from Vanessa, he stood naked beside her bed in the afternoon shadows of drawn drapes. He hoped she remained asleep while he dressed and eased through the kitchen to the garage.

He was backing the staff car out when he saw her face at the bedroom window. She was crying. He blew her a kiss and nodded, thinking that she would keep her word about his transfer. Vanessa was a special lady.

Crusty finished showing Ben Alexander the command center at the Hill. Ben said, "I heard, but it was hard to believe. This is as well-equipped as the small war room in Washington."

"Good enough for us," Crusty said. "Any bigger would mean more people and more mouths to talk about it."

His granddaughter carried a sheaf of papers into the room, and Crusty turned to pour coffee for her. As an afterthought, he filled cups for Ben and himself.

Gloria accepted hers and sat at her desk. "My reports are caught up through June," she said. "The eight Nazi saboteurs captured on the Florida coast, the British defeat in Libya, and the Chinese losses at Lishui and Kweiki. Then there's the Russian admission—late as usual—that they're being pushed back on the Kharkov front."

One phone buzzed, and Crusty picked it up; a teletype rang two bells, and Ben Alexander went to it.

"Yeah," Crusty said, "we figured the Japs would round up civilians, too. Just keep track of where they locate the PW camps. And Willie—don't let anybody lose the names of those camp commanders. Any shit"—he glanced at Gloria—"any stuff from them and they get their necks stretched after the war. How about names, prisoner lists? Okay, keep trying."

Hanging up the phone, Crusty went over to pat Gloria's shoulder. He was sorry she'd never been a lovely girl, but she had a special strong beauty, like that of a cleanly efficient weapon. She was damned sharp and, since she'd come back home, would take no crap from anybody. That might lessen her chances of another marriage, a good one next time, but that was okay with Crusty. He'd take care of her.

"No word on Penny Belvale, but she's a strong girl. If she made it this far, she'll hack it all the way. There's better war news coming," he said. "Not all that much, but starting a trend. We're not flat-out running away now, and we aren't losing *all* the fights."

Ben Alexander came to the desk and lifted a thin haunch to sit on one corner. "Colonel Belvale's report on Dieppe was a masterpiece."

"Always is," Crusty said. "The boy has one of those photographic memories. But he damned near got his ass—I mean career—in a sling, going in with those Canadians. What a mess that raid was, so many KIA and taken prisoner, and for what? Casualties are acceptable if there's a reason, but not just to make a show.

"Chad was lucky he was with the right boat. He gets stupid, too. That's what most medals are for—temporary stupidity. If Terrible Terry Allen wasn't CG of the First Division, Chad would be hung out to dry. The army just don't give a damn for its battalion commanders out playing shoot-'em-up."

Ben put down his coffee cup. "Now Terry de la Mesa Allen will pin another Silver Star on him, to go with the British citation. Our allies appreciated his saving one of their officers."

"So did that limey captain. More coffee, Gloria?"

She shook her head, and Crusty thought she had nice hair, always loose and shiny. Gloria said, "Something came in early this morning on a Sergeant Donnely. A transfer from Hawaii to New Caledonia, to the Americal Division. Is he one of the family?"

Crusty looked around for his pipe. "Nope, but he ought to be. We're keeping an eye on him. Rough as a cob and a soldier to the bone. Slick as owl sh—owl droppings around the ladies, when he wants to be. If by some off chance he ever shows up around you, Gloria, back off. He's not for nice girls like you."

Grinning, Crusty turned to Ben. "Would you believe it? This boy's specialty is officer wives. Where he's headed now, he won't find anything but Japs, but I wouldn't bet against finding him in bed with some slant-eye general's wife. Wait—I'll pour a shot of booze for a toast. May Eddie Donnely stay lucky all the way."

"Lucky," Ben Alexander repeated over his shot glass.

"All the way," Gloria said, taking Crusty's glass and tossing off his drink.

He stared at her in surprise.

CHAPTER 14

Special to *The New York Times*—Washington, D.C., Sunday, October 4, 1942: President Franklin Roosevelt ordered freezes of wages, rents and farm prices to take effect tomorrow. He also announced that he would issue an order on all dwelling units in the nation not subject to the current law. The earlier rent controls were applied only to 190 defense areas.

Food ceilings will apply to butter, cheese, evaporated and condensed milk, eggs and poultry. Prices also were held on flour, dry onions, potatoes, fresh and canned citrus, fresh fish and peanuts.

Something bitter always lurked in the guts of a blue lizard, so Keenan scooped out the tiny entrails before crunching the body. Two more blues and a hooded brown lizard dried in the band of his converted Japanese cap among fresh green leaves and brittle ferns. He hadn't tried the browns and would use his bad-to-eat test: a nibble and wait. If it was bitter, he'd spit out the shred of meat. If not, he gambled another tiny bite and waited. If no pain hit, if his stomach didn't burn within an hour, another item made his shopping list.

The same test worked for grasses and berries, and he

never worried about snakes. Whatever their color or head shape, poison or not, their flesh was always good. They were better roasted in ashes, like the big beetles and grub worms, but he didn't often make a fire.

One of the little bones nicked the inside of his cheek, and he grinned. Aunt Minerva, as much as possible, avoided serving finger foods at Kill Devil Hill. They were not, she said, quite proper.

Keenan lay upon his left side, the butt of his Arisaka rifle along his hip, its muzzle in the crook of his left elbow and free of the dirt. Some time back—he had lost time as a thing to be measured—he had stained his arms, hands and face with dark berry juice; spotty with mud, the camouflage was still good and had stopped itching. He didn't hide in the jungle; he *was* the jungle and the earth and the thorny moss hooked into his ragged clothing.

Wind flicking higher along the ridges left chill tailings, although he was on the down side of some strange mountain chain. Keenan knew he was off course, that first a Jap battalion and then a Nationalist Chinese combat patrol had turned him from his drive north for Chiang Kai-shek's headquarters in Kunming. As usual, the Nationalists didn't give a damn who or what was in front of them; they just opened fire.

Gray spider bites poisoned him after that, and when the swelling went down and his head finally cleared he found he had been moving west southwest. He would continue in that direction, reading the sun and stars until he found Mao's troops or the British—if they were still in this part of the world. Meanwhile, there were the Japanese and any who helped them. There would never be enough of the bastards to pay for the killing of Chang Yen Ling, for the deaths of Father Lim and the rest of Major Hong's company.

Yen Ling—had she ever journeyed this way? He wiped his mouth and fed a pinkish tuber into it; the stuff had little taste but was filling and gave some strength. Yen Ling would know its name. As a nurse, she used curative herbs where she found them. Yen Ling—her name was honey in his mouth. He couldn't remember whether the communist army's Long March had traveled through here or if she had been with it in the early days.

But he would never forget the woman herself. She was one woman and all women, and unforgottable.

Sitting up by slow degrees and remaining screened by brush, he peered down slope and listened to Yen Ling speaking her poetry, telling him of that Long March:

> . . . ten thousand waters and ten thousand mountains
> are only places.
>
> The five peaks undulate with small waves;
> Sandy water beats the cloudy cliff. . . .
>
> After ten thousand snows of Minchan Mountain
> and the whole army smiles.

Down the hill something moved. Keenan remained still to stare at the spot. Look for a right angle, he thought; nature abhors right angles. Watch for movement against the wind, jerky movements. Look for something standing in the wrong side of a shadow, for the upside-down Y that could only mean a careless man standing with his feet apart. Trees didn't grow that way.

Wait.

Much guerilla warfare was waiting—for the right time and place, the right opportunity. In the brush you sensed the other guy and waited for him to become impatient, to get edgy and move. Then you killed the son of a bitch.

Keenan ranged his eyes slowly left to right and back, scanning the brush line below the hillside clearing. A man stood up, rifle slung and field glasses to his eyes, looking up at the ridge and checking it closely. He looked away from the late-afternoon sun, so he had the edge. Chewing the pinkish root, Keenan inched his weapon into ready position but didn't zero in. The Jap was too casual, too ready to expose himself. He was bait, so it was smart to let him live a bit longer.

When the man moved into the open Keenan blinked. Dressed in a mix of Japanese uniform and native clothing, this guy was probably a bounty hunter, a mercenary working for the blood chit Japs paid for Americans and Brits, dead or alive. Small enough to be a Jap, too chunky for a Laotian or Thai, the man might be a well-fed Burmese, and there was the head rag across the forehead, a flicker of faded red—a damned foolish color that would turn this hunter into the hunted.

Burma? Keenan tongued the lizard bone out of the corner of his mouth. Had he made it all the way to the Burmese border, to the Shan State? Maybe the man easing along down there was a drifter strayed into Yunnan Province.

Inch by careful inch Keenan seated the butt of his rifle into his shoulder. Maybe the bastard had been sent especially to chase him down. He was becoming known for the headless bodies he left behind. What had the old women in the last rain-soaked village called him? Their dialect was close enough to Mandarin for him to pick out words.

He had gone into the collection of pitiful huts because he needed salt and casaba flour and pig meat, but mainly the salt. Children fled from him, and the only man in sight, ancient and bent, shrank even more into himself at Keenan's approach. The women stood with arms folded and eyes down in resignation, as Chinese women had done for five thousand years. He took what he needed and left a Jap bayonet, all his yen notes and the last of his Jap tea in trade.

It was when he slipped again into the wet jungle that one old woman called after him, telling him how he had been named: The One Who Will not Die.

"Ahhh," Keenan sighed, because two more Burmese—if that's what they were—came into sight behind the leader using the field glasses. All carried rifles that looked like Keenan's own Arisaka.

Spread out, they moved slowly up the hillside, rifle muzzles swinging back and forth like the noses of hound dogs sampling the air. Keenan sighted upon the man to his right. When he worked the bolt for following shots the movement would naturally swing his muzzle left to line up on the other two. Still he waited, for there could be another group behind this, and he didn't want to be forced into running in the wrong direction.

Impatience is the failing of foreigners. Japanese Major Watanabe quoted that from his lofty heights of the code of Bushido. It had been so long ago and far away in another part of China; it had been in that other life before Chang Yen Ling.

If Keenan could believe in an afterlife with Yen Ling, he would stand up right now and let the hunters nail him.

Maybe. Once, back at the start of his own Long March, on the beach of that damnation bay where his love lay full fathoms deep, or shredded in the bellies of sharks, there would have been no doubt. He wasn't certain of that now. He was sure of only one thing—killing the enemy, whatever shape he might take.

The men were halfway up the sparsely bushed slope. Keenan started his trigger squeeze, his sight centered for a heart shot, when the leader made a sweeping hand motion and they all stopped climbing.

Camp; they were about to make camp for the night, and the leader had chosen the site well. No patrol would stumble upon it by accident, because jungle soldiers never walked out in the open. Taking watch turns, the campers could keep all directions under observation and hide themselves under existing cover. This bunch was good, and Keenan should sneak far around them. Let them continue to search ahead while he disappeared into the jungle on their back trail.

Lowering his rifle with the same care with which he'd

brought it to his shoulder, Keenan knew he wouldn't fade away. He had become The One Who Will Not Die, but these men surely would. Settling back upon the damp earth, he ate the rest of his food, salivating at the thought of rice, peppers and dried fish. If they carried tobacco, he would save that to pay for things he took. He had never enjoyed chewing tobacco, and in the jungle a cigarette could be smelled twenty yards away. At night and in the open the red spark could be spotted at half a mile. When Keenan went into the jungle he had stopped smoking.

The sun dropped slowly, staining the hilltop. Keenan's nose twitched at a drifting of woodsmoke, but he couldn't see a fire. They had dug a pit and were cooking a stew. Keenan swallowed once to clear his mouth and again to force food out of his mind. Then, as the sun dipped into the far tree line, he lifted himself to all fours and began a cat crawl down the hill. He had learned well and moved with no sound that reached beyond himself, placing his rifle on the ground ahead, then easing out one hand, and another. When he lifted a hand his knee moved forward to recover the same spot. Left hand, left knee; right hand, right knee; move the rifle and repeat—the cat crawl, patience stalking a bird.

When his spread fingers told him of dry twigs he didn't move a muscle until a puff of wind rattled the brush and stirred dry leaves to cover any noise he might make. Keenan tasted the night upon his tongue, a heavier flavor than the vagrant drifts of cooking that rode the air.

He was close then, too close to be the cat, so he became a snake, a great and deadly serpent. Sliding forward upon his left side, he used an elbow and one knee to pull himself along.

Now he could see a faint glow upon the faces of men hunkered around a pot, and one of them whispered, harsh and warning. Topped by headbands, three faces lifted to listen, high-cheekboned and narrow-eyed. The wind hushed, and they looked back into the pot. One dipped a gourd and brought it out to blow upon the hot stew.

When Keenan rose to one knee and shot him in the face the guy slammed backward, flinging hot liquid into a companion's face. That man screamed, and Keenan tilted to the right to kill the remaining hunter. The last man pawed at his scalded face and snatched up a bolo. Firelight winked off its wide blade as Keenan swung the rifle butt and knocked him down.

The man grunted on the ground and tried to inch away. Stepping over him, Keenan raised the rifle high and smashed down with the iron-plated butt. The skull broke with a wet and satisfying sound.

Beginning with this one, Keenan knelt and sawed his knife deep across the brown throat. He did the same to the others, being certain they were dead, hotly wetting his arms to the elbows. He found the gourd and dipped some stew. It smelled great, all rich and peppery. Sitting cross-legged beyond even the pale reflection of the fire, he decided to take the heads later.

Right now he was hungry.

CHAPTER 15

ASSOCIATED PRESS—October 5, 1942: War news summarized—

U.S. forces pushed west in the Aleutian Islands to pin down Japanese invaders reportedly dug in upon both Attu and Kiska.

Allied Nations Headquarters, Melbourne, announced that Australian bush troops fought up a steep 12,000-foot ridge of the Owen Stanley Range to reach Efogi. This village in New Guinea is only seven miles from the mountain backbone, an ideal attack position.

Moscow: Russian counterstrokes inside Stalingrad and south and northwest of the Volga broke German offensive power and regained many positions.

Tokyo claimed the sinking of "several" U.S. heavy cruisers off Guadalcanal and the downing of 18 American planes. Pacific Command calls the propaganda "wishful thinking" and reports that U.S. Marines are more than holding their own in the island fighting.

British Intelligence has warned Allied planes away from Johor Province in Malaysia. Aerial photographs have pinpointed prisoner-of-war campsites around the jungle town of Keluang. This is about 100 miles northwest of enemy-occupied Singapore.

Penny Belvale carried her head as high as Stephanie Bartlett when the point of the ragged, weary column of prisoners trudged into the new compound. As the only military female, Stephanie had been appointed leader of the civilian women by the Japs, although they thought it hilarious that the British needed their women to fight for them.

It wasn't a job she wanted, and it was dangerous because in Jap eyes it made her personally responsible for any transgressions of the complicated and ever-shifting camp rules.

Penny hadn't wanted to be next in line, either, but their captors read her WASP semi-uniform of blue coveralls and cap as military, too. The job did keep her near to Stephanie, and they had become personally close, more than just one caged animal seeking another's company. They seldom got a chance to exchange confidences. Conversation was limited to food, medicine, the possibility of escape and rumors of the war.

On the march Penny had to save her strength, and when they fell down at night only the evening bowl of rice gruel could keep them awake for any length of time. The U.S. wasn't coming to free them; the British weren't coming, and the war was being won by the Japs. In this new camp there would be plenty of time—maybe years and years—for them to share every day of their lives, past and present, with each other.

Nobody here would talk of the future.

Losing sweat she couldn't afford, Penny stared with glazed eyes around the camp. The stretched lines of barbed wire and tall, sharpened walls of giant cane were the same; the bamboo barracks with palm-frond roofs were familiar. The major change was that everything was new and unused, even the cemetery marked by a stack of wooden crosses piled in the corner of a low fence.

That was different, too. In the other place the women had to make their own markers.

Some Jap officer was playing games, pretending to be thoughtful or being more subtle in deliberate cruelty. New this camp might be, but it exuded the same thin stink of hopelessness.

Penny flinched. Despite the airfield bombing and fighting she was still not hardened to death. Combat killings were bad, but she would never forget the corpses left unburied beside the road on the long march from Singapore. The sick and suffering women who staggered out of the column; the poor little kids fallen into the brush; maybe those who were bayoneted or had their heads slashed off by swords or beaten in by rifle butts were lucky. At least they died quickly and didn't know the ticks and spiders crawled up to feed on them, didn't know the goddamn ravens and horrid vultures pecked out their eyes.

They were better off than the miserable creatures so weakened by malaria and breakbone fever and bloody flux that they couldn't even brush off the gray lice that sucked the last thin blood. And in the end the jungle got them all.

How she hated these slant-eyed sons of bitches. She snugged her hate close, depending upon its dark strength to keep her alive. Even though at times it could be much easier just to give up and let go, she had to live long enough to even up something—anything—with these bowlegged little monsters.

Tomaru! Tomaru!

Sergeant Katana bellowed "Halt!" the way he ordered anything, loud and guttural in his throat. All of them yelled that way, putting a false deepness to voices they were afraid wouldn't sound military or male enough.

The column stumbled to a stop, and two women lowered the small children they carried; others propped sick friends between them. A girl gasped and raked hands down Penny's back before she fell, giving Penny a chance to turn and keep her from going down. Feet set wide, she held to Ilona Hodgkins with all her strength. Even though the road march was over, the guards might still murder any who fell.

Hidari-hidari! Katana tried to say "left" in English and

mangled the word, but nobody smiled. It was long past smiling time, and Penny wondered if she had forgotten how. Wearily she faced left with the ragged double line and looked across bare red ground to the building set on pole foundations. The Rising Sun hung limp in shimmering heat above its doorway. A squat officer hobbled out upon the covered porch, bobbing stiffly to his right because of a twisted knee.

Japs didn't need excuses, but this wound, as much to his pride as to his body, could make this one an exceptional son of a bitch. Face without expression, he stood looking down at his prisoners, and Penny realized that the headquarters building had been raised that high for more reason than to escape the ground heat.

He drew out the waiting to impress them, she thought, to humble them in the sweltering sun. His short-sleeved uniform was clean and form-fitting, high black boots glistening. A pistol hung at his right hip above that crippled knee, and a long samurai sword thrust its woven hilt forward at his left.

"Pay attention," he said in the standard gravel voice. The surprise was that his English was unaccented, Americanized. "I am Major Watanabe, camp commander. My orders will be obeyed to the letter. Violation of rules and any attempt to escape means swift and severe punishment. Do not expect preferential treatment as women. You are the enemy.

"You will bow in respect to all Japanese soldiers—repeat, *all* Japanese. Senior Lieutenant Ohiri will appoint group representatives and assign barracks. Name the Malaysians and Chinese as barracks commanders, Lieutenant, so the British learn the truth of the Greater East Asian Co-Prosperity Sphere."

He paused, scanning the ranks below, and his eyes came to rest upon Stephanie Bartlett and upon Penny. His lips curled. "Prisoner leader and second in command, substitute warriors for men afraid to fight. Remain in this compound until I send for you. Lieutenant Ohiri, organize the rest and dismiss them."

Bowing at the waist, the lieutenant snapped, "*Hai, hai!*" and shoved the women into groups.

Quickly Penny passed the Hodgkins girl off to the Kirk sisters, rangy Britishers who exemplified stiff upper lips and the upper classes—though old girls who might have learned dignity from the Widow of Windsor.

After he turned back into the building Stephanie shifted the shoulder band of her little knapsack. "Don't sit down. A bloody toff, is he? But the sma' clot will be watching for us to show weakness and lose face. Sounds like a Yank, doesn't he?"

"Okay," Penny murmured, "but I'd rather lose face than fall on my butt. He may really *be* American, and that might help." She tried to lick her cracked lips, but her tongue rasped more than soothed.

"Not likely, dear. Major Wobbly is a true clot and near daft. Toffs go daft when they get dirtied up, like that leg. He'll keep us standing out here until he realizes that we'll not get down on our knees."

Penny started to put her bundle down but straightened up and held on to it. "Oh, boy—if he ever hears anybody called him that—"

Stephanie brought up a grimace that was almost her old impish grin. "Aye, and won't it hurt the puir wee man?"

"Hurt us more. They're touchy about being short and yellow-skinned as it is, and any cripple resents—"

"Oh, never say it direct, dear—just so he knows the name is passing round. Prick air from his ruddy balloon."

Sergeant Katana strutted onto the porch. "*Naru-sa!* You come!"

After Stephanie Penny moved into the shade of the big room and felt the stirring of air from an overhead fan. She looked up to see the plaited palm fronds swishing back and forth and followed the thin rope down to a small Malaysian boy. Squatted in a corner, he tugged and released the rope in a steady rhythm. She smelled his sweat and coffee—*coffee,* not tea. She choked down saliva and thought for sure this Jap was at least Americanized. A tin pot steamed on a tiny charcoal stove, and she forced her eyes from it.

Watanabe sat upright behind his table, looking at two sets of papers, one in English, the other marked with Oriental brush strokes. When he glanced up he snapped, "Bow! Bow! Have you already forgotten to show respect?"

"Give him his ha'penny," Stephanie muttered, and she dipped her head.

Penny saw something flicker in his black eyes and made her bow deeper.

His eyes remained on her, probing. God, she hoped she didn't look attractive. Rape had passed by the group captured at the blazing airfield, but many other women in Singapore had been mauled, beaten and killed.

He pointed. "You—this is your true name: Belvale? What is your rank? No rank is listed here."

"I'm a civilian, a transport pilot. And of course that's my name, Mrs. Farley Belvale. My husband is an army officer."

He repeated it, "Belvale, Belvale. In Japan there are many Watanabes, Oharas, Tanakas. When I was in the States I heard common names, but this one is rare, I think. In China I was told of Belvales by another man of the family, one called Carlisle. This officer you married, this Farley Belvale, is he, too, related to the Carlisles?"

She didn't know how to play this, didn't know how much information he already had or what he might find out. Glancing at Stephanie, she got no sign and decided to tell the truth.

"Yes. The Carlisles and Belvales have intermarried for hundreds of years, becoming an extended family of military professionals."

Making the toothy hiss of the surprised Oriental, he frowned. "Yes, a family of samurai even in America. It seems long ago that Keenan Carlisle fought and died beside me in China."

Penny drew a deep breath and lowered her pack to the floor. This could be a break for all the prisoners, a personal contact she might use. "That would be my uncle by marriage. I remember when he went missing in action. He was related to my husband's father, Colonel Chad Belvale."

Watanabe's eyebrows lifted and he nodded.

Stephanie Bartlett buckled at the knees, and Penny reached to help, but her friend recovered quickly. "*Chad*—Chad Belvale? Oh, my God! I never put it together—Farley, Chad, you. I mean, with everything going on, and we never spoke of—oh, my God! I've been in love with Chad since the first time I saw him."

Now Watanabe yelled: "Love? There is no goddamn love, only war. Get out, both of you!"

Scooping up her gear, Penny hurried out to the porch, where Stephanie leaned her forehead against a post. She didn't know what had happened, but Major Watanabe had forgotten to make them bow before they ran off.

CHAPTER 16

ASSOCIATED PRESS—Headquarters, COMPAC, Melbourne, Australia, October 12, 1942: Early reports on the fierce fighting on Guadalcanal blame jungle conditions for as many casualties as those caused by the enemy. Malaria and dengue fever strike down American soldiers battling the Japs in thick insect- and reptile-ridden jungle.

Medical personnel are engaged in their own around-the-clock war to get these men back on their feet. Many soldiers and Marines leave front-line aid stations on their own. They return to combat while still sick rather than remain in safety while their comrades are shorthanded and in danger.

Farley Belvale hugged the damp and stinking earth, trying to make himself smaller, trying to concentrate on the wonder of what had happened to him rather than the obscenity of what was happening now.

Penny; pretty Penny Belvale; how had he been so lucky? Aunt Minerva sniffed that Penny had no sense of values, that by all that was traditional and holy she should not have married again so soon. Walt's body had not been found behind enemy lines, and in violation of good taste she turned to another family member. Did that signal something venal about pretty Penny Colvin-Belvale-Belvale?

No, Farley said; not only no, but hell no. Penny didn't care for money; Walt's death had left her plenty. She had come to Farley naturally, sensing his deep need for her, feeling their love reaching out and meshing.

Whap-whap-whap! Bullets snapping hot above him, probing for his life.

Oh, Jesus. Not now. Not with Penny waiting at home for him. He wished for a drink; a few steadying drinks would help him put down this urgency to flee, to take his fragile body out of danger and back to his beautiful wife. A lifetime of training told him that would be the greatest of sins, to panic and run to save his hide. But Jesus, how he wanted to get back to the love and warmth he had left behind.

There was a smell to fear, and it hung close around him. There was a feel to fear, a weight and furriness. Farley lay very still in a black night that would not be still, a night that cheeped and twittered and made insectoid scrapings, that tore itself open with machine-gun fire. The darkness pressed upon him, filled him with the sense of being alien in this bestial, growing, feeding world.

The dark was heavy upon his sweating body like the obscene intrusion of a rapist, penetrating his secret places despite his disgust. Farley shuddered. This was phobia upon phobia, the layering of one fear upon another so that they ran together and got lumpy like too much chocolate icing. A man could choke on too much of anything.

Such as love? No; those last few times with Penny failed because of overseas combat looming, and not for any weakness, not because he drank too much.

Prinngg!

Oh, Christ; so close. He tried to forget the sweat and the crawling of many-legged things over his face. He tried to bring back the wedding, the honeymoon nights with Penny, but the jungle crowded in upon him. He moved his head so that his cheek pressed the backs of his laced fingers. Something gouged the outer edge of his cheek, so he moved slightly and without sound. He was so damned scared and about to piss himself. Turning a bit, he fumbled with buttons and just made it, biting his lips and hoping the sound wouldn't be noticeable. Somewhere out in the vast and unseeable blackness the Japs slipped silently about their business, at home in the night and the jungle.

Farley didn't want to die, didn't want to have his own headstone in the garden of honor at Kill Devil Hill. Honor—oh, Christ. What honor was there in dying in this miserable jungle? He would rot here, melt into the stinking earth.

Ahead and off to the left something rustled. His platoon sergeant was several yards behind him, and the point man somewhere ahead. Farley heard a sharp intake of breath and held his own deep breath so he could listen better. There were no more sounds, and he wished the first noise to be some small and nibbling animal.

Eyes shut tight, he tried to picture his squad, the group that led him to stick his neck out, proving himself to be one of the guys. Oh, shit. He remembered only that men were planted on both sides of the narrow and barely discernible trail that snaked off into deeper jungle. Ambush according to the training manual; the men were not firing back, and the Japs were supposed to come down the trail to check out what they were firing on.

Ambush; even Japs deserved more chance, more dignity, than cattle approaching the slaughter. Farley gagged at the thought of grisly rump roasts and bloody rib steaks.

A softened *clink!* came back on the thick air, and Farley crammed his cheek harder against his hands, wishing, praying that it would not happen. All the while he knew it would. He knew the ambush would come off in a red, raging blowup that would shred him in a meat grinder.

He was in front of Sergeant Murawski, and Murawski was supposed to be trigger happy, not quite right in the head. He didn't wear a helmet and carried a BAR and was trigger happy; everybody knew that. Farley wanted to throw up the dark that had infiltrated him, needed to blot away the sweat gone chill in his armpits.

Rapp-rapp-rapp!

The burst from the BAR jolted him and tore open the night with quick thunder and red and yellow muzzle flashes. Farther along the path a grenade flowered hot and screaming metal, and the blast whipped over Farley. More weapons got into action, slamming into the dark, biting swift wasps of fire into bamboo and vines, scattering leaves. Another grenade sledged the ground, shook it briefly, and rolled vicious echoes through the brush. Instinctively Farley burrowed deeper into the rotted mulch of the jungle floor, flattening himself, clawing into oozing ground. His helmet slid forward and axed him across the nose.

He prayed for his men, prayed for himself. Murawski cut loose another burst; the crazy bastard didn't give a damn where he was firing. The bullets snapped over Farley's head.

Another grenade, this one Willy Peter that opened the night and seared the jungle with white phosphorus. Bamboo caught fire, and scattered patches of sawtooth grass flared up. He was numb, yet the numbness seemed to spread outward from his bones to stop just short of his outer flesh. His hypersensitive skin flinched from bits of mud and scraps of bark that skipped across him.

The nonfeeling was in his mind most of all, a bright blankness like a spotlight aimed into an empty room and showing only the dusty corners. He could not think; he could not concentrate because there was this intense, pinpoint focusing throughout brain and body, but it was not of his conscious doing.

Never had he been aware of so much body, so much feel of meat and framing and fluids. He ached in every cell as fibers pulled themselves tight, and he tried to rationalize that this was only the pumping of adrenaline, the quickened intake of oxygen, but he could not be rational. He was afraid, and his body was setting up its defenses for survival.

The scream lanced into him and wailed around inside his head, a high and keening scream packed with hurt and shock. An odd quiet hung after it as both sides stopped firing for a ragged moment.

"Lieutenant—Lieutenant! Oh, my God—"

The ground was soggy against his mouth, flavored by ancient rot and desiccated crawly things. The ground was warm and black, and he could hide in it.

"Lieutenant—I'm hit—help me—"

No medic with this little unit. But why yell for an officer? Because officers were supposed to have the answers.

"Lieutenant!" Sergeant Murawski took up the call. "Is he hit? Anybody see that goddamn lieutenant?"

Bracing against the dirt, Farley pushed and got himself lifted partway up. Close by, bamboo splintered, and shards of it speared past him. He got to his knees, not really understanding why, knowing only that it was against all human instinct. He moved a foot, then the other, and squatted like a hunchback frog. He stood up among the snapping noises and the popping spots of flame and stumbled toward the screaming man.

"Crazy bastard!" The sergeant crawled forward, snatched at his leg. "Get down—crawl to him—right over there—get down!"

Flame bloomed ahead as a grenade went *ka-whoom!* and angry bees spit by Farley. He heard the man groan and saw the upturned whiteness of the face as the jungle burned nearby. Kneeling beside him, Farley tried to ask where he was hit, but his voice wouldn't work. He felt over the man and found the wet place in the upper chest, felt the blood and splinters of bone.

Fumbling at his first aid packet, Farley spilled sulfa powder into the wound and pressed gauze hard into the hole. It turned quiet, so quiet that he could hear flames frying the jungle.

Sergeant Murawski shouted it: "Anybody else hit?"

One by one the squad sounded off. Farley worked an

arm under the man—a kid named Young, he thought—and braced the head for a drink from his canteen. Then, on Young's good side, he strained to lift the man and suddenly found help. Murawski was there, taking Young's weight on his hip, levering an arm across his back for support.

From behind the flickering fire somebody said, "Body count? I got my foot on one of the bastards. They shagged ass in a hurry."

"Good goddamn thing," Murawski said, "or they'd be blowing your ass off. Pull out—it's all over. Easy now, one at a time."

It was rough going with Young in the dark; they wobbled into thorn trees and sawtooth grass, but they held onto the wounded man. When the outpost challenge ripped through the night Farley almost sobbed in relief.

Murawski yelled back the password, and they weaved in with their load, with the limp wounded man.

"Okay, Lieutenant," Murawski said. "Here's the medic. You did good, man."

People faded into the dark, going to other places in the perimeter, saying little to one another. The ambush squad dissolved, and it would never be the same again. The men would be different in small ways, and the combat situation would not resolve itself in the same confused fashion. The next patrol or ambush or recon sweep would not be the first action for Farley Belvale. In a sense he was blooded now. He had been there and come back, and only he would know how afraid he had been. Only he would have to wonder if he could make it through the next time.

CHAPTER 17

SECRET—0100, 8 November 1942, French North Africa: Two infantry and one armored division plus a Ranger detachment and paratroops landed on the African continent today. All wore American flag patches on their shoulders. Commanded by Lt. Gen. Dwight D. Eisenhower, Operation Torch is the official opening of the second front in the European Theater of Operations.

Three prongs of the Western Task Force from the Mediterranean punched in at Port Lyautey, Rabat and Casablanca in Morocco. The Center TF objective is Oran while the Eastern TF attacks Algiers, capital of Algeria province. Air drops are scheduled south of Oran to nullify Tafaroui and La Siena airfields.

SECRET—0700, 8 November, Operation Torch: First reports from the beaches say that Foreign Legion resistance is spotty, fierce in some areas and light in others as defenders are confused by conflicting orders. A seaborne armored regiment is suffering heavy casualties in Oran harbor. From ten miles at sea battleship HMS *Rodney* duels with French naval vessels in the harbor and coastal defense guns at the ancient forts of Mers-el-Kebir and Hamman-bou-Hadjar high above the port.

Ashore, two scarlet flares flamed high into the black night, dripping comet trails of bright blood. As the bow of the HMS *Duchess of Bedford* slid through the calm sea Chad Belvale gripped the troopship's clammy rail with both hands.

"Two flares. A green one means no resistance, one red if the French want to fight. How the hell do we read *two* red flares?"

Captain Lucien Langlois said, "Take for ourselves a quick rear march?"

At his elbow Chad felt the solid presence of his new executive officer. The Cajun had arrived in England as a last-minute replacement for a kiss-ass officer. Not regular army, but fresh from a Louisiana National Guard unit, Langlois had already proved he was as good or better than any West Pointer in the regiment. Tough and smart, he was a southpaw with a deadly punch.

During the last weekend pass from ships anchored off Grenoch, the Cajun scattered unconscious Scots all over a Glasgow pub for making too much of the way he talked. The fuse lit when some kilted highlander called him a "bloody *sitzkrieg* Frenchie."

But the losers wouldn't get up and walk away from this coming fight.

"Ready as we'll ever be, us," the Cajun said. "Them powdered green eggs don't sit so fine on my belly, no, but look like everybody ate."

Chad heard the thump of landing nets going over the side and the muttering of troops crowding the lower decks, the dull clunk of helmets and the sharper rattle of rifles touching the rails. The landing craft creaked below swung-out davits that had once held white lifeboats. Like most English troop carriers, the *Duchess* was a hastily converted pleasure liner.

He glanced aft, to starboard and port, where he could make out only the forward gun tubs. The 20mm Oerlikons, three along each side, were manned by his son's company.

The crews had ridden the rough autumn Atlantic all the way from Scotland, bitching through the cold nights, strutting as they bucked the chow lines with gun crew passes.

Grenoch, Scotland and Stephanie Bartlett—a world away, an eon past. That special woman killed by Japs in Singapore, or a tortured prisoner like the poor bastards forced upon the Bataan Death March. He had to push her from his mind, for he had others to think about in the coming battle—the thousand men whose lives could depend upon his decisions. Thousand and one; Chad was just another poor bastard hoping to make it through.

Hang tough, Stephanie; make it through, darling.

The battalion's heavy weapons outfit would stay in position to search the dawning skies for German planes while the rifle companies splashed ashore. H Company would be last to off-load, but if stiff resistance—*two* red flares?—was met on the beaches, its guns would be needed in a hurry. The British civilian sailors could, after a fashion, man the 20s as they were supposed to handle the other armament: the Chicago Piano, the pompoms, stern gun and deck rockets.

Chad didn't trust them. The crew of the typically filthy British troopship had gone all out to hustle the GIs with everything from house-odds gambling games to selling late-night sandwiches. And for anyone tired of sleeping in hammocks or on the cold deck, a private stateroom was available for a price. What would it cost to have the ship defended from a down-and-dirty air attack?

"You want me to stand by the nets?" Langlois asked.

"Thanks, I'll do it. I'd appreciate it if you'd see that H Company is on the stick, ready for a quick off-load. If they're in good shape, my compliments to the company commander." Chad hesitated. "No—take the nets for a few minutes, Cajun. I'll do H Company."

Compliments to the CO, hell; a private moment to say good luck to Lieutenant Owen Carlisle, to his son.

"Yes, sir. The captain driving this boat, he's pushing in at land like a shrimp boat with a Gulf storm coming fast."

Chad turned from the rail, tasting chill salt spray and knowing the eager coiling inside him, the pre-combat tension that made everything brighter and sharper.

"Remember the last briefing? The captain said he'd ram this ship into the sand so if the Krauts bomb the *Duchess*, she can't sink."

"*Merde!* Black as a muskrat's ass out yonder. How does he know sand's ahead, and not a big old rock? I been on a shrimp boat what hit a little bitty cypress stump, and—*bing!*—I'm swimming around with bull alligators what don't give a damn who they bite. I figure we ought to get our asses off this bow immediate, us."

Grinning, Chad slapped the man's shoulder and went to find his son. Langlois was just the kind of guy every combat outfit needed, one who could ease any situation with a joke.

He found Owen by his voice at Starboard 5, the midships tub, a shadow among shadows. His shoulder against the cold iron ladder, Chad waited until Owen finished briefing his platoon leaders and they hurried off.

Then he said, "Lieutenant—ahh—son."

"Colonel?"

Even standing close he could only see Owen's face as a blur. The ship rocked, and he put a hand on the boy's arm. "All locked in?"

"Yes, sir. After the ship grounds and if there are no raids, we go below and just step into the LCPs for a short ride. H Company will be right behind the reserves as ordered, sir."

"Oh, hell, Owen, I knew you'd be on the stick. I came by to—just to—wish you luck, son. This thing might get sticky, so—"

Owen's hand slid his down and held it. "So good luck—Dad. And thanks."

"Yeah." Chad wheeled away and shoved through the troops. He could talk with anybody else, why not his sons?

And why was it that he could say it all to Stephanie and not to Kirstin? Stephanie might not be around to listen again.

Be there, Stephanie; good luck.

Good luck. It was what all soldiers said to one another, not good-bye or farewell or see you again; just good luck. It meant hope your transfer works out; don't stray too far before you re-up; hope you make that other stripe, that silver bar or railroad tracks.

In combat good luck had a different meaning, a stupid, hopeful meaning: Don't get shot, man; don't get killed.

Weaving through the crowd on the lower deck, he found the advance troops of George Company climbing down the nets and found the Cajun close by. "Captain—this is Change One. I'm going in with this company. You stick with the original orders and bring in H behind Fox Company. They're in reserve. See you in Africa, Cajun."

"Wait, Colonel—the boss ain't supposed to—oh, hell. *Bonne chance.*"

Thankful that the ship wasn't rolling, Chad put one leg over the rail and smelled vomit.

Halfway down the net a man said, "If you puke on me, I'll throw you off this fucking net."

A weaker voice answered. "Be two asses hitting the water."

Chad grinned; these men would do all right. He slipped in among them and went carefully down the crisscross of ropes, feeling for a lower foothold before changing grips with his hands. His carbine hung over one shoulder; his helmet and light pack snugged into place. He was much better off than the troops, who were loaded down with more weight than they had ever carried in training.

They struggled under full field humps with overcoats strapped on top; six cans of wet, six of dry and three D-bars, the C-rations for two days. Then M-1 rifles and bayonets, ammo belts and extra bandoliers, hand grenades and the new rifle grenades nobody had tested. Then canteens and entrenching tools, and some clowns wore World War I knuckle-duster trench knives.

Oh, yes—and the clumsy gas masks they had even been forced to take on pass in London. Now the gas mask carriers held only cigarettes and personal items. The masks themselves were deep in the Atlantic, and he didn't blame the troops for dumping them. If Hitler hadn't doused London with mustard gas during the blitz, the Vichy French here weren't apt to try phosgene on Americans.

At least half of that overweight gear would be discarded, if not on the beach at Arzew, then along the thirty miles of road between there and the city of Oran. Back at Tidworth Barracks he had lectured his battalion on the importance of hanging onto two things—a weapon and an entrenching tool. He told them of digging in with a bayonet and scooping with a helmet at Dunkirk, and they laughed. But would they remember?

Hands helped him down into the boat, and seconds later the coxswain called, "Boat away!" and the Landing Craft, Personnel, pushed off from the nets. Its motor bubbled underwater as its flat nose pointed for the unseen beach and French *colon* vacation homes of Arzew. More than a resort waited along this crescent of sand; a Foreign Legion coast artillery post threatened on the right flank. Its eight-inch guns could blow away the beach and everyone on it, including the troopships bobbing at sea.

Rangers, the newly formed outfit that had trained with British Commandos, were assigned to take out those guns, to slip in ahead of the first landing wave and silence the batteries before they fired a salvo. Battle planning was always exact, pinpointed, to the letter. It never worked that way. Back at Dieppe Captain John J. Merriman wasn't supposed to linger atop that damned hill and get blown up.

And back in London, an un-shot-at, very English brigadier thought to lecture Chad for risking high-rank capture to haul down his friend. Piss off, Chad said, and the brigadier said indeed, and saluted. Then he pinned the medal on

Chad and shook hands. Johnny Merriman had lost *his* hand, and England one hell of a field soldier. He'd want to be here now, and Chad sure wanted him, but Merriman was done, a cripple.

Spray wet Chad's face, and the LCP waddled in shallow-water waves. He listened for gunfire. Had the Rangers knocked out the coast guns? In this first-ever ETO landing anything might go wrong. He was lucky to have combat experience, to expect the unexpected. Two of the regimental brass had been under fire, but in World War I. Nobody else had been to see the elephant, his Civil War ancestors would have said.

Rocking, the boat pushed steadily for shore, its men silent, huddled with their thoughts and fears, with their prayers. Chad scanned the sky for more flares and listened hard for the warnings of small arms fire, for the fearful rush of a big shell. He balanced up front at the landing ramp, bumping against a platoon leader. Straining, he couldn't remember the guy's name. So much for all that combat experience.

The LCP jolted, and Chad grabbed for support. It shuddered and rocked, then the ramp splashed down and Chad jumped off with the lieutenant into water knee-deep and cold.

"Go—go—go!" the lieutenant yelled, and they waded a few yards to the beach, weapons held high.

The objective, Chad thought, and he checked the situation map inside his head. No thunder from the big French guns; no whiplash of machine guns along the sand. They were running lucky and would make it to the racetrack. Wasn't that a hell of a military objective, a racetrack? G Company was to hold it until daylight and then regroup to move inland. Two bucks on the nose of a reluctant nag called Vichy France.

Behind Chad boat after boat growled ashore, and noise grew—clangs and rattles and shouted orders. The battalion came ashore expecting a fight, and so far the landing was a walkover, so the tension broke and the men relaxed. Chad moved up beside G Company's CO as Captain Mulick sent his skirmishers ahead.

"No problems, Johnny?"

"None, and that bothers me, Colonel."

It worried Chad, too. For all the radio propaganda, air-drop leaflets and political underground work, that didn't mean the Legion wouldn't resist. Marshal Philippe Pétain, enthroned in his dotage amid what remained of technically free France, would order battle as soon as he learned of the invasion. After the blitzkrieg crushed the French army the ancient hero had no choice but to collaborate. It saved a small corner of the country from storm troopers, but the word was he went too willingly with the Nazis.

So he would bleed the Allied invasion of North Africa to save the vineyards of Vichy. Chad tightened his grip on his carbine. Somewhere soon there would be a fight.

Pom!

He went to earth at the curved wooden rail of the race-track. The dark clubhouse bulked to the front, low stables to the right front, threatening shapes against a sky going gray.

Pom!

Two seconds, three seconds wait, and *pom!* again. A bolt-action Lebel from that other war, Chad figured.

Ka-chung . . . ka-chung . . . ka-chung!

No doubt about the distinctive reply of an M-1 rifle. Some GI had picked up the muzzle flash or just tried his luck with sound shots. Either way it was a good sign; soldiers under fire for the first time often just sweated it out or waited for orders.

It was quiet again, the beach noise dampened by the brief gunfire, and Captain Mulick moved his troops forward, leap-frogging one squad past another according to the infantry manual. No other sniper fired; no mortar shells hissed down. Inside the clubhouse Chad kneeled beside Lieutenant—Schneider; that was it, Dutch Schneider.

"Oh, hell," Dutch said. "I thought we'd see some real action, not just some A-rab farmer with a shotgun."

Chad didn't say be thankful; he knew how eager the young officers and men alike felt. They had sweated and strained preparing for combat, had drawn brain and body tight against the possibility of not measuring up. They still had their inner selves to face, to wonder how they would walk among the bullets.

Touching the back of his neck, Chad felt cold skin and lifted hackles. It was coming for them all. He could sense it.

CHAPTER 18

ASSOCIATED PRESS—London, November 9, 1942: U.S. expeditionary forces are wiping out effective resistance along 500 miles of Africa's western Mediterranean coastline. Today the conquest of Oran, Algeria's second city, is expected to be complete.

An intercepted German report said the Bey of Tunis had granted President Roosevelt's request for passage of American troops to Libya.

On the Atlantic coast, resistance at Casablanca is fast crumbling under all-out naval and air assault. Heavy warships and dive bombers are plastering holdout positions as American armored columns penetrate the city's eastern suburbs.

Preston Belvale took a deep breath of Algeria. The smell was a pungent mixture of urine and garlic, date palms, wine and olive oil, with overtones of ancient shit, animal and human. The smell didn't match the imagery of Oran in pictures, those glistening white buildings and red roofs at a crescent of dazzlingly blue sea that evoked memories of *National Geographic* magazines.

This wasn't the big-city objective, only a small town whose name had never been known to the world before the landings and would be swiftly forgotten by all except the men who came to war here. And the next of kin of those who might die here. Light resistance didn't mean a free lunch, only that casualties were fewer. A man killed by light resistance was just as dead.

From this vantage point Africa didn't look like the Sheik of Araby and festooned-war-camel domain of *Beau Geste*. This was the rich and rain-cooled agricultural coastal strip, but the harsh reality of the burning desert was never far away. To the north waited the empty plains and rocky mountains of Tunisia, and farther west a bright German general named Rommel was giving fits to the British Eighth Army. Altogether this was an Africa that would confuse Tarzan; Johnny Weismuller would have no rivers to swim.

Sitting in one corner of Danger Forward's hut, the First Division command post, Belvale was very much a spare part. Being outranked by an observer of sorts didn't bother Major General Allen—Terrible Terry Allen—so long as Belvale didn't horn in, and he didn't intend to. Still, the CP brass sweated him out, watchful for anything a three-star stool pigeon might report to Washington.

He wasn't reporting a damned thing to the War Department that it didn't already know. The good and bad word would go out to his own War Room at Kill Devil Hill, to be sifted there by Crusty Carlisle. Suggestions for implementation or correction would be passed to the right people, but individual fault finding wasn't part of the observation tour. Unless some officer was so stupid that relieving him of command became necessary to save lives and win battles.

"Damn," a colonel said, "I wish Roosevelt would have waited until we took the damned city before announcing victory to the world. Everybody hear that radio message?"

"That's why Eisenhower wants Oran taken by the tenth," Allen said. "Send this order to the regiments: Nothing in hell must stop this attack."

"That'll do it," the colonel said.

Belvale got up and wandered outside to lean against the building's whitewashed wall of mud. He lighted one of the cigars he'd carefully protected during the landings. In general, the invasion had gone okay for a first time out. Flying in the 503rd Parachute Battalion was one of the not-okay moves; Eisenhower's HQ in London gave them the idea that this would be a peaceful landing, and during the C-47s' flight from England the planes lost the homing radio beam off Oran, and the flight fell apart.

Kee-rist; one plane landed at Gibraltar, two in French Morocco and three in Spanish Morocco. Word had just radioed in that some planes sat down so close to the city that the civilian gendarmes grabbed and jailed the troopers. He'd bet that airborne history books would ignore that snafu—situation normal, all fucked up.

Belvale would also like to know the silly son of a bitch who dreamed up the pyrotechnics, the hundred-foot-long American flag of fireworks to be fired high by huge mortarlike tubes. It was supposed to make a Lafayette-we-are-here announcement that called upon the French to lay down their arms. The only one to burst dazzlingly in the night sky called forth a blizzard of small-arms fire from legionnaires originally confused about finding a target.

His part of the invasion convoy coming directly from the States, Georgie Patton was doing all right at Casablanca, roaring around with his tanks and shooting up everything in sight. Anywhere in Africa the French armor was 1914 vintage and not much better than cardboard. And the mostly English operation had little trouble beating its way into Algiers.

Drawing a long pull of smoke, Belvale thought of the Zouave cavalry, blue jacket and red fez, ballooned red pants; he mourned for the gorgeous Arabian horses dead and dying at Rabat and out of Sidi-bel-abbes. The brilliantly uniformed officers had it coming for sending cavalry against modern infantry, and although the lancers had to follow orders, still they were men capable of decisions. But the poor damned horses had no choice and no chance. It was always that way—hell on women and horses.

Hell on pretty Penny Belvale, and on Chad's Englishwoman trapped at Singapore; hard on Kirstin Belvale-Shelby sweating it out at home.

The fighting man's gods must have smiled down last night, those wingless angels who wore not halos, but burnished helmets. No doves carrying olive branches perched on their armor, and the dogs of war snarled at their sides. Cry havoc and unleash the dogs—at the enemy, please. Those junior gods stood watch over Valhalla and guided the Valkyries, rode with the Crusaders and walked Fiddler's Green. Often capricious, last night they had smiled upon Operation Torch.

Not one but two coast artillery forts had fallen to the Ranger Battalion without major bloodletting—Fort de la Pointe and North Battery. One fort was caught that Sunday morning with its big guns stripped and left over from Saturday inspection, taken-down internal parts covered by canvas, waiting to be put back together on a duty day.

He looked across a long and bare drill field ground toward a large and brooding barracks that worried the division brass. Belvale worried, too; the building was supposed to be occupied by a troop of Tunisian Fusiliers, and nobody on either side had made a move or fired a shot—yet.

Ash dropped from the end of his cigar, and he watched its fall. He had checked; the 16th Infantry, Chad and Owen were doing all right. But the 18th Infantry was catching crossfire hell in the village of St. Cloud, and two battalions of the 26th still had the towering, well-defended Djebel Murdjadjo to take. Now the Foreign Legion was gathering itself, over its initial shock and preparing to live up to its reputation.

Nothing in hell must stop this attack, Terry Allen said. Belvale had a hunch that tonight might turn into a concentrated slice of sulfur and brimstone. He felt a little tired, just a little old, and his bad leg throbbed. Crusty could be right, and old dogs ought to stay curled before the hearth.

He stared at the barracks again, remembering the knock-down and drag-out battle continuing on Guadalcanal. The family was represented there by Farley Belvale, with Major Dan Belvale on the way. Friendship was marked by other, older officers, but especially by Captain Jim Shelby, a U.S. senator volunteered as an infantry company commander.

Kee-rist—Belvale had sent Eddie Donnely to Shelby, to ride shotgun, upsetting the whole Hawaiian Department chain of command. Donnely had been fighting for transfer to a line outfit, but his ladies maneuvered to keep him at Schofield Barracks. Lover he might be, but a soldier first, and maybe his military expertise could help stubborn Jim Shelby in the thrown together Americal Division. But this was the first war for Donnely, too.

Belvale dropped his cigar. Three men strode across that open parade ground toward the Tunisian barracks, officers of Danger Forward out to break the stalemate on their own, just a casual stroll. From narrow slits in the high, thick walls machine guns opened fire.

Nambu machine guns; bastard Japanese playing it smart with three-round bursts so it was tough to spot their positions. No more than two flanking guns, he figured, but they were holding up the company advance. Bellied down behind his BAR in jungle mud, Eddie Donnely watched the undergrowth. The little shits were masters of camouflage, but if he couldn't see the positions, he might pick up leaves jumping away from a muzzle blast. Less than a month on the Canal, he'd learned that much and a few other things that kept him alive.

Insects buzzed at his face, and something crawled on his neck, but Eddie didn't move. Eyes slitted against sunspots filtering through the green canopy overhead, he watched, right forefinger curled lightly upon the trigger of the automatic rifle. He'd inherited the extra weapon from the corpse of a Marine, lost and forgotten in some earlier fight. The Browning was heavy, but a solid, trustworthy weapon with more firepower than the Garand, and jammed less often than the carbine in these miserable conditions. No Table of Organization and Equipment on Guadalcanal, so a platoon sergeant packed whatever he was capable of handling. Neither did the TO&E state that a platoon sergeant should be out on point, but the rule books had gotten thrown away back on New Caledonia. The Marines wrote new ones, and some of that hard-learned information drifted down to this 164th Infantry Regiment.

Eddie had never thought to soldier with a National Guard outfit, the butt of RA jokes, but this unit was doing okay since it had been federalized. Its survivors were as tough and dedicated as any professional soldiers. Allowing himself a tight grin, Eddie thought that his old man would offer to stand up and fight out that opinion. But Big Mike was clear around the world in a different kind of war, one where a guy could see the fucking enemy.

Eddie watched. A gray spider marched many-legged across the back of his right hand, and he felt it pause to sample the base of each hair where tiny sweatballs gathered, where jungle rot was taking hold. Some of these little gray bastards could kill you with a bite, or just make you wish you were dead.

Brap-pap-pap!

To Eddie's left rear a man grunted and mumbled "Oh, shit" as if he were talking through a mouthful of blood.

There! Leaves swayed back, a cluster of three flat-bladed leaves flipped up by the Nambu muzzle blast from the left flank. Eddie centered his sights below the jitterbug leaves and shifted his elbows just a bit, slid his feet carefully into a better position.

Drawing a long breath, he let out half of it and started his trigger squeeze. Hell, it was habit. The BAR jumped against his shoulder, its bipod holding solid in the jungle floor. *Bambambam!*

He moved the muzzle an inch to the right and an inch down to kick off three more shots. *Bambambam!*

In the undergrowth a Jap screamed, and it sure as hell wasn't *banzai!* When one got hit he forgot that deep-throat command voice horseshit and screamed like a woman. Eddie swept down and left for three more rounds, then shut down the BAR and rolled hard right, spinning over and over like a kid playing in grass.

The right flank gun was closer than he thought. It kicked up greasy mud across the imprint his body had left, the gunner loosing a long, pissed-off burst. Eddie tasted the smoke and didn't try to change the BAR magazines. He could damn near smell the Japs, so he stayed put on his left side and took a grenade from the belt on his hip. You couldn't wear them in front and crawl on your belly like a reptile.

Barracks room chatter, Coney Island barker talk echoing at Fort Jay—hey, hey—she walks, she talks, she crawls on her belly like a reptile—

He pulled the pin, let go the spoon handle and counted: one . . . two . . . and three—hurrying the last count a bit. Then he flipped the grenade over a vined bush and past the shaggy bole of a palm tree.

Barracks chatter on payday in the dayroom, hustle from a winning blackjack dealer—around and around she goes (like Eddie Donnely rolling in a ball to get away from the blast) . . . and where she stops, nobody knows but God . . . and He won't tell. . . .

The explosion slapped him along the head, and his helmet was a washtub with somebody hitting it with a club. He tasted slimy mud and some green shit while his ears rang and rang and he couldn't pick up the phone. "Sarge—Sarge! You got the bastards!"

On his back Eddie blinked up at the kid standing over him, standing straight up with his rifle at port arms.

"Jesus—get down! Get your dumb ass—"

The kid went down, arms flung wide, driven back and

down as his helmet flew off. His rifle skidded the wet earth behind the flat sound of an Arisaka rifle.

Sniper high in a coconut tree, strapped at an angle where he couldn't spot anyone lying flat, Eddie thought. He cursed the kid for dying stupid, a yellow-headed ammo bearer with a long nose and pimples but no name Eddie wanted to remember. It was that way already, not wanting to get close to anybody who might be killed tomorrow. Already the guys who first came in with the outfit were running out of luck, and damned few replacements got through. When one showed up Eddie wanted him to be a blank face and a pair of hands, nothing more.

Sure, he had a couple of buddies, and he had Captain Shelby. And at this moment he had a sniper staring down at his platoon. Turned to his belly again, he considered options. If he stood up and fired a full clip at the trees the Jap might miss him, and somebody else might see the fucking monkey on a limb and take him out. "Boof" Hardin had a sharp eye and was good with an M-1, but Eddie didn't enjoy being a target.

He couldn't play Roy Rogers and hold a helmet up on the BAR; the Japs had caught on to that trick right away. The leaves; sure—the same giveaway leaves that had cost the Emperor a couple of machine guns. He snaked to a yea-high thorn bush and sawed through a thin vine with his gold-plated pocket knife.

Thanks for the gift, Vanessa Hammond. A bayonet won't cut worth a damn, and I ditched mine a while back. Thanks for crying when I got my orders. I cared, baby—I cared, too.

And in case I didn't mention it, Mrs. Captain Doetz—Marilyn—thank you for not making a scene at the dock.

"Boof!" He hissed it low to the ground. "Boof, you bastard—do you read me?"

The whisper came back: "Five by five, Sarge."

"Keep your big head down but look at that kid. Try to

figure the angle the sniper used, and watch it close while I draw fire."

"With your money-making ass?"

"By shaking a goddamn bush."

He was ten yards back when he jerked on the vine. The bush shook and settled; he put less pull on the vine next time.

Pranggg!

The Jap's bullet punched through the bush and kissed low off a tree trunk.

A bunch of rifles fired together, a drumfire roll interspersed with the clings of empty clips ejecting.

"Got him!" Boof Hardin yelled. "He's shot to pieces and hanging upside down from his rope. Bad day at Black Rock for that son of a bitch."

Eddie sat up and changed magazines, folded the bipod into place. "Move the guns forward, but watch it. This was probably a rear guard, but there have to be more of the little bastards."

There would always be more. This war was just getting started.

Barracks talk—Mama said there'd be days like this; she just didn't say they'd come in bunches like fucking bananas.

CHAPTER 19

TOP SECRET—2400, 9 November 1942, Algeria, North Africa: Agents within the city of Oran report that the two British cutters, *Walney* and *Hartland,* came under intense fire as they entered the port. Carrying 393 men of the U.S. 6th Armored Infantry, they were hit point-blank by shore batteries and emplaced machine guns, and by naval fire from submarines and destroyers. The only survivors are 47 POWs, this count unverified.

The 18th *Regimental Combat Team* has twice been repulsed in attacks upon St. Cloud, where the lives of 4,000 civilians preclude artillery bombardment.

A major ambush closed on 2nd Bn., 16th RCT at 2240 as it passed through Assi Bou Nif on its advance toward Oran. Casualties unknown as heavy fighting is continuing.

Private Sloan Travis hated slogging along in the dark beside the cart stolen from a poor Arab farmer back at Arzew. It was a rickety thing piled high with the platoon's machine guns and equipment. It was dragged by a dirty white mule, if you could believe that; a stolen white mule that practically begged to be the bull's-eye for a nighttime target. Oh, these professionals were so frigging smart, and so damned tough that they couldn't pack their own gear for twenty-five miles, even broken by what had amounted to an all-day picnic.

He also hated the socks that had dried too late to keep wrinkles from blistering his feet, the pack rubbing his shoulders raw, and even his stained and stinking uniform. Rotten luck had shoehorned him into this company of regular army misfits, and worse luck gave him an overdose of Belvales, father and son, colonel and lieutenant.

They should have allowed him to finish college, but even as an early draftee he ought to have made it into a noncombat unit, or at least to a new post being filled with inductees, his own and more intelligent kind. This bunch of New York street sweepings and down-home hillbillies had the collective IQ of an escargot; they signed away at least three years of their lives for room and board and twenty-one dollars a month. The officers weren't much better.

But having scorned the commission offered by the Great Family, he'd be damned if he asked them for anything. As the only known "handcuff volunteer" in this war, the only malcontent whose blood carried the holy military genes and who had not ecstatically volunteered to be shot, he was a pariah.

The night was cool, and the olive trees spaced along each side of the blacktop road moved past the shuffling column like stunted telephone poles. Yesterday ignorant GIs had chewed on green fruit plucked from those trees. Of course they spat and bitched and threw the bitter things at each other. Sloan adjusted his carbine sling and sighed. The overloaded cart creaked and rumbled. The white mule farted.

Sloan said, "My sentiments exactly."

The army had a public relations branch, and, as a journalism major with a literature minor, he should be there, using his skills. That wasn't the army way that placed civilian cooks as mechanics and turned plumbers into medics. The Carlisle-Belvales frowned upon such lowly within-the-army trades, the noncombatant, rear echelon support groups.

Blood and glory, the holy mission of the warrior born—great-grandfather General Carlisle reigning over Sandhurst Keep like Attaturk himself. But paladins weren't Christian, so the simile didn't fit. God had ever been on the side of the Crusaders; he just fell asleep when the scimitar overcame the broadsword.

Sloan's left legging had somehow gotten twisted and scraped at his shin. Canvas with hooks and laces, if you could believe that, while the Germans had high leather boots. It was a frigging wonder the U.S. Army didn't still issue wraparound leggings of felt that were good only for soaking up water.

At the tail end of G Company somebody coughed, and a canteen rattled. The army's strategy was to divide H Company's heavy weapons in support of the battalion's rifle outfits. So here went the leadoff 5th Squad of 2nd Platoon and its mechanized supply cart.

The white mule farted into the wind, and Sloan caught a whiff. Then bullets slapped the cart and kicked sparks off the roadway; bullets snapped and whined, and Sloan dived blindly for the ditch on his left.

Oh, God . . . oh, God . . .

Machine gun firing *down* the ditch! *In* the frigging ditch with him, and somebody's feet in his face and somebody else tight behind. Popping firecrackers just inches above his helmet were bullets, an unending stream of bullets. So close, they burned air at his cheek. He couldn't lift his head. Hot metal would rip it off if he lifted his face from the mud. Something flashed, so brilliant that it lit the ditch, and somewhere up ahead men screamed before the light blinked out.

Guns beat horror in the night, and he was scared, so frigging scared. He wanted to piss, and the bullets kept searching him out, gouging dirt from both sides of the ditch. The machine gun—on a low tripod like 5th Squad used on field problems; lock the traversing clamp and use the knobs—two clicks right and fire; two mills down and fire.

Oh, God . . . oh, God . . . don't let that gunner come down two mills. Two mills lower and he'll kill everybody in this ditch.

The gun stopped.

Jammed or being fed a fresh belt, the gun stopped firing!

Sloan hurled himself up and over the low stone wall to his left, away from the open grave of the ditch. Other guys crashed down with him, but not that many; his squad leader Pelky, the section sergeant.

POP!

A white flare, a blinding white parachute flare drifting high above the field, above the field of cropped grape vines like curled brown snakes.

"Don't move!" Pelky hissed. "Bastards won't see us if nobody moves."

Jammed against the wall, Sloan stared across the orchard—and found two men kneeling at another machine gun. In the stark white and black light he made out odd helmets and long overcoats, the pale watching faces. He saw the machine gun swivel to aim at his part of the wall.

His carbine surprised him. It oozed up on its own, something wrong with the thing, firing slow motion. He counted the rounds as they marched halfstep from the muzzle . . . eight . . . nine . . . ten.

At the gun only one man went down, and the flare hung up there forever. Deep and sticky, a lake of Karo syrup held him back as he waded toward the gun, as a full clip crept into his hand and clicked into place. Struggling against the clinging tide, he pushed shots back at the fireflies that swam past him.

Time snapped back when he stood over the dead gunners, when he kicked over the smoking machine gun. He dropped the empty clip and fumbled again and again, getting a fresh one into his carbine. Trembling, he went to his knees as the frigging flare at last sizzled out and left him in blessed darkness.

* * *

Owen Belvale sent another runner to bring up Cannon Company. His radio was out on the road, chewed up like the operator, and he was out of touch with everybody.

He crouched behind the farmhouse, confused and angry, his command scattered. That white mule stood quietly as bullets sparked around its hooves and ripped at the cart. Metal rang as a slug hit something—gun or tripod piled useless there. Road to his left, a long row of skinny windbreak trees to the right; his men spread God knows where, G Company pinned down. Who screwed up and didn't put out flank guards?

Where was Battalion and his old man? He hoped the colonel wasn't up with the point playing hero again. It was stupid for a battalion CO to leave his command to a subordinate and go cowboying for more medals. By God, he was going to tell him so.

Oh, these French bastards had set a good ambush, letting the point through and firing on the main body. They used the ditches, too—guns set in them, waiting for GIs to go to ground there.

But it was chickenshit to drop that high-voltage wire in the ditch far forward. G Company's runner came panting up to find Owen and say, "Fried like fucking eggs, sir. Half the squad dived on top of that goddamn wire and got fried like fucking eggs, sir. Big-ass white sparks like a goddamn electric chair. Captain Mulick, he says get him some fire on both flanks quick as you can."

Covering fire where? Not up the road, not too close on the flanks. He didn't know where his troops were, where anything was. Do something, West Point doctrine said; do something, even if it's wrong. Taking a deep breath, he felt the cold wall of the farmhouse against his shoulder and smelled gunpowder and the sour sweat of fear.

BLAAMM!!

It took a moment to shake off the hurt numbness. It was like fireworks going off too close to your hand, except this was a giant cannon cracker, and pain spread all over your body. Coughing acrid smoke, Owen felt around for his helmet and shoved it on. Mortar; the bastards had this farmhouse zeroed in; they planned on the instinct of men surprised by murderous fire to duck for cover here.

"Medic—medic!"

Turning to his first sergeant, he said, "Mike—"

Big Mike Donnely was gone.

Owen yelled, "Get the hell out of here! Take off down those trees and dig in. Spread out! Platoon leaders? All noncoms—"

BLAMM!!

"Medic—where's the fucking medic?"

Smoke thick and blackout lens flashlights probing; men down, gone flat because the life ran out and left collapsed shells. Dead men propped against the wall, heads angled, staring at nothing. Owen's first KIA; his stomach churned.

"Haul ass to the right flank! Dig in!" A sergeant's voice—Murawski? Things coming together bit by bit.

Chuff! Chuff!

Oh, Christ—beautiful! H Company's mortars in action, hurling finned shells out into the dark. Beautiful! Owen knew where Big Mike went—to set up the mortars and do something, anything.

Chuff! Chuff! Chuff! The deep coughs of the 81mm tubes, beautiful, firing back at the unseen enemy. The heavy thump of explosions there in the unknown beyond the farmhouse and line of skinny trees; silencing the enemy mortars, making the bastards keep their heads down.

Now the farmhouse wasn't so dangerous, but he was glad for the line on his right. He'd have guns set up facing the road and stone wall on the left. E and F Companies were to the rear, no doubt as bewildered as everyone up here, but in a loose perimeter defense. French machine guns fell silent in the ditches and beyond that wall, and no more flares popped. But anything could come roaring out of that field, and he had to meet it.

"Sir—5th Squad. I got the gun off that damned cart, but the tripod—"

Sergeant Pelke. No section sergeant or 6th Squad leader; two other squads spread along the tree line and chopping at the hard earth, the sound of pick mattocks and shovels drawing only occasional rifle fire. No machine guns in position to stop an attack.

"I'll get the tripod." Unknown voice, a volunteer.

Firing slowed along the road, and the white mule stood unconcerned. They owed that animal. If he'd bolted with the guns—

The GI brought back a folded tripod and went right back for an ammo box and the water can. Tracers zipped past the mule and the man back at the cart unloading other equipment. Pelke set up the gun and yanked the bolt handle to half-load.

The 81s chuffed again and again, comforting, protecting. Big Mike must be searching blind, but he was doing great, and now Owen picked up the sound of G Company rifles, a burst from one of their light 30s. The first shock was over, and the outfit was fighting back.

"Pelky," Owen said, "who's the kid risking his ass?"

"New guy, sir—smartass draftee. I don't believe it."

Everywhere firing slackened, a rifle pop here, the quick hammering of a BAR there. Men continued to dig, and the smartass draftee made another round trip to the cart.

CLANK-clank-CLANK-clank . . . "Right front, two o'clock! See that little blaze? Knock it out! Right through the window, and knock out the whole fucking house!"

Cannon Company's halftrack clattered to a halt, and its 75mm gun blasted. In the muzzle flash the white mule reared. Owen saw the draftee catch its bridle and bring it down. The 75 roared twice more, and flames rose high above the windbreak trees, a building and its group of hidden ambushers shattered and burning.

Good.

"Damn," Pelke said, "he unhooked the mule, and he's bringing him back here. It just ain't natural for that guy."

Fumbling and muttering in the dark, noncoms came up to gather their guns and stragglers, to report casualties. The halftrack rumbled and clanked up the road, and the 81s stopped firing. An eerie stillness descended on Owen's CP and along the road. The ambush was broken, but the battalion wasn't moving ahead in the night, a wait-and-see halt or the burnt child avoiding another painful blister. Colonel Belvale was being careful for a change.

Not fair; his father was only careless with his own life, not with those of his men.

Lieutenant Gladstein checked in, and Owen asked about the platoon sergeant. "Sergeant Murawski bought it. Sergeant Jordan, too."

"Okay—runner! Find Sutter and tell him he's got the platoon. Pelky, that gives you the section—find your own squad leader. Everybody dig deep and button up until Battalion says what's what."

Pale lights bobbing, medics worked on the wounded laid out on litters. Owen sat down beside Lieutenant Gladstein, sat with the dead propped against the wall. Cupping hands inside his helmet, he spun his Zippo wheel at a Lucky and drew deeply on it. He held the cigarette hidden inside the helmet close to his chest and noticed that his hands didn't shake. He hadn't been the perfect West Pointer, reacting by the numbers to a tactical field problem, but he hadn't really screwed up, either.

He said, "Thank God for Big Mike Donnely and that white mule."

When he reached for his canteen Gladstein said, "Try this. Second section loaded up on wine and edible olives yesterday. They paid the family with invasion bills and cigarettes, mostly cigarettes."

The wine was cool, and Owen drank thirstily of it. "From here on they won't pay. The good guys are pissed at their allies killing them. When we get into Oran every Frenchman had better watch his ass."

Gladstein drank and passed back the canteen. "So soon, you think? It stands to reason—*un*reason—that men change drastically in combat, but so many of these kids—"

"Look next to you. Those were kids. Now they're just meat, but nobody in this outfit will ever forget their names or who killed them."

Up in G Company an M-1 ran off half a clip. Behind the thin trees—poplars, that's what they were—somebody said, "Shit! You hear that ricochet? This hole ain't near deep enough."

Owen ducked for another drag on his cigarette. Then he said, "Daylight's coming, and we're a long way from our objective. I don't think the French left all their fight here, and they won't let us just walk into Oran."

The *pom!* of an enemy rifle left an echo behind the farmhouse.

CHAPTER 20

The New York Times—November 10, 1942, War news summarized:

U.S. smashes Japanese fleet in Solomons, sinks 23 ships, damages seven in three-day battle. American losses, eight ships; Rear Admiral Daniel J. Callaghan killed in action.

In North Africa fierce fighting continues on the outskirts of Oran and Casablanca. U.S. commanders predict victory within hours as infantry and armored pincers close upon the objectives.

Stalingrad, Russia: 1,500 Germans die in assault within the rubbled city and the Red Army gains in the Nalchik region.

Gen. Douglas MacArthur goes into New Guinea to lead American and Australian troops pressing on Buna. Meanwhile, Marines and soldiers on Guadalcanal continue the jungle battle against desperate and fanatic Japanese.

Imphal, India: Maverick Col. Orde C. Wingate heads some 3,000 British, Gurkha and Burmese troops gathered for penetration into enemy-held Burma. This raiding party is undergoing rigorous training even during the monsoon season.

They half circled Keenan Carlisle, guards hanging back with bayoneted Enfields at their hips, urging him toward the Britisher at the field desk. Keenan stood beneath the damp and blowing tent, feet spread wide and head sagging. He was so damned tired, and chills shook him every few minutes.

"Sir!" The leftenant popped his heels and saluted. "This man was picked up at the Burma border carrying Japanese arms and equipment. He claims to be a Yank officer. But he also says he walked—through the jungle, sir—across Indochina and Burma, beginning somewhere in China proper."

The fever dried his mouth; Keenan said through cracked lips, "From Hainan Gulf."

The British officer was naked to the waist and propped bare feet on the folding desk. Long-armed, he scraped at his feet with a rubber brush. "How long ago?"

Blinking, Keenan swayed, but when the leftenant put a hand under his elbow he shook the man off. Whoever this big shot was, he was a slovenly bastard, a condition virtually unknown in the English office corps.

"A year—fifty—whatever. What year is this?"

The man took his feet off the desk and sat up. "November, forty-two, Yank. Leftenant, get this man a chair and send for a doctor. Damme, use your head. Does he look like a sodding Jap infiltrator?"

"Only ten months," Keenan said. "Seems longer." He sank into a canvas chair and looked up as the man came around the desk with a bottle in hand.

"Colonel Wingate here. Cheers. Your legend has preceded you, the ghost the natives call the One Who Will Not Die. Every bleeding Oriental on the continent is frightened of the Jap *yurei* who comes by night and eats human heads."

The whiskey burned all the way to his gut, lovely warmth. "Sawed off their heads and hid them. Psy-war."

Wingate crouched beside the chair, nodding, bright-eyed, offering Capstan cigarettes and a light. "Tons of jungle knowledge, the ultimate guerrilla. Man, what a prize you are to me—oh, bloody hell. You are no doubt posted as Killed in Action, so give me your name, rank and such. I shall wire it to America immediately, and then—"

Keenan passed up the cigarettes for another pull at the bottle. "Stopped smoking in the bush. Smell reaches too far."

"Wonderful. What about the spark?"

Somebody else shoved in. "For God's sake, back off, Colonel! This man is seriously ill." A white shape smelling of antiseptic; kind, deft hands and cool instruments. "Stretcher bearers—get this man to hospital. Colonel, if you will allow—"

Keenan took a long swallow from the bottle, already dizzy, a stranger in a strange land. "Carlisle, Keenan, captain, United States Army. Serial number—serial number—I forget. How the hell does a man forget his serial number?"

As many hands lifted him from the chair and lowered him to a canvas litter he heard Wingate say quietly, "By surviving as a jungle animal, a bloody dangerous animal. Damme, sir—I hope you'll not want to race home immediately. I need you here; my entire operation depends upon—"

The doctor cut in. "Colonel, this patient is starved to a skeleton. He has malaria and dysentery and God knows what else. Here, remove that bottle—"

"He keeps the sodding bottle! Captain Carlisle, when you are fit you may of course go home. But if you insist upon leaving—"

Raising his head, Keenan said. "I came here to kill Japs."

Wingate laughed. "Man after my own heart. Take him along, doctor—and be damned careful with him. The captain and I have much to do together."

Arms pulled behind her and tied around the post, Penny Belvale closed her eyes against the beating of the sun. Stand straight and lock your knees, because if you sag or pass out your weight will jerk your arms out of their sockets. Dead weight to kill your arms. It was so hot, so hot that she was already drifting, and she'd only been here two or three hours.

Only?

Fight it, Penny—don't give that goddamn Katana a chance to gloat. He was down on the Someday List anyhow, and now she added a check mark beside his name. Concentrate on the list, start at the top and run it slowly through your mind—slower, so it will last longer and keep you from fighting the sun. Feeding upon hate keeps you alive.

Can't win against the sun; just try to break even. Win against the Japs so you can go through every name on the list one by one and see that they pay. Collection will come by court martial or civilian trial or in their slimy goddamn blood. Penny preferred the blood, enough to pay for Theresa Menasco and their plane, for the rotted corpses left along the tortured march from Singapore.

Here in Keulang Camp the debt had grown with every ready-made cross that was driven into the cemetery dirt, with every humilation forced upon weak and hungry women. And the three children remaining in camp; mustn't forget what the Japs were doing to them.

A drifter kind of breeze touched a passing kiss upon Penny's cheek, and she was so grateful that she wanted to kiss back, so thankful that she wanted to cry.

Watch it. Never cry; it's a sign of weakness and a loss of fluids you can't afford. Hold your shoulders back; don't droop; a lady does not slouch, Penny.

Sorry, Mother.

Oh, Christ . . . sorry you're dead, Walt Belvale; I apologize for pushing you into going overseas, Farley Belvale . . . hey, listen, everybody: I said I'm sorry, so can't I come out of the corner now?

The kids, remember. What about the kids? Oh, yeah—the Japs pretended they really liked children, and some guards slipped them bites of food and petted them. So the kids prattled about everything that happened in the huts, and who said what.

Funny noise; somebody clearing her throat, definitely a her. Forcing her eyes open half an inch, Penny looked across the baked ground and through the wiggly heat waves. Stephanie Bartlett defied the guard duck-legging beside her to shout, "Hold on! I'm off to protest to Major Wobbly."

She stumbled when the guard shoved her, then caught her balance and marched on with the arm swing of the English soldier on parade. Penny's lips hurt when she tried to smile. Give the buggers naught, Stephanie said, but always mind that Major Wobbly is daft, a regular bampot not to be pushed tae far.

Aye, Stevie; aye, lass, and thank you.

Her eyes closed, and she saw Sergeant Katana against her eyelids, squat and ugly. He had found her taking her early-morning shift in the garden patch, pulling weeds and watering while it would do some good. Before the sun sucked all moisture out of the earth. Sneaking up behind, he caught her as she stood up to massage the small of her back.

Clutching both her breasts, he ground himself against her. The stink of him clogged her throat. With both hands she jerked one of his free of her breast and bit down on his thumb. Katana threw her against the hut wall. She bounced off and ran around the hut, into the open. He caught her at the hut steps and raised a fist to strike. . . .

Penny pulled herself up and eased the drag on her shoulders. Hold on; damn it, she would show them she could hold on as long as she had to, forever or to the end of the war, whichever came first.

Katana had realized where he was, realized that his own men were watching. He dropped his hand, but Penny's reaction was automatic, and she slapped him hard.

"You attacked a Japanese soldier," Major Watanabe said, cool and polished behind his desk while the native boy pulled on the overhead fan. "There is no reason, no excuse for—"

"He tried to rape me."

"—no excuse for your crime," Watanabe said, as if he hadn't heard. "You are second in command of the prisoners and should be a model for the rest. You will demonstrate what happens when my rules are not obeyed. Obedience should be most natural to a woman, especially one of a samurai family."

She had looked him in the eyes, stared into those black and glittering eyes. "The Belvales and Carlisles don't make war on women and children. They're soldiers—not animals."

So she braced against the post, sliding her feet out and apart to help. Her shoulders ached, and the sun burned into the top of her head and seared her cheeks. Her lips were great puffy blisters. Water would be nice; a sudden rain squall would be nice.

Pull up and lock your knees. Think about the list—no, about Stephanie Bartlett and Chad Belvale . . . B & B . . . some kind of expensive liqueur that Mother insisted upon for the coming-out party, with pink champagne, of course. It was a group coming-out, because none of us could afford it alone.

Champagne would be nice.

No, concentrate on Uncle Chad and Stephanie—loyal, married Stevie, whose husband was behind wire in the men's compound down the trail, if he was alive. He had been captured; the grapevine brought her that much news. It couldn't tell her if Dacey Bartlett had fallen to the bloody flux or burned up with fever or kept his neck safe from a sword blade.

"I do love the lad," Stevie said, "in a certain fashion, you ken. It's not the way I love Chad Belvale, nor ever was."

"Did Uncle—did Chad ask you to marry him, or at least

come to the States with him? He could have arranged whatever you wanted. The family is very rich and powerful."

"Aye, he asked both of me, and I mind how hurtful and angered he looked when I said I could not . . . not so long as Dacey was posted to Singapore. It would not have been fair. You ken my reasoning, don't you?"

"I don't know. The war—not the war so much as this miserable damned camp and the Japanese—values have changed around, turned upside down. Now I would do anything to—to love and be loved, to live like a human being, even for a single day."

"Puir lass. Is it that you have your Dacey but have yet to find your Chad?"

"I may not have Farley, either. He's somewhere overseas. Oh, this stinking war."

War is the family business, pretty Penny. That's what Walt told her when they got engaged; Walt whose grave was empty in the grove at Kill Devil Hill. You must realize that we're born to the uniform and all it means, he said. And she said I accept that before she kissed him.

It hurt to yell. "Damn you bastards. I'm the uniform, too. I'm Walt's silver bars and Farley's gold ones and the battle flags in the great hall. Goddamnit—I'm a Belvale, and I am *family!*"

Her throat was raw, and her eyes burned. She opened them to shadows inching across the blistered assembly ground. Major Watanabe stood before her, left hand upon the long black hilt of his sword. Katana waited at his right and two paces behind.

"It is sundown," Watanabe said.

Chin lifted, she looked beyond him to the double line of prisoners called out to see her, to learn from her torture. Stephanie braced in position out front.

"Kaiho suru!" Watanabe ordered. "Release her."

Katana hopped to obey, and she barely felt the twist he gave her wrists before she fell to her knees.

Turning his head, Watanabe called to the prisoners: "Woman leftenant—bring another woman to help."

Penny fought upright and clung to the post with dead hands. "I'll walk." To prove it, she took two steps and fell.

"You cannot walk."

She twisted her face up at him. "Then I'll crawl, goddamnit."

Something flickered across his face. It couldn't be respect.

CHAPTER 21

ASSOCIATED PRESS—Washington, D.C., November 12, 1942: The navy has closed all routes for the Japanese to supply and reinforce their garrison on Guadalcanal, Secretary of the Navy Frank Knox said today. This, he pointed out, is due to the recent overwhelming naval victory in the Solomons, won against seemingly hopeless odds.

The blockade of the island by sea and air effectively seals off the Japanese and gives them little chance of holding out much longer. Meanwhile, American troops have pushed forward and extended their lines.

Crusty Carlisle snorted and pushed back his chair. "Feather merchant newsmen make it sound so easy. Technically, the enemy can't win, so the fight's over. But the Japs don't know that, and if they did, they wouldn't give a rice-fed rodent's rectum. That miserable island will have to be cleared Jap by lousy Jap, burned out and pried out of their rat holes."

Ben Alexander came over to look down at the bank of teletypes. Holding a mug of coffee, he said, "It's worse than the Indian wars. Cavalrymen knew there could be no mercy given or expected. Apaches, Comanches, the Yaqui—torture was a rite of honor, of passage into the spirit world. But the Japanese are an ancient civilization, and reports from the Canal—"

"Civilized, batshit!—ah, sorry, Gloria. The Europeans tried to civilize warfare, but war is barbaric, and it takes a mean-ass barbarian to win it down and dirty. We wiped out the tribes by out–Indianing them, improving upon their own tricks—and by superior firepower."

Crusty got up and stomped to the coffee table. "It has to be done again. Use any weapon, employ any trick, just so we kill their shiny yellow asses. And you can bet your money maker that the doggies and Gyrenes on the Canal are getting good at it."

Alexander said, "Did you see the communiqué from Preston? It came in while you were having lunch. I don't know whether to envy him or feel sorry for him."

She came across the room from the situation map, Gloria with her going-somewhere walk, straight as any Comanche maiden. "I gave him the communiqué right away. Who dares feel sorry for Preston Belvale? He wouldn't allow it, no more than Grandfather would."

Gloria fit in now, busy with a dozen War Room jobs and good at all of them. Crusty was glad she'd agreed to come down to the Hill with him. These days Sandhurst Keep in upper New York State was only a way station for family members passing through on orders or furloughing there. The Hill was close to Washington, where the Congressional peanuts could be headed before they lost the war.

"Preston got into action at Oran," Crusty said. "Damned right I envy him for that."

She said, "He admits he's tired, that war is for the young."

"Line troopers are young," he answered. "But can you imagine teenage commanders? Bat—stuff."

"There'll be some. Oh—not field grade, but the survivors will have to take command at company level. Look at expansion in the air corps—"

"You look! Goddamn flyboys, pretty kids driving their

cutesy toys. You don't win a war riding on toys. A war is won when our infantry—foot soldiers, by God—plant their feet on enemy ground and hold it."

Alexander said, "Any weapon, remember? The air corps is our best long-range weapon. I'd say that Preston's leg will hurt until it shows and embarrasses him. Then he'll come home."

"Wouldn't let *me* go, damnit."

Ben Alexander said he had to get back to Washington and kissed the top of Gloria's head.

Sitting down to file intelligence reports, she murmured, "Grandfather, you're the first to say it takes at least four support troops to keep one front-line GI in action. Everybody has a job to do—some of them like this one, unglamorous but necessary. There's no glamour for the poor foot soldier, and you know it. Pilots, paratroopers, nurses—"

She hesitated, and he said, "That woman—you're talking about that woman who divorced Keenan. Don't you think I know she got into the Nurse Corps? Lord, another female lieutenant."

"Then you know the woman has a name—Nancy Carlisle."

He grunted. "Not Carlisle anymore."

"She earned the right to wear the name. Keenan would admit that, and she's going overseas to do a vital job. I've been thinking—"

"This is vital! The country needs this War Room a hell of a lot more than another hospital bed maker. And Keenan can't admit anything, dying like he did." She scared him; he didn't want to lose her now.

He looked at her bent over the stack of reports, brownish hair drawn back and tied with a pink ribbon, her only makeup a little lipstick. Her perfume was flowery, not a sensual musk like most women wore. Gloria would never be called beautiful, but she was well put together and attractive, damnit. She would find another man but not have a husband pushed on her by Crusty. This time he would be her own finding, and the man would be damned lucky to have her.

Lieutenant-forever Johnson—or resigned-commission Johnson—either shivered out the war high in Alaska or was trying to stay ahead of the draft board.

He hadn't been the man for Gloria. She would know that one when she met him herself. But not yet; she wasn't ready yet.

Meddling in her destiny? Kee-rist! Belvale was doing it itself.

Eddie Donnely whispered it: "Regiment wants prisoners. Let them come in, but watch them close."

"Yeah," Boof Hardin said, "real close. The Marines said these bastards deal all kinds of dirty tricks."

Kneeling behind a bush with knifeblade leaves and snugging the BAR to his hip, Eddie stared at the two Japs across the grassy clearing. They stood side by side, hands upon their heads, buck naked except for dirty crotch rags and twisted headbands. It was the first time Eddie got to examine live Japs reasonably close.

These were scrawny, heads shaved, their sweaty hides yellow but no darker than Eddie's, with its malaria-treatment Atabrine tan. They wore split-toe rubber sandals and were flat-faced, droopy-eyed, alike in every respect—except the guy on the left had a leather strap around each shoulder and across his belly. Some kind of equipment carrier?

Boof hissed, "No guns, and if they even got grenades, they're stuffed up their asses. Want me to wave them in?"

"Call them in. Don't stand up."

"Yo! Come here! Come over here, you little turds."

For a moment the Japs hesitated, then shuffled slow and stiff through the ankle-high grass, sticking close together, elbow to elbow. Sunlight gleamed off their greasy skins and off the leather straps as they inched across the open space. Their eyes were glassy, fixed.

"Look at them little bastards," somebody said. "Head on, I could kick the shit out of both of them. What's the matter, shitfaces—Tojo run out of fish heads and rice?"

"Yeah," another GI said, "they ain't so tough, walking like they got a hose up their asses."

Bushes rustled behind him, and Eddie yelled, "Stay under cover! Don't make a target—"

Too late. The left-hand Jap dropped to his hands and knees, and Eddie saw the machine gun strapped to his back, the short Nen Shiki Kikanju. The other Jap straddled his partner and fired the gun.

Eddie shot back, trigger held back on full auto. The BAR slammed both little bastards back and down, the 30-caliber bullets sledgehammering them, ripping their bodies and smashing their heads.

The gunner's dead hand fired three more rounds, kicking up dirt and grass.

"Jesus Christ," Boof Hardin said, "and I ain't cussing."

"Medic!" A kid yelled. "Medic—oh, God, Jonesie's hit bad—"

"Never mind the medic," Boof said. "He's dead."

Eddie clicked a new clip into the BAR and continued to watch the jungle screen. "How many more?"

"Only Jones. You got them too quick."

"Too slow," Eddie said. "Those fucking straps—I should have figured." He screamed it over his shoulder: "You dumb sons of bitches—I told you to stay down! The next son of a bitch that gets off his belly without orders I'll kill myself."

Boof said, "They could have wiped out the whole squad. Close, Sarge—damned close."

Barracks talk: Close only counts with horseshoes and hand grenades.

Second Lieutenant Nancy Belvale wasn't ready for her first salute, and her return was shaky. It didn't seem to bother the Medical Corps soldier in hospital whites. He walked on by the bus and passed beneath flowering trees. The air itself was laden with the scent of exotic blossoms she couldn't recognize. She stretched and breathed deeply of the ocean, of Oahu and the warm excitement of Hawaii itself.

She had expected a tough duty post, was looking forward to it, in fact. Rushed through nursing school, she took special training in what the other girls avoided. She admitted it was mostly because she couldn't picture herself an OR nurse, blood to her elbows and having to throw away body parts. She got queasy in dissecting class.

The dirty stuff didn't repel her; she could scrub vomit and empty bedpans with the best. She could clean suppurating wounds without holding her nose. It was just the blood that bothered her. And death.

"Your gear, ma'am." The shuttle bus driver set her bag on the pavement. "I'd tote it for you, but I got to keep a schedule. Wounded coming ashore down at Pearl."

"That's all right, I understand—"

The bus pulled away, its fumes soiling the Hawaiian air. The driver was going to Pearl Harbor, where the battleship *Arizona*'s top still leaned sadly in the water. It was all she had seen of the destruction that had happened here less than a year ago. She didn't want to think of how many sailors were down there with their ship.

"Help you, ma'am?" His smile was young in a thin, tanned face, and he wore the maroon jacket and pants of an ambulatory patient.

"Why, thank—are you sure it's all right?"

The smile spread wide and bright. "I don't break easy. In fact, I'm going back to action tomorrow." He lifted her bag to his shoulder and led the way into the lobby of Tripler General Hospital.

When he lowered her duffel bag to the tiled floor it was before the reception desk. "This it, ma'am? All the new nurses check in here. Excuse me—I have to go get ready. The ship won't wait."

"Thank you," she said, and she watched him go back out through the double glass doors. She turned to the gray-haired woman behind the marble counter. "Isn't that something—a wounded soldier so eager to return? I thought—"

Reaching for Nancy's orders, the native woman shook her head. "The only place he's going is to the neuropsychiatric ward at Letterman General. Oh, I see you're an NP nurse, so you'll get to see a lot of George."

"But he said—"

"Look out the door, dear. Some patients kid around and call him George the Greeter, or the doorman. He sits out there all day and waits for buses so he can tell his story."

"Oh, God, and he can't be more than—"

"Just turned seventeen; lied about his age to enlist." The woman picked up a phone. "NP ward—hi, Lettie, your new girl is here. I'll get her set up in quarters, and she can report for the 1900 shift, right?"

Nancy blinked. Now there was more hospital smell than the perfume of flowers. "So soon?"

"They're coming in every day from Guadalcanal and Tulagi, or fished out of the ocean."

Turning, Nancy looked out to where a boy named George sat on the steps, waiting for the next GI shuttle bus. "Seventeen years old," she murmured.

The woman at the reception desk said, "We can't figure out if George is the lucky one or not. His twin brother got blown apart at his side. So welcome to the Pacific Theater, dear."

Chad Belvale took a swallow of the rich purple wine. It had a licorice flavor. He passed the bottle back to Owen and said, "General Roosevelt is coming by to hello the battalion and maybe hang on some medals. Regiment figures about 1300, but Little Teddy runs on his own time. I have the awards list."

"I put in for two of my guys. I thought about putting

that white mule in for at least a Silver Star, but only General Roosevelt would appreciate that."

Laughing, Chad slapped his son on the shoulder. "I heard about that mule. If there was any way, I'd ship him home to the Hill, personal attention of General Belvale."

He sobered. "The battalion did all right in the end. An ambush the first time out is rough, but they shook it off."

"The flank guards—whose fault was that?"

"My responsibility. I told Johnny Mulick to keep his men close and move fast up the road. Flankers move slow among these orchards and farmhouses. They would have been left behind and probably run into friendly fire. At times we gamble. Captain Langlois left the regimental CP at Ste. Barbe du Tletat—and ain't that a mouthful? He's making the battalion rounds at St. Louis, La Siena and Tafaroui. I'm good at delegating. What's your security here at Château Neuf?"

"House Nine of the Foreign Legion is still being debedbugged. We had to burn every straw mattress and torch the iron bed frames. Never saw so many damn bugs, and the men are already coming down with the shits. Security? G Company has the perimeter guard. I put a gun on the roof and another close by on the wall. S-2 says to expect dive bombers coming after the docks, and they have to pass right over us on this hilltop. If you think I might need the other guns—"

Chad reached for the wine and ran his thumb over the label. "Malaga—a good year, do you think? No more of it'll be going to Vichy France and the Jerries. No, you're right to hold guns in reserve, but it wouldn't hurt to have some BARs on the roof, too. If the Stukas come visiting, they'll keep the extra men busy.

"There's still sniping in town—Arabs glad for a chance to pop any white man, or goddamn Frenchmen pissed because we disturbed things, upset the goddamn political status quo. *Vive* Darlan, *vive* Giraud and don't forget Le Grande de Gaulle. All jockeying for power before the war's won, and nobody giving a goddamn about killing American soldiers."

Tilting the bottle, he said, "*Santé*—and piss on all their houses. This regiment is stuck with policing the city and standing guard at the airports. The air corps stumbled over an orange peddler who had a Schmeisser machine pistol tucked among his merchandise. Naturally they're yelling for infantry protection."

"We're not going to make it to Tunis in time."

Chad looked at his son. The boy was good and would get better; he had a grasp of the immediate picture and the overview, too. "It's wet and it's cold in Tunisia, where the roads are swampy and there's only one railroad track from here to there. We'll get just enough armor and people up there to get the hell kicked out of them—and us later when Rommel wheels on us. What the hell, everybody screws up. Have a drink to screwups."

Owen held the bottle. "Speaking of which, one man I put in for the Silver Star is Sloan Travis, a true fuckup pee-vee-tee. Know the name?"

"*Travis*—oh, Christ, not old Crusty's great-great-something or other, the family eight ball who got drafted?"

"Him. First he charged a machine gun and knocked it out. Then he made six trips under fire to haul equipment off that mule cart. Last, he brought the mule to cover. But he told Big Mike what the army could do with its frigging medals and says he won't accept one."

"The hell he won't. Send that smartass to me before Little Teddy gets here."

Leaning back in a rickety chair, Chad looked down at a courtyard straight out of *Beau Geste*—featureless walls thick and high, a Legion officer walking across cobblestones with grass growing between them. A guardhouse across the yard, armed civilian chasers too ready to kick scrawny prisoner asses, a dark tunnel leading to the massive main gate.

Beau Geste was only a paper hero long overdue for retirement, and La Légion Étrangère no longer a schoolboy glamour, just a bad dream.

He drank, and the taste of licorice was mild now. Do you dream, Stephanie? To sleep, to dream—aye (and how often she said that: aye), there's the rub. Nobody knew if the dead dreamed.

"You should have married me," he said. "That goddamn Colonel Blimp shouldn't have shipped you off to Singapore. All the shoulds and ifs and maybes—oh, hell. I have to believe you're alive, Leftenant Bartlett, and it's a long, long trail awinding from here to you. But I'll be there. I will be there."

CHAPTER 22

REUTERS—London, November 25, 1942: Sharp fighting took place today in several sectors of Tunisia where Allied forces are advancing on Tunis, the Axis-held capital, and Bizerte, the vital naval base. There has as yet been no major clash, although air activity is increasing as opposing forces maneuver for position.

Radio communiqués from both sides were misleading, but indications were that the Allies are advancing on a broad front while the Axis continued its hasty preparations to make the Tunis–Bizerte corner a sort of Tobruk. That embattled city in Libya has been attacked and defended by both British and Germans.

UP/AP/INS POOL—Casablanca, French Morocco, January 27, 1943: President Roosevelt, Prime Minister Churchill and their staffs ended a conference here in which a program for military strategy for the coming year was worked out. The president paid a surprise visit to U.S. troops stationed in Morocco and sent belated New Year's greetings to men fighting in Tunisia.

Gavin Scott tooled the Lightning low over the drab mountains of Tunisia, hugging the wide valley floors when he could. He looked for German tanks reported to be nosing out from Tunis, a crappy mission for a hot fighter pilot. What he wanted to find was an enemy plane. His fifth kill, his rank as an ace, so long overdue.

But he was in the air again. Goddamnit, he showed them—the shrinks, the surgeons, the fucking family and the women. He was here and as good as ever, probably better, and the women could attest to that. No broad would deny him, and no lousy Nazi would ever sneak up on him again.

Something was out of place in the gray-brown brush below his wings, and Gavin goosed the P-38, climbed a couple of thousand feet and dropped his left wing tip to begin a slow circle. Whatever that was, he intended to shoot the shit out of it. His hands trembled, and he forced them to stop.

North and west, the port city of Bizerte was shrouded in mist only touched by weak winter sun, and the blue Mediterranean was a mudhole. The Jerries unloaded replacements there, and their planes flew sorties from Sicily. The Jerries—*krauts,* for chrissakes, *krauts;* he was well away from the RAF and their cute talk. Damned well away from Limeyland, too.

And Stevie Bartlett.

"Shit!" He said into his windshield, and he angled his plane sharply for the ground.

She'd wanted it as much as he did. She dated him for a first-class night in London, didn't she? In spite of his fucked up face she went out with him and got drunk, right? She didn't mind swapping spit in the taxi, and prick teasing was just a game they all played. He gave it to her good on the back seat, and she—no, she didn't *laugh,* goddamnit! If she didn't like it, she was either too drunk or a fucking lesbian, and she didn't laugh; she *cried!* That's why he got away from there fast; he couldn't stand to hear a woman whine like that. Twin motors roaring, twin booms like the spread tail of a striking hawk, he dived for a patch of brush just off a dirt road. This plane was supposed to have gremlins like disintegrating wing tanks and leaks in the intercooling system. This baby showed him no problems, and another plus was that she could lose one engine and still bring him home.

If she wanted to call it rape, why hadn't Leftenant Stephanie Bartlett reported him? His face; the left side of his smashed face, that was it. The bitch couldn't take it any longer, for all her sympathy crap. Up close it had finally been too much for her. It didn't repulse all the other bitches since; he made certain of that. He would allow no more plastic surgery; shocking them was better, making them feel guilty if they didn't screw a terribly wounded hero.

There! Armor; not a tank, but something flatter with tracks. He thumbed the firing button for the 20mm cannon and laid five seconds of HE into the machine. Dirt exploded and bushes ripped. He blurred over a black cross on painted camouflage steel.

Screaming up so sharply that G-force slammed him against the seat, he clawed for the sky and whipped over again. A string of bright orange tracers floated by the plane as he cut loose his four 50-calibers and raked the bastards good. Shoot back at him, would they? Too bad armor didn't score, but it would be okay to get known as a tank buster. Like the balloon buster so famous in the other war, Frank Luke. Tank killer Gavin Scott climbed and victory-rolled.

And came out of it roaring straight up at the belly of the biggest bomber he'd ever seen that close. It loomed so near that reaction got him only a one-second burst with all guns before he peeled away. The P-38 rocked, and he could swear he almost brushed the swastika on the bomber's tail.

The ass-end stinger reached out and popped holes in his right wing. The slick skin on his face itched, too late for a warning. Aircraft ID pictures flashed his mind as he whipped around and down in a tight bank—Heinkel 177-something; Jesus! a pair of 20mm cannons and *seven* machine guns!

Plexiglas cracked at his right ear, and the fiery ball of a

Roman candle kicked off the nose of his plane. No time, no worry about why a fat Heinkel would cruise along without fighter escorts. He got a cannon shot into the left engine and toed just enough rudder to rake the length of the fuselage with his 50s. Fire and smoke blew out, and the big bastard heeled over to pinwheel for the desert floor.

Score! Magic number five! Oh, you beautiful goddamn—

No confirmation. Who the hell could have seen the Heinkel crash down there in popcorns of flame? American troops, maybe. Some GI outfits were in Tunisia, too late to grab the original objectives. He'd have to radio the time and map reading to them and get confirmation. That's it, head up and locked, Gavin. On the ball.

His face prickled, and without hesitation he threw the plane into a chandelle and came around on a Messerschmitt. The bomber hadn't been alone, but the ME 109 got caught with his heils down. Gavin blew him apart and took cockpit hits from a wing man. The P-38 was armored there, and he did an Immelman to get on the surprised bastard's tail. Now he was moving; now he was cooking. Who the hell said the Lightning wasn't a dogfighter? That depended upon who was flying it.

The 20 ran out of ammo, but there were at least two bursts left in the 50s, because he smoked the next kraut with the second burst. He yelled; he screamed like a fucking banshee and beat one fist against his canopy. Three down, three! How could anybody not see three kills in a row?

Turning in a sky he had swept clean, Gavin headed back for Tafaroui Airport outside Oran. No hurry, since the Lightning's tanks were good for a thousand miles round trip, and he'd watch for targets of opportunity on the way home.

Aren't you sorry, Stevie? See what I did. Look who I am now. Up yours, Stevie.

* * *

Dragging their Bren gun out of position, two grinning Tommies stopped to point out their shallow hole. The lance corporal said, "All yours, Yank—and welcome to it. There's a bloody Eyetie gun down there somewhere, but we've not caught him out. No sign of Jerry except the sodding planes, of course. Didn't you bring any planes with you?"

Corporal Sloan Travis shrugged and thumbed at a likely spot for the 5th Squad tripod. Behind him Sergeant Pelke said, "Yeah—we got a shitpot full of planes, but they have to stay in England to keep the island afloat."

"Arsehole," the Tommy said. "Seen a world of action, have you? I wonder how cheeky you'll be when Jerry comes for this hill."

"Jerry who—Jerry Lewis, Jerry Colonna?"

"Bloody Yanks. In Blighty they say you're overpaid, oversexed and over there."

Pelke made his Donald Duck imitation: Quack . . . quack . . . quack. "The women don't say it, Tommy."

Sloan stepped between them. "We've got enough war."

The lance corporal hefted his Bren and walked back along the hill. Just before the team turned out of sight he looked back and called, "Protect your bum, Yank. More than Eyeties and A-rabs out there."

"Yeah—good luck, Limey."

Sloan groaned softly. It was all so frigging childish, the jokes and camaraderie. His Silver Star and promotion just as stupid. Back in Oran, when he tried to refuse them both, Colonel Belvale called him in and gave him a choice: follow orders or get his ass kicked and have to obey anyway.

The old bastard meant it and was probably capable of carrying through. He was chunky and face-scarred and had this pair of gunsight eyes. The colonel had said, "Brave men die for this medal, and good soldiers become leaders to care for the not-so-good ones."

"Brave?" Sloan laughed. "I was scared out of my frigging mind—sir. I simply saved my own ass. And I don't take responsibility for anyone else."

"Only idiots aren't scared. A soldier faces his fear and acts in spite of it, and as for responsibility, you brought that white mule to cover."

"I never claimed to be a soldier, and the family didn't face that. You remember the family, sir? As for the mule, he wasn't there by choice—like draftees."

"General Theodore Roosevelt, Jr. will arrive soon to award decorations. You will stand tall when he pins on the medal, shake hands and salute. You will assume responsibility for the 5th Squad. You have no choice. Now haul ass. Do you read me, Corporal?"

"I guess so—yes. Yes, sir."

So now he had a squad, to wipe their noses and tuck them beddy-bye in holes deep enough so they wouldn't get shot. Not right away, anyhow. The army; the frigging army.

"Dig in," he said. "Zigzag your holes behind the gun. Forrester, Sands—make a real hole for the gun. Cover for you both and room for ammo. Deep slits in a vee ought to do it, so we can traverse that valley."

Pelke said, "Sixth Squad, put your gun over there about twenty yards, same layout. I'll be up here between you two. Travis, how did you get so fucking smart all of a sudden?"

"I read a book," Sloan said, and he unsheathed his shovel.

"Evidently not the Articles of War. You'll be broke for the next six months, wise guy."

"You mean I can't go out for a malt?"

The soil was rocky but damp on the surface and not too hard digging. The 1903 Springfield he had inherited with his new stripes lay beside a growing pile of raw dirt that he would have to camouflage. The vintage bolt-action Springfield was the only rifle adapted to fire the new rifle grenades, but its rickety springs-and-tin aiming sights were already ripped off. The grenades would have to be fired by guess and by God, with Kentucky windage. Sloan didn't trust them any more than he trusted anything about the army.

They'd made so much of him making trips to that mule cart under fire. He did that to bring out guns, tripods and ammo, the water cans. When the guns were set up Sloan Travis had a better chance of protecting himself. The mule had been different. It wasn't the mule's fault that he was caught in an ambush.

Out of the heavy overcoat and field jacket, OD shirt open to his long johns, Sloan sweated in the deepening hole. If rain held off, every new cave dweller could snug in under shelter halves, home away from home—or a grave.

The damned Belvales had outsmarted him, not only about the medal and promotion, but about forcing him to keep the stripes. Every night at Château Neuf he'd gone through a hole in the high iron picket fence for an evening of cheap *vin rouge* at the first joint down the hill. On the rue de Révolucion the Bar de Sous Marines waited. His high school French came in handy there, especially with the owner. Madame Wanda Sanchez had married a Spaniard now off in Morocco and was most happy to help Sloan practice the language. He traded her cigarettes and the GI margarine that would melt only on a stove, and only for the garlicky food—rabbit, duck or escargot. It beat hell out of C-rations. The trouble was other language helpers hanging around the place, usually friends of Señor Sanchez.

When the air raid sirens went off he timed it back to the rooftop in four minutes flat, arriving ahead of German bombers and Lieutenant Belvale. Another problem with Wanda Sanchez was her traditional step-by-step coquetry, and he didn't have a real opportunity to get into her pants before the outfit moved out to Tafaroui airport. On pass to Oran on Christmas Eve he was faced with a decision—catch the returning trucks to a soggy pup tent or stay in the deep feather bed with all-out hungry Wanda. Going AWOL meant losing his stripes, of course.

Fat frigging chance. One night and one day over the hill bought him a special court-martial, but it was fixed. Colonel Belvale didn't bust him but laid out a fine of two thirds pay for six months. Smiling like a rattlesnake, he said then, "Expensive piece of ass, boy. And you've still got the squad."

Sloan dug into the hillside. The bastards were jealous because he'd found a girlfriend while practically everybody else had to line up at whorehouses, enlisted men at Chancre Alley and officers at the Villa de la Rosa. A whorehouse by any other name?

When his hole was belly-button deep he paused for rest and a pull at his canteen. The water tasted of metal and purification tablets. He looked out over the valley 5th Squad was to cover, and to the towering ridge on the right front. Conical Hill, the officers called this knob, actually more of a saddle between higher mountains. Low ground between two high chunks; was that by the book? No defensive expert—or offensive either, for that matter—he'd rather be looking down on the enemy than up.

That night, with G Company dug in out ahead and thinner on the flanks, half the men at a shift on Conical Hill went for a hot meal. A quarter mile down and a half a mile to the rear in the stumbling dark, to find the mess truck hidden in a fold of ground.

The food was hot, and it didn't matter that you couldn't tell what layer you were eating. It was all one pile in the mess kit and lid, and as always the rolled lip of the canteen cup blistered your lip until the coffee inside cooled. But anything beat the frigging C-rations. There were only three kinds—meat and vegetable stew; meat and vegetable hash—which nobody could tell apart except for the color of the grease—and the meat and beans favored by rear-echelon troopers who stole them before the cases got packed up to the line.

By the time you climbed back up the hill you were hungry again, and mightily pissed at the U.S. Air Corps that couldn't keep the Luftwaffe from controlling the Tunisian skies.

For days nothing but sunshine happened on Conical Hill, and Sloan lazed it out. But for the food, it wasn't a bad war, as wars go. He did have to discuss targets with the instrument corporal and get information for the range card. The gunner picked out a ravine-side patch of brush at 800 yards, because it looked like a bull's-eye, Forrester said. He got exact range and quadrant of elevation for other areas, and there was one narrow draw of dead space that worried him.

"Rifle grenades." Sloan said, "and the 81 mortars behind us."

Sands said, "Me and Forrester don't like that hill looking down our throats."

"I don't, either," Sloan answered. "Anybody know General Allen's call sign?"

"It ain't enough he don't want this squad." Sands had a walrus mustache and smoked a pipe, both out of place in an RA outfit. He was also a draftee but had stopped talking to Sloan before the Arzew landings. "That ain't enough. He's a fucking comic, too."

Forrester grabbed his crotch. "I got his comic swinging."

So much for frigging camaraderie. "Just don't screw up the range card, the dial or the clinometer."

"I know," Sergeant Pelke said, "you read a book about indirect and night firing."

Another night and the chow hike, and a cook slopped spinach on top of his rice pudding. He ate it anyhow. When he bedded down above ground with Pelke for the night, one blanket and shelter half down, one each over them, he quivered, uncovered, unhidden by the night.

Despite cool darkness without a shot fired or a challenge hurled, Sloan napped, fragile and exposed.

Like a white mule.

CHAPTER 23

Berliner Illustrierte Zeitung—January 20, 1943, with the Afrika Korps in Tunisia: Field Marshal Erwin Rommel's panzers appeared suddenly before Bizerte to startle American troops as yet untried in the crucible of warfare. Shouting their "Sands of Africa" song, desert-hardened panzer soldiers promised to rout the cowardly mongrel representatives of the Jew Roosevelt.

. . . Heiss über Afrikas boden,
die sonne glüht—
unsere panzer motoren,
singen ihr lied . . .

(Burning over African sands, the sun beats down;
our tank motors are singing their song . . .)

Feldwebel Arno Hindemit chewed on the last of the captured British rations, spitting out bits of kidney. "They did not boil the piss out of this lot before putting it in the tin. Those goddamn panzer *truppen* are full of it, too. Listen to the bastards sing—as if they didn't run off at El Alamein and leave it to us to cover their tin-can asses."

Hauptman Franz Witzelei thumbed down the pages of

his book when the damp wind ruffled them. "Philosophy, Sergeant. Consider the thinkers, and the stomach relaxes and forgets hunger."

"Not my stomach, and if you insist on carrying books, get a thicker one to deflect those Ami bullets, if ever they fire at anything but each other. A better body armor would be the army directives on the care and handling of ass wipe."

"This is only an old copy of *Die Truppenführung,* but a philosophy of sorts nonetheless. Listen—"

Arno munched on the steak chunks and cold gravy, running his dirty finger around the inside of the tin for the last of the grease, picking up bits of sand with it. Captain Witz was a regular fellow, too much so to be an officer, and they had been comrades all through the Libyan desert campaigns. Now they were part of the high command's "screening force" in the cold Tunisian hills before Bizerte.

But Witz had his habit of lecturing, and worse, of trying to find reason and logic in this abortion of a war. That was only natural for a schoolteacher, but here in the high desert lessons did not come from books. Arno sighed and hoped the cold, miserable rains would hold off, and that the newly arrived Americans would not become eager and instead remain sensibly in winter quarters.

"Each new weapon, so say the wise men, is the death of the infantry. The infantryman silently pulls on his cigarette—"

"If he is lucky enough to capture cigarettes. Otherwise he smokes camel dung."

"—pulls on his cigarette and smiles. He knows that tomorrow this new weapon will belong to him—"

"If he does not get his balls blown off. New weapons backfire, which is why they are tested first by the infantry."

"There is only one new factor in the techniques of war that remains above all other inventions. This new factor is the infantry, the eternally young child of war—the man on foot, even as Socrates himself was, the only and eternal, who sees the whites of the enemy's eyes."

Shoving the steak-and-kidney ration can deep into hard sand, out of habit Arno covered it so no sun would reflect. "Some Luftwaffe general wrote that, no doubt. Did Socrates ever carry a mortar tube? Eternally young child of war! *Scheissen!* I never heard such shit. Do I look eternally young? My mother would think I am my own grandfather. And the whites of your eyes, Mein Herr Hauptmann, are puddles of horse piss."

Closing the field manual, Witzelei leaned back upon the rusted track left behind by a panzer repair unit, his ragged khakis blending with the dirty sand. "Field Marshal Rommel says the English are unhappy with their American allies and their tendency to disappear under fire. One disgusted general called them the Italians of the British Eighth Army."

Arno grunted. "Can we transfer all our Italians to him? They would be more useful to us on the other side. The Amis are new at this *scheissen* war, while Mussolini's brave ones have been running back and forth for years. The Amis will soon learn to fight—worse luck. It is the everlasting curse laid upon the miserable infantry."

Taking off his glasses, the captain rubbed the lenses with a stained handkerchief, then peered up at the weak winter sun. "The Emperor's Roman legions probably complained when they battled wild Arabs along here. Close by there is a city named after Constantine."

"Italians must have been different in those days, but I have a theory that a bastard Roman brought this curse upon the infantry."

The captain put away his troop manual and stared. "And how is that?"

"The legionnaires were foot soldiers, correct? And that one *verdammt* bastard could not be content with easy sentry duty. Like our own Private Langen—that one could find trouble if he were assigned to sweep Fräulein Braun's bedroom. A bad example, for to think upon it. Even I might ignore my duty in such a case."

The sound of motors stopped as the panzers found cover and their crews hurried to camouflage them.

"Thank God, the shits stopped singing as well," Arno said. "The Amis must have airplanes, and I would as soon listen for the sound of their motors."

Witzelei said, "Yes, yes—and the Romans?"

Eyeing the rugged mountains, Arno saw nothing but low gray clouds. "That *landser* troublemaker at the foot of the cross. He had to stick his spear into a dying man. Jesus laid a curse upon him and all others like him for war after war after fucking war—a permanent curse upon all *landsers*. We will be marched into hell itself, and then what? Some stiff-necked *obergruppen führer* will order us to dig in. Of course, being of high rank, he will be privileged to wear a helmet of ice."

The captain laughed. "Ah, *mein* friend Arno—you are the ultimate pessimist."

Arno drank sparingly from his canteen. "Is such permitted to a lowly rifleman? Damned little else is these days. Once a soldier did not have to be ashamed of his profession, but that was before the fucking Gestapo and the fucking SS and the goddamned politicians in uniform who play at soldiering."

Witzelei looked around. "Speak with care, old friend—there are still those who—"

"So? Let them send me to the front."

"There is a worse front than this."

Arno blinked. "You are right, professor. Russia is hell painted white, and I would sooner burn than freeze. But if our general staff of monocled Vons and sainted Junkers is so brilliant, why are we fighting on so many fronts? One learns better than that in noncommissioned officers' school."

"The corporal didn't attend leadership schools."

"Ach—the corporal." Arno stretched out beneath a

scrubby bush and pillowed his head upon his helmet. His platoon was in position, well hidden in a wadi, but still he watched the skies. "What is it that floats up in the air and grows bigger and bigger?"

"The corporal's ambition?"

"*Nein;* Hermann Göring. A giant sausage, our air marshal."

Abruptly the scream of a diving plane burst upon them. Arno's reflexes were swift and automatic, rolling him into his foxhole before he even looked up. "The thing has two tails," he called across to the captain's hole, "and he's after that Balkenkreuz half-track."

After the first strafing run of the American plane he lifted partway from his hole and yelled through his cupped hands: "Sing, panzers—sing!"

CHAPTER 24

Supreme Headquarters, Allied Expeditionary Forces (SHEAF)—London, January 30, 1943: Russian troops have killed or captured all but 12,000 desperate German holdouts trapped at Stalingrad. More than a quarter million of Adolf Hitler's best troops had surrounded the city at one time.

REUTERS—Melbourne, Australia, January 30, 1943—A large force of Japanese planes approaching Guadalcanal were driven off by American fighters, and four Zeros were shot down. United States ground forces consolidated their positions at Kokumbona village.

On the Canal you rot. If the fucking Japs don't put a bullet through your head or sneak up and cut your throat, you rot. If malaria doesn't shake you to bits or burn you up, amoebic dysentery runs bloody shit down your leg until you think your asshole is falling out and wish it would. Then you shrivel to tight yellowed skin over sharp bones.

And speaking of bones, there's plenty of dengue fever to go around, and the better name for it is breakbone fever. You feel like every major bone in your body has snapped and the splinters are breaking out through your flesh. You go right past pain to *son of a bitch!*

Or you just sit in the rain and rot.

The leeches; oh, those fucking leeches. It isn't enough that they fasten their slug bodies to you with so many tiny teeth that they must be forced loose with glowing cigarettes. They suck your blood; they leave rings of flesh that turn sore and black with pus.

Bug bites, spider poisons, the razor edges of elephant grass, and speaking of elephants—

Elephantiasis; everybody was scared shitless of that disease, ever since the guys saw that native hauling his swollen balls around in a wheelbarrow. That's how huge they were—like giant, aching watermelons.

But sneaky rot always worked on you, jungle rot that ate into your ears so deep that the medics couldn't scrape it out, and you couldn't hear the Jap sneaking up on you. Its fungi cousins rotted the soles off your shoes and ate your fatigues to shreds; dhobie itch worked between your toes to make agonized balloons of your feet.

"Hell of a place to fight a war," Eddie Donnely said. He sat cross-legged on twin coconut tree stumps, huddling beneath ponchos stretched to make a semi-dry platoon CP. "Worst thing we could do to the Japs after the war is make the bastards live on this fucking island forever."

Captain Shelby held a cigarette cupped in both hands, protecting it from the drizzle. "Remember the first prisoners the Marines took? Some of them thought they were in California, and the rest didn't know where they were."

Boof Hardin said, "You mean this ain't Hollywood?"

Eddie stared down at water too thick to swim and too thin to walk on; a sluggish brown river, it moved through the jumble of makeshift shelters. Rain dotted it as a palm leaf floated by. He wondered if North Africa was anything like this, and how Big Mike was making it. Outside of that one weakness, that single obsession with a cunt who almost made him lose it all, Big Mike was unshakable, immortal through two wars and as many more as might be coming.

He'd go out when and where he wanted to, and not before: Africa, Italy or Berlin itself.

Sometimes a dribble of secondhand radio news from the outside world reached them here, enough for them to know that nothing came easy for the Allies fighting anywhere in the world.

He knew what Big Mike would say: "This is what they pay us for. It's not for squads right on the drill field, son, and not for command inspections. The eagle shits for combat soldiers, and everything that goes before is just to provide us with a spoon."

"Marines left us the Jap POWs and those live bastards out yonder when they pulled out," Hardin said. "Damn—I'd give my left nut and my front seat in hell to get off this stinking island."

Shelby drew on his cigarette. "The Marines took the worst beating here, and now they have to make a landing on some other stinking island and stir up more fresh Japs."

Fresh Japs, hell, Eddie thought; stinking Japs puffed up like they had all caught elephantiasis, swelling bigger and rounder until their cartridge belts cut through their bellies and they softly blew up. Then they stank more.

If you couldn't get to dead GIs and bury them quick, they smelled different, and in this heat it didn't take long. The only thing with an odor exactly like a dead American was a dead rat; they had the same penetrating sweetness that pushed you close to vomiting.

Shielding a cigarette, Eddie needed three of the damp C-ration paper matches to light it, even though he kept the folder pocketed next to his skin. The company was damned lucky to have a CO like Shelby; the man was a natural, quick to learn and no bullshit, a respected leader but one of the troops, too. That combination wasn't easy to create.

He had guts to spare, maybe too many. And replacements coming in—as few as they were—never failed to be shocked when they learned their company commander was a United States senator. Then they thought he was flat-out crazy for being on the Canal instead of riding a desk, fat and safe in Washington.

"Sun's going down," Eddie said.

Hardin put on his helmet. "How can you tell? Those little bastards ain't tried nothing yet."

"They will," Shelby said. "Not enough of them to overrun our lines, not enough of us to shove them the rest of the way off the island. Just so we kill more of them until MacArthur or some lesser god gets us aboard ships and leaves them to starve." He dropped his cigarette butt into the flowing mud, then stepped down after it. Water reached almost to his knees. "I'll get back to the company CP before the first soldier goes ape. Good luck for the night, gentlemen."

"You, too, sir." Eddie watched the captain slog through the flooded area, then he put on his tin pot and waded out to check his platoon positions before dark came slamming down as it did in the tropics. Anybody moving through this area after dark was SOL—shit outa luck—password and countersign be damned in most cases. But sometimes events made you take the gamble.

The Light 30s were okay, but the 60s were short of mortar ammo, and he promised them more as soon as Battalion brought some up.

"Save it until you get a fire order from me. No grenades to your front unless you actually see slant eyes, and then try to beat his head in first. Remember, you're too close on the riflemen."

He found his hole with Boof Hardin and squatted ankle-deep in the mud to wait out the night, to listen out the night and maybe pray a little. Maybe, hell; everybody prayed in one way or another.

Barracks talk: tell your troubles to Jesus; the chaplain's on pass.

He napped in turns with Boof Hardin, swapping their only GI watch each time, thankful for its radium dial. Eddie never slept deeply, always tense just under the surface of his skin. On the Canal deep sleepers often didn't wake up, and neither did snorers.

Before midnight it happened.

The moan was low, caught in the throat and filled with nameless agony. Who? Oh, shit—which one got caught and hauled out there in the blackness?

"Ohhh! . . . Oh, God . . . help me, please . . ."

Hardin sat up, whispering. "Sounds like Taylor."

"Might be a Jap."

"Uh-uh—listen close. It's that fucking Taylor."

"Who was with him?" Was, because they didn't drag one man out of a double foxhole unless his buddy was dead.

"LeCroix, I think. Shit—he was a good kid, but that goddamned Taylor—"

"Oh, God . . . oh, God . . . please . . . please . . ."

Eddie turned his face up; the drizzle had stopped. He slid the torn bit of poncho over to protect his BAR anyhow. He said into Hardin's ear, "Give me your grenades and some of that commo wire."

"You ain't going out there with just a .45? Goddamnit, you told us never to do what you're—and Taylor probably went to sleep on his shift. He's such a fuckup—"

"He's *our* fuckup," Eddie said, and he slithered out over the edge of the hole.

Barracks talk: I want three volunteers—you, you and that son of a bitch hiding in the latrine.

Nobody volunteers, especially to slide through the mud like a water moccasin in order to reach a bunch of waiting snake hunters. The Japs had Taylor pinned out there in the dark, probably with a bayonet in his guts, twisting it every so often to make him moan. If he was real unlucky, he might last all night long. If the Japs got lucky, some fool might try to rescue him. He was probably wired, too—booby trapped with made-in-Tokyo grenades whose fuses had already been knocked against something hard so they'd blow when weight lifted off them.

Maybe the Japs didn't really expect anybody to try for him, the trick was so old. But being Japs, they kept repeating it. They did the same stupid things in open combat because they wouldn't or couldn't change orders. Eddie was grateful for that, and everybody else ought to be.

He moved a few inches, thankful this time for the rising wind that made noises to cover his own. Moving a few inches more, he aimed all senses in the direction of Taylor's moans. Far to his left rear an M-1 rifle banged twice, and a flare popped above the trees. Eddie had to wait until the light drifted out to belly forward again.

The wind changed, and the stench of a dead Jap made the mud on his lips taste slimier.

"Oh, my God . . . Mama . . . Mama . . ."

Closer now, much closer; Taylor crying for his god and his mother, not necessarily in that order. Eddie couldn't remember a dying man calling out for his father. If *he* got hit bad, he might ask Big Mike for help, or just to listen, since his mother heard and saw only what she wanted to. It had taken Eddie too many years to realize how cold and narrow and priest-ridden his mother had been.

"Please . . . goddamnit, please! Help! They're tearing my guts out. . . ."

Rain came down again, scouts-out drops at first, then a driving sheet of the main body; wind lashed the palms and almost muffled Taylor's agony. Now even Japs would crouch under some kind of cover, Eddie thought, probably those woven straw capes or a roof of palm leaves.

So he reached out in the flowing ink and touched Taylor's face. The man grunted, and Eddie clamped a muddy hand over his mouth. When he had his lips touching Taylor's ear, he let go.

"It's Donnely. How they got you?"

He gave the guy credit; Taylor choked back a groan and whispered, "B-bayonets—through my balls—belly and chest—pinned me to the fucking ground. Hands and feet tied. Oh, Christ, it hurts—oh, Christ—"

"Christ can't help you, but I will. Grenades?"

"Wh-what?"

Rain slashed beneath Eddie's tin pot and made Taylor choke and cough.

"Listen up," Eddie hissed, "did they wire you, stick grenades under you?"

"Yeah—I think so—oh, Christ, they shoved it through my lung . . . I . . . I can't breathe. . . ."

Working quick and slippery fingers, Eddie ran the commo wire around Taylor's left arm and looped it. Wind shook the cocoanut fronds, and Eddie put his mouth to Taylor's ear; it was cold. He said, "You know I can't get you out."

"Yeah—yeah. Just stop it for me, Sarge—for God's sake, stop the fucking pain—"

Holding the Marine knife in his left hand, Eddie felt down the throat with his knuckles and found the jugular. He clamped his right hand over Taylor's mouth and whispered, "Good luck."

When he cut the guy's throat hot blood leapt over his hands.

After the gush stopped he slid both hands through the mud and backed slowly away, playing out the wire as he went. Ten yards, fifteen, and the end of the wire. He lifted to his knees and pulled the pin on a grenade, cocked his arm back and hurled it as far as he could. He wanted it to land beyond Taylor's body.

It must have. The brief red-flame flower didn't blow the Jap booby trap, so he pitched another grenade the same way, ripped out his .45 and got off three quick rounds before falling on his face. A hurt Jap screamed in that high, womanish voice, and other Japs shouted.

He gave them time to work up a *banzai* charge . . . count five . . . count six . . . count seven. Then he set himself and yanked mightily to drag Taylor's body off the Jap grenades.

Caught the little shits! The booby trap blew high and wide, its bright explosion showing a flash of three Japs twisted in midair, mixed with chunks of Taylor. Eddie didn't think Taylor would mind.

Spinning, he headed back for his foxhole, hissing louder each time: "Coming in—Donnely coming in!"

Funny he should think about it now, but tomorrow was payday—would have been payday—the high point of garrison life when the dayroom readied for crap games and poker, when the twenty-percenters waited to get back their loans. It was a holiday from the moment the bugler blew pay call:

> Payday . . . payday . . .
> What you gonna' do with a drunken soldier?
> Payday . . . payday . . .
> Put him in jail until he's sober.
> Payday . . . payday . . .

Or just leave the poor bastard scattered in the jungle.

CHAPTER 25

Special to *The New York Times*—Constantine, Tunisia, French North Africa, January 31, 1943: American and British First Army hilltop positions were hit hard at dawn by German infantry, armor and air strikes. Early reports indicate that the Allied forces are hanging on, but a fallback in order to straighten and strengthen defense lines appears possible. This is according to headquarters sources at this railside city named after a conquering Roman emperor.

When the first incoming mortar shell exploded atop Conical Hill Chad Belvale had just hiked into the draw behind it, where H Company's 81s were emplaced.

It was barely daylight, and he glanced up through the light tree cover to see a thundering ME 109 loose a hundred-pound bomb and peel off. The ground rocked, and he wanted to run up the hill to help. But there was nothing he could do, nothing anyone could do, except George Company and H's 2nd Platoon dug in up there. It was a bad position, and they had to make out as best they could.

Supporting fire from a battery of British 25-pounders might beat off the first attacks. The Royal Horse Artillery had an observation post forward on the hill. He grabbed the mortar section sergeant.

"Targets, Sergeant Lord?"

"Anything past G Company's lines—everything."

"Radio!"

"Sir—clear to—"

WHAMM!! Heavy mortar, too close.

"Clear to battalion, Colonel."

Spitting dust, ears ringing, Chad yelled into the radio handset.

Craack! Craack! High and behind them this time.

"Them ain't mortars," the radio operator said. He was on his knees now. "Goddamn 88s, that's what."

"Battalion!" He forgot the call sign, something cute and goofy. "This is Belvale, damnit! Where's artillery support?"

Whipcrack explosions of the fabled 88mm ripped the hilltop while mortar bursts walked up and down the sides. Chad could see only rolling clouds of dust and smoke. He couldn't hear the automatic weapons fire but knew it would be tattooing the ground up there, the 9mm stuff chopping and tearing at every foxhole lip.

The 81s around him coughed steadily—*carumph—carumph*—spitting back without definite targets. A voice crackled in his ear: ". . . knocked out . . . the limey OP on the hill got knocked out! The battery is blind—"

"Tell them to fire extreme range—anything! Get shells in the air!"

It wouldn't be enough. The Germans were laying heavy covering fire on the hill, killing and maiming, forcing survivors to keep low in their holes. Meanwhile, in the classic pattern, the enemy infantry advanced.

The plane came again, the wail of its bomb cutting through the hell that blazed atop the hill. Dirt and shards of rock showered among the mortars; a piece rang off Chad's helmet and wobbled him.

Sergeant Lord gripped his shoulder and shook it. " 'Scuse me, colonel, but you ought to haul ass. I got to pull my mortars soon as the first Schmeisser zeroes in on us. Can't afford to lose these tubes, or lose you neither."

Dizzy from the wallop on his helmet, Chad said, "Right, right, thank you." Walking back beyond a protective shoulder of the ridge behind, he shouted into the radio, demanding artillery, air support, something to help George and How companies on Chronicle Hill.

All the while he knew help wasn't available. All along the steep sides of Faid Pass, tucked into little patches of trees on the wide valley floor, the battalion was stretched thin. Hell, the entire regiment was spread over too much ground. There'd be no counterattack to relieve the pressure. He could only hope that Captain Mulick and Lieutenant Belvale hadn't run out of luck.

Good luck, Owen, my son.

Then he heard the metallic growl and grind of armor—German tanks.

Owen Belvale dropped the handset. The radio's guts spilled out and mixed with the operator's. For a weird shifting moment Owen tried to believe he was back in the company CP, tried to teleport himself two miles down the road.

A fistful of bullets whacked by his head, and he pulled deeper into his hole. He didn't know what guns were still effective, but between the whir of metal and rapid explosions he heard one going on the other side of the hill, a second section gun.

Peeping from his hole, he used field glasses and saw riflemen scrambling back from the forward platoon. As he watched, men fell and others ran crouched for the hill itself. But there was no protection here, only the thin comfort of misery in company, the herd instinct. A man turned and emptied a clip at an enemy that Owen couldn't see.

He ducked and bobbed up again, carbine at the ready. No orders could come from battalion unless by runner, no fire from the 25-pounders, and of course no air support. He couldn't just pull out; he was in support of a unit getting the shit kicked out of it, and he couldn't get his men off the hill until G company passed through.

Slaamm!

He tasted bitter smoke and dirt that had been crappy when Roman legions marched through this pass. He couldn't find a target for himself, but he saw the platoon sergeant's body, what was left of it after a direct mortar hit. He wanted a drink of anything, wanted time for a smoke. Doesn't the condemned man always get a last cigarette?

There! Sixth Squad's gun laid a long, protective burst over the heads of the retreating riflemen, lancing into the enemy chasing them.

Fifth Squad was alive, too. Its gun sounded off on the left flank, a continued pounding that said the gunner had a good target, and one that would call adjusted enemy fire down on him within minutes. Last war figures showed that a machine gunner's life in combat averaged a minute and a half. Now weapons and tactics were supposed to be improved; did that include life span?

"Sir—sir!" Sergeant Pelke, the section leader. "I'm hit, Captain. Can I get off the hill?"

Slaamm!

"Get out while you can! Medics—"

"No stretcher bearers left, but I'll make it. Fifth Sqaud—Travis has the gun himself. Almost everybody else is down."

"Go!"

Wishing he'd paid attention during compulsory attendance at West Point chapel, Owen searched his memory for the right name and rank, for the god of infantrymen and lost causes. Naturally they were the same. Saint Jude, yeah—help us hang on, Saint Jude, even if some of us aren't Catholic.

Raprapraprap! A machine pistol spraying the hilltop. Kraut infantry in among them now.

Catholic, Baptist—no, Church of England, the Belvales

and Carlisles; the church of the Crusades and altar of the sword. Give us a break anyhow, Saint Jude?

A Kraut loomed spraddle-legged over Owen's hole, puffing and blowing from the climb, blue-black Schmeisser cradled in both hands. His eyes were wide and blue, his mouth hung open.

Owen shot him three times and knocked him backward. Fifth Squad's gun hammered and hammered.

There at 800 yards Sloan Travis watched them come across the open ring of earth and down into the bull's-eye of ragged brush. It was on the range card that Forrester had laid out. Forrester was gone; maybe he'd make it back. Sands was dead, and Murphy had a hole in his belly. Moore limped off to the rear dragging one leg. Somebody had to serve the frigging gun, and where were all the professionals?

The Germans carried something, a crew-served weapon. Crew-served? He was beginning to think like a damned soldier. Anyhow, he hoped it was a mortar. He hated frigging mortars. Flipping up the battle sight, he set the leaf sight at 800 and laid directly onto the bull's-eye. Nine guys had gone into that brush; he'd see how many came out.

WHAMM!

Waiting until his eyes cleared, he found the target again and fingered the trigger. The gun ran half a belt smoothly, and the flavor of burned powder tingled his mouth, his nose. Up two; count four for a five-round burst; down four, another burst. Work two mills right and back four to be sure the beaten zone completely covered the target. I read the book, Sergeant, Lieutenant—I read it close, Grandmother Carlisle, and what do you know? I still don't like it worth a damn.

Something glinted left at the edge of his vision, down the slope where only friendly riflemen were placed to protect the gun's flank. That, too, was by the book, but somebody had thrown away that set of instructions, AR-dash-whatever. Downhill a German soldier stood with his arm drawn back, a potato masher grenade in his fist. He looked straight up at Sloan, and the sun flashed off his mouthful of wet steel teeth.

"Shit!" Heeling the elevating clamp forward, Sloan dropped the gun muzzle and poured fire into the big bastard. Too many shots; firing too long gives the enemy forward observers a dead sight on your position, and they'll make you dead with it.

The guy rolled and rolled, dirt kicking over and around a flopping rag doll as the bullets tore through him and whined away. Sloan couldn't let go the trigger until the empty belt writhed through the receiver and snaked into the bottom of the hole. The bastard had been too close, far too close. What had happened to the screen of riflemen? A heavy machine gun couldn't last without flank guards.

The Kraut grenade went off far down the hillside, and Sloan fed the brass tip of another belt into the gun, jacking the bolt handle twice. Blasts shook the earth, and he held on. As a kid he'd sneaked into a field behind Sandhurst Keep and crawled onto one of Great-grandpa's horses. The horse bucked at every jump, and like a fool kid Sloan gripped the mane and stayed with the beast as long as he could. His crotch was sore for weeks.

It was like that now, the ground heaving and bucking when one of those hundred-pound bombs exploded anywhere near. He gripped the pistol handle of the Browning and hung on, but this time he wasn't a childish fool. He was a grownup fool with his testicles so deep in a crack that he couldn't just let go and hit the ground.

Sixth Squad's gun rapped and rapped again. Small arms fire chopped across the hill as the barrage lifted, which meant Conical Hill was being lost. What the hell was he supposed to do about it? When they moved here in a defensive position that meant twenty-five boxes of ammunition per gun, grunted and sweated step by step up from the road at night. He looked at the bottom of this hole, then leaned over to peer into the one adjoining. Three boxes; 450 rounds including that in the gun.

He watched where Marks fired the other gun. A German slipped over the high ridge to the right front, then another and another, never in the same place. Marks was trying to hold them off, so Sloan joined in, taking the left flank and yelling to Marks to hold the right.

The next few Krauts slid down the near side, but not alive.

Ammo, damnit—he needed ammo and would have to crawl back to the other holes to get it. The hill went quiet—an eerie kind of silence. He didn't know what it meant, except that the second section guns had stopped firing, out of action.

What had he done with his Springfield and the rifle grenades? God, but his mouth was dry, and he noticed that blood oozed from a creased hand. He didn't remember getting nicked. Ammo, damnit, because they were coming up through the narrow valley he was responsible for.

A thump startled him, and he snatched for the .45 that Forrester had left in the hole.

"Figured you to be getting short," Lieutenant Belvale panted. "Stay on them and I'll get more ammo."

Damn! The man was above ground and crawling around for extra belts. Sloan caught one glimpse of a dirty, determined face before looking back into the valley and finding targets.

Into the valley of death rode—make that strode—the five hundred. Make that about two hundred on and around the wrong frigging hill . . . theirs not to reason why . . . theirs but to do—to *do*.

Let the Germans die.

CHAPTER 26

SECRET to Kill Devil Hill—Battle of the Atlantic report, 9 February, 1943, 1300: The provision of naval escorts and air cover is not keeping up with the output and increasing menace of U-boats. Approximately 17 enter service each month. At 12/31/42 there were 212 operational enemy submarines compared to 91 operational beginning the year. Destroyed were 87 German and 22 Italian, not in sufficient losses to offset the construction rate.

During the year in all waters Axis submarines sank 6,266,000 tons, while other enemy weapons raised the total lost to more than 7,790,000 tons.

Preston Belvale settled back into his big leather chair and sighed. The cigar was good, the whiskey exceptional, his leg didn't ache much and he was damned glad to be home.

Crusty said, "Hell, me and my arthritis could have lasted that long. You get up into Tunisia and fall off a camel or something?'

Belvale smiled and sipped bourbon. "You got my TWX about the boys? And tell me what's happening to get more planes over there."

He said thank you to Gloria for bringing ice and the bottle. He liked the way she moved, easy on her legs as a champion mare, with the grace and power of true quality. He thought of Kirstin and how Chad let her slip away. Special women always reminded him of good horses.

"Good to know they were all right as of the last report," Crusty said. "Damned little else is good news—except for Keenan rising from the dead. Soldier's luck, by God and guts. But the hammer head got tied in with that crazy limey Wingate, a real Section 8, from what I hear. I tried to order Keenan back, and he told me go to hell, says he doesn't want to come home."

"I did. I told myself that I was needed in Washington to push for more air power, more and better armor, more of everything. But it was Tunisia, cold and rainy and full of Erwin Rommel. He's liable to give us a whipping and a half, at least for a spell. I've come home—winter in Tunisia and an admission of age, Charles."

"Charles?" Crusty thumped the table, and Gloria snapped around to stare at him. *"Charles?* Maybe you can't help getting long in the tooth, but by God, that don't have to turn you into some kind of fu—fancy peanut. Gloria, why the hell don't you find something to do in the kitchen?"

"Because you need me here. Because Minerva and her staff run everything else in this house except the war room. Because I'm my own woman, and if you can't talk without doing your Georgie Patton imitation, go ahead—damnit!"

Belvale laughed. "No doubt that she's family."

Grunting, Crusty shook his head. "I guess. The factories are just now reaching for high gear on everything, planes and tanks especially. The shipyards are doing okay, and they'd better be, just to keep up. Do you know that the—"

"—goddamned Heinies," Gloria said.

"—goddamned Heinie U-boats are sinking our ships within sight of the Florida coast? Civilians go out and watch as if it's a—shut up, Gloria—some kind of picnic."

Drawing on his cigar, Belvale allowed his eyelids to droop. It had been a long flight, and he could still feel the cold and threatening mountains of North Africa around him. He rubbed his bad leg and thought that those mountains would soon explode. Driven hard by the British First Army in Libya, Rommel would be forced to turn and protect his ports of supply in Tunisia, and Eisenhower simply hadn't gotten enough American units up in time to shut them down by land. Most of the Mediterranean was still a German–Italian lake, so Tunisia wasn't the quick and easy campaign predicted by the War Department planners. It would be hard and bloody.

The air corps interdicted ships and troop-ferrying planes that Berlin had hurrying across from Sicily, and that was one reason for little or no ground support. And enough enemy troops and supplies were getting through for a major buildup. The U.S First Armored's too-light tanks had already taken a beating, and Terry Allen's First Infantry was spread over twenty-two miles of scrubby ridges and flat valleys that were wide open to armor attack. Belvale had a hunch that the Afrika Korps was winding up to throw what could be a Sunday punch.

Knock*out*, no; knock*down*, yes. Rommel might kick the Allies back into Algeria, but they couldn't be held there long. Even with the French commanders jockeying around with their usual politics and power grabs, enough fresh U.S. reinforcements would be fed in to finally overrun the Afrika Korps. The men there now would take—were taking—the beating; they were the sacrifices. It was always so for the first soldiers thrown hastily into the fight; the regulars on call, living bored payday to payday through the peacetime years for their moment to burn in the sun.

Belvale hoped that most of the Axis survivors could be trapped and not get away to Sicily and Italy and regroup to fight another day. The "soft underbelly" of Europe would have to be invaded in time—soft only to the armchair commandos and newspapermen who had named it so. Any campaign in those mountains would be a bitch. It was going to be a long war.

"I'm not up on the Pacific, Crusty. What are we doing there?" He was afraid to ask about the girl directly.

"A couple of rays of sunshine. Farley's wife was taken as a PW, and she was alive a week ago. Kee-rist, Preston, money is always useful, but never as good as when it can pry news out of a Jap prison camp. We even know which camp Penny is in, and we're working through contacts in Malaysia and Burma. Smuggling in food and medicines is about all that's possible right now. We can think about escape later."

"That's great," Belvale said. "That's great news." The whiskey tasted even better, warming his belly and making him younger. If only a moment, it was a good moment. If it were anybody but Japs, and Japs in the full arrogance of their victories over the hated white man, it might be possible right now to get pretty Penny out. Bribed guards to spring her from the compound, then tough Burmese bandits who would take her through the jungle to the sea; Malay pirates there waiting to sail her within reach of the U.S. Navy. Payments to be made in gold at every stop.

It would have to wait until Allied wins in the Pacific made the junior samurai uncertain and scared the uniformed peasants not long out of rice paddies. Then a few non-fatalistic Japs could be greased.

One teletype machine made two dings and clattered. Gloria went over to watch it roll out a message. Crusty added a dollop of rich bourbon to his glass. "We kicked the Japs off Guadalcanal on February ninth, officially and technically. Lots of beautiful suicides, but I'd bet my left—arm—there'll be fanatics hiding out in that jungle years from now."

Gloria tore off a sheet from the machine and said over one shoulder, "Why is it always the left—arm? Are all soldiers right-sided?"

"Is it just because you grew up with soldiers, or are all women so—so—"

Gloria's chuckle was throaty and fun-loving. "All of us. I'd bet my left whatever on it."

She was coming out of it, Belvale saw, ridding herself of any lingering guilt for her bad marriage. Crusty knew damned well who was to blame and was trying in his hard-shell way to make up for his mistake. Gloria didn't need help; there was a glow to her, a sparkle now and then that a wise man would note and appreciate.

Again Belvale thought of Kirstin gone to Jim Shelby and of Jim Shelby gone to war. Neither were actually of the family now, but Kirstin wore the mark, and Jim had always been a friend so close he might have been of the blood. Pretty Penny, too; of course pretty Penny.

"MacArthur has been in New Guinea for a while," Crusty continued. "I guess he means to island-hop clear across the Pacific. He got the airfield on the Canal—and that's where a lot of the bombers are, flying for MacArthur. He claims we're stripping him of everything he needs and sending the stuff to Europe instead. But he has practically the whole navy and all those blue airplanes as well. All right—before you say it I'll admit that we need some air power and some navy, even a few Marines. But the infantry is still the queen of battle."

Enjoying the taste of fine tobacco, relaxing by degrees, Belvale said, "I never understood where that term originated. The words queen and infantry do not set well in the mouth."

Tired, he concentrated on problems at hand. "FDR grows weaker every month, and too much of the war will kill him. He can't last much longer, and our Douglas has his eye on the presidency. Or Mother MacArthur does. He's expert at keeping himself bigger than life, building the legend in the public eye. And he would finally outdo his daddy—General Arthur MacArthur never reached the White House."

Crusty snorted. "No goddamn chance of Doug making it either! Mommy might see that he runs for king, though. In the meantime, the British are trying to get back into Burma, and Vinegar Joe Stilwell is still tangling with Clare Chennault over who gets what in the CBI theater. In a weak moment Chennault let slip that he thinks Madame Chiang Kai-shek is a beautiful princess that he will never forget. You think old Clare's putting the blocks to the Peanut's wife?"

Gloria cleared her throat. "I think I will make a quick inspection of the kitchen."

Belvale opened sleepy eyes. Generalissimo Chiang Kai-shek did seem to be receiving an inordinate amount of money, arms and supplies for the scale of actual fighting his Nationalist troops were doing in China-Burma-India. Maybe he was correct about the communists in his country being more of a threat to his dictatorship than the Japanese invaders. But they were not that to the United States, and Belvale tended to agree with Joe Stilwell that more strings should be attached to China aid so the "Gitmo" would be forced to fight the common enemy.

Perhaps he nodded off; maybe he just drifted. There was Sir Erwin Belvale, lately Earl of Derbyshire, and his lady Abigail; there stood Sir William Carlisle and his wife Susan. Belongings gathered about them, they stood looking out over the green and rolling hills.

"A softened land," William said, "despite being wilderness. I'll not bide here long. A man needs harsh stone about him, else he softens of himself."

"A quiet and beautiful land," Erwin said. "Ripe and luscious. Somewhere near I shall build a great hall."

William snorted. "And squat in it like our penurious majesty Charles II? Best you had also taken a Portuguese bitch to wife, and not my fair sister."

"I am content," Abigail said.

"Women must say so."

Susan Carlisle spoke then. "Not true. I am greatly happy, but if I were not—"

"May God preserve the ears of all men," Erwin said. "Will you stay beside us until we build a shelter, William?"

"That I will, but I promise naught beyond it."

Crusty mumbled something, then said, "FDR is about to clamp federal control on wages and prices, and no war worker will be able to quit one job for a higher-paying one. Private Joe Louis says we'll win the war because we're on God's side. Nice turnabout, that. You think somebody told him about the family fixation that we're God's chosen? It would be the northern branch, of course."

Rubbing his knee, Belvale said, "The planes and tanks—we must speed up delivery to Africa."

"Somehow," Crusty said.

Second Lieutenant Nancy Carlisle kept shoving down the thing that wanted to choke her, the powerful eel thing in her stomach that tried to make her quit. She could just say she'd had it, that she'd made a mistake specializing in NP. She could demand that administration put her on straight duty and threaten to resign her commission.

She would not do that. Once in a while she had to hide in a latrine or linen closet and have a short cry, but not as often now. She would make it, just as Keenan had. They said he fought for hundreds of miles through trackless jungle and the Japanese army, Lazarus rising after the army declared him dead. He'd come through if only to show the War Department that it was wrong; that was so like Keenan. She could admire him for that, and maybe she had always admired him when he was her husband. She just couldn't love him anymore.

But she was happy he was alive, and so far as she knew, Colonel Chad was alive, and Lieutenants Owen and Farley; Captain—the kid who flew airplanes—was back in action after losing half his face. And Major Belvale—Dan Belvale, the one who lost a son in Poland. Not all the Carlisles and Belvales were lucky, then. Not all the ex-family members either. She heard recycled reports from Kirstin regularly and shared her worry about Jim Shelby, about everyone they knew. Even the old general was overseas.

She walked down the hall toward the NP ward, her starched whites making those swish-swish nurse noises. Her patients weren't the holy fighters of a family traditionally dedicated to war. They were just kids coming in from those rotten islands, bringing the rot with them, a corruption of body, a corrosion of soul and mind.

The books said that in another war it had been called shell shock; now the medical designation was combat fatigue. The GIs called it battle rattle; funny, ha-ha, because if they didn't joke they might break down, and that was taboo. They could kill without mercy and lay down their bodies to protect a friend, but it was against army regulations to cry.

Did he lose a leg? Hell, call him Stumpy. Is he blind? How about Blackout, or maybe Pencils?

If he flipped out in combat, if he just couldn't take another minute of hate and hell and terror, he called himself a squirrel and his ward the Fidget Farm, Pecan Place or just the Nut Ward Ha-ha, nurse; who's in the rubber rooms tonight?

It wasn't a damned bit funny when they screamed in the night or ripped their faces bloody or crawled under the cots—and into some unplumbed depth of their minds to hide. Oh, it was hard to reach them there; too often she couldn't get deep enough even to touch them.

Captain Zimmerman never reminded her that he was the psychiatrist, but the head nurse did. Flora Harris was also a captain, and the railroad tracks always shone brightly upon her collar.

"You do not usurp the doctor's duties," Captain Harris said. Not said; lectured or read off as if they were on the parade ground: Attention to orders! Uniform of the day is . . . details for the day . . . Officer of the Day is . . .

They never told you that the nights were much worse.

"You are only a nurse, and a junior nurse at that. The doctor will make all diagnoses. Is that understood, Lieutenant?"

So she mumbled yes ma'am and tried to limit involvement with her patients to the standard twelve-hour shifts. But if she was on nights, some poor kid needed her to talk with him in the day room, or to crouch inside one of the locked rooms and quietly sympathize just by being another human in the steel box. And she would forget she wasn't supposed to be working.

She knew the jargon—the manic-depressives, the schizophrenics, the catatonics; projection and rejection and denial; guilt and Freudian fantasy. The labels slid around and overlapped and at times lied, for these boys had suddenly been turned into bitter and shaken men older than their fathers.

Ten minutes early this evening she checked in and received the keys from Lieutenant Linda Fielding—this key for the ward itself, this one for the restraints, this bunch for the rubber rooms, the executive suites. And the key with red nail polish on it, for the narcotics cabinet.

"New man on the officer's wing, bed six." Linda pinned her hair tighter to clear the collar; uniform regulations for women. "We expect another planeload before 2200, so you'll have an extra ward boy tonight. Oh—bed six may need another shot in about half an hour. He's not too bad, but you know—"

Nancy knew; she'd seen too many come awake scared out of their heads and not knowing where they were or why they were here. So she went to check on the new patient before starting her regular rounds.

No restraints strapped him to the bed, and he looked like any recent arrival—Atabrine tan from malaria pills, scabs around the ear announcing jungle rot, unshaven tensed face showing the mind clocked too tight. His chart said he'd been hit in the shoulder—thanks, Linda; you never mentioned the physical wound.

Nancy's fingers closed hard upon the metal frame of the chart. It was typical that she had read off the medical information first; names came and went, and she tried to forget them. She couldn't forget this one. She rechecked the tag and then stared hard at the man's face.

"Farley," she said. "Farley Belvale—does the family even recognize combat fatigue?"

Of course he didn't answer. He didn't see her, either, although his eyes were open.

CHAPTER 27

CLASSIFIED—Headquarters, His Majesty's Forces, New Delhi, India, 12 February, 1943: In reply to Member of Parliament enquiry regarding background and present status Brigadier Orde C. Wingate.

Speaks Arabic; reprimanded as junior officer: uniform and discipline violations. In 1936, Palestine, organized Zionist Special Night Squads to contain Arab raiders and protect oil pipeline; exceptional results. Alleged offer to lead Jews against British mandate; recalled England 1939.

General Wavell (CIC, Africa) brought then–Major Wingate to command Ethiopian partisan army. His force of 1,700 caused surrender of more than 15,000 Italian troops. Emperor Selassie restored; Wingate refused to communicate with superiors and disobeyed orders. Ordered Cairo, felt his work not appreciated, slashed throat with knife. General Wavell blocked dismissal for instability.

Temporary rank of colonel, in charge of guerrilla activities in Burma. Proposed long-range penetration unit, 77th Indian Infantry Brigade, nicknamed "Chindits"; prime minister expresses interest in operation. Training intense and difficult. Wingate advanced temporary rank brigadier. Present whereabouts and operations SECRET.

They had cleansed him inside and out, wormed, pilled, injected and fed him, beginning with whole blood. The diet progressed from juices and vitamin pills through steak-and-kidney pudding and mutton stew to fresh water-buffalo steak. Keenan filled out in a few days, with the help of raw eggs in Wingate's whiskey and pints of half-and-half.

"You realize, Colonel," Doctor Ferguson said, "that it's far too soon for you even to leave hospital, much less go back into the bush with that madman. You've made a swift and somewhat amazing recovery, but there are things in your intestines and bloodstream that—"

"They'll still be there for your laboratory tests when I get back. Thank you, doctor. You've been great, and the staff made me feel special. But don't worry. I'll keep up with Wingate and his Chindits."

Ferguson passed one hand over his retreating hairline. "I rather believe you will. Why is another thing. I understand the vengeance of men who have lost homes and entire families in the Blitz, but America hasn't been bombed, and military casualties are to be expected."

Wriggling his toes inside English army shoes, Keenan picked up his kit and stood away from the cot. "And we joined the war late. But a few of us have been at it as long as the British, long enough to hurt and hate."

"Sorry."

Keenan smiled; he hadn't had a lot of practice at that lately. "No need, doctor. I know people have been curious because of all the commo traffic back and forth from the States, and I know it's unthinkable for a British major to tell a lieutenant general to go to hell and be promoted for it. It is in my army, too, but that general is my grandfather, an ornery old bastard who expects everyone in our military family to die with our boots on. If we're lucky, we probably will."

Shaking hands with the doctor, Keenan walked outside to blink in the hot, bright sunshine. For a moment the image of Chang Yen Ling blotted agony against his eyelids. We hurt and hate, too. Even soldiers can love.

After the Japs, what? After he killed every slant-eyed son of a bitch he could reach and after the goddamn emperor surrendered or commited *seppuku,* what then? Keenan didn't much give a damn about any kind of future without war.

But there would always be open season on sharks. If he lived through the war, he could hook and poison and blow up sharks. He despised those monsters almost as much as he hated Japs . . . triangle fins slicing the waves, blood spreading on the water, men screaming . . . he couldn't have hacked it if Yen Ling had screamed then. He prayed that she died in the explosion.

Wearing a donated Aussie bush hat, he went slowly across the compound toward Wingate's headquarters. He wore no insignia of rank, and none of the busy Chindits—a name derived from stone lions of legend that guard Burmese pagodas—spared him more than a glance as they hurried to and fro. They were neat-bodied Burmese only a bit taller than their Enfield rifles, turbaned Gurkhas wearing sets of their sacred curved knives and Tommies volunteered for the great adventure Wingate promised.

Crusty Carlisle and the family wanted Keenan home. Where and what was home? It would have been anywhere with Yen Ling, a blanket shelter in the mountains or a flowered couch in a Mandarin's secret garden. But a desk in Washington or a training command—never.

He had been too long in the jungle, so closely mutated to a predator that he wasn't even comfortable here in an outpost of civilization. How could The One Who Will Not Die exist jammed among unseeing, uncaring civilians and imitation soldiers in the U.S., a country that didn't even know it was at war? How could that far land accept the *yonsei* who ate heads?

In the bush he walked the stripes of the tiger—that fine line between madness and sanity, however sanity happened to be gauged at the moment. In civilization the sidewalk tigers wearing watercolor stripes would fear him and gather in packs to destroy him. They could not understand that a real tiger always walks alone, especially after he has lost his mate.

Wingate wasn't bare-assed this time. He wore threadbare khaki shorts and shirt; atop his rickety desk sat an old pith helmet shaped like an inverted coal scuttle. A kettle steamed over a Sterno can, and Keenan stared. The goofy bastard was straining tea through a sock. Wingate offered a cup, and Keenan shook his head.

"I'm not completely daft," Wingate grinned. "Some of this is a calculated attitude. Some, of course, isn't, but with English of a certain class the unforgivable sin is to be a bird apart from the flock, unorthodox and doing the unapproved. Then the only way to be tolerated is to alter one's difference into eccentricity. Do sit down, Leftenant Colonel, and congratulations—upon your promotion, refusal to be evacuated and recovery. The mind, sir—the mind drives the body. It is written in Ecclesiastes: 'For him that is joined to all the living there is hope, for a living dog is better than a dead lion.' "

Wingate sipped tea and lifted an eyebrow. "Of course, a soldier accepts only the first part of that verse—survival, but not at any cost. Dead or alive, a cur is still a dog. I am partial to Ecclesiastes, but in edited form."

Taking a folding camp chair, Keenan accepted a whiskey and turned down a cigarette. Wingate launched into a description of the upcoming operation, an insertion of conventional forces far behind enemy lines. Supplied by air, directed by radio, the group would cut communication lines and raise all-around hell in the enemy's rear areas. The man's voice was mesmerizing, his enthusiasm infectious, but Keenan didn't have to be sold, even by this offbeat character.

"Sir," he said, "I'll be honored to soldier for you."

"First rate!" Reaching behind him, Wingate brought out

an M-1. "I anticipated. This is the weapon of your preference? Plenty of ammo to hand."

"Thank you, sir. More firepower than an Arisaka, better range than a Thompson."

Nodding, Wingate said, "You are assigned as my aide, and I shall draw upon your guerrilla expertise. In the field you may be called upon for any sort of duty. Please draw a battle kit and be ready on the LOD at 0500 tomorrow."

At 0530 Keenan left the line of departure beside his commander, crossed the Chidwin River and plunged back into Burma's jungles. As the green twilight closed about him a thin skin of civilization peeled away scale by scale, and the dark urgency filled him again. Somewhere in the deep bush Japanese waited to die for their emperor.

It was an odd time to be thinking of his ex-wife; Nancy Carlisle-whatever-now and the Burmese jungle didn't belong in the same thought pattern.

This did. He touched the cool handle of his big knife, a haft made to fit solid in a man's hand, the metal shaped and honed by a gallant old Chinese. He murmured it against his teeth: We are ready again, Father Lim. We are ready, Chang Yen Ling.

Gavin Scott's P-38 flashed just above the thinly brushed mountains of Tunisia, and after a first glance he pulled back on the stick. Low ceiling and drizzling rain couldn't mask the enemy buildup beyond Kasserine Pass. A long column of moving armor spaced itself along muddy roads and through the winding valleys. Climbing high and fast as both engines gave him their throaty roar, he banked left and radioed Tafaroui airfield. He might reach them from here, even through the charged clouds, and he'd keep trying as he flew south.

Maybe the Afrika Korps gathering had already been reported and the ground troops knew what was coming at them, but a verification wouldn't hurt. You're damned good at scouting, the brass said. Of course, you're a top-notch fighter pilot, too, but a lot of pilots can't read ground action the way you do. And you seem to find Kraut planes, whatever your mission.

Damned right, and the newspapers knew it. Every few days GI or civilian cameramen took pictures of him posed at his plane with the Nazi swastikas painted in a row, denoting eight kills since he caught the Stuka over Tebessa.

They said, "It would make a better shot if your plane was named, Captain—something catchy." Then they insisted that British Bitch would be censored, so he had to change bitch to Witch. The limeys thought he was giving them a backhanded compliment, and Stevie Bartlett would know what he meant anyhow.

"Tafaroui—Tafaroui—I say again, come in—come in, damnit! Over!"

What the hell, if he couldn't pick them up, maybe they could read him. "Krauts zeroing in on Kasserine—tanks all over the place."

(Crackle.)

"Say again. I read you three by two—maybe less. Tanks—tanks . . . Tear, Able, Nan, King, Sugar! Beaucoup fucking armor at Kasserine—Kasserine."

(Crackle—buzz.)

The burned side of his face itched.

Ziiippp!!

What the hell—there went the son of a bitch—ME 109 . . . no, yes . . . something different about it, juiced up, faster. The Kraut rolled back at him behind converging streams of tracers. Gavin kicked over and dived into the cloud blanket, feeling his way, sweating out mountain ridges.

Zooming out, he looked all around for the Jerry plane, rolled and checked the sky above and below. Where was the bastard?

There! Oh, shit, breaking out of the clouds, too. Below Gavin and climbing faster than he ought to be—the modified Messerschmitt firing, deadly fireflies popping off the

British Witch's wing, armor-piercing bullets ripping away chunks of metal.

Standing his plane on the good wing, he went straight down at the guy, tripping all guns, the 20mms and 50s blasting together. Winking red, the Kraut kept coming, and when he exploded the boom kicked Gavin's plane sideways, and pieces of wreckage slapped it.

"Come on, come on, bitch"—he fought to pull out of the dive and almost made it—"stay with me, baby—nose up!"

He cut air speed when the hillside blurred gray and green before him in slashing rain. The plane smashed the earth, bounced and skidded, then bounced again. Something banged Gavin's head as the Witch tore apart.

Get out! . . . out before she burns! . . . no English Channel this time . . .

Blinded by blood, he shook out of the harness and fought the shattered cockpit cover. The son of a bitch was jammed, but he fisted it loose and struggled over the side to land hard on his side and right shoulder.

Pawing at his eyes, he crawled downhill, raking hands and knees on jagged rocks.

Hurry . . . get as far as you can . . . hurry, damn it!

He stumbled, tried to catch his balance and fell into a muddy gulley. Christ, his ribs hurt.

BLAMM!! A heat wave rolled over him, and a series of smaller explosions beat upon him as the ammo blew up.

Goodbye, Witch; you stayed with me and never laughed. We fucked them good, you and me, and you never shamed me.

On his knees, smelling the greasy funeral pyre of her death, Gavin palmed cold water over his forehead and fumbled out his handkerchief to bind the cut. He sucked dirty water and bent over the pain in his right side, feeling beneath his flight jacket and hoping like hell not to find bone sticking out. Ribs were cracked, but they hadn't penetrated the flesh. He was still running in luck.

Under his left arm the .45 pistol hung weighty in its shoulder holster. What was he supposed to do with it? He couldn't hit the side of a hangar with a small arm, but with it he might bluff a stray Arab into leading him to the American lines. If he had any hope of making it home, he had to get away from the signal fire of the P-38, and quick.

Pointing south, hunched over his bad ribs, he followed the narrow gulch, putting one careful foot ahead of the other, sloshing in his fleece-lined boots. Bastard things to walk in; hey, Uncle Chad! How about a pair of ground-pounder shoes? No extra issue for the flyboys, Colonel?

Goddamnit, he could hike all the way back to Oran. He was as tough as Chad Belvale or any other man wearing the crossed idiot sticks of the infantry. Keep walking, but try not to stagger, and for certain don't fall . . . we stagger on but we never fall . . . we sober up on wood alcohol . . .

What college was that? Not the U.S. Military Academy at West Point. He could use a drink right now. He pictured a glass of bourbon, a bottle of Scotch, a jigger of gin. Even water, he thought, and he stooped to feel wet ground but no puddle of water, so he turned his open mouth up to the chill sprinkle of rain.

Mistake. The sky wheeled gray and dizzying above him, and he braced his feet wide to catch himself. Then he threw up, and that hurt his ribs so goddamn bad that he fell on his ass anyway. It took a while to get back on his wobbly feet.

Where the hell was an Arab? There were always baggy-pants A-rabs selling eggs, oranges and dates around the airfield, always looking for a way to steal something, especially the GI mattress covers prized for making more baggy pants. It was predicted that the Muslim savior would be born to a man, and the wide-bottom pants were designed to catch him when he dropped.

Gunfire rattled beyond the ridge to the west, and Gavin remembered that, per orders, he carried a compass and an area map folded into a leg pocket of his flying suit. There had also been a mission map on a lap clipboard, but that was gone with the plane, with the aid kit and canteen.

Finding an overhanging slab of rock, he crawled beneath it and blinked for long, dulled moments at misting rain. Searching his inside pockets, he found a crumpled pack of Chesterfields and the Zippo he'd meant to have engraved with an ace of hearts—a lover's red heart marking his status as a live air ace, not the ace of spades, symbol of death.

He had just inhaled a second drag on his cigarette when the bullets chopped pieces high off the rock and flying bits stung him.

"Kommen aus!" the German shouted. *"Schnell, schnell!"*

CHAPTER 28

AGENCE FRANCE PRESSE—Guadalcanal, February 12, 1943 (Delayed): Advance parties of the Americal Division loaded aboard transports here for movement to somewhere in the Fiji Islands. Marine and army intelligence sources estimate Japanese losses during the campaign at more than 32,000. U.S. infantry rear guard units remain to sweep the Guadalcanal jungle and root out the few enemy survivors hidden on the island.

Instinct pulled Eddie Donnely's head down when the plane thundered over the treetops. Even though he knew it was American, his body reacted out of reflex. Over the months there had been the night visits of Washing Machine Charlie and his bombs falling Christ knew where. Worse had been the sudden air raids in force, flights of Zeros howling down to nullify the hard-won airstrip of Henderson Field, but just as willing to bomb and strafe infantry positions.

More nerve-racking was the shelling from the Tokyo Express, destroyers flying the Flaming Asshole that ran The Slot. That was the busy stretch of ocean which began off the tip of Bougainville and narrowed to Sealark Channel between the Canal and Savo and Florida islands. And there had been Oscar, the Nip submarine surfacing every night to lob lazy shells at anything within range.

Eddie sniffed the air and signaled the patrol to halt. He didn't have to tell them to hit the deck; that, too, was instinctive, and the difference between the quick and the dead. Again he wished that Captain Shelby had stayed behind in the company CP, but what the hell could you do with a guy who really wanted to be out with his men? Not to rack up points with the high brass or get a write-up for a medal, but just to show the troopers he was one of them.

As platoon sergeant, Eddie wasn't taking the point for that reason. He was better at it than most, his senses honed to a cutting edge by so much experience, a tested-in-the-field knowhow. It was backed by scouting and patrolling classes hammered into his head by Big Mike and successive first soldiers, so that he could practically quote the field manuals, and a lot of that past war information worked.

Combat maxim: killing is the sixth sense; the other five just support it.

On one knee, the butt plate of his BAR resting against his hip, he scanned the area foot by slow foot. Checking the treetops, then the lines of banyan networks, into broom and thorny creepers and over new beginnings of slim bamboo shoots, he bellied down to sight low along the damp ground. And to listen: to high leaves rubbing each other, to a click beetle searching green fungus; hearing the far cry of that goofy bird that sounded like it was coughing up blocks of wood; hearing the drip of his own sweat.

The very earth of the Canal stank of swampy rot, and its miasma rose to thicken air already heavy with moisture. But he smelled something else—the unmistakable odor of death unburied. Jap corpses; their putrescence was different from that of dead GIs.

Lightly tapping the stock of his weapon twice, he let the men behind know that he was scouting forward alone. Boof Hardin and J.C. Gibson would make up the connecting file, and Captain Shelby was supposed to stay put somewhere in the middle of the patrol.

Eddie slid along the ground, pulling himself along with

the butt of the BAR. Even though he'd stripped away its bipod, the weapon was heavy, but he wouldn't trade its firepower and dependability for an M-1, carbine or Thompson. Breathing deeply again, he sorted another odor from the overall stink—a faint echo of burned powder, the residue of a 105 shell that had screamed into this section of jungle and caught some Japs out of their rat holes. Mark one up for the redlegs of the 245/246/247th Artillery, whichever battalion had fired the mission.

The shelling must have been for effect, concentrated along what Eddie made out to be three coconut-log bunkers, staggered for connecting fire in the tree line beyond a little clearing. Or what were once bunkers; the artillery had flattened them, scattered the logs and blown the Japs to hell and gone. Or to be resurrected in four days to slant-eye paradise, where beautiful geishas and plentiful sake awaited the heroes who died gloriously for their emperor. Whichever didn't matter. On this island and in this life they were dead.

Barracks talk: S.O.L., you bastards—shit outa luck.

Three raps on the gunstock, louder. Remaining in the shadow of a tree bole, Eddie stood up and slowly traversed the blown bunkers with his gun muzzle; nothing. The stench got to him, and he propped the BAR to pull a grimy handkerchief and wet it from his canteen. Knotting it across his nose and mouth, he picked up his weapon and advanced into the clearing. Behind him he heard the patrol following and gave the hand signal for advance as skirmishers, spacing them wide just in case.

"Boof!" snorted Hardin, making the lip-blown sound that nicknamed him. "What a stink. You find any samurai swords?"

"Someday you'll get your ass blown off hunting souvenirs."

J.C. Gibson said, "Not by any of them puffed-up turds. Looks like an officer over yonder. He'll have a sword."

Captain Shelby passed Eddie a lighted cigarette. "Artillery did a job here. The area must be clear, or this bunch would've been dragged off."

Puffing smoke beneath his handkerchief, rolled higher, Eddie said, "I don't know, sir. The Japs probably quit worrying about us counting their casualties when they pulled out what they could save."

He rested the weight of the BAR against his right leg and allowed smoke to trickle past his nose to mask the odor of dead Japs. Watching Boof Hardin fix his bayonet and prod the officer's swollen carcass over, he blinked and rubbed smoke out of his eye.

That's when the live Jap rolled away from a pile of corpses with a pistol in each hand. Up on his knees, wild-eyed and screaming, he blazed away with both Nambus.

Eddie swept up his BAR as the first shot knocked Captain Shelby off his feet. He got off a burst that went high when a sledgehammer blow spun him around. Somebody yelled "Oh, Lord!" through the *raprap* of the gunshots, over the mad shrilling of the Jap.

So damned heavy, the BAR sagged in Eddie's hands. He turned and fought it up again as Gibson shot the Jap and Hardin lunged to pin him to the ground with the bayonet. Hanging on to his weapon with an effort, Eddie moved stiff-legged to where Shelby lay. The platoon medic kneeled beside the captain and looked up to shake his head.

"He never felt it, Sarge—heart shot. Hey, man—you're hit."

"No shit." He didn't want to see the captain's face. He took three steps away and sat down.

The Jap kicked and wiggled, squeaking as he pawed bloody hands on the forestock of Hardin's rifle. Noticing a sucking noise, Eddie pressed the heel of his left hand against the hole in his chest so he could breathe easier.

"Hey," the medic said, "that's a lung wound, man—oh, hell, man."

"That Jap is no man," Eddie said. "He's only a fucking animal. He lived in with those stinking corpses so he could get off a free shot. Keep him on the bayonet, Boof. Let him take his time dying. *Banzai,* you slimy little son of a bitch."

The medic said, "Hold still, Sarge. I think I can plug this hole."

"Gibson!"

"Yeah, Sarge?"

"Get their dicks—take every set of balls. Chop them off or blow them off, but get them—you hear me? If he's still alive, start with that one."

"What the hell?"

Captain Shelby was dead. Oh, goddamn; he lit a cigarette and gave it to Eddie, and Eddie had let him die.

The pain whistled through his chest, and Eddie gritted against it. "In case the sons of bitches may be right. In—in case they rise and go to warrior heaven like—like the Shinto priests tell them. Cut off their dicks and smash their balls so they can't fuck the angel geishas, only sweat them out for all eternity. . . ."

Eternity flowed up black to spit in Eddie's eyes.

On Stephanie's early advice Penny Belvale had hidden everything she owned, any object that might possibly be of value. Long ago cigarette lighters and fountain pens had been traded to the guards for food. An egg was sinful luxury, an extra bowl of rice gruel a blessing, and a spoon of rancid fish oil promised one more tomorrow.

Everybody in camp went to bed hungry and got up hungry. In between they dreamed of food, and Penny didn't want to hear course by course about any banquets to be savored when some woman got home. Going home stood a good chance of being never, even if the war ended soon. Odds were against that, too, so she hoarded her engagement and wedding rings against the years of starvation ahead, as did Stephanie Bartlett.

Penny couldn't imagine how she would have made it this far without Stevie. The British stiff-upper-lipism rubbed off, but it was more than that, more than her determination to outlast Major Wobbly Watanabe and pay back the rest of the lousy Japs.

She had never known a closeness like this, even during her childhood in Virginia, when of course there had been a series of bestest friends exchanged almost every summer. Or at the beginning of each school year. Now she had to think hard to bring back the name of her college roommate: Leah—ash blond, and proof that a girl could wear glasses and still be sexy. Leah something; yes—Leah—Ireland? Nobody could think straight on a stomach shrunken for so long.

And their friendship was sealed tighter because of Chad Belvale, Uncle Chad, who had been Stevie's lover, who was still the man she loved. Even if her husband had survived the fall of Singapore and was in one of the male-only prisoner of war camps, Stevie would choose Chad. It showed in the way her eyes deepened when she talked of what they had together, the tenderness softening her voice when she spoke of the short, wondrous times remembered. Stevie was so eager to hear every tiny detail about Uncle Chad, and when Penny couldn't come up with the right words at the right time she made up something.

Penny didn't think she had ever loved like that, not even when she first went to bed with Walton Belvale. Giving up the burden of her virginity was exciting and couldn't be matched on her wedding night with Farley. She hadn't faked the ruptured hymen, and Farley was smart enough not to ask.

Squirming inside, she tried not to dwell on the sensuous memories of Walt—how he caressed her, and the hunger of him as he tasted her mouth and her breasts. So hesitant, so gentle, until she surprised him by forcing him into her body. The quicksharp pain didn't last long enough.

She shut her eyes and fought the warm rush of her cheeks. Did being hungry all the time make you horny?

Standing beside prisoner CO Leftenant Bartlett, Penny

stared across the parade ground at Watanabe's polished boots. She'd be damned if she'd look up; that's what he wanted when he made announcements from the headquarters porch stairstepped above their heads. Besides, Japs would think she was being properly humble as a woman. If at any time an average woman couldn't outsmart these jerks, it was only because they kept changing the rules.

"Labor outside the camp is voluntary," Watanabe said. "Volunteers will work in the old rubber tree plantation that new jungle has reclaimed. You complain that you have little food; now you will clear the fallen trees, chop down the young ones, and dig up all roots. Then you will plant the land."

Before he could turn away Stephanie stepped forward, snapped to attention and saluted, all very proper.

"Sir!" She made it sound like an epithet. "The lack of food has made us weak and ill, unable to do such heavy labor. No one is physically able to volunteer, and—"

"Of course you will volunteer," he cut in, "tomorrow morning. I order it, Prisoners dismissed."

Penny touched her hand as they walked back to the huts and latrines they had to finish cleaning. "Vegetables—think of what kind we'll plant, all the things to eat."

"Bloody hell—if any survive long at such difficult work. No one is near strong enough. Look at us, Penny—take a close look at everyone and ken how incapable we are."

"Hey, we can do whatever we have to."

That was the family talking; centuries of knights in armor, of fighters wielding swords, sighting down muzzle loaders and machine guns; the Belvales and the Carlisles as one. That was herself talking honor to her husband, and now maybe wishing she hadn't pushed him into volunteering for overseas duty. She fit into the family pattern better than Farley. Still she didn't think she could have respected him if he hadn't; he had the name and the blood. Farley would do okay.

And she saw that Stephanie needed her as much as she

depended upon Stephanie. Green and black, the flies rose thick around Penny as she trailed Stephanie beneath the low palm roof of the latrines.

Slapping at the buzzing cloud, Stephanie muttered, "Sod that whoreson. He'll bury us all then."

"Not us. We'll do the Viginia reel on his grave, or that Highland fling. Do Japs get buried just like people, I wonder?"

No soap, of course. Stephanie dipped a hand-tied brush into the wooden bucket and scrubbed water at the tree boles laid across an open trench. The rough bark saplings had been rubbed down to the smooth grain by a thousand seatings of skinny butts often bleeding from dysentery.

Penny used one hand to clamp her nostrils against the stench and to protect her nose and mouth from the flies. The other used a brush like her friend's. Family was a fine word; friend was a great one.

Stephanie said, "This trench ought to serve for that *gammy*, evil cripple that Major Wobbly is. Oh, to see his shininess put down in this terrible mess—"

"Spinach, cabbage, carrots. Tomatoes, do you think? No, we can't stuff Wobbly into the latrine."

Her friend stared at her.

"We have to keep the crap clean for the vegetables—pure manure."

Exploding into laughter, Stephanie said, "You're daft, you know."

"It helps. We'll outlast them, Stevie."

"Of course we will."

CHAPTER 29

SECRET to Kill Devil Hill—14 February 1942, TWX delayed for new security clearance check. Quote, original report—II Corps HQ, Algiers, 14 Feb: General Eisenhower attributes severe lack of transportation from Algeria to Tunisia for piecemeal commitment of the 1st Infantry and 1st Armored Divisions and resultant losses.

The Afrika Korps attack at 0600 this date designed to smash through Kasserine Pass, turn northwest through the Tebessa supply base and reach the coast to cut off Allied units. 1st Arm. Div. suffered losses and was pushed east into new mountain positions, exposing XIX Corps flank. 1st Inf. Div. withdrawing slightly to plug gaps and fight series of holding actions.

Chad Belvale marked another circle on the overlay of the situation map and turned to his executive officer. "What did Regiment say?"

Langlois put back the field phone handset. "Take our best shot and they let us know when the other battalions pull out."

"Yeah, thanks a lot."

The Cajun said, "Uh-huh. That's what I told them—*merci beaucoup, ma fois*. Little bit of French confused them like hell, they figure we over in the Foreign Legion sector. Your boy, he's still all right?"

"At last word. But these fight-and-fall-back actions are messy. I saw it in France. Sometimes an entire unit is cut off and never gets home."

"Good thing their damn tanks can't climb straight up, then. We all be cut short where it hurts."

Battalion CP had been pick-and-shoveled into one side of a wet and shallow wadi; its cover was a cook tent fly camouflaged with grass and leaves. From up high it might fool the Luftwaffe dive bombers and Stork pilots spotting for artillery. Kraut air worked over anything that moved and were sharp at picking out vehicle tracks, especially in this drizzly weather. Knowing that a dearth of friendly aircraft was caused by the good guys working over enemy rear areas didn't keep Chad from wishing they were here for close support, and low ceiling be damned.

They'd pulled out and set up again three times since the Krauts attacked, and Chad thought they would soon be retreating again. Rommel's troops were damned tough, battle-hardened in Libya, and when his tanks broke through they ran wild, cutting communications and blowing up command posts. And the only thing that stopped that damned armor at any time was point-blank fire from 105 or 155 artillery, a lucky mortar hit, or accidentally throwing a track. The U.S. Army's antitank gun, a pipsqueak 37mm, was about as useful as throwing rocks at an elephant. And that was for tanks lighter than the new Kraut monster, the Tiger. It had been guesstimated at sixty tons or so; none had ever been knocked out in this sector.

Armor, direct air support and troops seasoned by long combat—Rommel had them all. The 16th Infantry had to run or stand him off with what they had, and with GI guts. Most times, pulling out in panic got a soldier killed quicker. Firing back kept the other guy's head down, and staying deep in your hole didn't make him eager to come get you.

Don't think, and try to stay busy; that advice kept a

soldier from worrying about losing his legs or eyes or balls. Or just your right hand, like Johnny Merriman. Fight back; then you didn't think on 4-Fs back home making that big money in defense plants and screwing your girl.

It helped Chad to shove his personal problems to the rear. If he dwelled upon the survival odds for Owen out there in the shot-up desert, facing German Mark IV and Mark V tanks with his pea shooters, or upon the unknown of the South Pacific where Farley soldiered, Chad couldn't do his job.

Certainly he couldn't think long about Stephanie Bartlett; her memory tore at him when he least expected it, and nobody had any information on her since the fall of Singapore. At least Kirstin was okay; there was something to be said for civilian loves, if they weren't caught in the London Blitz. Kirstin was safe at home, not at the Hill, but in her new home in Texas, with her new husband.

Why think on Kirstin now? Hell, a man couldn't live with a woman, a good and solid woman, for twenty years plus without her keeping a place in his head.

On the radio to his line companies, Chad stayed on top of the situation, and it didn't sound good. He couldn't reach Fox Company, and Easy's CO asked for help that Chad didn't have. George was ass-deep in trouble as usual, and Howe's gun platoons were attached to everybody, its mortars running low on ammunition.

The phone made its buzz-ring noise, and Captain Langlois picked it up. Nodding at the S-3 sergeant to change the overlay, he said to Chad, "Regiment reached 9th Division Arty; they say we get fire support from them soon, us."

The angry snarl of an .88 shell passed overhead to explode down the road behind the command post. Chad reached for his carbine and said, "It had better be soon. We're about to be overrun."

Nancy Carlisle was never comfortable in the Officers Club. It was too much like partying in Washington, where the only signs of war were the crowds and the uniforms. It was different on the ward, where some of the men had never gotten free of the jungle and screamed back at charging Japanese every night.

Now she was more edgy because she barely knew the light colonel across the table, and because his very name brought back a time she would rather forget. Like Keenan and the family; like the Hill and Washington and a slick, sexy Congressman who had used her to keep tabs on the family.

"We finally irritated somebody in the War Department and got my orders cut," Dan Belvale said. "I wanted the ETO for personal reasons, but you know the old general. Soldier where you're sent, he says—except for himself, of course; he sent himself to North Africa. And Crusty is too busy giving all of Washington a bad time. I'll have to get out of here and into a combat command as best I can." He glanced around the club. "The Andrews Sisters singing 'Don't Sit Under the Apple Tree' on the jukebox, frangipani blossoms and a waterfall behind the bar. Lord, Lord—since Pearl Harbor this command is only technically overseas."

The look, she thought; that certain aquiline cast of features that was the family stamp, the look of the hawk. That same suicidal eagerness to go into combat and climb the ladder of rank or die on the way up. Not fair, Nancy; this one had already lost a son to war: Walt Belvale, first of the family to fall this time around. The invasion of Poland seemed so long ago; the time for her had been a divorce and Representative Marshal Bailey and another lover of sorts; a short moment of sharing that was almost incest, if a brother-in-law counted that way. Sex for Chad and her had been a deep need for closeness and release, and she refused to be shamed for it.

She could only remember one Belvale-Carlisle who was rank-happy—Luther, whose eagles rode heavier upon his shoulders than the chaplain's cross. Family members became colonels and generals because they were good at the family business, and since an era lost in the mists of time their stock in trade had been war.

And there on the ward, where she would be on duty at 0700, Farley Belvale lay staring at the ceiling. He was paying one hell of a price for his blue-chip share in the corporation, his uniform now only convalescent blues. For him even that label was out of place. Convalescent, walking wounded? Not so; Farley would be flown to the mainland strapped to a litter, catatonic, the next thing to a corpse. Maybe the dead were better off. The highball glass was chill in her hand, so she drank her bourbon on the rocks. It tasted brown and slippery cold.

Signaling the waiter for another round, Dan said, "It's habit for me to check the officers' roster at every new post, looking for friends, enemies or the family, which can be either. I'm glad you kept your married name, Nancy. We're so scattered that I wouldn't have known you were here, or what happened to Farley. On the Hill they know, because bits and pieces of information about family members are fed in behind the important war reports. Will Farley ever come out of it?"

"Possibly; probably. It will take time, but we're learning more about combat fatigue every day."

Names and faces passing, forgotten as the new casualties came in, the psychiatrists trying to distinguish between a frightened kid not allowed to admit it and the frightened kid whose mind had refused to accept any more horror. The learning was that often not much separated them. Nancy tried hard to erase all the faces and sometimes succeeded; the names echoed awhile before they went away.

Farley wouldn't go away; she had known him when he was a boy, as a cadet, and thought it was stupid for his brother to attend West Point while he was at VMI. The family and its goddamn traditions; Keenan a part of it and twice—twice!—carried as MIA or KIA, pushing his luck beyond the limits in China, Burma or wherever the hell he was now. She knew he was alive—a bit, a piece of information passed to her as an afterthought, after the important war reports. She drank her icy bourbon.

Dan lifted his hand, but she drew it back to the tabletop, a hand alive and warm. "I'd better not have any more; I'm on day shift, 0700."

He said, "I never thought to see you in uniform, but you're doing fine and looking great."

She thanked him for the compliments and the drinks, and for going to see Farley and talking intelligently to him as if the boy could hear and understand. Then she insisted upon getting the cab for herself. Leaving Dan Belvale behind, Nancy walked out of the club before the cigarette smoke made her eyes water, or too many drinks made her throw up. It wasn't Dan, Farley or even the family itself. It was the ward following her into the bar, and the sobs, the screams that came faintly through the music.

Crusty Carlisle roared and waved the sheet of paper. "What the hell do they mean—delayed for new security check? Is J. Edgar Hoover off his trolley, or is this the work of some equally stupid bastard in counterintelligence? Are they tapping our goddamn teletype and taking pictures when I go piss?"

Preston Belvale lighted a fresh cigar. "I just called Ben Alexander to check it out, but I'll bet on General Skelton."

"General, my aching back! Tom Skelton wouldn't make a pimple on a PFC's dick. Tell him to take a flying fuck at a rolling doughnut. Better yet, I'll go to Washington and stomp a mudhole in his ass."

"Too late. Skelton finally got overseas—to London."

Crusty ripped the TWX to shreds and tossed them into the air. "To command some underground mess kit repair division and put himself in for the Legion of Merit. Oh, that revolving son of a bitch."

"Any way you look at him," Belvale agreed. "He took a nip at us and ran. Ben Alexander is tracking how he did it and who helped—probably some clown on the president's staff. While you were at chow the personal follow-ups came in—delayed, of course. Farley is en route to Letterman General, battle fatigue; Gavin Scott shot down in Tunisia, no further word; no word on Chad and Owen since the start of Rommel's attack at Kasserine Pass; Keenan is somewhere in Burma with the Britisher Wingate. And, damnit"—pausing to take a comforting drag upon his cigar, Belvale stroked his mustache—"Captain Jim Shelby went down on Guadalcanal in a mop-up operation. The press will milk that story: Senator dies on front lines. It will make other legislators in service look patriotic, although they're nearly all tucked away in safe jobs. Kirstin doesn't know yet. I'll have to call her before the War Department telegram gets to Texas and the reporters swarm in on her. Damn, but I hate this. Jim Shelby was a good man, a credit to the service and the country. His death will hit Kirstin hard."

Crusty kneeled and made a project out of collecting the bits of paper he had scattered over the carpet. He dropped them into the wastebasket and looked up. "Somehow it's different when a friend buys the farm. I mean, it's never easy to lose somebody, even if he happens to be one of the family's particular sons of bitches. Like Luther C. Farrand, that phony fucking sky pilot, and what's his name—that flyboy kid was no big winner.

"The family knows there'll be empty chairs at the table. We expect it—acceptable losses. But Jim Shelby didn't have to work at soldiering and had damned little practice. I'm glad you'll be talking to Kirstin instead of me. I'd screw it up."

Bells went off at one teletype, then on another. Belvale discovered his cigar had gone out and relighted it while Crusty checked the machines. Bending to read the clacking messages, Crusty then half turned to say over one shoulder: "Withdrawal at Kasserine, my ass. We're getting the holy shit kicked out of us."

CHAPTER 30

UNITED PRESS—Kasserine Pass, Tunisia, February 15, 1943: Led by wave after wave of tanks, the Afrika Korps slammed against Allied defense lines at 0400 today, in an icy gray rain. Heavy panzers attacked through this valley of rocky sand and scrub brush, preceded by artillery barrages and followed by self-propelled guns and infantry.

Stretched thin and undergunned, especially in armor, the II Corps reeled under the fierce onslaught. Major General Lloyd Fredendall's HQ admits to loss of some ground but says the troops are "holding all strategically important positions."

These troops are a mixed bag of American and British armor and infantry, and French Legionnaires that include Algerians, Moroccans and Senegalese. Officials here say privately that French politics and resentment of English commanders present a more difficult barrier than the language differences.

Meanwhile, to the east in Libya, "Desert Rats" of the British 8th Army are not only holding fast but initiating a series of probing attacks.

Radio traffic was heavy and spooky as messages flew in: The English battalion up the road just lost fifteen Honey tanks because their popguns can't stop the Tigers. . . . The Tigers are coming! . . . Everybody better shag ass. . . . The fucking A-rabs are selling out every hidden position to the Krauts. . . . This outfit is about to break,and that one already panicked; nobody knows what happened to first battalion. . . . Tigers . . . Tiger tanks . . .

Damn the Tigers. There had to be a way to trap them, a way to stop the big bastards if it meant running out and prying off a track with a crowbar. But who had a crowbar? The antitank rocket launchers had arrived yesterday, two of the goofy things the men immediately named "bazookas" after the strange musical instrument tooted by Bob Burns in the movies.

Pamphlets on how to work the recoilless, shoulder-fired, 2.5-inch weapons came up with the ammunition, but nobody had tried firing yet, and nobody much wanted to. They looked weird and clumsy, and their range was short; you had to be looking a tank in the gullet to launch the rocket. Would it explode and penetrate the armor? Nobody knew; the book said the ass end definitely was dangerous, that if the loader was to kneel directly behind the tube he'd be fried by the backfire. In desperation, someone would have to try it first, and who but Owen Belvale? He wouldn't order anyone else. RHIR—rank hath its responsibilities.

Maybe it wouldn't be as dangerous as the English sticky bombs. Those things actually had to be hand-slammed to the side of an enemy tank, and its goo was supposed to hold it there until the timer went off and a shaped charge blew a neat hole in Jerry's vehicle. How did the human tank destroyer get within arm's reach? How did he get away from his own explosion and the machine gunners? Nobody explained the little things.

Owen hid from the cold rain under a shelter half which the wind jerked from time to time. He couldn't hide from the fact that the whole division was in trouble, and maybe the entire Corps. He knew they'd gotten on line too late to hit Rommel's rear area and cut off his supplies. Now they were bogged down in the muddy Tunisian winter, where only German tanks seemed able to cover any distance—even those damned sixty-ton Tigers. The British Honeys and Valentines and the U.S. Shermans sank deep into mudfields or immediately threw a track. Kraut armor commanders must have learned mud lessons in Russia; their tank treads were much wider and flatter.

This was miserable country—rocky desert cold, gray and wet, only bits of stunted brush straggling over landscape too poor to support Arab goat herds. Owen's regiment was dug in on the left flank of the pass in low, rolling mountains that offered some cover. The 26th Infantry was caught more in the open and was paying dearly for its unlucky position. He didn't need field glasses to see the puffs of smoky dirt that were 88mm explosions battering troops along the valley floor. And the enemy tanks came rolling, so many and so heavy that Owen could feel the earth tremble.

Big Mike Donnely's helmet dripped water into his gray-black beard as he stuck his head into the CP. "Fire mission on my own, sir? Plenty of targets out there—infantry riding on those tanks or following them."

"Bracket and fire for effect," Owen said. "Battalion said they'll get you more ammo ASAP."

If any vehicle could run the gauntlet in time; if not—and there was real danger of being cut off—Sergeant Donnely would hold back enough propellant increments to help hand grenades destroy his mortar tubes. The trouble for all would be no place to hide; any major retreat would put everybody out on that open plain, straggling, accordion columns fat and helpless targets for Kraut artillery and armor, and if the low ceiling lifted, the Stukas and Messerschmitts.

"Sanya!"

"Yeah, lieutenant?" PFC "Boots" Sanya grinned. He enjoyed carrying messages and made a game of dodging incoming fire like a broken field runner, pretending to be Crazy Legs Hirsch or some other famous back.

"Nobody pulls out until orders from me—only word from me. Then we'll do it by the numbers—no panic."

"Got it, boss!" He scuttled from the hole.

Karumph! Karumph! The 81s coughed, and Owen wiped his field glasses lenses to peer through the drizzle. So much damned armor fanned out through the pass, rumbling ahead and firing the whipcracks of their 88s. They were oblivious to the poor limey tanks waiting hull down to face them, to hope they would come into their shorter range.

A Honey blew up in a ball of flame; two Valentines exploded as Owen watched, and there smoked a half-track and a pair of sizzling Shermans. The 1st Armored called their Sherman tanks "Ronsons" because their high-octane fuel tank was so thin it flared up at any hit. The Germans came on and on, and Owen could see tiny figures bailing out of blazing tanks and running until machine guns cut them down.

It was massacre and butchery, and within minutes the battle of Kasserine Pass turned into a rout as blind, unreasoning panic swept the Allied troops. Owen wished to hell that his gun platoons were back with him. Below him on the flat, GI trucks filled with troops barreled to the rear, and many of the men had no weapons. His people were more heavily burdened than these runaway riflemen; they had fifty-one-pound tripods and thirty-seven-pound guns to carry; they had water cans and ammo boxes and their personal weapons.

And the stubborn bastards would try to bring everything out, come hell, high water or Hitler himself.

Wham! Wham!

A Cannon Company half-track turned wide and fired back across the field, its gunners throwing 75mm shells at extreme range. Owen took a deep breath as he watched mortar bursts make a deadly pattern behind the last vehicle of the ragtag convoy in flight. The last was an ambulance, and Big Mike had waited it out. Damn! Was Kraut armor that close?

Not every outfit was running.

"Sir!" His radioman passed him the handset.

"Fall back," his battalion commander said. "Stick to the hills as long as you can, because the whole front is collapsing. Stay off the main road and head for Sbeitla. We'll try to collect there."

"Yes, sir. My attached gun platoons—"

"They'll have to hang tough with their companies," Chad Belvale said. "We're losing some radio commo, and all wire is cut. Owen—"

"Yes, sir?"

"Good luck, son."

"You, too—Dad."

The standard parting of soldiers: good luck. In peacetime it meant find a happy home in your next outfit, a good post and maybe a boost in rank. In combat it meant don't get blown into bloody little pieces; don't die.

Big Mike's mortars coughed again and again, hurling projectiles out onto the rocky land. Owen yelled it: "We're shagging ass! Load the jeeps and stay together! Sanya—"

"Yeah," Boots said, "I know—see everybody gets the word." And he was off again, zigzagging, carbine tucked under his right arm, his left hand pushed out for a stiff arm.

KA-WHOOM!

Spitting dirt, ears ringing, Owen flinched at the ball of fire that rolled uphill when the half-track blew up. Direct hit by a German tank; small-arms ammo popping belatedly; damn, damn!

The tank's machine guns raked the wadi . . . *brrrppptt* . . . *brrrppptt* . . .

Owen saw the bastard now, squatting out in the open as if it owned all of Kasserine Pass and everyone in it.

"Get out!" he told his radioman. "Run to the mortars."

The hell that Mark IV owned the pass or any part of H Company. He fumbled for the bazooka and found it clammy in his hand as Lieutenant Gladstein tumbled into the hole.

"Aaron—haul ass out of here!"

"You need a loader. I don't know where the hell the other Buck Rogers gadget is, but here are a couple of rockets."

Lifting, Owen threw back the shelter half and braced the launcher on his shoulder to stare through the big open sight at the tank below.

Brrrpppttt! One of its machine guns walked a long burst along the lip of the gully, throwing mud, dirt and rocks.

Owen felt the rocket push into the tube. "Aaron, you clear?"

By the book, Aaron Gladstein slapped his back in the all-clear signal.

"Fire in the hole!" Owen yelled, and he pulled the trigger.

The flashes were almost simultaneous, the electrically fired rocket hissing out in smoke and rearward flame, and the hit just below the tank's turret, a much bigger *whoosh!* and *crash!* One machine-gun muzzle tilted upward, and the Mark IV lurched.

"Does the son of a bitch work?" Gladstein shoved another round into the tube.

The long gun swung toward Owen and stopped halfway, the turret jammed. The tank shuddered around on onc track as Gladstein slapped Owen's back again.

This explosion knocked a hole in the side plate, and the turret lid flew open. Smoke boiled over, and a German soldier lifted out. The muzzle blast of Gladstein's carbine almost seared Owen's cheek. The German toppled over the side and flopped to the ground. Inside the machine a man screamed, and black smoke poured from the turret.

"Here comes another one," Owen said. "Load, damn it!"

The hillside exploded and banged him into the side of the wadi. When the smoke and dust cleared his first shot missed the tank. His next one tore off a track; it didn't stop the men inside from working over the hill with machine guns as the muzzle brake of the 88 cannon reached around for Owen.

Shoosh—blamm!!

Dropping the bazooka, Owen reeled from the flash and nearness of a blast that slapped him across the mouth and glazed his eyes. Mortar—it could only be an 81 dropped right in the tanker's lap. Close, so damned close that steel fragments whirred hot by Owen's face. He just got Gladstein pulled down as the panzer blew up with a roar that deafened him and almost buried them both.

"Out!" he screamed, hearing his own voice tinny and far away. "Get the hell out of here!"

Up the gully until it flattened, then crouching low, he ran with Aaron until they fell into the deeper dip of the mortar position.

"Last rounds!" Mike Donnely shouted. "Fire!"

Chuff-chuff! Chuff-chuff! Four mortars fired almost together.

"Grenade the tubes! Blast the sights! Don't leave anything for the bastards!"

Gladstein's hand helped Owen to his feet, and he trotted with the rest as grenades dropped onto handfuls of powder increments and exploded with muted roars.

"Follow me!" His voice was hoarse, scratchy in his throat. "We can't all ride, so jeep drivers load the wounded and go! I'll take the walking point and get us out of here. Everybody keep your distance, but stay together, damnit! Donnely—drop somebody fast back as rear guard. Sanya—"

"Sanya's dead," some kid called out. "He was my buddy, so I'll do it."

It was stupid to yell out good luck, so Owen only said it inside his head.

CHAPTER 31

Völkischer Beobachter—Berlin, February 15, 1943: Minister Joseph Goebbels announced today that the *Gessandante Kultur* would forward all messages to their families from Afrika Korps troops in the field. Disruption of mail services caused by indiscriminate Allied bombings will soon be remedied, he said. He added that the morale of German soldiers has never been higher since their shattering defeat of the American forces at the battle of Kasserine Pass in Tunisia.

Field Marshal Erwin Rommel stood up in his command car, the Mittlerer Kommandopanzerwagen. The attachment of the bulky, armored command post on wheels had been left under netting and behind protective dunes. It wasn't needed at the moment; communications were excellent in this half-track.

General Wilhelm Witter von Thoma made himself as comfortable as possible upon his seat with the extra layer of padding. Let Rommel stare into the rain and any blowing sand while presenting his best profile to the cameras. To shine in the public eye was all very well to attain higher rank and glory, but that also kept close attention of the general staff focused upon today's hero. Worse, the Führer himself scanned the newspapers and films, in addition to reports from the field. Von Thoma had long ago learned the value of a careful facelessness, so that he would never join Hitler's Reserve, that group of officers retired in disgrace from active duty: von Manstein, Halder, von Rundstedt . . .

He would remain officially anonymous here, too. Whatever the Field Marshal might think of his assignment from Berlin, von Thoma acted the part of an observer only, offering no advice and asking no questions. He also smiled often, although with a hidden bitterness after Rommel's incredible luck at Kasserine Pass. The great Desert Fox had no idea he was just five days away from being shipped home on medical orders from Professor Horster.

Or perhaps not, after the highly successful strike through the passes of Tunisia. It had been arranged for him to leave by Field Marshal Kesselring, "Smiling Albert" come to Africa to work out difficulties between Rommel and Colonel-General von Arnim. Rommel, son of a schoolteacher, had never gotten along with the northern aristocrat, descendant of a line of generals. Von Arnim had been given the Tunisian theater of operations and practically all available reinforcements and supplies, while Rommel strove to hold off the British in Libya with his 14,000 Germans and 15,000 Italians. Certainly Rommel did not suspect that von Arnim was scheduled to replace him as overall commander in Africa the moment he was flown out. Kesselring had arranged that as part of the compromise.

Now? Von Thoma cupped his hands around a cigarette in a short ivory holder and drew hard upon it. Now the ragtag forces opposing Rommel, *Amis*, French and British, were scattered through the rainswept mountains. Swiftly beaten and demoralized, they had abandoned guns and equipment to flee in panic, especially the inexperienced Americans.

Zap-zingg!

"Sniper," the *oberleutnant* driver grunted. "Out of range and only firing to make himself brave."

"Left front," Rommel said, peering through his glasses, "three hundred yards. Gunner, give him a burst."

Easing down in the seat, von Thoma pulled on his cigarette and flinched when the machine gun loosed a string of sharp explosions. Generals should not be this close and vulnerable; they should be controlling the nerve center, the command post where the big picture could be clearly seen and its many components controlled.

The half-track ground forward as shell casings clattered on the floor. Von Thoma thought of minefields, teeth locked around his cigarette holder. He concentrated upon bringing an earlier scene to mind, a scene he had witnessed in the Führer's headquarters just last November. It assured him that the great Desert Fox was neither immortal nor irreplaceable.

Von Thoma had stood back against the wall, taking notes as Rommel stood stiffly at attention before the Führer and Reichsmarschall Hermann Göring.

". . . defeated at El Alamein, despite air superiority, more tanks and artillery. Why?"

Rommel muttered that he ran out of fuel, and Göring laughed. "Enough gasoline for hundreds of trucks and panzers to flee in shame down the coast route."

Rommel then complained of ammunition and weapons shortages, and Hitler turned livid, pounding the table and shouting. "Your cowardly men threw away their guns. Any soldier without a gun should be shot."

Watching closely, von Thoma saw Rommel's jaw muscles twitch and realized that the man was about to lose his temper, a dangerous thing.

"Only luck allowed the Afrika Korps to escape the British," he said. "Now we are expected to fight not one army, but two. Unless we immediately withdraw to Italy the Afrika Korps will be destroyed."

"Nonsense!" Hitler leapt to his feet. "You will defend North Africa as Stalingrad is being defended. The American invasion army must be beaten there, not in Italy! That is an order, Feldmarschall!"

"Yes," Rommel replied. "*Heil* Hitler."

Then, against all odds, he became once more the Desert Fox of old with this sweeping victory over the Allies at Kasserine. Luck; a stroke of blind, incredible luck, and Erwin Rommel was once again the darling of the press and back in favor with the Führer, to a point.

Something slapped the armor of the half-track, a ringing blow that tore off a splinter of steel and shrieked it past von Thoma's head. Wide-eyed, he saw gouts of mud march away to the right flank.

"Spitfire!" the driver shouted. "*Verdammt* Britisher!"

"Gunner," Rommel said.

"Yes, sir! But I will not have a shot; he's flying straight away. It does not look as if he is coming back."

Rommel lifted his glasses again. "A stray, I hope. If not, then the British Eighth Army is closing faster than I thought possible."

Raising his head von Thoma said, "But Eisenhower can be pushed right out of Africa."

For a long moment Rommel did not turn around. When he did, he said, "So," as if he had never seen von Thoma before.

Gulping von Thoma plunged on. "I mean, sir—intelligence reports that the U.S. First Armored Division has lost ninety-eight tanks, fifty-seven half-tracks and twenty-nine pieces of artillery. Without counting the huge infantry losses, surely that unit is no longer combat-worthy—"

"Of course you would be familiar with intelligence reports; your duty to Berlin, *nein?* Then you must know that we are even now on our way to attack the *Amis* at Gafsa oasis. Led by Colonel Menton, Special Group 288 is at this moment clearing mines from the road. But in haste to reach the objective, naturally some mines will be left."

Von Thoma's mouth went dry. "Naturally, sir."

CHAPTER 32

Field Dispatch to Reichsminister Joseph Goebbels, dated 20 February 1943, marked SECRET—Tunisia, with the Afrika Korps:

Your sources here beg to report that Feldmarschall Rommel's drive is not going well. He was warned not to risk his limited supplies of men and machinery by General von Arnim but plunged ahead recklessly.

Rolling into the oasis at Tebessa, waving his celebrated fly whisk at Arabs pillaging wrecked and abandoned Allied vehicles, he accepted their acccolades as if he were their individual liberator. Repeatedly the ragged throng shouted, "Rommel! Rommel!" and only as an afterthought, "Hitler, Hitler."

In asides to staff officers who remonstrated against an ill-prepared attack in the wrong direction, Rommel said that his motto had always been Exploit! Exploit! Exploit! and here was a situation ripe to exploit.

He silenced von Arnim by reminding the colonel general that the Americans had retreated as von Arnim wished, and was not the smaller solution achieved? Why not drive to Bone on the north coast and run wild in the rear of the Anglo-Americans? His illnesses and pains seemingly forgotten, Rommel outlined his new plan. The town of Feriana had been left far behind them, so now who knew how far they might advance?

Before ordering the attack and ignoring his gathered commanders Rommel ate a heavy lunch of couscous with a local Arab sheik.

After the 10th Panzers were decimated by direct fire from hidden artillery Rommel appeared to have lost all interest in the battle, and as a cold, heavy rain beat upon the sides of his armored command post the *feldmarschall* became exceedingly despondent.

Despite radio calls from Kesselring and frantic attempts by his chief of staff Westphal to dissuade him, Rommel called off the offensive.

Since Rommel is shortly to be relieved of command and returned to Berlin, further orders concerning observation here will be appreciated.

"Miserable cold and rain," Arno Hindemit said, "or either burning heat and sand. There is no middle ground for those who bear the curse of the *landser*."

An enemy machine gun fired a desultory burst and fell silent. At what target, Arno wondered; those left of his platoon would not be acting the hero along the fireswept ridge top. They had climbed the mountains all right, marking their progress with corpses. As Arno had thought, there they found *Ami* mortars and machine guns sited to cover all approaches, and they joined with the artillery to stop all forward movement.

For when the infantry halted, so must the panzers. Lacking cover by *landsers*, the tanks were inviting targets for the *panzerfürst*, that personal rocket launcher that made tank killers of individual soldiers. Of course, there was a drawback to the new weapon: Any thoughtless soldier caught in its back blast became an immediate casualty.

He had also predicted that the *Amis* would learn to fight; he had not thought how quickly.

The *hauptmann* lay facing Arno, the right lens of his glasses cracked, a scratch along the same dirty cheek. "After the war I will write a paper on curses and the superstitious illusions of infantrymen."

"Ah, schoolteacher, first you must realize that war is never over. War merely sits down for a breather."

"Not the same war."

"Who is to say there was not simply a long breather between the last war and this one? And this one—France, Russia, Africa—where next, China, the North Pole? That is it, Captain. We must paint ourselves white and attack polar bears for the glory of the Third Reich, for *lebensraum*. But no, not a single *verdammt* Prussian will be sent to settle among the igloos. They will be busy preparing to defend from an attack by the South Pole. And look about you—would any family worth being called German wish to settle in this forsaken land?"

Witzelei listened with him as an *Ami* light mortar crew searched the hillside—one shell, two, three. A blessed silence followed; no scream of a wounded man. Witzelei said then, "The Sudetenland, Poland. It is true that there were threats and that Germany needed room to grow, to grow and progress. Our population—"

"Is much less now, so we will go home?"

"Of course not. You refuse to understand. We are committed to our country, and despite your antagonism, I know that you, too, serve honorably and faithfully. More so than most."

Cold rain dripped from the rim of Arno's helmet; some found its way to his chest, and he cursed. "I serve my uniform, *mein hauptmann,* not what my country has become. I believe that is so for the professional soldier of any nation, and you, schoolmaster, do not completely understand the professional. But then who does? Besides, *landsers* must practice a while here before they take the blitzkrieg down to the one real hell, although I cannot imagine hell being worse than this."

Pap-zinggg!

"Poor sniper," Witzelei muttered. "Far off his mark, but a bastard nonetheless."

"Ah," Arno said, "now you are beginning to understand."

Few men did, and practically no women, especially those who married the uniform. Those he divided into two classes: *dummköpfe* who didn't know what they were doing and expected no more from life than a meager but dependable income, and outright sluts.

Ilse had never been stupid, but her true nature appreciated the romantic opportunities presented when Arno was often absent on duty. When an *oberleutnant* grew serious she said *auf wiedersehen* to the sergeant she had first married. The opportunities would remain, and the money was better.

Perhaps there was a third group and a few Lili Marlenes existed, or else the song would not be so popular. *Ami* prisoners taken at Kasserine said that the "Krauts" had two exceptional inventions that their troops would certainly appropriate or copy—the 88mm and Lili Marlene.

> *Vor der Kaserne, vor dem grossen Tor,*
> *stand eine Laterne . . .*
> (By the barracks gate, in the lantern light,
> a faithful woman waits always . . .)

Take the 88, *Amis*. It can always be depended upon.

Pap—zinggg!

"Closer," Witzelei said, "but not by much."

"Sounds more like one of ancient Lebels of the French, or perhaps the English rifle. The *Amis* seldom fire a single shot with their M-1. It is more likely to be a burst of three, for a rich nation does not worry about expending ammunition."

"Then we should seriously consider occupying America, where we might all be rich."

"There you have it, Captain, but for one thing."

A lone mortar shell whispered in to burst on the valley floor.

"What is that?" Witzelei asked.

"The *Amis* will not allow it."

CHAPTER 33

Völkischer Beobachter—El Guettar and Maknassy passes, Tunisia, February 21, 1943: A fierce counterattack by a panzer division drawn from defense positions in the Mareth Line struck hard at American forces today. Fifty tanks from General Fritz Von Broich's 10th Panzers rumbled into these narrow defiles, followed by mobile guns and troop carriers filled with cheering infantry. Messerschmitts dived out of the morning sun to bomb and strafe American 1st Infantry Division foxholes and gun emplacements. The latest attack led by the Desert Fox, Field Marshal Erwin Rommel, was called devasting by observers and staff officers.

UNITED PRESS—El Guettar, North Africa, with the II U.S. Corps, February 23, 1943: Noting enemy tanks roaring perilously close to the 1st Infantry Division's command post, a staff officer suggested a hasty retreat.

"I will like hell pull out," snorted Maj. Gen. "Terrible Terry" Allen, "and I'll shoot the first bastard who does."

Feldwebel Arno Hindemit shouted at one of his stupid soldiers: "Drop the *verdammt* rations, fool! Run for cover!"

A shell exploded too close by; he tasted burned powder

and the sweat of his own fear. When dirt fell back and the smoke cleared he saw the ration box, its tinned guts spilled out. He saw his fallen *landser* in the same condition, but the twisted strings of guts were not metal.

Private Langen, the poor bastard who could trip over trouble on his way to church. Of course it had to be Langen; the infantryman's curse rode even heavier upon him. A simple task, bringing up rations; simple to remain in a safe hole to the rear when the shelling began. Nobody here was starving.

BLAMM!

Ears ringing, Arno hugged the ground. They were caught in a narrow neck of this pass in the wet mountains, catching hell from *Ami* artillery cleverly concealed on both slopes. Why? Because some brilliant general ordered them too far forward, probably von Arnim himself in a great hurry for a victory to match Rommel's at Kasserine. Word had filtered down to the troops that the generals of a divided command did not get along and were competing to remain in the Führer's good graces.

So Private Langen died here, and a good many more would follow. The goddamned Prussians would still be around after the war because men without a von before their names had died in their places, following their stupid orders. It was little wonder that Rommel fought with the aristocrats; he was a common man, but what could a common man do against the Prussians?

"*Scheissen!* Number two squad—dig in where you are! Number three squad, fall back around the bend!"

BLAM-BLAM-BLAM!

Ahead a panzer blew up, its machine-gun ammunition popping after like a string of Chinese firecrackers. Two other Mark IVs whipped around fast, their tracks squealing and throwing dirt. One of them caught a shell and staggered, a crippled monster helpless to run straight. Its crew jumped out and scattered. The other tank made it around the bend to safety.

"Battalion radio wants to know what is holding us up." Hauptmann Witzelei lifted his head from behind a boulder. Light glinted from his glasses. "Can you see the enemy?"

"Hell, no! I am not *trying* to see them. Schoolteacher—back behind your rock, *bitte!*"

Arno was too old and weary for breaking in another officer. The next one might be altogether too eager for an Iron Cross, and a prick in the bargain.

A pair of tanks roared past for the rear, hatches clamped tight and with their turrets swung around. Their long guns pointed behind like threatening stingers that no one took seriously. Hornets bent upon serious damage did not fly away. Even if Arno could hear over the roar of motors and thunder of enemy guns, he doubted if the armor *truppen* could sing with their balls drawn so far up into their bellies.

Lying on one side and scratching at the hard earth with his digging tool, Arno said *"Scheissen!"* again, knowing that for him, that was a lie for the future—if he had a future. *Landsers* were not to be blamed for soiling themselves when caught under heavy artillery fire, for rifles could not range in upon cannon, and fighting back made you feel a bit better, as if you were doing something to help yourself. When you could do nothing but pray, the bowels took over on their own.

But for Arno, as experiences in the past proved to him that he probably would not be able to shit for a week, his asshole drew up protectively tight.

"Sergeant! Room here for you also!"

Like cattle or ducks and less harmful animals, we always need company, Arno thought; we are not born alone, and so we are terrified to die alone. Besides, the ground was too hard for him to scrape out a proper hole. Following one shell burst, he took a deep breath, rolled over and ran like hell for the captain's sheltering rock, shovel in one hand, machine pistol swinging in the other.

The barrage fell off after he dived in next to Witzelei, only an occasional explosion now that the remaining panzers were out of sight. But no *landser* would move forward into the bottleneck defile. No doubt enemy mortars were waiting to add their voices to those of the artillery pieces, and even the rawest recruit realized that the crossfire of machine guns would be ready also. The only way through this pass would be straight up the ridge slopes and into the machine guns. It was not a pleasant thought.

Wounded, the radio operator pressed a bandage pad hard against his bloody shoulder. Lance Corporal Derbein was capable; he would make it, not like that poor bastard Langen. There was barely room for him, the captain, the radio and Arno in the natural pit behind the boulder.

Blam!

That blast was high up on the ridge, but Arno had no inclination to go out and look around for different cover.

"What?" Witzelei said into the radio mouthpiece. "Repeat, please."

Please; always the schoolmaster.

"What? Continue the attack? But Colonel, there are no panzers left, and the pass is a death trap. Oh—yes, sir. Yes, of course. *Heil.*"

Clicking off the handset, the captain looked at Arno. "Our colonel says more panzers are on the way."

"Of course," Arno said, head cocked to listen for an incoming round, "but to where?"

Witzelei wiped at his glasses and settled his helmet snug upon his head. "But we must try; orders are orders."

"*Scheissen, mein hauptmann.* Into the valley of death rode the—how many men have we left? We did not even start with six hundred."

Peering from beneath his helmet rim, Witzelei said, "You are a constant surprise to me, Sergeant."

"Because I can read? What about those lines in "The Charge of the Light Brigade" where it says someone had blundered? What about that?"

Another *Ami* shell struck the hillside above them and showered them with pebbles.

Arno hugged his Schmeisser close. "They are walking the barrage. It will soon be landing behind us, unless they mean to herd us forward into the machine guns, into our own valley of death."

"All right, sergeant, we shall wait the arrival of the panzers. But we will follow them wherever the orders lead us. You know that *landsers* do not think—they obey."

General von Thoma worked another American cigarette into his ivory holder. The brand didn't matter; all *Ami* tobacco was better than anything to be had in Germany these days. When that nation of mongrels—Jews and Negroes and the refugee scum of Europe and South America—was beaten to its knees it could continue to produce good things for the Third Reich. Mixed-blood shopkeepers and peasant farmers could not stand up to the motivated Aryans of Hitler's legions, but they could sweat.

The proof was all around him as the little convoy wound through the unbattered village of Tebessa, the unharmed trucks and piles of fine equipment abandoned when the Americans fled in blind panic from Afrika Korps panzers. Knowing full well that these same Arabs who turned from their looting to cheer had also cheered the enemy, von Thoma casually lifted his gloves to them in answer. Probably the same kind of heathen blood was also accepted into the mainstream of *Ami* life. Occupation would change all that.

Rommel's *panzerwagen* turned off into a narrow road between Arab mud shacks and tile-roofed French colonist houses on the other. Von Thoma, riding the newly captured vehicle called jeep by the Americans, tapped his gloves against his driver's shoulder in a signal to follow. He could not miss any off-the-record meetings of the Afrika Korps staff, for the delay in completely uncorking this end of Kasserine Pass had not further endeared the famous Desert Fox to General Kesselring in Rome. Von Thoma had nothing concrete to go on, only the intuition that had brought him so far up the ladder of rank. That told him that Rommel would not avoid his medical transfer for long, despite his earlier sweeping victory.

Smiling, von Thoma turned the thought in his mind that command would not necessarily be given to von Arnim. In his own hands Afrika Korps would be a plum indeed. No more losses of ground need occur; troops facing the Britisher Montgomery on the Mareth Line could hold defensive positions until Berlin, freed of the popularity threat of Rommel, sent in the supplies and reinforcements so badly needed. The Allies in Tunisia were already defeated, running back to their headquarters in Algiers.

There had been no opposition to the panzers on the Thala road, and even Italian tanks reported no resistance. Rommel had been correct in insisting on breaking the stoppage established by *Ami* artillery and a British force, but he was a fool when he grew this cautious. He still hesitated, even in the midst of this easy conquest, even though Intelligence told him that the way was clear for a continuing drive deep into Allied territory.

Von Thoma climbed from his vehicle and strolled to the gathering of staff in the building shadows. The smell was still that of Arab urine that had soaked the clay walls for a hundred years. A few daisies and scarlet poppies bloomed along a fence, only a shadow of the spring drifts of flowers that had shone back in the pass before the six-barreled Nebelwerfer rocket launchers began firing. The rockets had screamed into artillery positions, and the wounded *Amis* screamed in the echoes. Reaching aside, he crushed a little stand of red poppies with the sole of his polished boot.

Rommel spoke as von Thoma closed on the little group: "The enemy is planning a counterattack by tomorrow at the latest—that much is obvious. I have halted the columns so that they may consolidate and prepare. Rome headquarters reports by radio that British and American reinforcements are pouring into this area to defend Tebessa and Thala."

Colonel Krause passed a canteen to von Thoma; it smelled of schnapps from home. Von Thoma took a long and grateful pull and handed back the canteen, which went in turn to the field marshal. Rommel shook his head. The fool seldom warmed his cold, middle-class belly with strong drink. What was he afraid of exposing while in his cups?

Krause said, "I quite understand, sir. The reports say that forty to fifty pieces of medium artillery are arriving to defend Thala. Shall I send word to General von Broich to hold up?"

Rommel showed his profile for an enlisted photographer, appearing to be deep in thought. A flashbulb went off. "Not yet," the great man said. "Sightings by the Luftwaffe tend to exaggerate, and we should at the least take Thala before halting."

At least, von Thoma thought. The man was finally cracking under pressure. The Führer had expressly forbidden any more withdrawals, and even field marshals were not excluded from his wrath.

He cleared his throat. "Independent reports have reached me that the guns are from the U.S. 9th Infantry Division, commanded by Brigadier General Irwin. These doubt so many guns but are certain that the *Amis* have just ended a forced march of four days from Algeria over these muddy roads. They are weary and unfit for combat."

Rommel's eyes below the lifted dust goggles were piercing. "So, independent reports?"

"Delivered to me only moments ago, Herr Feldmarschall."

Rommel did not look away. "Delivered horseback, one would suppose, while you rode behind me."

"Motorcyle messenger, sir. I would not presume to tell the Feldmarschall when and where to halt."

Grunting, Rommel put his leather back to von Thoma and Colonel Krause, lowering his voice as he spoke to his officers. "Broich's group will attack and attack again until all of the Tebessa road and Thala is ours." He glanced around again. "And this staff—all my staff—will ride in immediately behind the infantry—immediately behind. Is that understood?"

Von Thoma swallowed; Colonel Krause managed a weak, "*Jawohl, mein herr.*"

Up ahead panzers rumbled onto the road, and the first *Ami* shell burst among them.

CHAPTER 34

Special to *The New York Times*—Washington, D.C., April 8, 1943: There will be no army commission, "at least for the present," for New York Mayor Fiorello LaGuardia. Secretary of War Henry Stimson said the mayor had offered his personal and patriotic services but was "too valuable" to the nation in his present position.

ASSOCIATED PRESS—With the II U.S. Corps in Tunisia, April 8, 1943 [delayed]: Two army sergeants, William Brown from Devonshire, England, and Joseph Randall, State Center, Iowa, stopped on the Gafsa–Gabes highway today to shake hands: Thus the British 8th Army out of Libya and Americans up from Algeria met as a gigantic trap began to close on the Afrika Korps retreat.

Staff Sergeant Eddie Donnely was eager to see her. He had been too long in too many hospitals, but at last the doctors thought they'd patched him enough to hold. From tent hospitals in the field through Hawaii, San Francisco and Halloran General on Staten Island, where he thought the specialists were done with him. But no, there was a hotshot doctor at Walter Reed, where Washington politicians and high brass were treated. He thought he could plug the holes in Eddie's lung for good and stop that damned whistling noise.

Doctor Silipo did what the others hadn't: he made Eddie breathe right, so he could work out in physiotherapy and get himself into some kind of shape.

Could that get him back into action? Well, the medics said, nobody could promise that; there were the parasites, the malaria and dengue fever; maybe other exotic diseases yet undiscovered in his system. He wasn't quite ready for active duty yet and had to remain in the hospital a while. Anyhow, he'd already done his duty on Guadalcanal, what with his Silver Star and Purple Heart. He ought to be happy to sit out the rest of the war.

The hell he would. His father was still overseas, and the Americal Division was marking time in the Fiji Islands, but he knew the outfit would be fighting again in the South Pacific. The war was a long way from over, and it was Eddie's job to be in it. No matter how many Japs other soldiers killed, it was his duty to exact a blood debt for Captain Jim Shelby.

Until that was possible, he could be happy about this three-day pass, eager for his first date with a woman who interested him more, drew him to her more, than any he'd ever known. She had electrified Eddie from the first morning she came to work on the wards as a volunteer for the Red Cross.

There was a thing deeply compelling about her, a quiet and secret sensual power that underlay her every movement and each throaty murmur. Lighting a Camel and closing his eyes, Eddie brought the image of her brightly against his eyelids. Sitting in the hospital waiting room, he listened to piped music, to Peggy Lee's great rendition of a new blues song: *"Why don't you do right, like some other men do . . ."*

That tapered into a softer, upbeat number by the Andrews Sisters, a song that had been popular before he shipped overseas: "I'll be with you in apple blossom time . . . I'll be with you to change your name to mine . . ."

Uh-uh, Eddie. The only thing that applies to you is the time of year. Apple orchards bloomed white and pink on small, rolling farms outside Fort Devens, Massachusetts, where he'd been shanghaied for a little while to a do-nothing housekeeping unit for punching out some officer's kid. Before the World War I post had been rebuilt and expanded for the First Infantry to move in, and upgraded from "Camp" to "Fort," Devens had been outer Siberia with apple blossoms, a punishment tour for eight balls.

Gloria; she remained imprinted on his mind, moving so graceful and easy, writing letters for guys who couldn't, pushing the library cart and trailing a clean scent of soap and flowers. She only showed up on Mondays, and nobody called her whistle bait. The patients acted as if she was everyone's sister, or an untouchable maiden aunt. It took a practiced eye to see that she was an exceptional woman.

". . . some day in May, I'll come and say, happy the bride that the sun shines on today . . ."

Hell, he had no intention of marrying Gloria or any other woman who might take a chance on him. Not only did he move among many women and would find it difficult to break the habit, he was already wed. She was a tough old bitch with a hard ass and OD drawers. He got hitched to her when first he raised his right hand and swore to defend the Constitution of the United States against all enemies foreign or domestic.

Right now his wife had her tit caught in a wringer, and what civilian could pry her loose? There were the undraftable 4-Fs busy building planes and tanks, doing all right at making ammunition and equipment. But it took ornery men to turn the crank handle and free the old bitch. Eddie grinned; some GIs claimed to hold a 4-F military rank.

Barracks talk: 4-F—Find 'em, fool 'em, fuck 'em, forget 'em.

That didn't hold true for Eddie; he never fooled a woman about anything. When he said he loved them he did, and he proved it. But he never mentioned marriage, and he tried never to forget any of them. Women who had shared their love with him were beautiful memories to be brought forth and savored during the lost and lonely times, and he didn't regret any of them.

Gloria said, "Hi, Eddie. Sorry I'm late."

Climbing out of the chair, he pulled his overseas cap out of his shoulder loop. "That's okay. I was just listening to the music. That's one of the things you don't think about until it's gone. Like dry socks and milk."

She looked great, standing there straight-backed and chin up, wearing only a touch of lipstick and no rouge or mascara. Her skin was clear and luminous, and her eyes didn't need accenting; they were warm and deep with hidden promises. He liked how her brown hair drifted loose and unfrizzed to wide shoulders held squared. Eddie cocked his cap over his right eye, the khaki cap with infantry blue piping, and smiled at her.

"I saved up my gas ration stamps," she said. "Since you have a pass, I got a short leave from my regular job, and we can take a long drive. It's up in New York, but I'd really like to show you the old family homestead. Is that okay? The nurses said this is your first time out, so if you'd rather go dancing and bar-hopping . . ."

"Whatever you want is fine with me," he said, and he meant it. He only wanted her. On their first date she would drive him home to meet her family? That was kind of strange, and he'd have to be as honest with her as he'd been with other women. Maybe more so, and that could turn the weekend into a dry run. Still, Gloria had that aura . . .

She drove the '40 Ford business coupe deftly, threading traffic lighter than normal, thanks to gas rationing. The car radio purred, its music rising and falling as broadcast stations fell behind and others picked up. ". . . we meet, and the angels sing . . ."

"There's an oldie," she said. "Nineteen thirty-nine, wasn't it? I always liked this song."

". . . you speak, and the angels sing, and I hear music in every word . . ."

Eddie was acutely conscious of her nearness, her fragrance, the smooth roundness of her thigh and the sculpted swell of her bare calf, the skin tinted brown to imitate nylon stockings difficult to find in wartime. He had been a long time without a woman, and this one was so vibrant. He sensed a hunger in her to match his own and forced himself to light a Camel and offer her one.

"No, thanks." It was a whisper that made him turn and stare blindly out the window.

Oh, hell; he was Eddie Donnely, in the old days known army-wide as a cocksman first class. So why was he acting like a scared cherry out on his first date?

Inching his window down, he let cigarette smoke out and the world in. The damned radio finally quit playing "And the Angels Sing:"

". . . and leave their music ringing in my heart . . ."

She turned the thing off, and they talked; rather, he talked. She asked him about his family and his life. Keeping his eyes off her legs, he told her of being born on an army post and never wanting life to be any different, about Big Mike still soldiering overseas. He didn't tell her of his mother, that dried and holy woman so begrimed by the black sins of sex that she drove her husband to the lying love of an officer's bitch.

Gloria didn't seem surprised that he'd known nothing but the uniform and chatted knowingly about what was happening on all combat fronts. He watched her damp mouth as she spoke, and the sleek, throbbing line of her throat.

"Here we are," she announced, and she turned the car through massive iron gates that might shield a castle or guard a prison. Gravel rattled beneath the tires along a road that curved often upon itself through barricades of tall trees.

And there was the house, the huge, dark towers, the dragon bulk tensed to spring.

"Jesus," he breathed.

"Not who the Carlisles had in mind when they first raised Sandhurst Keep," she said. "That would be George of England and his bloody lobsterbacks."

Eddie stared. "It's so—so damned—"

"Yes. I wanted you to know what you're getting into. This ugly pile of granite and petrified logs represents my family—tough and hard and at times unforgiving. We Carlisles have always been military, too."

When she climbed down from the car Eddie got out and went around to meet her. "Not my kind of military. Your name tag said Johnson, but you—damn. This is officer country. General Carlisle—*Crusty* Carlisle?"

"My grandfather. I was married to a man named Johnson for a few months—half a man, half a marriage. I should have said something, but I didn't want to scare you off."

He bumped one tight fist against the other. "I didn't know that you—oh, hell, woman. I come from Soapsuds Row, not Field Grade Avenue. It's not true that the colonel's lady and Judy O'Grady are sisters under the skin, and you damned well know it. Kipling also said that never the twain shall meet. Why don't we forget this mistake and start back to the hospital?"

"Why don't you shut up?"

She turned against him, and his arms came around her. She fitted the fullness of her rich body to him warm and eager, her mouth lifting for his kiss. Oh, God—she tasted of pink apple blossoms and leaping springtime, a sweet purity he had not known for a long, long time. The hesitant flick of her tongue was soft and unsure, the love offering of a young girl.

He said it again: "Jesus."

She drew back a single step and took his hand. "Oh,

yes—Jesus. Come with me, Eddie Donnely. I knew who you were all the time. I heard about you from my grandfather and from General Belvale. But I didn't tell either of them that you were at Walter Reed because they'd have made a fuss over you. I want this first weekend at Sandhurst Keep to be ours alone. The servants are gone, even Molly the cook. Especially Molly; she'd be shocked—not at you, but by me. Prim and proper Gloria doesn't do wild things."

Shaken more by her kiss than the news that he was off limits, he allowed himself to be led into the big room. She turned to him again, and this time his hands tenderly wandered her body as his tongue probed her gasping mouth. Gloria trembled beneath his caresses, and she lifted on tiptoe to move her pelvis against him.

Panting, she broke away to stare into his eyes, surprising him by the glint of tears in her own. "Oh, Eddie, Eddie—I know I'm not beautiful, and even though I was married I'm dumb about—about love. But I know it has to be better than what I—than what m-my husband did to me. I know it has to be more than hurt and anger. Tell me, Eddie. Show me how—please show me."

He didn't ask where was a bedroom or carry her to one of the long couches. Her knees went weak, and she sank easily to the carpet when he drew her down with him. Slowly and carefully he undressed her. That luminous skin went pink as he stroked the perfection of her tip-tilted breasts and palmed the hills and valleys of Gloria's marvelous body.

When he started to remove his clothes she pushed his hands aside and did it for him, face down and blushing, fumbling at buttons and belt but determined to finish. Then the awkwardness went away, and she flowed beneath him. He admired the way her naked thighs were jeweled connections to her hips, a delightful framing for the soft centering of her mound. Lightly he thumbed those joinings, tantalizing himself as much as her. And then he loved her slowly,

slowly, despite her sudden abandon and repeated sobbing cries of completion.

"Never," she murmured, "never, never—"

And he was no longer certain that he had ever loved before, either. He was sure of only one thing—that Gloria Carlisle was beautiful.

CHAPTER 35

RESTRICTED—New Delhi, India, HQ, CBI Theater, 0700, 3 May, 1943: Enemy radio communications intercepted here report a large raiding party has been observed by air patrols. This is understood to be Brigadier Wingate's band of Chindits, which has successfully sabotaged the Mandalay–Myitkynia railway in several places. These guerilla actions, plus cutting roads, destroying bridges and attacking outposts in enemy rear areas, have caused the Japanese to commit two infantry divisions to the field with orders to pursue and destroy.

Keenan lay flat, watching the narrow dirt road that curved into this opening in the jungle. Even filtered through the leafy canopy overhead, the sun beat down upon him, and the moist air was thick to breathe. Sweat slid down his ribs and dripped off his face. An insect walked the back of his neck, and he only blinked. This was a well-used Jap supply trail, and a convoy of carts was due soon. He didn't move; the grasshoppers and crickets chirred on; a bird shrilled from a treetop. The smell of rot oozed around him.

This ambush was Keenan's operation; Wingate had his main body of Chindits miles from here, its mission to blow a major bridge and to knock out an enemy position astride the main supply route. Raids had hurt the Jap MSR, and they were beefing up protection.

On each side of this trail a Bren gunner waited in the brush, his automatic weapon angled to sweep the target area without firing into his own troops. Gurkhas hid in tangles of vines, ferociously eager to open fire and then rush close for bloody work with bayonets and knives. They waited for the signal, a blast from around the curve.

Back there two men waited in a camouflaged hole. When the tail of the plodding Jap column cleared them they would detonate a spread of antipersonnel mines to start the show. Besides killing off a few spare Japs, the explosions would spook the draft animals and stampede them into the loaded carts ahead, creating more panic and squealing confusion. It was a good ambush, and Keenan hoped the Japs would be hauling more food than ammunition.

Lately the British air drops hadn't been getting through with any regularity, forcing the men to live off the land and eat the pack animals they'd brought into the jungle. The diet change made little difference to the Burmese and Gurkhas, who got along well on roasted locusts, monkey meat and the shoots of jungle greenery; they also prized stews made from great pythons. Keenan had already proved that he could subsist on almost anything.

Staring at a red ant that explored the bolt of his M-1, Keenan ran his tongue over dry lips, sweated, and thought on Wingate. The man had turned weirder the longer they were gone from the base camp in India, and he hadn't been all that stable to begin with. True, the mission of the 77th Indian Infantry Brigade was being accomplished, but Wingate's personal quirks might screw it up before long.

"Whatsoever thy hand findeth to do, do it with thy might" was his favorite quote from Ecclesiastes, but it had nothing to do with the brigadier's belief that staying on the move and marching fast prevented malaria. Hell, the *Anopheles* mosquito flew faster than a man could run, and the forced pace on a road march only ground down men already weary from weeks of fighting the hostile jungle, as well as the Japanese.

Leg ulcers, fever and dysentery were weakening about everyone, but so far Keenan's group had managed to stay together. He didn't want to think ahead to the time when some man might have to be left behind. If wounds or illness made him a drag on the team, Keenan would just walk—or crawl—off into the jungle. Wingate had talked of that himself.

And the only time Wingate didn't talk was when he was part of an ambush. In camp he would pace and quote the Bible; he would deliver lectures on ancient or modern literature and eighteenth-century art. The British soldiers whispered that he was really Brigadier Bela Lugosi and hung upside down to sleep. Most of the Gurkhas and Burmese bandits didn't understand him anyway. But Wingate had one thing going for him: he had an expertise in killing Japs, and that made him okay with Keenan.

Lifting his head an inch or two, he listened harder and picked up the creaking of cart wheels and a fainter *ting* of harness metal, the smallest tremble in the earth. The Japs were coming up the road.

Bram-blam-WHAM!

The antipersonnel mines went off, and Arisaka rifles popped wildly in response. A donkey brayed and a camel squalled, and the head of the ragged column boiled around the curve. Shouting, an officer wheeled his skinny horse and waved his pistol.

Keenan shot him in the back and knocked him off the horse. The M-1 kicked lightly against his shoulder, and he smelled gunsmoke. The Bren guns opened up, and the Gurkhas fired their Enfields into the chaos. Keenan tasted the tang of burned powder, rolling it upon his tongue as the shooting deafened him.

Animals went down in the hail of bullets, a gray mule kicking, a knobby-legged camel trying to buck, donkeys dropped in their harness. But the men fell with them, jungle caps flapping and spinning off. One Jap twisted in midair, caught by a burst as he leapt for safety. Clinging to his rifle, another outraced all odds, the bullets kicking dirt all around him.

When he reached the jungle edge a Gurkha rose from the brush and took off his head with one mighty swing of a curved *kurkri* blade. The body spurted red for several steps before it crashed into a thorn bush.

The firing stopped, and Chindits came out of hiding to move cautiously into the road, weapons at the ready. Keenan moved among them to catch the reins of the Jap officer's horse and tether the survivor to a sapling. Then he walked over and put the muzzle of his M-1 to the back of the sub-lieutenant's head.

He pulled the trigger and blew the bastard's face off. Maybe he had still been alive, maybe not, but it wasn't a mercy killing. It was always better to kill them twice and be sure. Turbans bobbing, the Gurkhas moved among the fallen Japanese, cutting every throat, making sure their way.

"Rice," British Corporal Wragge said. "Plenty of sodding rice and dried kippers, like. I say, now—no tea to brew, but here's a few bottles of Nip whiskey. Get all the food and drink, lads—it'll hold off chewing on bloody snakes for a fortnight."

Singsonging among themselves, the Burmese got busy, dressing out the downed animals for meat, ignoring the blowflies already gathering in clouds. Buzzing greenish black, the flies settled to feed upon dead animal and gory Jap alike.

The Gurkhas hustled through the carts for anything usable. The rest—Jap weapons, ammunition and some gear—got piled onto a single cart. Keenan set the booby trap himself—a rifle stock wired to the pin of a British grenade centered in a hidden nest of Jap grenades. The trouble with a Jap grenade was that after the pin was pulled the starter had to be knocked against something hard, usually the helmet. In the jungle silence a tapping sound meant a handful of hell was on the way.

Without orders a pair of Gurkhas worked the camel free of its harness and dragged it aside. Keenan backed a step and looked over the heaped cart; it appeared as if it had been stacked up to haul away. The Japs would think that the guerrillas had been scared off before they could move the loot, and some simple bastard would be ordered to unload it. Bingo!

He pointed. "The headless Jap."

Grinning beneath his tended black mustache, the chunky Gurkha sergeant took another man and brought back the slow-dripping corpse. The horse snorted and rolled white eyes at the fresh blood scent, but Keenan stroked and calmed him. They strapped the dead Jap across the saddle, and Keenan led the horse back upon the road. Heading it back toward the rear, he slipped its bridle and slapped the bony rump, forcing the animal into a trot that flopped the Jap's dangled arms and legs.

"Load up and move out!" he called. "Let's get the troops out of the hot sun!"

Somewhere down the line horse and rider would be found. That would remind the Emperor's soldiers that a horrible *yonsei* still roamed the jungle. They would become more superstitious about the ghost that fed upon the heads of men. Maybe they would whisper again of The One Who Will Not Die.

Penny stomped hard upon a rat and broke its back. She crushed its head with her heel and kicked it aside to use later. This shabby little room was all they had for a nursery, kid's hospital and school. A boy and girl, both seven; two-year-old Haig, too sick to be told he was now an orphan; three unlucky babies born behind wire. If these kids were the future of women in this camp, the future was starting with short odds: five against millions of goddamn Japs.

It was her turn to play nurse and teacher, and she started

by bathing little Haig. The rats had eaten the last slivers of soap, so she wiped him down as best she could with a rag and cool water. "Little" was a word that could be applied to all the children; they were all stunted, half-starved and wormy. They probably would never catch up to their proper size, if they lived through the war.

There was nothing Penny could do about that, beyond trading with pliant guards or stealing scraps of food when her nursery shift was coming up. What she did was to make damned sure the kids remembered a better world outside, and that they hated Japs deep and hard and would someday take revenge. Some of the guards played with the older kids and even slipped them fruit or a bit of raw fish. That was okay; anything that brought food was okay, even to what a few of the women were doing—screwing pet Japs. Penny just wanted the kids to know that the Jap—any Jap—was a mean and miserable bastard and the cause of their mothers being prisoners, their fathers being tortured or murdered.

"Penny?" Sarah had round blue eyes and hair once golden. Vitamin lack had turned it dingy. "I'm scared to take my nap. I saw a big cenni—centipede in my corner."

"Don't be a baby," Harry said. "Hit it with the stick."

Sarah tried to cry. "It's big and ugly—"

Penny said quietly, "Harry's right, dear. You have to take care of yourself. You might be alone." She handed the girl the stick, the only weapon in the shack, used at night to beat off rats that came down out of the thatch roof.

Swallowing audibly, Sarah inched over to the corner and prodded at the floor. The centipede got away through a crack.

"See, dear? It's more scared of you, and you'll get it next time."

Penny cleaned the babies—Susan, Roy and Daisy. She fed them a paste of coconut oil, chopped sweet potato tops and rice. She rocked them and teased them, then induced them to play with each other. They really didn't know how and tired easily.

She put in an hour on math and spelling, using a twig and the shallow baking pan filled with sand. Nobody recalled where the pan came from, but it served as a makeshift blackboard. It began to rain, and she moved the babies and Haig to the dripless corner, away from the open windows. The roof hammered and rattled, but Harry and Sarah wanted to run outside in the rain, and Penny said all right.

Then she looked over at the rat she had killed and wondered if she would sneak it into the pot tonight or trade it for something. The tears gushed suddenly, and she wiped at them.

"Surprise," she said. "I thought I was all out. It's the damned rat—options on what to do with a damned rat." Burying her face in her hands, her rough and callused hands, she wondered what had become of a girl that had once been called pretty Penny.

"Hello there." Stephanie crawled barefoot into the room and shook water from her sawed-off hair.

Practically all the women cropped their hair now; it was easier to keep clean and free of lice. They used the clippings to stuff patched-together rags as mattresses for the babies. The damned rats came in the dark to gnaw at those, too.

Stephanie said, "Truly the biblical deluge out there. You'd think the bloody camp would float out to sea. Perhaps a Yank submarine would torpedo us and we'd drown all the Japs. At least Major Wobbly would get his boots dirty."

"Maybe drowning wouldn't be so awful. The sea must be cool and peaceful."

"Wheest, lass; are you that sad, then? Not my Penny Belvale. Is it the children? I'll care for the bairns if you—"

Penny pointed a finger. "It's a dead rat. Stevie, I couldn't decide about it. The thing turned so damned important. Oh, God—how much longer can we survive this hellhole?"

Stephanie reached out, and Penny tucked her head into her friend's shoulder. "We will last it out because we must. You braved the day tied to that post and made the bastards respect you. The war goes on, and our men will return for us. We canna allow our Japs to win either. We canna let Wobbly defeat you and me and these babes."

This time Penny was right about the tears; she had used the last of them. She kept her face buried in the comforting vee of Stevie's shoulder for a few minutes more.

When she murmured thanks and sat back Stephanie said, "He sent for you, did Wobbly, and gave no reason. I can convince the whoreson that you're ill, and—"

Penny said, "He'd only punish you instead. I can't think of anything I did, but if you watch the kids, I'll see what he wants. Maybe it's only me."

She tried to smile at Stevie, but Stevie didn't smile back.

CHAPTER 36

REUTERS NEWS AGENCY—With the British 8th Army in Tunisia, May 13, 1943: Today German Colonel-General Jürgen von Arnim surrendered himself and 250,000 soldiers of the Afrika Korps to Field Marshal Harold Alexander, commanding.

Alexander treated him with courtesy, gave him supper and lodgings for the night and said, "He expected me to say what a splendid fight his men put up. I disappointed him."

The marshal cabled Winston Churchill: "Sir, it is my duty to report the Tunisian campaign over. Enemy resistance has ceased, and we are masters of the North African shores."

INS FEATURE SYNDICATE—Algiers, North Africa, former HQ of Free French forces, May 13, 1943: Papers translated here show that French General Henri Giraud, then heading Legionnaires in Tunisia, asked General Charles de Gaulle, overall commander, for an additional ten divisions of troops. De Gaulle replied: "Why should any Frenchman give his life to liberate France when her allies can do the job, leaving France stronger?"

It all seemed so damned pointless. A new and bloodier campaign started as soon as the old one ended, each battle only trading men's lives for real estate. But Jim had believed and given all for his faith; so must she.

She tried hard, but Kirstin Belvale-Shelby remained hollow. She knew if somebody flicked a thumbnail against the deadness of her skin, she would echo like an empty washtub. All about her as she sat waiting in the cab of the pickup life went on little changed in Boerne, Texas.

Cibilo Creek still wandered through town to cross South Main/Highway 87 and plunge suddenly underground southeast of town. The same spiced odor of mesquite rode a light and muggy breeze; folks never failed to lower their voices in deference as they walked past the Robert E. Lee house where he rested many times when he was a U.S. Cavalry colonel.

Mothers, wives and sweethearts of Boerne men overseas still knelt to pray in St. Peter's old stone church. Maybe their appeals would protect their loves; Kirstin's prayers had not. Jim Shelby's dead body was buried on a jungle island nobody could even name until last year.

Oh, Jim's name would be long remembered here, for he had truly been one of the people, and they were proud of his climb to represent Texas in the Senate of the United States. Fame and memory, or what the family in Virginia called duty—none of that helped her through the lonely nights or brought back her husband's smile.

Upbeat victory stories in the *Boerne Star* didn't keep her from worrying about her sons. Owen was off fighting in Africa, and Farley was hospitalized in Hawaii; the army wouldn't fill her in on what had happened to him. She only knew that he was physically whole and might be shipped back soon. She wouldn't have that much information if Nancy hadn't written directly. It was hard for Kirstin to believe Nancy had become a nurse, an important part of the war effort, and was taking care of Farley. Life was so screwed up, only sometimes coming out right.

Sighing, Kirstin admitted that she also worried about Chad Belvale. Jim had been a beginner at soldiering and was given so little time to learn combat. Chad had been a professional since birth, but he was so damned duty oriented that he would defy fate, and a bullet didn't differentiate between professional and amateur.

No woman could live with a man as long as she had been married to Chad, and bear him two sons, without fretting that he might get his fool self killed. Chad had not been a complete bastard. There was tenderness in the beginning, and the boys they had produced, and sometimes it had been good being part of that special family—

The pickup bed bounced, and she flinched, then remembered she was at the loading platform of Ramsey and Palmer Feed Store. Men dropped heavy sacks of grain and slid salt blocks into her truck, and she'd soon have to drive home. She never looked forward to walking the empty rooms where old laughter lingered in shadowed corners.

Home was the Bar-S Ranch north of town on the Guadalupe River. She wished she could change the river's name; it always reminded her of Guadalcanal. Partly because of it, for a time she had considered selling the ranch and moving. Not back to Virginia, just to another place. It wouldn't help. She'd never forget where and how Jim died anyhow.

So it was better to keep his ranch going, producing beef for the army, no longer showing her horses but caring for them, doing whatever to stay busy. After the war she intended to build the ranch library into a lasting memorial to Jim Shelby, but now it seemed she wasn't doing enough. She headed up scrap metal drives, helped collect grease and old rubber tires for the defense effort and planted twenty acres of vegetables for a charitable victory garden.

It didn't seem nearly enough, but each time General Belvale called to update his reports on Chad and the boys he said ranch production was what the country needed. Unconvinced, she didn't know what else to do, what other jobs would make her tired enough to sleep through the night.

"Okay, Miz Shelby, all loaded."

"Thank you."

She drove through town and past Kreutzberg Road. Its name always reminded her of the Germans who had settled here to found the town and spread through what was now Kendall County. They'd been sturdy and hardworking, standing against the wild hill country and wilder Comanches. It was ironic that much of this war was being fought against the homeland of those pioneers. And before that time there had been the Kaiser.

Pushing the truck along Highway 474 with hot wind in her face, she crossed the Guadalupe River bridge and turned onto the Bar-S private road, where dust rolled up thicker behind the bouncing Chevy pickup. She passed the house, deliberately ignoring the pillared front porch where Jim had liked to sit in the evening and look out over the twilight pastures.

Kirstin stopped between the high, thick walls of the round breaking pen and the pole arena where started horses were brought for polish. The ranch hands gathered at the rail as her foreman swung open the gate and one of Jim's quarter horses skittered in with a strange kid on its back.

She strode forward. "Gregorio, what the hell—"

Gregorio Venegas turned and spread his hands. "*Señora, por favor*—it is my brother's son who demanded—"

"Demanded? Damn it, if you let one of Jim's colts be spoiled by—"

She cut it off when she saw the bandage covering the boy's eyes, when she noticed that he wore the green work utilities of the Marines. Then the horse took a short run and crow-hopped. When the bay stallion spun the rider lost one stirrup.

"*Madre mia,*" Venegas said. "I begged that one, but he would not hear."

Blind; the kid couldn't see a damned thing and was trying to sit a rank young horse. He'd get his fool neck broken. The ranch hands hollered "Ride him, cowboy," and yipped their high-pitched yells of excitement. One slapped the top rail with his hat. Chico Guerra, she saw; Moose Moran and José Lorenzo. If that crazy boy got hurt, they could draw their time and go on down the road, along with Venegas.

The horse squalled and jarred the earth on four stiff legs, squealed again in rage and bounced up to sunfish. He left the kid high in the air to come wheeling down and slam the ground hard.

"Goddamnit!" Kirstin ducked between the rails and ran to the sprawled rider. On the edge of her vision she saw Gregorio reach the bucking horse and snatch its headstall.

She helped the kid sit up. "Boy—are you hurt?"

He spat dirt. "Boy, hell! I'm a goddamn Marine, lady."

Holding to her arm, he wobbled up. The bandages slipped from his eyes and exposed scarred sockets and flat, wrinkled lids. He pushed the bandages back into place.

Kirstin wanted to brush the dust from his face and hair but didn't reach out. She said, "You're a goddamn fool, and that's my horse."

He brought out an olive-drab handkerchief and wiped his face, his feet braced wide, puffing some. "You're Miz Shelby, then. I'm Manny Venegas, and I guess since the Canal I'll be just an ex–Marine when my hospital leave is over. Don't blame Tio Gregorio—I kind of forced him.

"Your horse—I was just beginning to rodeo when the war started. Then I got hit right off, and they sent me home. Oh, hell, lady, I had to find out if I had any guts left. So I had a wreck on your horse, and didn't make the horn, but for a few seconds on that bronc's back I felt like—felt like I was a whole man again."

She kept her fingers on his arm and guided him to the gate. The ranch hands had unsaddled the horse, and Gregorio led him snorting back to his stall.

Kirstin said, "You're a man, all right—crazy, but *mucho hombre*. My husband . . ."

There was no point in talking about Jim; this boy-man had been there, too. A hazy idea began to form in her mind.

"I heard he bought it on the Canal," Manny said. "A lot of guys did. Maybe they're better off that way."

Shaking him, she said, "Damn you! Do you think I wouldn't want Jim home, blind or crippled or in little pieces? You're not buried on that stinking island, you're right here, so live, damn you—live!"

He said, "Sorry, ma'am," and he put an arm around her shoulder; she clung to him for a steadying moment, smelling dust and horse and man. Then she moved back and said, "Other guys in the hospitals—like the Harmon General over in Longview—do you think it might make them feel better to ride? To take a better hold on their lives? Of course they'd be on school horses, not some hammerhead bucker—"

"You know what they say: The outside of a horse is good for the inside of a man. Sure, I figure any crip could get his confidence back if he didn't have to depend on somebody to move him around. You feel taller on a horse."

Kirstin said, "That's it, what I've been looking for. Manny Venegas, come on back here as soon as you get discharged. If you want it, you have a job helping me with a riding program for wounded vets."

In Bizerte Chad Belvale celebrated by getting drunk with his son. Through bottles of Malaga wine they spoke in hushed tones of Djebel Tahent, Hill 609; they detailed the taking of its neighboring hills and being pushed back off them by counterattacks. They remembered names that should go down in history—Faid Pass, El Guettar, Gafsa and Gabes, Fondouk; they remembered the Mateur Plain and the final drive through the hard, choppy country, that last, weary offensive that rolled up German resistance on the II Corps front.

"Who'll know those towns a year from now, much less the hundred dirty little fights without a name or number? Who'll count up so damned many casualties?" Chad said. "So many friends lost, good soldiers—"

"So many friends still alive," Owen said, lifting his wine glass. "That's how I hold it easy in my mind, by the ones who are still around." The kid had grown up fast and now gave good advice to his old man. Chad drank; the packed café smelled urgently of garlic, red table wine and sweaty OD wool. The cigarette smoke had different odors—black French/Arab, stale English, crisper American tobacco; it puddled blue and drifted above the tables, gray tributaries fingering through loud talk. Laughter cut itself short by quick silences when somebody remembered too much. It picked up with frenetic spurts of energy as glasses were raised to the dead by the living who knew the guilt of survivors.

Somebody across the room sang:

Dirty Gertie from Bizerte
Hid a mousetrap 'neath her skirty,
Baited it with fleur-de-flirty,
Made the GI peckers hurty . . .

Chad leaned across the table to say, "Your promotion came through, and you earned those railroad tacks, Captain. I bitched, but I'm still being moved up to regiment. Terry Allen insists on his own people getting the promotions because a lot of unshot-at replacements are coming in loaded with rank. That made little Teddy Roosevelt bang around with that mortar-aiming stake he carries for a cane. He threatened to fly to Washington if division men got shoved around."

Combat aged everybody, and Owen was no exception. At odd angles his face was a stranger's, drawn and moody. He would stop in the middle of a sentence, and the thousand-yard stare of the battle-worn infantryman would glaze his eyes.

He came out of one drift-off to say, "Sorry, Dad."

"Happens to us all, son."

By far most of the English 8th and 1st armies gathered

in Tunis, a few guarding the main body of obedient Kraut POWs. There were almost a quarter million Aryan supermen who had had their asses kicked good and realized it. But some Brits collected in Bizerte, and one lifted a penetrating voice to sing back at the GIs:

Bless 'em all, bless 'em all,
the long and the short and the tall,
For there'll be no promotion
this side of the ocean,
So cheer up, me lads, bless 'em all!

Then the guy yelled, "Except for the bloody RAF! They get promoted for shining their arses in Cairo!"

Chad stared through the smoke. "Holy shit!"

Owen blinked at him. "What's the matter?"

Leaping up, Chad elbowed through the crowd, knocking over chairs and one table. He roared, "Merriman! You sodding Cockney son of a bitch—"

The Englishman banged into him, hammering his back. "Belvale! Bloody Yank bastard—where've you been hiding? An effing colonel, are you? What a balls up! Now we've lost the war for certain."

Chad stared at the shiny steel hook at the end of Johnny Merriman's right sleeve. "You're out of your mind. Captain, what the hell are you doing back in a combat zone—and with that thing?"

Merriman reached up and tapped the hook at his left shoulder. "Still three pips, I'll have you know. Sir, Captain Merriman, J.J., reporting. But a bloody wounded hero, and didn't it piss them to exalt me, not knowing I refused to walk civvy street right off."

Shaking his head, Chad said, "Come to my table and meet my son. You can't be a line officer with that thing—"

"Well, you fucked off and didn't bring my hand back from Dieppe, so I had to become the highest-ranking motorcyle courier in all Africa. My hook fits this loop on the gas grip, and I zip along arse over teakettle. You can imagine what the lads call me—Captain Hook."

He put his good hand on Chad's arm. "Your boy—what would he know of Stephanie? Wouldn't want to sully old Dad's reputation."

"No, I haven't said anything to him about her. Johnny, is there any word of her? In England they promised to let me know, but we've been on the move so long."

The celebration howled and shook around them. A limey and a GI got into a fight, and glass crashed. But it only upset the French barkeep, and nobody else pitched in. A Legionnaire sang teary verses that nobody understood.

Merriman put his head close to say, "She is definitely listed as a prisoner of war, and now a bit of late word is coming out of Malaysia. Contraband radios, border crossers, coast watchers and the like. Leftenant Bartlett was alive a month past."

It's something to hang onto, Chad thought. That brightness and love of Stephanie still lived. The Jap prisons were torture camps run by sadists where men who had made it through the Bataan death march were beaten, starved and beheaded. The civilian internment camps wouldn't be much different, if any. Japs were Japs, just as Krauts would never change.

Which was why the Big Red One would have to trek back through the scene of its humiliating defeat at Kasserine Pass. Orders were already being processed at headquarters, before the smoke faded and the echoes of Tunisia died. The division would head all the way back to Algeria for new arms and equipment, and to train for anything new in tactics in seaborne landings.

Oh, yes, and a rest period. A damned short rest, because odds were being laid on a quick assault before the Krauts recovered from their beating here. The target would be what Churchill and the press called the "soft underbelly" of Europe—the tip of Italy's boot, the islands of Sicily or Sardinia; less probably northern Italy and southern France.

Soft, hell. The Nazis had another half million troops waiting on those beaches behind ramparts of steel. Filling their glasses with wine that Algerian *colons* had kept hidden from the German armistice committee, Chad lifted his own.

"Here's to us, and here's to now, because that's all there is."

"Hear, hear," Merriman said. "It's enough."

Owen Belvale only nodded.

CHAPTER 37

Berliner Illustrierte Zeitung—North African theater, May 15, 1942: Betrayed by vacillating leadership, certain units of the Afrika Korps have left Africa in order to defend important positions in Sicily, by orders of Field Marshal Kesselring in Rome.

Long commander of the elite Korps, and known to the world as the Desert Fox, Field Marshal Erwin Rommel had returned to the Fatherland for medical treatment before the tactical troop movement and is considered blameless.

The names of Colonel General Jürgen von Arnim, General Wilhelm Witter von Thoma and other traitors who surrendered to the enemy have been stricken from the rolls in disgrace.

The New York Times—Cap Bon, Tunisia, May 15, 1942: An estimated 150,000 Axis prisoners jammed this small peninsula as the vaunted Afrika Korps collapsed in total disarray. Few, if any, escaped to Sicily, and those who did had to run a gauntlet of murderous air attacks.

Twelve generals were scooped up as hordes of dispirited German and hangdog Italian troops surrendered at the first approach of an Allied tank. Desert Fox Erwin Rommel, who led his men to stunning victories against the British in Libya and who crushed green, outgunned American troops at Kasserine Pass, was not among them. Sources said that the field marshal was ill and had been evacuated to Berlin some time before his once-proud Afrika Korps fell apart.

Mein Gott, Arno Hindemit breathed as the forked-tail American planes climbed high and headed back across the Mediterranean. Two of the motorized rafts had been chopped up and had disappeared under the strafing runs, and when Arno looked back he could see no heads bobbing in the sea. It was water frothed and bloodied by the accurate 50-caliber shells.

Three rafts were left of the round dozen that had started out from Cap Bon while other men, tired of war and therefore sensible, milled around without leadership and waited to become prisoners of war. This group climbed into unsafe craft, stored for God knew what grandiose landing plans. Because they were stupid, and Arno could think of no other answer, they hoped to make landfall in Sicily or wherever the tides might take them away from the *Amis*.

Why, in God's name? Arno had been fighting for five years. Why should he opt for more, and especially in a war that was sliding downhill?

"Because you wear a uniform," Hauptmann Witzelei said.

"Not a word," Arno grunted. "I did not say a single *verdammt* word."

"You did not have to."

The tides they expected to ride had their own ideas. They had turned vicious and permanently taken two of the flimsy and overloaded vessels. The equally overloaded soldiers, pulled down by packs and weapons and ammunition, drowned. They drowned battling a stretch of water that was worth nothing to Arabs or Italians and certainly not to the Fatherland.

Then there was the enemy aircraft. *Schiessen!*

Arno still didn't quite grasp what he was doing here, water-soaked and uneasy in his stomach. This was no way for a confirmed *landser* to travel. He had always loathed troopships, but these floating condoms were much worse.

He could have been in a semicomfortable prisoner of war camp by now, smoking good *Ami* cigarettes and telling brave war stories. But no; the *hauptmann* and the few survivors left in their company insisted upon seizing these dangerous little rubber boats and risking their lives at sea. There was no cover out here from sudden, fierce attacks by vengeful airplanes.

All right, so no one had forced him to go along. A soldier did not desert his comrades; some honor was left.

The Afrika Korps was *kaputt,* finished for all time. It should have been better supplied, better supported by air, had more replacements. If those things were not possible, then any fool knew to retreat, to pull out and leave the miserable continent of Africa behind.

But the von fools and the fool corporal kept the Korps grinding away until it was too late. Caught between the sledgehammer of the British Eighth Army and the armored face of the *Ami* anvil moving north and east, what had been the best fighting unit in the world was beaten flat. Now the ragged remainders were headed for another desperate stand on Italian soil. If they made it.

Choppy, the sea moved beneath the little raft, and its motor sputtered.

"Not now, damn you," Arno said. "The time to misfire was back on the beach in Tunisia, not out here in the middle of the ocean. Cursed though we are, it is the destiny of *landsers* to die upon the land or not at all—which means those unlucky ones stay at war through eternity."

Captain Witzelei's cough was harsh and wet. "Those men in the other boats—"

Arno stroked with the paddle, keeping the craft's blunt nose pointed toward the misty blue land mass on the horizon. "Transfers from the Luftwaffe or the *Volkssturm*, possibly seaman. The German navy has been known to run aground. They were not regulars anyhow. I hope we can get close to land before nightfall. Schoolmaster Witz—would it be possible to drift all the way back to Germany?"

"Not from here."

"Even if we try?"

A wave rocked the raft. Wiping his face, Arno tasted wet salt and shouted at men up front to bail with their helmets. Softer, he asked the wounded radio operator how he was doing. The man nodded and grunted; a true *landser*. Arno thought of what his old sergeant had told him years ago, when he was a raw recruit: "We are all *rechte narren*, regular fools, professional soldier and conscript alike—we both get screwed. The difference between us is that the professional expects it."

He came erect. "Paddle, paddle! The tide works against us."

Looking up and back over his shoulder, he thought he saw black specks moving high against the bright blue of the sky. More enemy planes, British or American did not matter, for where were the fat man's Stukas and Messerschmitts, flying cover over Berlin?

Even that protective net of planes had not done the job. What had *der* Hermann said to Hitler? If a single bomb falls upon Germany you may call me Meier. A month later the first British bombers soared over the homeland, but fat Meier still commanded the Luftwaffe and did not wear the yellow star of Jewry.

"Karinhall," Arno said. "I wonder if Hermann keeps a harem there, Oriental potentate that he acts. A swastika of pearls, they say, diamonds upon his pretty uniforms, and those designed by Omar the Tentmaker. No, I do not think Hermann can appreciate a harem. It puzzles me how he does it with one woman, or even how he can be sure he has his *schmuck* in hand so as not to piss down his leg."

Men laughed, and Lance Corporal Derbein laughed, too,

pressing a pad of cannon wadding against his chest wound. The saltwater getting under it must hurt like hell, Arno thought.

"Göring's castle?" Witzelei removed his cracked glasses and wiped them against the underside of his shirt. "We are about to be strafed and sunk, and my sergeant prattles about a *reichsmarschall*'s palace. We will never be invited. But in fairness, Göring was wealthy before."

Resting his paddle upon the side of the raft, Arno said, "His wife was wealthy. Do you suppose she is now called Frau Meier?"

Nobody laughed this time. A wave swept the little raft sideways and almost swamped it. Arno lost his paddle but hung onto his machine pistol, the Schmeisser he had carried for so long. It had never jammed, never betrayed him. A good weapon was faithful so long as you cared for it properly; a woman was not. He wondered if his wife's lover was back there in the tangled mass of prisoners, or if he had died on the Russian front.

"Look there." Captain Witz pointed. "It is not far to land now. Paddle, boys, row! We can make it."

Arno stared up at the sky and cradled his Schmeisser. "If the *Amis* allow us. Here come the planes again."

CHAPTER 38

INTERNATIONAL NEWS SERVICE—Tunisia, May 17, 1943: Allied officials here are hard put to feed, shelter and provide medical care for more than 150,000 Axis soldiers who surrendered in the final mop-up operations. Caught between the hard-driving British Eighth Army from the west and the American-British-French armies advancing from the south and east, the Afrika Korps collapsed suddenly.

Surrender stories are coming in by the dozens: Germans flagging down American tanks to give themselves up, Italians volunteering to lead their captors to arms and ammunition caches, native Arabs turning suddenly helpful and small quiet heroisms.

One such tale concerns an arrogant German general, spit-shined and bemedaled, who "refused" to give up to a lowly enlisted man and "demanded" an American officer of equal rank be brought forward to receive his formal surrender.

Somewhat disheveled, he was happy to give up seconds later.

Von Thoma had deliberately allowed others of the staff to get ahead of him. Farther along the road was chaos, teeming with undisciplined soldiers turned cowardly. Allied planes, fighters and bombers, circled high above the seething, dusty rout, and he expected them to come plummeting down at any moment, bombing and strafing.

If he were the enemy commander, he would order it. Such attacks would considerably lessen the logistical problems of moving and caring for so many prisoners of war. He did not wish to be among the eliminated. Glancing at his driver, he saw the corporal's face white and strained beneath its layer of dust. Possibly the man was worried that he would be shot because he drove an *Ami* jeep, but the Afrika Korps had long fed upon abandoned and repaired vehicles, placing new markings and sometimes paint over the stars or circles of the enemy. The Allies were slow to use the technique, and until now they had not had overwhelming opportunities. Still, he would wager that no converted German panzers would lead the way in the next landings; too much trouble for a wealthy nation, even though the German armor was superior.

"Here," he commanded the driver. "Stop so I may get out here."

"But sir, there is nothing—"

"Here! And then drive on."

"*Jawohl,* General."

Stepping carefully so as not to dirty his boots, von Thoma walked beside the road. The *Ami* might not like a general riding in their captured jeep, so let the driver bear the responsibility. Tattered soldiers gave way to both sides for him as he strode proper and erect through them. No one saluted, and he felt a sullen animosity, a muted threat that his rank did not diminish, and some of them still clung to their weapons.

He feigned a limp and got off the road to sit awhile on the hillside beneath a scrawny tree that gave little shade. The column of trudging men passed on, and he lighted an *Ami* cigarette. He would rid himself of the pack before he surrendered. Surely some officer would replace them for the newly appointed commander of the Afrika Korps. By radio from Rome von Arnim had been relieved and himself given the leadership. That had to mean he was not in disfavor with Hitler; the scapegoat had been found and the blame for this catastrophe placed.

He heard motors ahead and watched a tower of dust grow slowly nearer, wondering if it might be better to surrender to the *Tommis*. The British were sticklers for soldierly tradition, while no one knew the reaction of the Americans. Certainly he wanted nothing to do with the so-called Free French.

Drawing hard upon the cigarette in his ivory holder, he thought about French auxillary troops, the Moroccan *goumiers* and the Senegalese. Savages both, unfit to be in any uniform. Intelligence reported that the standard pay of the Moroccans ceased once they entered combat. From then on they were paid according to the pairs of ears they turned in.

He shuddered. The Senegalese were worse, so black they were, and their teeth were filed to cannibal points; they wore red fezes, huge knives, wrap leggings and no shoes. They came silently in the night to take the heads of men on outpost duty, always leaving one man alive and asleep in his hole. That one spread panic, and the heads were found next day, minus the ears. The raids had some benefits, though; no Senegalese was ever brought in as prisoner.

What if those jungle beasts rode up there, chattering like the black apes they were and showing their sharp, wet teeth? What would they do to a German general, a white man? Surely civilized officers would prevent them from the barbarism of taking ears from a prisoner, and one of such high rank.

He peered up the road. Those did not appear to be *Tommi* trucks; they were American. Yes, the *Amis* were the answer. They were new at warfare and easily impressed.

The lead jeep swung an air-cooled 30-caliber machine gun and had a tall wire cutter mounted up front. Grinding out his cigarette butt, von Thoma remembered how his own engineers had strung thin wire across the roads, just high enough to decapitate a jeep driver and the man riding in the front seat, if the windshield had been laid flat on the hood.

He stood up and brushed his trousers, then walked slowly out to the roadside, hands held shoulder-high.

The jeep slewed to a stop, raising dust that tasted bitter. The two trucks and armored half-track behind stopped in place. The trucks had gunner holes cut into the roofs of their cabs, and 50-calibers were mounted there on rings. The *Amis* had adapted their equipment quickly, fitting it to the situation. The half-track bristled with guns.

Chest out and head back, Von Thoma halted and clicked his heels together. In practiced English he called out, "I am Colonel-General von Thoma, commanding officer of the Afrika Korps."

A grimy soldier, his helmet straps dangling, stepped down from the jeep, rifle held casually in both hands. He stared a moment, then called back over his shoulder, "Damn, Smitty—looka' here. Claims he's the sure-enough big dog."

"Soldier!" von Thoma snapped. "Call your highest-ranking officer immediately. I will surrender only to him."

The man spat and slouched forward. He was dirty and ragged and had not shaved in several days. He stank of whiskey.

"What say, General—you ain't surrendering to nobody but an officer?"

"Correct. Now I demand that you—"

"Oh, shit, General, we ain't got no officer on this party. If we did, he'd tell you that you just ain't in no position to demand a goddamn thing."

"Soldier, you know who I am, and yet you—"

"Uh-uh," the man grunted. "I know *what* you are, and that's just another Kraut son of a bitch."

Then he smashed the butt off his rifle into von Thoma's face.

On his knees in the dirt, hatless and holding his broken, bloody mouth with both hands, von Thoma mumbled, "I surrender, I surrender."

"How about that?" the *Ami* said.

CHAPTER 39

UNITED PRESS—Allied Headquarters in North Africa, June 3, 1943: Some 400 Allied bombers hammered Sicily yesterday for the third straight day. The ports of Marsala and Catania were left in flames, while other planes smashed at the island of Pantelleria. Returning airmen said that Flying Fortresses, Mitchells and Marauders had virtually wiped out the towns. British bombers worked over Pantelleria. All told, 15 enemy planes were shot down over Marsala on the west coast of Sicily, while only one Allied plane was lost.

The New York Times—New York City, June 4, 1943: Federal grand juries convened in Brooklyn and Manhattan today to investigate price gouging in poultry and other foods. Six wholesale poultry firms and 13 of their officers have been arraigned and held on $1,000 bail each.

The grand jury indictments are part of an ongoing Office of Price Administration drive, in cooperation with city and state officials, to wipe out black markets in foodstuffs.

Belvale climbed down from the old stallion and thumped Ric Arana's heavy neck in appreciation. "We're both kind of stiff, old boy, but we cover the ground."

Walking the big chestnut to cool him out, he inhaled the good perfume of horse sweat and thought what a great champion Ric had been, and how glad he was that Kirstin had made him a present of the old guy. Since his service in the cavalry Belvale had never been quite comfortable with the family's Thoroughbreds, the jumpers or the racing stock. The army had chosen Morgans for excellent reasons—calmness, stamina and good sense. Too many Thoroughbreds lacked one or all those qualities.

He unsaddled Ric, led the horse into his box stall and turned him to face the Dutch door before slipping the headstall. Ric expected his rubdown and brushing and stood quietly for it. Working happily on the satiny, dappled hide and feeling the solid muscle tone, Belvale combed out mane and tail.

It would be great if he were in that condition. He matched his age to the stallion's at four horse years to each one for a man. Since he had just passed his sixty-seventh birthday, and Ric was foaled twenty-five years back, that made him—good God!—not one hundred? Little wonder that the horse creaked some.

"Like me," Belvale said. "I only hope I can keep on the job as well as you."

Limping only a bit, he left the stables and walked to the house. He went through the kitchen where Minerva was in the midst of instructions to the cooks. She broke off to trail him down the hallway.

"Preston, I do hope you won't come down late for the soiree tonight. The Wellborns are attending—Mother's second cousins from North Carolina, you know. Senator Folsom promised to make an appearance, and the speaker of the House, and those people who have something important to do with airplane factories—"

He walked faster. "Kissing Jim Folsom ought to liven up the evening."

"Do try not to smell so horsey, Preston. And please see to Charles's tie yourself. He always gets it crooked."

"Okay, Minerva. There *is* a war on, but we'll take time out."

He climbed the stairs, favoring the game leg. Minerva, from the Latin, highest goddess of Rome, coupled with Jupiter and Juno, as an equal and not in the literal sense. This Minerva had coupled only with his brother, and that reluctantly, he had little doubt. Born to be the perfect maiden aunt, she had left destiny's path to be widowed by Sam Belvale.

Now she was the perfect hostess and keeper of the family tree, down to its smallest twig. Minerva was necessary for Kill Devil Hill, like for the party tonight, another social maneuver for political leverage. Roosevelt had come down hard on management during a Montgomery Ward strike, even ordered troops to haul the president bodily out of his office. But he backed off when John L. Lewis called out the coal miners and threatened the entire defense industry. The coal strike caused rationing of artillery and mortar shells in some units. FDR's illness caught up at times, and he had to be prodded into better decisions.

Minerva was at her best directing power plays, and only the family knew that she was often a pain in the ass. He had hoped one of the other women would replace her in time, someone like Kirstin, but there was no chance of Kirstin now.

He hadn't faulted Jim Shelby for volunteering but wished him alive and back in the Senate. Since the Guadalcanal and North Africa victories, and the big naval wins in the South Pacific, some legislators had stacked arms. For them the war was already won, and they looked more to votes than to the good of the troops on line who had a hell of a lot more combat ahead.

Maybe more than straight combat; every war had its share of rumors about terrifying secret weapons, but this time they were stronger on both sides, more believable. If Hitler got off first, the balloon would go up all over again.

Before heading for the shower Belvale went through into

the war room. One teletype clacked, the shortwave radio buzzed without words and Crusty hung up the phone with a bang.

"Son of a bitch won't mess with me again."

Belvale brought forth a cigar. "Any son of a bitch I know?"

"That shitty Finance colonel. Pay got shipped late to Algeria—some excuse about overprinting the greenback seals another color. I told him that Treasury did it on time last year and to get off his ass. Three things soldiers won't stand being fucked with: their women, whiskey and payday."

"Gloria back yet?"

"Yes and no. She spends more time at the hospital, and even drives up to the Keep on weekends. She used to bitch how she never liked her own home—too gloomy, she said. Now when I need her she's up there, and wherever the hell else she runs off to. So I called Colonel Belvale's wife—"

"Adria."

"Adria, whoever. She said since Dan got out of Hawaii and into the Americal Division she needs to keep busy. She's willing to move to the Hill with her daughter."

"Joann."

"Whoever. It's a good thing the women of this family can soldier, too. Somebody has to take up the slack, with the men shipped out and Gloria goldbricking so much. Damn, she used to have good sense, but I don't know what's gotten into the girl lately."

Belvale drew on his cigar. "She's in love."

"Batshit! My Gloria? After her experience with that goddamn peanut she married—"

"The peanut *you* married her to."

Crusty got up and stomped across the room, pausing to read the teletype. He poured coffee for himself, hesitated, and then topped off the cup with bourbon. He turned. "She hasn't said anything to me. How come you know?"

"I talked to her, and later I saw them together, and it only took a glance."

"Yeah? You playing Dorothy Dix, advice to the lovelorn? Gloria'd say something to me if she was getting mixed up with another man. But if she is, the guy'd better not be another fucking loser. I'll run him over the hill."

Rolling cigar smoke inside his mouth, Belvale found the taste faintly bitter. Maybe he shouldn't have mentioned Gloria's romance; Crusty was hurt that she hadn't told him.

Belvale said, "She might be afraid to let you know. Not exactly afraid—it would take a panzer division to spook Gloria—but she could be nervous about your attitude—"

"Batshit, godamnit!"

"That attitude. She probably doesn't want to upset you or him at the moment."

Crusty drank his coffee royal too fast and burned his lips. "Him—*him?* How come *he's* so important all of a sudden? Don't tell me he's a civilian. Gloria knows better than that. And even if he's a pill roller, I may not like the son of a bitch, but that don't mean—"

"You like him," Belvale said. "It's Eddie Donnely."

Crusty dropped the coffee cup; it broke. He sputtered, "Eddie—Sergeant—*Donnely?* Eddie put the meat to half the officers' wives at Schofield Barracks. He'll screw anything that's wet and grows hair, and I ain't all that sure about the hair. Hell, he'd screw a goddamn snake if somebody held its head. That's not the kind of man for my Gloria to—"

"*Your* Gloria only to a point. You don't want to lose her to any man, but Gloria is her own woman. And she is his, if she wants it that way. It's evident that she does."

"Goddamnit, Eddie Donnely's how old—twenty-six—seven? Never been close to being married. Doesn't that tell you something? He don't want to be tied down because he has too much fun dicking officers' women. Wait a minute! That's the reason he's messing around Gloria. She's no beautiful movie star, no Carole Lombard by a long shot, and he's taking it out on her—this secret hard-on he's got for the brass."

Belvale tapped his cigar into an ashtray, the polished and cut-down base of a 105 shell. "We weren't informed that he had been admitted to Walter Reed, and he didn't know who Gloria was. At the hospital she's Mrs. Johnson, and she kept it that way until she was sure about him."

"She told you that?"

"Some of it. The rest wasn't difficult to figure. Like Donnely being able to find a beauty in her that other men are blind to. You'll admit that he's a connoisseur."

"Too much so. And he's an enlisted man."

"Going rank happy in your old age, Charles?"

Crusty toed the pieces of the broken cup against the wall. He filled another one with straight bourbon and took a swallow. "Charles, your Secessionist ass. You know what I mean, damnit. Sergeants don't want us crossing over to their side of the line either. He'd be uncomfortable and probably refuse to mix with the family, while Gloria has known nothing but officers and her own people."

Finishing his drink, he snorted again. "No sweat. Donnely won't try to marry her anyway. I'll talk to Gloria and show her—"

"You'll just prove that you're acting stupid again. Remember that she won't be pushed anymore. She'll tell you to go to hell and walk out if you confront her about this."

"Okay, okay! You're such a smartass—do you want to *bet* that Donnely won't drop her like a bad habit? Fifty thousand—hell!—a hundred? And a public apology, public like at a party of big wheels. The winner to pick time and place. That'll hurt you worse than losing money."

Belvale considered.

Gavin Scott had thought about touring Italy after graduation, but not by banging around in Jerry trucks with worn-out shock absorbers. Officers rode and EM hiked during this move out of the POW camp in lower Calabria. Walking might have been better. He stretched and rubbed his sore ass, then the shoulder that had ached ever since the crash, and stared out through the newly strung wire. Raw and hastily thrown together, this camp wouldn't be nearly as comfortable as the old one; no barracks, just a rickety mess hall and some shabby tents.

The escape committee's clandestine radio had informed them why they were being moved. The overwhelming defeat of the Afrika Korps had put Allied troops in command of that shore of the Mediterranean, much closer to the Italian boot and the possible liberation of Allied prisoners. It also screwed up the best laid plans of mice and the ranking limeys who ran the committee. RAF pilots shot down and ground pounders taken in Libya, some of those guys had been POWs for years. The stuffy Englishmen were too damned careful, nit-picky and slow moving.

He wanted out; he wanted back in the air so he could blow up the kind of bastards who had worked him over in Tunisia. Goddamn Kraut infantrymen beat him down with gun butts and kicked him in the ass every few steps as they herded him to their officers in the rear. When he climbed back into a P-38 the whole Kraut army and Luftwaffe would pay for it.

Security at this new camp must be uncertain and full of holes, so the time was right for individual breakouts. If the committee didn't have a date for him, he'd try to get away on his own, and the committee could kiss his rusty dusty. The problem was—get away to where? Any direction he took had to include an ocean voyage. If he was back in his own world, he could buy a damned ship and a crew to run it. Here the family money wouldn't buy an extra helping of goat meat.

It wasn't food he missed most, or even the freedom. Gavin missed women, any woman who would stroke his ruined face and tell him how sorry she was. He needed a woman's submission, the giving softness to counter his driving hunger. Behind the wire there was too much time for the memory of one woman to irritate him—Stevie Bartlett and the heartless way she had humiliated him. When he escaped and somehow made his way back to England he meant to find that little bitch and tell her what it was like to be locked away while she played around with Uncle Chad or some other old bastard.

This time, when he got through with her, she wouldn't laugh.

CHAPTER 40

Brigadier Wingate to Chindits—CBI theater, June 3, 1942: "Put yourself in the position of the enemy commander. His one aim will be to prevent anyone getting out alive. We can take it for granted that from now on the Jap will do everything in his power to wipe us out. The first thing he will do is make a strong effort to prevent us recrossing the Irrawaddy."

The brigade split into smaller groups and made a headlong run at the river. Keenan was two paces behind Wingate himself as they burst out of the jungle at the riverbank, 220 bearded—except for the hairless Burmese—and weary soldiers looking toward home.

Poppoppop!

The Nambus spat fire and lead from brush on the far side, kicking up spurts of muddy water and scything down the lead troops. The river splashed bloody.

Karump—karump!

They had the crossing zeroed in with mortars, and a hot fragment whizzed by Keenan's head. A grenade exploded too short. This time the Japs had them cold, outthinking Wingate for once and beating him to this part of the river. They blocked the only route back for his guerrillas.

"To the rear, men!" Wingate's voice lifted above the

gunfire, and Keenan sloshed back to the bank to wheel and drop on one knee. He laid covering fire into the trees with his M-1, spacing his shots until the clip *pinged!* out and he thumbed another into place.

A machine gun chopped a line of sand beside him, and he bellied down to roll left. He got off four quick rounds that reached just below a thin puff of smoke that eddied above a thorn bush, then rolled to his right. No answering fire came from the gun, but he spread the rest of the clip low through the masking elephant grass to make sure.

Oblivious to enemy fire, Wingate stalked the riverbank as bullets whipped about him, his long beard rippling, a ragged blanket flapping from his shoulders. To Keenan he looked like some mad prophet out of the Old Testament and about as untouchable.

"To the brush!" Wingate roared, and he strolled after the fleeing survivors. The dead and badly wounded men drifted in the river. Never exposing themselves, the Japs continued shooting at the bodies, and the wounded were dead, too.

Reaching deep cover, but with enemy mortar shells searching the jungle beyond them, the Chindits sprawled wet and gasping. Checking his ammo and reloading, Keenan watched Wingate.

"We divide again," the brigadier announced, and he took off his sun helmet to mop at his face with a grimy handkerchief. "Each leader to find his own way."

He pointed to one man. "Leftenant Dennis—take that group. Sergeant, your lot is the lads lying beneath the teak trees. Where's Leftenant Singh? Oh—downed in the river, was he? Bad luck. Sergeant Sindhi, it's your command, then. Take to the high ground until you overlook a spot where the Jap relaxes, then make your way across the river as best you can. Good luck, gentlemen, and good hunting. We will meet again at base camp. You men here remain with me and Major Carlisle. You also, Leftenant Sheffield."

The mortar fire slowed, and Keenan imagined the Japanese cautiously easing from the brush to try the river in pursuit. They would be slow and jumpy; the Chindits had bloodied them too often before. Wingate put on his pith helmet and pointed the way from the low ground of the Irrawady valley and up into the foothills. Keenan volunteered to drop back with five Burmese as rear guard.

It was like old times in the jungle, when Keenan had been the prey sought by many hunters. A dangerous prey to be sure, one who ambushed and slew his pursuers and sought them out in return, but for him to stop moving would have been to die. Now it was true for the forty-two other men Wingate led. The man was about over the edge, but still as wily and deadly as any jungle animal.

Motioning to the Burmese to divide on each side of the trail, Keenan used Corporal Pangrit's limited supply of English and his own hand signals to give orders. All went to work putting together a pair of giant fly swats, those squares of sharp bamboo daggers vine-lashed to a drawn-back pole. Thin, almost invisible vines became the trip wires that would loose the killing swats one by one. Whether they impaled or just scared hell out of Jap scouts, their presence would slow the chase considerably.

He moved the rear guard farther up the trail and halted them along a straight stretch to whittle *punji* stakes, slivers of razored bamboo. The thicker butts of these were driven into the earth at a downtrail slant and angled inward, the needle points awaiting the Japs who would dive for cover when two Chindits fired upon them and ran.

Keenan was half a mile along with Corporal Pangrit and another small, turbaned man when the gunfire rattled. He smiled at his men and waved them on while he waited for his gunners to catch up. Squatted off trail, he went immobile and thought that they could remain in the jungle forever, harrassing Japs and cutting their supply lines—if they had more air drops and some fresh troops.

Alone, he could survive off the land, but many men

required much food and equipment. Now that the enemy knew the Chindits' approximate location, their Zeros would make the skies dangerous for C-47 Dumbos, and parachute drops would probably fall in Jap held areas. Wingate's raiders were on their own.

The trotting Burmese hissed in surprise when he rose silently from the brush, then they showed betel-stained teeth in broad grins. The One Who Will Not Die was their legend, and they were happy to live it with him.

Keenan trotted with them, clamping his lips against the malaria chill that began to shake him. Illness was a major enemy for what was left of the brigade; men were going weak from fever, being eaten by festering sores and drained, as well as infected, by the omnipresent sucking leeches.

He was almost exhausted when his rear guard closed on Wingate's main body, which was less than platoon strength. The chills had stopped and the sweats were underway, his bones aching by the time he found the others. They were tucked into a dense patch of jungle at the foot of a lightly wooded ridge where the Burmese scouts had found a flowing spring. It was a good hideout. Abrupt and gray, dusk closed down as the Gurkhas dropped the remaining two pack mules and cut their throats.

"Sir," Keenan reported, "the rear guard set swat traps and fired on an ambush with emplaced *punjis*. Enemy casualty count unknown, but pursuit slowed."

He watched the Burmese dig deep and narrow pits to hide small cooking fires as the Brits gathered dry twigs and unslung their pots. Mule stew for tonight and tomorow's mess; he hoped the Burmese would find edible greens to add.

"Thank you, Major," Wingate said. Stroking his beard, he sat with his back propped against a tree bole. "What do you think are the relative merits of Popeye and J. Wellington Wimpy?"

"Sir?" Keenan could barely make out the man's face in

shadows. Popeye and Wimpy—what the hell did cartoons have to do with anything?

"Power and passivity, Major. The food supply and the feeder, the dinner and the leech."

Shrugging, Keenan hoped his sweats would soon break. He couldn't afford the loss of salt. He said, "I never thought about it, sir."

"Odd, Popeye being a Yank tradition. Pity we have no spinach, what?"

Keenan nodded and closed his eyes. He had little doubt that Wingate was now all the way around the bend. Wingate's interminable lectures on eighteenth-century art were preferable to "I'll gladly pay you Tuesday for a hamburger today." But the man made no strategic mistakes—so far.

"We have succeeded in our mission," Wingate said. "We have harassed and disturbed the Jap. We have forced him to use two entire divisions in pursuit of us, and we have cost him men, supplies and transportation."

Breathing slowly, smelling the risen cookfire smoke before it dissipated high in the jungle ceiling, Keenan said, "Yes, sir."

"Even if we had not been militarily successful we would not be at a loss. As Edwin Markham once said, 'Defeat may serve as well as victory to shake the soul and let the glory out.' "

Let the glory out? Keenan knew Wimpy better than Edwin Markham, and that wasn't saying much. These days, only idiots fought for glory. "I'll set the perimeter guard, General."

"Thank you. I expect to remain here for some time, weeks perhaps, until I am certain the Japanese have gone after the other commands. Then we shall be able to cross the Irrawaddy unmolested. If we should be discovered, we will of course fight our way through."

They did rest for twelve days, gathering strength in sleep, good water and enough food. When the mule meat ran out, Burmese soldiers dressed out pythons to boil with certain roots and leaves. Other greenery and mud packs were used as dressings for sores that mostly refused to heal; mosquitoes, leeches and red spiders were constant irritations, and malaria shook and sweated the men in turn. Still they fattened and grew stronger. When the scouts reported no enemy waiting in the brush beyond the river, men had stopped listening to Wingate's compulsive monologues on religion around the world.

Keenan's advance party of six led the way across the river and drew no fire. He breathed deeper but waited ten minutes before signaling Wingate it was safe to come ahead. Pausing, he smelled the rich perfume of an unseen flower, and the image of Chang Yen Ling leapt brightly and painfully to mind. Flowers blooming in a Mandarin's secret garden, and the loveliest of them all unfolding her petals for Keenan Carlisle.

What poetry would she write of this *here,* this *now?* She had seen beauty in every place and time they shared. He needed her. He couldn't bring her back, no matter how many goddamned Japs he killed, but logic would not keep him from trying.

He heard her soft whisper:

> Listen to the sun, my love;
> he speaks of warmth.
> Taste the wind, my love;
> the flavor is honey.
> Tonight, pillow the moon,
> For she is me.

Was it the fever? *Yen Ling!* he cried only in his soul, clamping hard upon his rifle, so hard that his fingers ached.

He didn't hear her again during the march, even when Wingate halted for forty-eight hours to camp beside Leftenant Sheffield, hoping the man's dysentery would ease up and he would gather the strength to continue. When Sheffield couldn't rise Wingate gave him his own Webley pistol and a canteen half full of water.

"We must go on, you know," he said.

White-faced, cheekbones protruding sharply, Sheffield murmured, "Yes, of course."

"We will send your effects to England."

"Thank you, sir—and good luck."

Oh, Christ! Luck from a dying man who had run out of it. Would he use the Webley or wait and hope the Japs didn't find him until he just wasted away? Keenan thought he knew which choice he would make.

Time lost any meaning, so either another week or ten years passed before they lost another man. British Corporal Wragge's leg sores had eaten to the shinbones, and although tired men took turns supporting him, nothing could be done to ease his agony. When Keenan woke from a short and fretful nap Wragge was gone; he had crept away into the jungle to die. Nobody had the chance to wish him luck.

Wingate saluted the place where Wragge had crawled off and scrawled his name in a mildewed notebook.

It took all the guts Keenan had to stand up and move out again. His M-1 was heavier than any weapon had a right to be, and he was out of water, his mouth gone dry and cracking.

If they ran into even a small Jap patrol, they'd be in real trouble. Even The One Who Will Not Die might. At this point it wouldn't matter, if he could be sure that he would meet Chang Yen Ling. . . .

Penny Belvale brushed her hair; she had let it grow, and it was just long enough to appear womanly if you didn't look too closely. Peering into a sliver of broken mirror, she bit her lips to redden them and then practiced a smile. It almost seemed as if she remembered how and meant it.

Rain pattered the thatch roof and leaked through. Kneeling before the upended box that held her few possessions and Stevie Bartlett's as well, she didn't wonder if she could go through with what she had to do. She had already made up her mind about that; the question was not only could she make him believe, but how long could she keep it up.

As long as the war lasted, or until Major Wobbly tired of her. She had to become an exceptional actress. It wouldn't be tough to mouth the lines, but what about making her body respond believably? She'd heard that many women faked orgasm, but she had never had to—not when Walt was her fiancé, and not with Farley after they were married. Sex was only natural to her, and wholly enjoyable.

Swallowing, she continued to brush her hair, to delay. At least Major Watanabe was clean; he kept himself spotless, which might be something psychological and a problem for her in the future. He was pretty nice-looking—for a Jap. He was a goddamn Jap, and no soap and water, no amount of boot polish would change that. Jesus; going through with this was the most difficult thing she'd ever had to do.

Rain thrummed harder on the roof, and a floor puddle spilled over to drain through a crack. If the downpour increased, Wobbly—she had better never slip and call him that—might have the women brought in early from the wet fields. She ought to be out of here before they came back, or else Stevie would try to talk her out of this. She was doing it for Stevie and the rest of the women in this hut, because they couldn't take much more of how Watanabe—what the hell was his first name?—was working them over. And of course Stephanie had caught the worst of it. The bastard was smart; he'd seen they were close and played that angle.

Penny got up and brushed at her skirt, the best one she had. It seemed longer than two months since she had turned down Watanabe's proposition, but time dragged on when the hut was called last to chow, when rations got shorter and shorter. Forever was when Stevie got set up for punishment over tiny infractions of camp rules. Starved to bones and slapped daily by grinning guards, she remained British and a soldier through it all. Sergeant Katana got a great kick out of beating her with his bamboo stick shaped like the sword he would never wear. The beating was not enough to incapacitate, but more than enough to make her choke back whimpers of pain through the night.

"Enough," Penny said, and she went out into the rain. "More than enough. I should have bowed to the little son of a bitch and crawled into his bed before he took it out on Stevie."

Without caring what the rain was doing to her hair, she walked slowly toward the headquarters building. Watanabe had ordered her tied to the punishment post, to stand all day in the blazing sun without shade or water because she'd slapped a guard who tried to rape her. When she toughed it out like any member of the family would have done, except perhaps her husband, she gained Watanabe's respect.

Oh, he wouldn't rape her; he was a samurai and therefore of great honor. He wanted her to come to him on her own, and he offered her a deal: become his mistress and have the best of food and all the cigarettes she wanted, and do no work beyond a face-saving secretarial job in his office.

The bastard surprised her; she bowed and said, "No, thank you."

He looked down and knuckled his bad hip. She tensed.

"We have little medicine for ourselves. My soldiers also suffer from malaria, but Japanese love children, and I will see to aspirin for them, perhaps some quinine."

She wavered but thought how no kid was deathly ill at the moment, how they had made it this far without Jap help, in spite of the Japs who loved them so. "There are native women. Your soldiers trade with them."

He slapped the desk, loud as a pistol shot. "I am no peasant soldier! I am educated in your own country, an officer from a famous samurai family."

"My family is also samurai."

"Which attracts me. Yes or no, woman. I will not ask again."

And he hadn't even spoken to her since. He applied pressure to her hut; he singled out Stephanie Bartlett for punishment. So now Penny was climbing the stairs to the porch where Major Watanabe stood proud and shiny to make his daily announcements.

She recognized the guard who stood up and slapped his rifle butt but didn't remember his name. He did his guttural call to attention: "*Hai-ryo!*"

Sitting at his desk, Watanabe looked up. He laid down his lettering brush and said nothing, just looked at her, black almond eyes showing no hints.

"The guard, please," she said.

"*Kaiho suru!*" he snapped. "Dismissed."

Penny bowed. "Thank you."

"What do you ask of me, woman?"

"Nothing, Major."

He leaned back in his chair and nodded at a closed door of split bamboo and rice paper. "*Ah-so.* There are towels in my quarters. dry yourself."

"As you wish."

"Obedience in all things is good in a woman."

Her throat closed, and she choked. Fighting off dizziness, she folded her hands in front and bowed again. Then she opened the door to his bedroom and walked inside. It was Spartan as she had expected—a short rice table, a hibachi for heating snacks and water for his tea, for heating sake in those little white bottles. His *yukata*, the sleeping kimono, hung on a peg above the neatly folded mattress padding, a flowered, silk-covered futon.

Another corner held wash basins and smelled of soap. Removing her muddy shoes, she crossed the rice straw tatami and took a towel to dry her hair. As she patted her thin blouse she heard the door open again. The rain stopped suddenly, and blue twilight held its breath just outside the window. Obedience, he said; she would obey and save Stevie from any more pain.

He didn't put his arms around her waist or kiss the nape of her neck. She had heard that the back of a woman's neck was sexy to the Japanese. She had heard a lot of things, and soon she would know the truth of them. Before it happened she already knew what a whore felt. At school a psych professor had said that all women fantasized what it would be like to enter a hotel room with a strange man and take off her clothes, to be paid for making love.

This wasn't the sensation she'd imagined, and she certainly wouldn't be making love or anything close. Penny would be an obedient body, fearful but unexcited. When she heard the soft slap of the unfolded futon she battled the trembling that threatened her composure and barely won. Maybe he wouldn't light the candle.

Twilight darkened, and candlelight flickered crazy upon the wall. Catching her breath, she turned, the towel still clutched in both hands and pressed against her belly.

"Stand before me as you remove your clothing," Watanabe said. "It has been long since I saw an American woman naked."

She couldn't avoid looking at him, a small, nude Buddha, hairless but for his crotch. He sat cross-legged, knees spread upon a silken field of scarlet flowers. The color was right for her, and the candlelight ought to be red, too. Hands shaking despite herself, Penny dropped her blouse; her bra had long since worn away. She eeled quickly from her skirt and thumbed the loose elastic of her panties. It hadn't been like this undressing for Walt or Farley. It would never be the same again.

"*Ah-so,*" he breathed. "You are beautiful, as I thought."

She couldn't answer. She only just made it to the futon before her knees gave way. Then she whispered, "P-please, the candle—"

"*Hai*. Modesty also becomes a woman."

Blowing out the candle flame, he turned to her in darkness, pulling her body against his. She lay passively beneath his caresses, grateful that he clung to Japanese ways and didn't kiss her. Did men kiss whores?

Surprisingly gentle, he stroked her breasts, her belly and thighs. Eyes shut tight, she prayed he would not demand that she caress him in turn. He didn't; panting, he spread her knees and mounted her.

Think of something else, Penny—anything else. No; don't lie still like this, unmoving as the deadness inside herself. That might anger him, and Watanabe raging was what she didn't want. She moved a little, and a little bit more, remembering how it had been with Walton, especially with Walton. Suddenly, impossibly, it burst insanely within her as her body turned traitor to her mind.

No! No! her mind shrieked—what was she, to let this happen? What kind of depraved bitch was she, to squirm in mutual orgasm with a goddamned Jap?

It should not, *could not* happen; not to pretty Penny Belvale. She had loved and been loved, and this animal coupling wasn't anything to compare. She didn't love this man buried within her, sweating atop her. Hell, no, she hated the cruel son of a bitch with all her heart and soul.

Then why, why? In the name of all decency, *why?*

All the questions screamed around inside her head, and she had never wished for anything as much as she wanted him to take it out of her right now. He didn't move; his hot breath was sticky in her ear; one of his hands clenched her buttock and the other hurt her breast. She needed to scream aloud, to curse and heave from beneath him.

All Penny could say aloud was, "Oh, God."

CHAPTER 41

Variety—Hollywood, Calif., June 16, 1943: Clark Gable enlisted more than a year ago, after the death of his wife Carole Lombard in a plane crash while returning from her war bond tour. In this reporter's opinion, Clark should not be allowed to be a soldier. The Selective Service System ruled that motion pictures are an essential war industry, and FDR appointed Lowell Mellet as Coordinator of Motion Pictures.

At a recent meeting with the industry's War Activites Committee he said: "We hope that you and your workers stay right here in Hollywood and keep doing what you are doing. Your motion pictures are a vital contribution to the total defense effort."

War is too serious a business for Clark Gable to be playing sentimental games. He has a duty, and Hollywood has a duty, and they should be made to stick to it.

Sloan Travis slouched at attention and stared at a flake on the adobe wall a foot above the regimental CO's head. He had caught on quick to that useful EM's trick of never looking an officer in the eye. It was easier to stay blank and play dumb.

He hoped that the slings and arrows of outrageous fortune would somehow backfire and rid him of Chad Belvale. The War Department should hurry and promote him to at least three stars, so he'd be forced out of division level and Sloan would never have to see him again. Bird colonels who continually cropped up were far worse than the proverbial bad pennies or a plague of locusts; they were powerful junior gods. Here in North Africa they held the balance of life and death. The war wasn't over; it was just on a ten-minute break, and pretty soon somebody would say saddle up and move out.

"Goddamnit," Colonel Belvale said, "pay attention."

"Yessir." Slur it, make it a single, toneless word, automatic and without nuance.

The omnipresent odors of Oran city wafted through the unscreened windows of 16th Infantry HQ, garlic and olive oil and urine. Sloan drew them in and decided he could also smell the faint licorice of Malaga wine and a salted blue hint of the Mediterranean Sea. It was no longer an Axis lake, and Il Duce ought to be getting nervous.

"You come in here acting as if you have a choice. You don't. I don't either, though I'd rather promote an Arab mule. Kasserine Pass cost the regiment far too many platoon leaders, and under pressure you react like an honest-to-God soldier. So you'll wear this gold bar or get it shoved up your ass, Lieutenant."

Sloan blinked. "I understand an officer can resign his commission—sir."

"I don't have to accept your resignation, but if I do, you will be called back to active duty immediately as a private. Then I'll detail you to Graves Registration, the most miserable job in the entire army.

"You'll collect rotten body parts and try to puzzle them into a recognizable corpse. You'll stuff poor dead bastards into mattress covers and truck them back for identification and burial. That means prying their mouths open for a dog-tag and making casts of their teeth, if they have teeth, if they have mouths.

"If they retain much of a head, you'll look anyway and run your fingers into the cavities anyway. You will learn to chain-smoke cigars because it's the only thing that you can count on to almost—almost—kill the stink you live with. You'll throw up a lot."

Accenting it differently, his stomach queasy, Sloan said, "I understand, sir."

"You'd damned well better. Boy, I don't know why a wild hair grew crossways in your ass, but I strongly suggest you pull it out. You're lucky to get a battlefield commission and even luckier to remain in H Company, where you're known and respected. You may even have friends there, although Christ only knows why."

Sloan braced a little straighter. "Sir, may I—"

"You may not. Pin on that bar, then get the hell out of here and do your job as a second john."

Outside in the yard Sloan passed a PFC who snapped him a salute. Sloan said, "Thanks, I guess," and he belatedly remembered to return the highball. From spite he wouldn't have saluted back, but that would have insulted the soldier, not shown the colonel that he still didn't give a good goddamn.

PFC—one stripe, a private first class or poor fucking civilian, which is what Sloan wanted to be. What the hell made the brass think he was so good at playing soldier? He only did what he had to, reacted to save his own precious ass. Okay, maybe some actions helped the guys trapped with him, but that was only for mutual protection. He was no flag-waving, parade marshal hero, and he sure wasn't destined to be a leader of men, an officer and gentleman by act of Congress. For one thing, he couldn't be a chickenshit.

"Hey, there." It was Owen, his captain, company commander and the one Belvale that Sloan could stomach; a good guy. "Congratulations."

Falling into step with Owen, he said, "I just got my first salute. Was I supposed to give the guy a dollar?"

"Tradition for the Academy and Officers Candidate School. I doubt anyone here ever heard of it. That's a buck saved for another bottle of *vin rouge.* Wetting down a new shavetail's bars and a noncom's stripes is an older and stronger tradition, and you pay."

"I'll drink to that. Let's see—yeah, there's the rue de Révolucion, and we're not far from the Bar de Sous Marines. Remember that joint?"

"More memorable is the lady who owns it."

For the first time that day Sloan smiled and felt like it. "You, too? The bar's not down in Chancre Alley, but the lady and her friends did okay by us common folk. I thought officers only frequented the Villa de la Rosa. It was off limits to peasants and guarded by MPs."

"Past tense—it *was,*" Owen said. "Tell you about the change over some wine."

The cobblestone street was downhill and uneven, Arabs drifting sullen along walls slitted by barred windows, their dark eyes also slitted. A charcoal-burning bus huffed around a corner and spilled bits of fuel for native kids to fight over. The Arabs didn't give a damn who won and who lost wars in their country-become-colonies. They sold out either side and cheerfully stole from both. From the conquering legions of the Roman Emperor Constantine to the time La Légion Étrangère established its headquarters at Sidi Bel Abbes, Arabs knew the ultimate losers would be themselves.

Turning into the dark café, Owen said, "Your commission—did my old man present it in person?"

"Who else?" The place was just as Sloan remembered it. Was it less than seven months since he first ducked in here, technically AWOL? It seemed much longer, for time was measured differently now. Midnight became 2400 when time was drafted and became regimented; time crouched on exploding hilltops and hid in blazing mountain passes to count who would hear the next tick or see tomorrow.

Owen Belvale squeezed into the thin wooden booth.

"Any first john or anybody else who outranked you would have served as well. But the colonel especially likes to give out battlefield promotions."

Sloan sat down and put his elbows on the table. It was early, and nobody was behind the bar; he looked toward the kitchen. "He doesn't like me. He's your father, and you call him by his rank? Family habit, tradition, what?"

"He doesn't like you because he sees a deliberate waste of talent. Yes, he's always been something other than Dad to me—a captain's bars, gold leaf, silver leaf, now the eagles, and for most of my life he was my mother's absentee husband.

"Jesus—did I come down on her because she divorced him. It wasn't because I was so much on his side. It was the idea of her leaving him for another man—a civilian. Women in our family weren't allowed the option. Four years at the Academy reinforced the traditions for me—girls who married cadets after graduation marched out of chapel through the arch of sabers. They were enlisting for the duration and accepted their lifetime duty with the ceremony. Now I wonder that more of the family women don't say the hell with bugle calls and post duty calls and opt for a normal life. That would be a life without shipping orders and husbands present when babies are born. It's not family burial plots with simulated graves because the bodies can't be found."

Madame Sanchez brought the good smells out of the kitchen with her, rabbit cooked tender in a spicy roux, or possibly escargot heavy with garlic and wine, as butter had been rare since the war began.

"*Ma foi! Mes amis,* you return to my poor café." She came around the bar and undulated to the booth. "You are not injured? *C'est bon,* my fine officers. *A bas le boche*—finish, *non?* You desire food and wine?"

"We desire desire." Sloan smiled up at her, this energetic *colon* with perfumed hair and a ripe mouth.

Madame Sanchez's return smile promised many things, but other services first, *mais non?*

"Your best of everything," Owen said, "now and later." And when she swung her skirts back into the kitchen he murmured, "I'm hurt. She doesn't remember my name."

"Or mine. Did we expect she would?"

Owen laughed. "No more than the corps MPs expected that gang of drunk GIs to hook a deuce-and-a-half truck winch to the gates of the Villa de la Rosa and tear them off. Officers-only cathouse, hell—they were the goddamn First Division, and that meant fuck or fight. Mean and hairy and horny, they brought their weapons to town, and who dared take them?

"Rear-echelon clerks and desk officers still catch hell for wearing clean suntans and campaign ribbons. For weeks back then every MP in Oran had to stay under cover. Damn, it was glorious! And when Corps Command tried to call General Allen on the carpet, know what he said? Terrible Terry said Oran belongs to us; we took this town once, and we can damned well take it again. Little Teddy Roosevelt probably added some choice words."

The wine was red, dry and cool. Madame Sanchez—Wanda?—poured, leaving the bottle and a trail of musky scent.

Sloan drank off most of his glass, a grapey sourness that would warm his gut. "I'm not knocking all officers or even the army as a whole. It's just not for me, especially as a career. General Allen's good at the business, and I guess the old man—your old man—is okay, too. I only wish he'd get off my back."

Holding up his glass, Owen squinted at the wine. "I felt the same way about him. I didn't want assignment to the same post, much less to be in the same regiment with him. I felt like a kid starting school where his dad is the principal. I'm only now finding out there's really a father under his uniform, that he struggles not to show how he worries about me. Hell, he sweats out every man's problems and bleeds with every casualty."

Sloan didn't follow that line of discussion or want to. He lifted his wineglass. "Here's to—not the old *Wings* movie about the Great War—pardon me, World War I. You know, where the gallant pilots drank one for the dead already and here's to the next man to die. We don't have a rock fireplace to break our glasses in. And please, no toast to the gold bars that may be too heavy for me to carry. What can we legitimately drink to?"

"Womanhood," Owen Belvale said. "To Madame Sanchez. Is Wanda her first name?"

"I forget," Sloan said.

Nancy Carlisle didn't slap; she swung a fist and staggered the ward boy into the green steel door.

Sputtering, he bounced off and reached for her. She hit him again, this time flush in the mouth. It split his lips and hurt her knuckles.

He snarled. "Goddamn you! I'll break your goddamn—"

"Come on!" She was so furious that his face was a red blur. "Come on and hit me! I'll see that you get a general court and five years."

He backed up, shaking his head, his mouth bloody. "You hit *me*, goddamnit. An officer can't hit no enlisted man neither. You'll get court-martialed, not me. I'm going right to the colonel and turn you in."

"I'll go with you, so I can tell him how you abuse patients. You kicked that poor boy—"

"Crazy son of a bitch tried to bite me. Some of them goddamn psychos ain't as crazy as they put on, and everybody knows it. They just fake it to buck out of the army on a Section Eight. Anyway, I got a right to protect myself."

She glanced at the drop bar on the isolation room door out of habit. It was in place, but when she got this nonsense settled she'd come back and let the boy return to his bed on the ward. He'd still be on his feet because T/5 Morrison hadn't injected him with a needle before she saw what was going on. That was something else; regulations said that only a doctor or nurse could give inoculations, not a ward boy. She hadn't caught this one doing it, but patients whispered to her.

And only the duty nurse carried a key to the narcotics closet, so a lazy nurse allowed Morrison entry to the hypos; an uncaring woman who had something, or someone, else on her mind. Or just a bitch who hated the NP ward assignment and blamed the patients.

Morrison was right that she couldn't hit him, but it felt good. Now she had to take it all the way. Brushing by the orderly in the narrow hallway, Nancy stormed for the locked mesh door that divided the ward from the office, the mentally wounded from the nominally sane. She keyed the lock, stepped through and tried to slam the door behind her. Morrison was a step behind and caught it. His slam was loud, a crash that caused one patient to yelp in fear and another to moan.

Morrison beat her to the nurse's station. "Cap'n Harris, ma'am. I'm sure glad you're here. This here woman—ah, Lieutenant Carlisle—just busted me in the mouth. See how I'm bleeding? Permission to see the colonel, ma'am."

Captain Flora Harris sat at her desk where every paper lay straight in file boxes, where pencils, thermometers and a clip-board covered down and dressed right as if on parade. She said, "Both of you get in here. Shut the door, Carlisle. Can't I leave the floor for any length of time without some kind of snafu?"

The woman's chubby face was flushed and her fresh lipstick off center; the nurse's cap leaned atop dyed hair cropped regulation length above the collar. "What is this nonsense? Lieutenant, did you actually strike an enlisted man? I realize you're only a recruit with little knowledge of army nursing, but a snafu like this reflects upon me as head nurse. I will not have a bad mark in my file because of—"

Nancy cut in. "I hit him twice. To protect the patient he was kicking. I will prefer charges, Captain."

Morrison wiped his mouth. "Cap'n, ma'am? I been with you a long time, and this woman, she don't do nothing except it's her own way. Acts like she's boss instead of you." His eyes flickered. "I mean—I reckon I might be willing to forget what she done if she apologizes and you ship her to some other ward."

Flora Harris tucked loose hair under her cap, and Nancy wondered which doctor thought her attractive. She had been in the linen closet with some officer; she was too rank happy to play games with a lowly GI. She said, "Carlisle, when you first arrived I warned you not to rock the boat, that the army does things by the numbers. A court-martial—either yours or his—will imply that I am incapable of enforcing discipline. I think you should accept T/5 Morrison's suggestion. I *know* you will perform better working sick call."

"You want me to apologize to one of your pet sadists? The hell I will! This jerk kicked a helpless patient. He's carrying an unauthorized hypo, and by God, I mean to stop that kind of crap on this ward. I demand to speak to the CO."

The captain leapt up and kicked back her chair. "I warn you, Carlisle! Colonel Hooper is old army. He and I have soldiered together on other posts. He will understand why I back my enlisted personnel over an insubordinate snip not worthy of her rank. This snafu—"

"Situation normal, all fucked up? Believe it—Captain." She leaned over the desk and picked up the phone.

"Told you she's crazier than them nuts on the ward," Morrison said.

Flora Harris snapped, "I give you a direct order not to call the CO. Do you *hear* me, Carlisle?"

Into the phone Nancy said, "Patch through to the mainland. Priority call collect to Kill Devil Hill, Virginia. No—it has its own exchange. Look it up."

"Lieutenant—"

"My name's been good enough all through this bullshit. You *remember* it." To the operator she said, "Yes, that's it. Person to person for Lieutenant General Preston Belvale, Nancy Carlisle calling."

Flora Harris tried to snatch the phone. Nancy threatened her with it as the ward boy opened the door and slid out.

"Oh, hell—he's not there?"

The smirk on Flora Harris's fat face was satisfied.

"Then give me Lieutenant General Charles Carlisle—yes, Carlisle."

Dropping back into her chair, the head nurse stared. Her mouth hung open, and a fleck of lipstick showed on one tooth.

"Crusty? Hi, there, sorry to bother you. Oh, yes, I enjoy being in uniform and nursing here at Tripler General, but no—I'm not calling about Keenan, unless you've heard anything. I thought not. Sir, I have never asked the family's help or used its influence, but there's a military problem here I'm sure will interest you. It's not as important as your investigation of the Pearl Harbor attack, but something more personal, the rights of wounded fighting men."

She half turned and lifted one hip to sit on the desk. "Yes, it can be boring at the Hill—how well I know. You will fly out tomorrow, as soon as General Belvale gets back? Fine, Crusty. I'll meet you at the field—and thank you."

Sliding off the desktop and turning to face Flora Harris, Nancy smiled. "Like they say, Captain: if you've got it, flaunt it."

CHAPTER 42

Special to *The New York Times*—Washington, June 18, 1943, delayed: Little information available to the press has filtered out of last month's meeting between President Roosevelt and Prime Minister Winston Churchill. Others attending have been named as three top British commanders in the China-Burma-India theater: Field Marshal Sir Archibald Percival Wavell, Commander in Chief in India, Admiral Sir James Somerville, commander of British forces in the Bay of Bengal, and Air Marshal Sir Richard Pierce, CinC of Air Forces in India.

Sources also included appearances by Lt. Gen. Vinegar Joe Stilwell, U.S. boss in the CBI, and Maj. Gen. Claire Chennault of the famed Flying Tigers. This gathering seemed to portend more attention to be given to a new offensive against the Japanese not only in the CBI, but also in the South Pacific.

SECRET to Kill Devil Hill, TWX scrambled—North Africa, June 19, 1943: Entire 1st Infantry Division concentrated near Algiers, command post at Staouelli. Practice landing upcoming near Zeralda; actual loading of landing craft to begin 26 June, following day depart for Tunis. Reinforced division to begin embarkation 5 July for rendezvous off Tunis 8 July. Long-range weather forecast: morning sea normally calm for time of year, afternoon tendency to choppy sea and moderate wind. Invasion jumpoff date, codeword and target destination TOP SECRET, Eisenhower staff eyes-only.

Belvale stood before the Mediterranean situation map and stared up at markings and pins that colored its overlay. If he were Ike, where would he land—Corsica, Sardinia, Sicily? Maybe the invasion would hit Italy proper, say at Reggio di Calabria. If so, that convoy would have to circle south of Sicily and pass close to Malta, which might be a break if that bombed-out, hang-tough little island could be turned into a gigantic protected airstrip. He couldn't recall news of heavy aircraft shipments headed that way; the North African command needed all it could receive. The convoy leaving Tunis must have powerful air cover.

If it was to be Corsica, the beach was Ajaccio, such as it was. Sardinia meant the Cagliari area, no better for a seaborn assault under fire and about half again as far from Tunis as Sicily. So he would place an even-money bet on Sicily but figure on no particular landing site. That was up to Ike Eisenhower, and Belvale didn't envy him the choice. G-2 information had German Panzer and infantry divisions being rushed down through the Brenner Pass, plus a steady Luftwaffe buildup on Italian airfields. Hitler placed little trust in Mussolini's reluctant troops since the wholesale *paisan* panics in Libya, and Italy was too important, too close to home. He would not allow its abdication from the war.

Belvale touched a button and the sitmap of the Pacific Theater slid down. He took a close look and flinched. So many islands were still being doggedly fortified by fanatic Japanese. Like moles they would burrow deep into hard coral rock and create a network of tunnels. Fanning out from main caves, these would set interlocking fire patterns, accurate and murderous. Air photos showed beach after island beach with underwater obstacles set to lead landing craft into fire zones tested and zeroed in.

One or two of the brighter militarists in Tokyo surely could see that their gamble on a limited war had gone down the tubes when they were unable to hold Guadalcanal and Tulagi. Like beads dropping from a broken chain their other island conquests were falling one by one. But just as surely, the only orders to come out of Japan would exhort the followers of Bushido to stay and die gloriously for Hirohito.

Not one island campaign would be a walkover. MacArthur's army troops and battered Marines would pay the blood price for every miserable little atoll as they island-hopped across the Pacific. Belvale hoped that more planning would prove the worth of cutting off naval and air supplies to all but the most important of those islands and bypassing the rest. Left behind, the Japs would wither and blow away or commit *seppuku*. Either way Americans lived and Japanese died, and that was the name of the game.

The war room entrance warning buzzed at the same moment a teletype signaled a semi-important message with two clangs. Joann looked up from her typewriter. "I'll get them, Uncle."

Smiling at her serious blue eyes, he said, "Never mind, dear. The door is probably Gloria ready to come back and give us a hand. I'll catch the teletype first."

Joann had immersed herself in the job. She had been one step from joining the Women's Auxiliary Army Corps, to help make her brother's death mean something more. A pretty girl, she had cut off her social life since coming to the Hill. She'd work around the clock if Belvale allowed, and she still took a moment every day to kneel at Walton's memorial grave.

He thumbed another button on the board that flashed the outside WAIT light and moved the maps out of sight. Then he stepped over to read the telex. It came from Letterman General Hospital in San Francisco, a report on the condition of First Lieutenant Farley Belvale. With all the medical jargon filtered out, the news was that he remained somewhat confused but was now ambulatory and often coherent.

Good, very good; perhaps in time, when Farley broke the shell of his own prison, he might be strong enough to be told about his wife languishing behind Japanese wire. *If* pretty Penny was still alive; that condition changed day by day for military POWs and civilian internees alike, and incoming reports didn't keep up. Savagely Belvale bit the end off a fresh cigar. The damned Jap butchers were going to pay for their animal cruelty. Family political power and wealth could serve no better cause than to guarantee swift and severe punishment for all war criminals. Hanging the bastards who started wars might establish a precedent to make other would-be conquerors of the world think twice when their own asses were on the line.

Tapping an electric switch, he swung the panel back and let Gloria Carlisle inside. She was followed by Sergeant Eddie Donnely, and Belvale thought that they both might as well wear neon signs announcing their love. The signal was that clear.

"Come in," he said. "Sergeant, I haven't seen you since we were at Schofield Barracks. How's Big Mike doing?"

"Made it through North Africa without a Purple Heart, sir. My old man is too tough for the Krauts."

"Agreed. This is their second chance at him. Oh, excuse me, Joann. Sergeant, this other lovely lady is Joann Belvale. Her brother was an observer, lost in Poland. Joann, the sergeant is on convalescent leave from Guadalcanal."

"Sorry, ma'am," Donnely said. "Thank you, sir."

Joann said, "A pleasure to meet you—Eddie. Gloria has talked about you. I understand that the Canal was really rough."

"I guess. Ahh—no hairier than the blitz in Poland, ma'am—ahh, Joann. At least we could depend on backup."

Crusty had been correct on one point in his objection to this pairing of his granddaughter and Big Mike Donnely's son. Donnely was uneasy at the Hill. What was the new simile the troops were using—jumpy as a T/5 at a noncom's meeting? Crusty would say as a whore in church.

With Donnely it was for cause; born into the rigid caste system of the old army, he wasn't socially comfortable around high brass. Belvale swallowed a smile; the man was more familiar with a number of officers' wives, but that would probably change.

One of the phones beeped, and Joann answered, then held it out. "Uncle? It's General Carlisle in Hawaii."

Belvale took the phone. "Will you pour coffee for everyone, Gloria? Thank you. Yes, Charles?"

"Charles, *Charles?* If you keep that up, you goddamn grayback, I'll piss in your mess kit."

"If the switchboard is open on your end, the scrambled line here won't help. You just set respect for general officers back a hundred years. Don't spend much time on Waikiki Beach—your wrinkles won't take a lot of sun."

Crusty made a rude noise. "I got your respect dangling. What rattled your cage? Did mighty Minerva give you permission to smart off? Can't loll on the beach if I want. Hawaiian Command has turned military as all hell. Now it's minefields and barbed wire and enough ack-ack guns to protect Washington itself. Somewhat *after* the Pearl Harbor fuckup, of course. Gives me a new slant on the old American Expeditionary Force; here the AEF means ass end first.

"I called so you can expedite the shanghais I'm putting through on some eight balls. Oh, pardon me. It ain't gentlemanly to call duty station transfers by such lowly slang. By any other name, get orders cut on these peanuts ASAP. All data coming by TWX. I busted a couple of shitheels down a grade—a bull bird administrator and a nurse captain now on their way to freeze their asses off on Adak for the duration plus. They didn't get time to draw long johns, either. A bunch of ward boys just made yardbird rank and became infantry replacements, and damned if they didn't volunteer to carry 81mm mortar base plates. Maybe they can figure out how, without busting their humps. Thanks to our Nancy—that girl is still good family, by God—no more bedpan commandos will screw around with battle casualties on the NP ward or any other wounded. What do you hear on that kid Farley?"

"He's coming out of it."

Crusty paused, and Belvale glanced over at Gloria. Murmuring with her head close to Joann's, she actually glowed. Whatever Donelly had been, whoever he might become in the future, just now he was the best man ever to come along for her. Belvale hoped it would stay that way. It might be called a quickie war romance if both of them hadn't grown up military. War had always been a possibility.

"I might take a look at some other islands," Crusty said, "and don't give me any bugle oil about it."

Belvale sighed. "I thought you jumped too quickly at a return trip to Hawaii. I won't try to block you. You have to learn how old you are, just as I did. Remember your shoulders."

"How can I forget the damned things? Preston—is everything all right with my Gloria?"

"Good—you can't imagine how good. She wants to talk to you."

Gloria took the phone. "Granddad, I'd like your blessing. Eddie asked me to marry him."

Belvale could picture the look on Crusty's face, but for all the old duffer's hard shell, this young woman was the chink in it.

She said, "Yes, Granddad, I am—very sure. Well, please—he has something to say. Will you speak with him?"

Donnely's face was pink, but his jaw was set. Damn,

Belvale thought, he was about to pay respects to an obsolete army rule.

"Sir!" Donnely said it loudly. "Request the general's permission to marry."

In the bygone days of boots and saddles and outposts in Indian territory, regulations called for enlisted men to obtain approval from their commanding officers before they could wed. Few soldiers today even knew the tradition, much less respected it.

"Yes, General. Yes, sir. *Hell, no!* I don't give a sh—doodly-squat about money or rank or any other goddamn thing but Gloria! If that's not good enough—"

Covering his mouth, Belvale masked a grin. Crusty just learned that he was butting heads with one of his own kind.

"All right, sorry, but the general goddamned well pushed me into it. Okay. Thank you, sir. We hope you can make it back for the wedding. Don't make it too long."

When he returned the phone to Belvale he smiled at Gloria. "He wants to give you away, if we wait awhile."

Belvale said, "Crusty, get back soon as you can. These kids don't want to wait forever, and you're worth more here than nosing around the Pacific."

"The sergeant's a real hard-nose, ain't he? He'd just better make her happy."

"Crusty—"

"Yeah?"

"Oh, hell—take care."

For a long moment the line hummed, then Crusty said, "If I have a choice, these damned lungs or Fiddler's Green, you know which way I'll go." He hung up then.

Closing his eyes, Belvale stood alone in shadows with the smell of the stables for company. Ghosts of cavalry horses whinnied, and far off a bugler softly played Call to Quarters.

So when both man and horse go down
Beneath the sabers keen—

Or when the hostiles crave your scalp
Just empty your canteen—
Put your pistol to your head
And go to Fiddler's Green.

Gloria touched his arm. "Will Granddad be all right?"
"Sure." Belvale opened his eyes. "Sure he will."

CHAPTER 43

INTERNATIONAL NEWS SERVICE—MacArthur's Headquarters, South Pacific, July 9, 1943: More than 100 Allied bombers joined warships and artillery in launching the strongest barrage to date against the Japanese base of Munda. The Japs sent 45 Zeroes over Rendova Island, but they were scattered and four destroyed. The enemy also tried an unsuccessful dive bombing on our base at Nassau Bay, New Guinea.

Wire Services Information Pool: AP, INS, Reuters, UP—Allied Headquarters in North Africa, Saturday, July 10, 1943: Allied infantry landed at a number of places on the rocky Sicilian coast under a canopy of naval gunfire this morning as the long-awaited invasion began.

As the Allies struck General Eisenhower broadcast an appeal to the French people, warning against rash actions that would bring Nazi reprisals. "When the hour of liberation comes," he said, "we will let you know."

SECRET—Algiers radio broadcast in English at 1240 today reports landings on the rocky western tip of Sicily, 260 miles from Rome. German and Italian air and land forces putting up "fierce opposition." Defenders blow up harbor installations that survived concentrated Allied attacks and shelling.

G-2 expects very heavy fighting from divisions of fresh German reinforcements moved into undestroyed defensive positions.

LT. GEN. PRESTON BELVALE: This landing is going to be exceedingly difficult. Everyone at Kill Devil Hill will please take time out for prayer. The troops going ashore need all the help they can get.

MAJ. GEN. CHARLES CARLISLE: Oh, batshit! We knew this would come off, but I thought there was more time. Goddamnit, I'll bet that Preston didn't keep me up to date on reports from North Africa. Maybe MacArthur will show us something in the Pacific. Meanwhile, kick ass, Ike—kick ass!

CAPT. GAVIN SCOTT: Something's going on, and nobody can figure exactly what. All kriegies know that our air has been raising hell off southern Italy, but the goons have been so active that the radio had to stay under cover. Latrine rumors say we're about to be moved again. I kept after the escape committee, but they dragged ass. Screw all those limeys; I'll make my own break when we get on the road.

KIRSTIN BELVALE-SHELBY: He was doing so well until the news this morning. Harlan rode with us—with me—every day, and it stopped tearing him up for anyone outside the hospital to see his missing limbs. He reins just fine with those clamps where his left hand used to be, real easy on a horse's mouth. And he learned to shift weight instead of legging the horse with the prosthetic that's now his right leg. His old outfit's landing in Sicily, and he can't be with them, so he thinks that makes him even less of a man.

He was suicidal before becoming interested in our horse

program, and then the doctors said his prognosis was good. But today when I called for him the nurse said Sergeant Harlan Edgerton caused an uproar this morning and got put back on the locked ward.

I know about NP wards; my son Farley is a patient on one. I know about invasions; my husband died on another island. My other son and my ex-husband are probably right in the middle of this landing. They could get shipped home crippled like Harlan or blind as Manny Venegas, if they come back at all.

Oh, God. Oh, God.

S/SGT. Eddie Donnely: When the papers put out generalities and background information but damned few details, you know the fighting is rough. Still, it's probably a good time to apply pressure in the Pacific. The Americal has been out of action in the Fiji Islands for months. I've been marking time for months, too. I wonder when it'll jump off. I wonder if it's the right thing to marry Gloria before I rejoin them, even if I have to go AWOL to do it.

NANCY CARLISLE: If they're attacking in Europe, they'll start up again against the Japs, and returning transport planes will bring us more poor damaged kids. Hospital ships will dock at Pearl Harbor to offload litters by the hundreds. Crusty left right after he shook out the bad apples so the good guys can do their jobs. But I'm not sure how long I can do mine properly. I'm so tired, and I have nobody to talk to.

MAJ. KEENAN CARLISLE: Wingate is a crazy son of a bitch, but he's my kind of son of a bitch. He's still going and keeping the rest of us going. The Japs have been snapping at our ragged asses every step of the way, and we're bleeding them in turn, beating them off. But this jungle is a worse problem. We're dying on our feet, including the Gurkhas, and they're damned tough. Even the Burmese are collapsing, and it's home to them, their jungle. The consolation is that it has to be every bit as bad for the lousy Japs, and that might just allow a few of Wingate's Chindits to make it.

PENNY BELVALE: I told Stevie. I worked up the nerve to tell her what happened with Shigeo Watanabe. Oh, yes, he has a first name, but I am not allowed to use it; that would show disrespect. I told Stevie, and first she gave me hell for attracting him in the first place, and then for shamelessly selling out to Major Wobbly. I said the only thing I was ashamed of was having an orgasm.

After, she cried a little and thanked me. Then she held my hand and said that women dinna have to be in love or even like the man to reach a climax. Orgasm, she said—as if she were lecturing her anti-aircraft girls in better times—orgasm is caused by repeated stimulation of the clitoris. Lassie, it is but a mechanical thing, Leftenant Stephanie Bartlett said. It has naught to do with your true feelings, and dinna fash yourself that the women call you names. There beside him you can keep others alive, especially the bairns. It's all mechanical, therefore I am a robot, a Frankenstein monster. And I swear by all things holy and unholy that I will one day kill the man who created me so—Major Shigeo Watanabe.

2D LT. SLOAN TRAVIS: When the wind rose before midnight everybody threw up in the landing craft. Through the dark I can see naval shell explosions and the bubbling white fantails from other boats, but not the beach itself. Between the shell bursts there are the firecrackers of small arms popping. Paratroopers from the 82d Airborne jumped in early, and a Ranger force is out there fighting ahead of us. I pity the poor bastards. I'm sorry for this puking, scared-shitless platoon, and I hope we don't lose any guns going in. I still don't know what the hell I'm doing here.

COL. CHAD BELVALE: Nobody slept, and I passed on midnight chow. We balanced on deck and eyed the tracers; then we caught sight of fires burning on the shoreline. Back in the ship's wardroom, I told the officers of Regimental Combat Team 16 that the latest intelligence reports indicate the beach is lightly defended. But G-2 considers any force less than an army corps as "light," and I know damned well that panzers are waiting for this RCT. We're going in not far from the prime objective, a two-bit town named Gela. Before we get there we have to take Pina Lupo, where tanks are dug in turret-deep on line with too many concrete pillboxes.

Pina Lupo—Wolf Point; if the name is some kind of omen, it's not a good one for our side.

Here we go.

LOOK FOR BOOK 3 OF THE *MEN AT ARMS* SERIES

A WORLD ABLAZE

In Europe, Chad Belvale leaves the U.S Army to fight with the Free Polish troops, while his cousin Keenan recuperates from his Pacific ordeal and signs up for the 442nd Infantry Regiment—destined to become the most decorated army unit in World War II.

General Crusty Carlislc's only regret is that he hasn't been there to fight this war firsthand. Now he's getting his chance. But when his troopship is torpedoed, Carlisle is plunged into a nightmarish battle for his life, as he and a handful of sailors survive shark-infested waters to wash up on an island far behind enemy lines. In Washington, his counterpart, General Preston Belvale, is fighting the tactical war, helping to engineer the dangerous alliance among Stalin, Churchill and Roosevelt that will propel the Allies to victory in Europe.